About the Author

Alex Charlton lives in Dorset with her husband, who manages her restless energy and constant flow of new ideas with equanimity. Her passions, apart from her husband, two beautiful daughters and close friends, are history, languages and philosophy. She has enjoyed success in diverse careers: financial management, a high profile educational position – and a sheep farm. She also loves travel, exercise – especially yoga and tai chi – and new experiences. Her writing philosophy is to explore the timeless beauty of life within a strong character and place-centred style.

THE CAROUSEL OF TIME

Alex Charlton

The Carousel of Time

Vanguard Press

A CIP catalogue record for this title is
available from the British Library.

ISBN 978 1 784 65 199 2

*Vanguard Press is an imprint of
Pegasus Elliot MacKenzie Publishers Ltd.*
www.pegasuspublishers.com

First Published in 2018

Vanguard Press
Sheraton House Castle Park
Cambridge England
Printed & Bound in Great Britain

Dedication

To my dear friend, who provided the inspiration for the character of Helen; and to Ash.

Love never ends.

Acknowledgments

Huge thanks to John for his infinite editorial patience; and to Hannah and Amy for their invaluable suggestions throughout the writing and production of this book.

.... the seasons they go round and round
And the painted ponies go up and down
We're captured on a carousel of Time.
We can't return — we can only look
Behind from where we came;
And go round, and round, and round
In the Circle Game

The Circle Game, Joni Mitchell
1970 Album *Ladies of the Canyon*

Prologue

Despairingly Æthelwulf looked at his land. It was dry, totally arid. The crops that he had planted had died in the ground. The hard won – so hard to win – land that lay in the centre of the great ash forest was dust in the unremitting drought. The river – never strong – had dwindled to a trickle, barely enough for the eorl's people to drink from, let alone water the sheep and cattle which sat listlessly, almost too weak to move.

The great ash forest! It had appeared as if the ancient gods were breathing a blessing on Æthelwulf and his people when they had first arrived in that place. There was one tree in particular – mighty, towering, a veritable Yggdrasil – around which, living and bearing leaf and fruit still, Æthelwulf had built his hall. It was as if it had always been meant that he should settle here: there were flat stones already, strongly placed, with no gaps through which soil or weeds could grow, which formed the floor of the great Anglo-Saxon hall.

He had tried everything he knew: prayer to Thor for thunder and heavy rain; prayer to Frig for renewed fertility. Nothing. There was one thing left – but as leader of a people he had struggled to civilise, this route he did not want to take.

Day followed blazing day. The sun looked like the great bronze disc necklace that Æthelwulf wore about his neck as a sign of his eorldom: unremitting, glaring, a symbol of death not life.

He had no choice…

In the darkest part of the night Æthelwulf left the hall. Silently he looked on his sleeping wife, Elfgifu, and slipped, quietly as a ghost, out of the great hall doors. He walked down the slope to the crossing over the dry river bed.

Moving into the deepest part of the ash wood, he made his way reluctantly to the shapeless black hovel. The land surrounding the building had been cultivated. At the entrance to the clearing was a raven, roughly carved of oak. Huge and dark, it almost looked alive. In the starlight he could see herbs that he could recognise – and some that he could not. There was the faintest glimmer of light coming from under the turf roof. He had been there before, sometimes seeing a huge shadowy figure melting away from the hut as he, Æthelwulf, approached. He felt a deep sense of disquiet when he saw such uninvited visitors on his land, but what could he do? Unnamma did not operate within his laws.

He opened the curtain covering the gap in the mud walls that served as the doorway to the hut.

'My lord! I was waiting for you!'

An ageless woman rose from the mud floor where she had been sitting by the fire in the centre of the hut. Tall, straight, with features of extraordinary clarity, she approached the eorl of Æscwyrd.

'You seek the solution to this endless drought.' She stated this as fact.

'I do, Unnamma.'

'But you know the answer Æthelwulf. You know it already.'

'Is there no other way?'

'No other.'

'How shall he be chosen?'
'By the casting of the runes.'

***

Godgifu turned to her lover. He was sleeping, facing her, the love and life in his dark eyes covered by his sweeping black lashes. His black hair outlined the strong contours of his cheek, his neck, curling softly on his shoulders. She gently stroked the face she loved so much – so much – and he shifted and murmured in his sleep. She would do anything for this man. Æsc had already proved himself, both as a man of peace and as a warrior. He worked closely with eorl Æthelwulf. One of the first generation of settled Vikings to be born in this fertile wooded valley, he had soon proved himself invaluable to his lord. Astute in meetings of the village, hard working on the land, fearless in battle, gifted in poetry and song, he was the flower of manhood in the tiny settlement of Æscwyrd. He had been given his name because his family had believed that he would become one of the greatest warriors and statesmen of the settlement, embodying the principles of valour and wisdom upon which it had been founded. He had fulfilled this belief, indeed he had surpassed it... and it was she that he loved. He had chosen her!

They had become handfasted nearly a year ago, on the anniversary of her birth – before this never-ending drought had plagued the land. They laughed, ran, hunted, sang and swam together: they were everything to each other.

She remembered how, that Spring, they had been in their favourite place, a high flower-filled field. She had been lying,

15

half-asleep in a hollow, lazily listening to the drone of an early bee; and he had stood tall above her, looking down at every feature that he loved so well. He had spoken her name quietly:

'Godgifu!'

And she had sat quickly up, blinking her eyes to try to adjust to the light.

'Æsc?'

Because of the brightness of the sun behind his tall figure, she had not been able to make out clearly his features and it struck her that he was almost like a figure from the sagas and myths that the bard sang in the mead hall, so perfect was he.

Later that year – she smiled when she remembered – on Midsummer Day, they were haymaking with the other villagers in the oval hayfield near to the mound that her father told her was an ancient burial site. Æsc had woven for her a garland of flowers which were already drying in the hot sun. As he placed it lightly on her tangled hair, he had slipped onto her slim finger a silver ring on which tiny runes spelled out the words

My Beginning and My End

She knew that she would remember this moment forever. She folded her hand gently around her ring finger, raising it to her lips to kiss… She loved this man so much it was like a physical pain.

***

The great bronze disc of the sun beat mercilessly down. Would it ever stop? The trickle of water was now dry and the desperate settlement of Æscwyrd had to send men fifteen miles to the nearest spring – and now even that was dwindling and was guarded by the men of the next settlement with increasing challenge.

***

The elders of the village stood uneasily in the centre of the great hall, in a circle around the tall stately timeless figure of Unnamma. She held a bag in her hands, worked with swirling patterns of vestigial beasts – an eye here, a tail lashing there, part of a sinuous body, all composing a disconcerting pattern and shifting picture in the shadows of the hall.

'You are ready?' she asked the men unflinchingly.

'We are.'

'And you will adhere to the outcome? You swear?'

'We will.'

'Whoever the runes choose?'

'Yes,' they replied gravely as one voice. Quickly the woman opened her bag, lifted up the runes and scattered them across the floor. The bone cubes had the letters of the futhark scratched upon their surfaces.

Each of the elders looked gravely at the shards of bone, holding the initial letters of the young and bold men of their village: Brighthelm, Guthlac, Kenric, Æsc...

The woman gave a low whistle and from outside the hall came a slow beating of wings. Through the great entrance a huge raven flapped, hovered for a moment over the silent figures, and fell instantly upon one of the runic bones. Holding this in his beak he hopped deliberately, directly, towards Æthelwulf. The eorl held out his hand. It was shaking slightly. The raven dropped the runic bone.

Ashen, Æthelwulf looked at his hand as he slowly unfurled the fingers – almost as if each was being forcibly pulled away from what it enclosed.

'A . It is Æsc.'

***

The crying, the screaming, the tears were over. Godgifu sat like one of the stone figures on her father's chessboard staring into space, into nothingness.

It had happened that morning – Midsummer Day – one of the most powerful days in the old religion and exactly a twelvemonth since that unforgettable day when he had given her the ring. Her betrothed, her lover, the brave and gentle heart of her heart had been sacrificed. The stone sacrificial knife, a relic of earlier brutal days, which was kept in the stone box deep under the hearthstone of the hall, had been used. The farce of crowning him Midsummer King had been gone through. The ceremonial bathing in water fragranced with rosemary, the unworn green tunic of fine cloth slipped over his head, his thick dark hair crowned with a wreath of leaves and roses. With a savageness that she knew had finally broken her heart they were married – to increase the potency of the fertility ritual according to Unnamma. The fine, cream cambric dress that she had woven with her dreams – dreams of long, full years with her beloved, filling this place with their children, with their love and energy, was now spattered with the blood of her husband. The wreath of fresh young roses and St John's wort – tokens of everlasting love – had slipped unwittingly from her thick dark hair and was disintegrating as the terrible pageant proceeded. Æsc had stood silent, his eyes – deep brown, mesmeric – fixed upon her as his life ended. Even as it was done the wind rose and grey clouds, gathered from the sea, swirled and built over the settlement. As his body, according to pagan tradition, was ploughed into the earth, the rain started to fall, gently at first and then tumultuously, like the tears that she could no longer shed.

The rain fell still.

***

Years passed. Godgifu remained unmarried. The ring that her lover had given her became worn as her hands relentlessly traced the runes:

My Beginning and My End

Like a storm gathering momentum, the intention grew in Godgifu, grew and swirled and circled throughout her entire being. Her love of sunshine and clear water and blue sky was banished for ever. She walked only at night, her head covered, her eyes downcast to the traitor earth which had swallowed her life and her future. And increasingly she walked towards the dark hut in the deep woods where the woman Unnamma still lived. Years had changed Godgifu beyond recognition. Her hair, once so black and thick was streaked with white; her eyes were almost colourless; her face grey and expressionless. Unnamma was unchanged.

***

Æthelwulf was dying. In the centre of the great hall, surrounded by his faithful elders, by his wife, and by his wraithlike daughter, he reviewed his life. His bard sang his triumphs and told of the way he had led his people over the seas to this beautiful part of the world so long before. How he had cleared and worked and built to create the settlement of Æscwyrd – 'the fateful settlement in the ash forest'. The long fingers of the silver-haired bard moved skilfully over the strings of his small harp, telling again the bitter story of how life in that place of good fortune had been threatened at the time of the terrible drought; and how Æthelwulf had turned back to pagan ways to bring rain and fertility to his people once again.

The eorl's face clouded as he re-lived this most terrible of times, which had robbed him of one of his finest young warriors and statesmen and had sucked away the life of his daughter.

Suddenly the scene was transformed. Instead of the measured grace of the bard's poetry, the respectful peace of the elders, a savage screaming woman towered in the midst of the hall.

'Cursed be you father, through whose will my love was torn away from me!

'Cursed be you, this settlement, which lives through my love's death!

'I curse you and the people who live in this settlement of Æscwyrd for ever!

'May they know the agony that I have felt. May all their good come to evil. May they lose the things most precious to them!

'My Beginning and My End! Here I was born and here we will all die!'

At this Godgifu, with almost supernatural strength, grabbed several of the blazing logs from the fire and hurled them at the wall-hangings which clothed and made beautiful the wooden walls of the great hall. Almost instantly they caught fire, as did the wood from which building and furniture were made. With her back to the great ash tree at the centre of the hall, surrounded by fire and smoke and screaming running people, Godgifu stood motionless, herself blazing, as the fire licked about her long skirt and cloak. Her last gesture was to *lift on high the ring whose words of love had become the substance of her curse.*

Behind her, hardly touched by the raging flames, the great central ash tree stood implacable. The other timbers of the hall burnt and fell into the mead hall space; the roof groaned and collapsed, sealing the scene of death and destruction. Outside, drifting through the shadowy ash trees, the terrible, black figure smiled and was gone.

TIME WAS

KATE

Chapter 1

1965

I could almost taste the acrid smoke that curled up from the ruined building. Blackened timbers were strewn here and there, lying where they had fallen, as slowly the whole structure of the great hall had been destroyed by the fire. I fought, as usual, to get out of the nightmare and to return to some sort of reality, but the terrifying recurrent dream would not let me go yet. Surreal, the silver ring spun at the centre of the ruin – held by an unseen energy that just would not let it fall; that would not let this tragedy cease. The scratched letters circled relentlessly, but I could not read what they said. There was crying and billowing smoke and such deep sadness and despair that it was tangible.

Eventually, the desperate, vivid dream released me. I lay, breathing fast and deeply, in my single bed, in the room that had been mine since childhood. The papered walls were blue, with small pink flowers that had faded over the years since I had chosen them. The curtains, stretched tight across the windows, were faded too; the furniture well worn. Nothing changed here – ever. I was eighteen and had been born in the house which my parents still occupied. My father's failing health and my mother's strange inability or disinclination to work meant that there was never enough for luxuries. Life was slow, repetitive. Even the annual holidays to the seaside had stopped.

I lay, as always, deeply shaken by the dream which had haunted me for as long as I could remember. It had no connection with anything that I had read, or seen, or been told. It had just arrived and seemed as real as my limited surroundings.

It was half-past two and I knew that I would sleep no more that night. If I got up, I would wake my parents and that would cause my mother to remark, tight-lipped, that my father's sleep had 'been disturbed; which isn't fair really as he has to get up so early to go to work...' Why on earth didn't my mother get a job, I wondered for the millionth time? She was fit, relatively young – but there was never any question of it. She continued to run the house – haphazardly; to cook – badly; to eat – incessantly.

In those quiet dark minutes of sleeplessness I thought of the fascination that most subjects – but especially languages – had held for me since I had gone to grammar school. In the half-light I looked at the rows of books above the little desk in the corner of my bedroom – *Jane Eyre, Pride and Prejudice, Wuthering Heights* – and latterly *Beowulf* and the tales of the pilgrims winding their riotous and complex way to Canterbury. My determination to "succeed" academically had not been onerous – I had analysed and empathised with the fictional characters which crossed my path with a passion.

I remembered the thoughtful smile on the face of my English teacher, appropriately called Miss Austen, several weeks earlier at the end of a debate about the merits of fiction versus biography.

'When is the last time you had magic in your life?' I had asked passionately of my debating adversaries. 'Not the wand-waving, illusionist type of popular magic – but heart-stopping joy, wonder, or freezing horror? These emotions and the elements that cause them are always present – they just need uncovering. We need to push below the mundane surface of life, to uncover the eternal elements of love and death, of good and evil.'

Connie Austen had challenged and encouraged me during my last three years at school and I replayed in my mind the arrival of the telegram earlier that week from the minor Oxford college to which I had, through her gentle insistence, applied and where, just a month earlier, I had been interviewed. My hands were shaking so much I could hardly open the ordinary-looking brown envelope.

'We are pleased to offer you a place on our English Honours course…'

And this was the start of it all, I told myself. I would, one day, have a house that people admired, that people wanted to photograph and paint. I would live in the country, not grey suburbia. I would move in middle-class society, I would marry an amazing man and live a perfect life. Well, these were my dreams – my daydreams, at least.

Chapter 2

1981

Our lives are measured by dates – by birthdays or anniversaries or the date we start school – but sometimes by a date which does not appear significant until many years have passed and we have the historical perspective to realise that, from this day, our life changed forever. In my life, 12 September 1981 was such a date.

The year was at that delicate point of change from summer to autumn. The narrow road along which we were driving was narrowed further by the banks of seeding rosebay willowherb – known locally, as I learnt later, as fireflower. It had been sixteen years since I had said goodbye to my respectable little childhood home, and to my puzzled parents, who could understand nothing of the ambition and determination which were an essential part of my character. But even then, I thought involuntarily of my mother. She had told me years previously that she had picked armfuls of this particular wild flower, only to be told by her mother that it was poisonous. Had she at some point then had a spark of spontaneity in her life? I hoped so, idly, as I watched the incredible beauty of the lush Kent countryside drift past the windows of the car.

Incidentally, when I had left home for university, I had also said goodbye to any sort of meaningful relationship with my mother, who could not, or would not – I think in her own way she was as stubborn as I am – forgive me for moving so far from 'home'.

I thought again of the poignant letter which I had received from my mother, written in her round, un-formed handwriting, when I had told her I was going to get married. She clearly expressed her hurt and disappointment that what she and my father could provide was 'just never good enough' for me.

I felt awful when I received her letter. I permanently felt guilty that I was not home more/didn't love her more/was ambitious/ and looked far beyond the suburban horizons that bounded her life. This feeling of guilt was entrenched and coloured, I came to realise, my relationships with other people as I grew older. I was too ready to apologise, too accepting of unreasonable demands. I knew already that, in the relationship with my husband, I was the compliant one, the one to step back and allow his opinion or decision to predominate.

My parents did not come to our wedding.

I had met Mark Summers, my husband, nine years before, over a tea table in a cricket pavilion. It was an idyllic late summer afternoon and I regularly supported my local cricket team in their home matches in the village near Tonbridge where I had managed to buy a tiny cottage.

'Are there any ham sandwiches?' he had asked, jumping the queue dramatically and thrusting his plate in my direction.

I looked up from the interminable routine of tea-pouring that was central to these occasions. It was hot and I was flushed and the huge metal teapot was making things even hotter – I certainly did not look at my best. Behind the plate was an almost unbelievably attractive man, mid-height, tanned and fit with dark hair and vivid blue eyes – and with an innate authority that helped him get away with behaviour that would, in gentler people, never have been tolerated.

'… or salmon?'

'Just cheese and pickle, I'm afraid!'

'Who's in charge of the menu here?' he scoffed. 'Someone who has gone to the Boring School of Cookery?'

The local Chair of the Women's Institute, who actually *was* in charge of organising the catering, was standing just behind me and flushed with annoyance.

'All these sandwiches are made voluntarily,' she said, tight-lipped. 'If you don't think they are adequate, perhaps you ought to make a contribution to the tea fund.'

Mark looked at her and, with slow deliberation, never losing eye contact with the organiser for a second, walked behind the tea table and tucked a ten pound note behind the large 'Women's Institute Chairwoman' badge which she had pinned prominently to her blouse. She flushed again – this time, I imagine, because of Mark's proximity to her.

And this was Mark – charismatic, a natural leader, funny, quirky, often to the point of rudeness – and for some reason that I have never fully understood, he was interested in me. Maybe it was my compliance, my readiness to be the butt of his ill-judged humour, that he found attractive. Until that point in my life, one of the most complimentary things that anyone had ever said to me was when an artist friend explained that she would love to paint me, not because of any claim to beauty, but because 'you could stand most people on their heads and they would look the same, but you change with every movement, every word.'

We had been married for eight years. The list of things which we had achieved within this space of time indicates the sheer pace at which we lived. We had moved four times, from flat, to a Victorian terraced house, to detached mediaeval cottage, to, now, the prospect that lay before us. A perfect historical gem hidden in the Weald of Kent: a country house built centuries ago, with acres of land, its own pond and woodland. Mark had qualified as a commercial lawyer shortly before we met and, mainly because of a heady combination of oratory, ruthlessness and insightful intelligence, had rapidly become a highly sought-after barrister.

Oh yes, and I had had a miscarriage, which had absolutely devastated me. When I knew I was pregnant, it was as if someone had given me fifty thousand birthdays and Christmases all rolled into one. Ironically I had just told my office that I would need to attend antenatal appointments, when I had lost the baby quietly and undramatically.

I never thought that I could be fully happy again. Certainly something in the intactness of our relationship had gone forever. The partying, the drinking, the steady pursuit of success and position increased to fill the void that one tiny, vulnerable human being could have passively healed. All that was months ago now. I had resigned from my London job when we knew that, unbelievably, our offer on this beautiful house had been accepted and my energies would have to be spent renovating and decorating, rather than dealing with what my husband regarded as the routine administration of my job in London.

'What are you brooding about, Kate? Thinking of writing a poem?' This was a typical Mark-type comment. Pragmatic to the point of insensitivity, self-confident to the point of brashness, he seized every opportunity to belittle quietness or reflection. Since I enjoyed both, this meant that I frequently caught the sharp edge of his 'jokes'.

I smiled without comment, which seemed to irritate my volatile husband. He accelerated far too fast down the tiny country lane, whistling tunelessly and sounding the car horn in time with the tune he was attempting to capture. Our long suffering Labradors, Rupert and Emma, sandwiched tightly in the back of the car, were roused from their half-sleep by the noise and attempted to stretch stiffly – the four-hour car journey must have seemed endless to them. Rupert started to howl softly at my husband's atrocious whistling, whilst Emma's tail thumped rhythmically against the window. There was no doubt that the Summers had arrived in Ashward!

I caught tantalising glimpses of the people who were to be our neighbours: a farmer slowly herding cows into a muddy field; a young man writing at a table in front of an upstairs window in a white, weather-boarded farmhouse; an elderly woman collecting eggs from her hens in the garden of an unkempt and dilapidated bungalow. Who were these people? What were their names? Would they become friends? Would their lives ever intersect with our own?

We rounded the corner. I can see it still in my mind's eye: the long slow bend, and then the amazing, startling view of Knight's Manor. From this direction – the north – you see the back of the house; and its sheer size and proportions are, strangely, more striking from this aspect than from its placid front south face, which is stately, symmetrical and graced by an ancient, wall-mounted sundial. This is the side that is always photographed. The sundial is priceless. But what the photographs never show clearly are the fading and eroded words that run around the sundial. They say:

TIME IS

TIME WAS

TIME IS NOT

All the secret, hidden, unpalatable bits of its history are visible as you approach the house from the north. I learnt later that the dairy, attached to the original farmhouse, had, over the years, become the dining room; the strange patchwork of stonework, with a soft covering of moss, indicates the site of the long filled-in well. A new wing cuts brutally into the gracious, steep clay-tiled roof.

The interior of Knight's Manor can be read almost as a social document. Pigs reared on the land found their last resting place on the heavy iron hooks driven deep into the central kitchen beam. The central hall – the dark heart of the house – was made even darker at some time during the eighteenth century by fine linen-fold panelling. Massive oak beams, some chamfered and carved, some plainer, give the house immense character and mark the passing fashions of the times as surely as fabrics do today. The enormous double-windowed drawing room faces south across the house's own land and east over the pond, rose garden and the tiny track along which we had just driven. A huge inglenook fireplace, whose oak seats provided comparative warmth and comfort to previous generations, still dominates this space. No-one sits on these worn, smoke-darkened seats any longer and now the massive circular chimneys make this room cold, as they funnel out any warmth from beyond the fireplace itself almost immediately. However, in the evening, by candlelight, when flames flicker and wood fire burns, and shadows dance in the uneven corners of the room, the chill can be dispersed a little. But the eastern reaches never become warm. From the front door, the grounds stretch nearly a quarter of a mile in front of the house until they meet the quiet flower-filled belt of woodland that is the boundary of Knight's Manor land.

'Come on Cheeks, let's take some photographs!' cried Mark, as he erupted from the car like some comet imprinting itself upon the unsuspecting Kent countryside. It was one of the least attractive aspects of Mark's character that he had to find nicknames for everybody and everything. It was part of his approach to life, which veered from taking things far too seriously, to ridiculing people and their attitudes. When he was in a good mood, he called me by this rather unprepossessing name and had done so for some time. When his mood was more abrasive, I was just 'Kate'.

He stood proudly, fearlessly, in front of this amazing place which we – well, he, as he would point out if I dared to suggest some measure of equality in our relationship – had bought. I took the picture. I still have it today, grainy, faded. He is a vivid contrast to the timeless elegance of the house in the latest sports clothes of the time – bright red tracksuit top and black tracksuit bottoms, T-shirt and trainers. He looks relaxed and yet defiant, as if he has just taken on an enormous challenge.

***

'Mm! Get me a coffee will you, love.' Mark muttered sleepily from under his impossibly long black lashes.

Although his eyes were shut, his face was still shadowed, cautious. I could never be sure that I had 'all' of him. 'Will the real Mark Summers please stand up…?' The thought came unbidden to my mind as I forced myself to move from the relative warmth of the duvet, which I had wrapped around myself like a cocoon, to the almost sub-zero temperature of our bedroom. Eventually I leapt out of bed and slipped quickly and as quietly as possible into my dressing gown. Crossing the bedroom, I noticed with a shiver how the valance sheet on the bed was moving gently in the cold draught leaking from the cracks between the floorboards, or maybe from the ill-fitting windows, or possibly the gaps between the ancient plaster of the walls and the heavy oak wall timbers. We had certainly taken on a challenge with this house! This was just one room. There were acres of rooms, of landings, of halls and staircases, of attics – and cellars? Cellars – I wasn't sure. I couldn't remember having viewed them during our inspections of the house, yet with a property of this size surely there would be wine cellars or storage of some kind.

I tiptoed down the uncarpeted stairs with an elegant turn and half-landing where a window overlooked the tiny road outside. The smears of noses and tongues were evident across the dusty glass – traces of our dogs' initial investigation of the vast and puzzling spaces to which they had been brought. If they couldn't smell or taste it, it didn't exist! That was their comforting philosophy. I smiled, despite being really very tired indeed. It had been three-thirty in the morning before the very basics had been established in the house, the beds made up, the kitchen essentials arranged and Mark's business suits hung in the dressing room that led off our bedroom. Those dogs! Really, sometimes they made life worth living! I was met with their usual ecstatic welcome as I went into the kitchen, which was big enough to swallow up the ground floor of my parents' tiny suburban semi *and* leave some over!

Yawning, I let out the dogs and sleepily put on the coffee machine. Watching the steady drip of the liquid, I thought through the previous evening. Until the end of my life I shall always associate the day of our arrival at Knight's Manor with two things: the dozens (it seemed like hundreds) of crane flies that crowded in through the windows open to the warmth of the late summer's evening; and the glowing colours and incredible scent of the final sweet peas that I managed to salvage from the garden. I put them in a very unsuitable plain glass vase, but they shone like jewels against the mellow golden pine of the old kitchen and the huge pale-blue Aga that dominated it.

The Aga was firmly *out*. Mrs Reed, from whom we had bought the house, had sold only because she had to. Such a place was too big and cold for a widow to maintain. This, basically, had been the reason that we could afford the place. Mark always prided himself on grinding down someone on the price of a house which they needed to sell and negotiating the purchase of Knight's Manor had been no exception. Any element of profit he required firmly to be his and his alone! The house had therefore been grudgingly handed over to us. Carpets had been removed, together with curtains and all lightbulbs except one. The vegetables had been dug up and burned. The whole place was filthy.

The coffee gave its final gurgling signal that it was ready. Still very sleepy, I walked to the low window sill and breathed in the exquisite scent of the flowers. A list had already been made of the 'musts' and the 'fairly importants' that I would have to tackle over the ensuing weeks and months – and years I thought ironically. High on the list was to get that Aga *lit!* It was freezing in this house. The central-heating boiler was approximately as large as a modern-day American double-sized fridge-freezer and took up the entire alcove to the right-hand side of the inglenook that housed the Aga. A tentative effort at turning on the boiler the previous evening had produced – apart from a series of minor explosions and surges of, presumably, hot water along the pipes – only a mild heat in some of the rooms. At the far end of the house, there was no heat at all in the bedrooms; and the attic rooms were icy. We had already decided that we would have to rely on open fires, a wood-burning stove in the study and the aforementioned Aga.

I could hear Mark's tuneless and very loud whistling upstairs. Bored of waiting for coffee, he had decided to shower. As I hurried upstairs with his drink he shouted:

'What have you ironed for me to wear today?'

'Get out of the shower and you will see for yourself!' I responded, wrapping my dressing gown more tightly around me as I saw my breath on the icy air of the bedroom.

He shot into the room, still towelling himself dry.

'Mark, aren't you cold?' I shivered.

'Ah! They breed them tough where I come from!' he grinned.

'My childhood home was only about fifty miles from where you were born!' I protested.

'Ah, but you have become soft through being over-indulged by your husband!' he quipped, pulling on grey suit, blue and white striped shirt and plain blue silk tie – all carefully ironed by myself the night before, despite my extreme tiredness.

'Oh for heaven's sake, Mark! It's freezing. I will see you in the kitchen. I'm getting dressed.'

Having pulled on several jumpers, jeans and socks, I had at least stopped shivering. As I went into the kitchen, I saw Mark gazing abstractedly out of the kitchen window, stirring milk into a fresh cup of coffee. Clearly he was already anticipating the challenges of his latest case during the day ahead in the city.

I cut across his reverie. 'I think I will ring the Aga engineer today,' I announced.

'Mm. What?'

'I said I think I will ring someone to get that range going.'

'Yeah. You do that. We will be OK with the Aga in the kitchen and the log fire going, won't we, Cheeks?'

He flung me a kiss, looking at his watch.

'Let's hope it's too early for the police to be patrolling the Kent countryside,' he observed wryly, realising that he had left himself only seven minutes to drive the six miles to the station he had chosen to travel from. This was not the closest and most obvious which most of the local commuters used, but a smaller station further down the line, which he had worked out would ensure a good seat, despite a hair-raising drive down single-track, wooded roads.

The gloriously long, golden and blue day stretched before me. The house was a mess – but never mind, I told myself, I had all the time in the world to tidy, to renovate, to restore, to discover. The dogs ran in and out following their own inane, self-contained doggy games. As for me – well, I walked slowly around the house, telling myself that I was just checking through the jobs on my list, but in reality just feeling its presence, smelling the earthy scents of autumn that flooded through the open windows, touching the silky softness of the huge wall timbers and the roughness of the bricks.

Chapter 3

The weeks that followed marked the start of one of the coldest, brightest autumns I can remember. The winds moved to the east and strengthened, causing the canopies of golden, red and amber leaves to become crisp carpets under my feet as I explored with my dogs the beautiful countryside which surrounded us. There is a stillness, a separateness, about Ashward that I have never encountered anywhere else.

The village is set within a triangle of roads – not even main roads – that effectively isolate it from the realities of everyday life. You don't have to drive through Ashward, you drive around it. There are beautiful houses, picturesque cottages, barns, a church – clearly very well-loved and looked after – but walking the bitterly cold, narrow lanes that first autumn I lived there, I seldom saw *people.*

At first I just took this for granted. I was so intensely preoccupied with cleaning, sorting, unpacking and discovering, that the need for company did not really arise. But as the weeks passed and October arrived and the pattern of my husband leaving early in the morning and returning late, sometimes very late, in the evening gradually established itself, I found that I started to miss the stimulation of conversation and human company. The impression that gradually formed in my mind was that, under the surface of Ashward life, people interacted, talked and met together. But exactly where and for what purposes was not clear to me: there was much that was hidden and secret under the outward elegance and history of the place.

It was 12 October, exactly a month after Mark and I had turned off one of the roads which isolated Ashward from the noisy, intense world we had inhabited together for the last five years. I quickly put on as many clothes as I could manage to move in to combat the cold, gusty wind, and it struck me that, since arriving in Ashward, I had seldom actually left the village. I decided to take the dogs on my favourite walk: it was short and sharp, in keeping with the temperature!

From the courtyard at the back of Knight's Manor, I turned left to follow the boundaries of our land down to the woodland, looking back again at the south face of the house. It looked so different from this aspect. Even in this raw weather, its appearance was warmer, the rosy red tiles gentle and welcoming, the proportions harmonious. It did not present the over-high and, I had to admit, rather threatening elevation that it did from the east; nor the random haphazard northerly aspect. The wood was a carpet of gold and ochre and red. The setting of the house within its land was magnificent; and the air was so clear that I could actually make out the far glimmer of the sea.

I walked past our woods and down another tiny road. This was like a voyage of discovery into a land that would become the dearest to me of all places on earth. I was sure that, forever, the glowing autumn colours and bitter, bright weather of my first weeks in Ashward would remain with me. And they have.

When I had first walked down this track, I had just been able make out the name on a broken piece of wood. The letters had apparently been burnt into it: 'Old Cruck Lane.'

More history here, I thought. I was acutely conscious that the past was all around me, but that I was too ignorant to decipher the traces.

Here and there trees appeared to have been planted into meaningful groups – tiny coppices or hedges, long overgrown. What appeared to be small orchards of fruit trees had been planted here and there on the banks of a meandering stream which appeared and reappeared now on one side, now on the other side of the road. But nowhere were there houses, or traces of houses. I later learnt that centuries earlier these small parcels of land alongside the stream had been granted to country people who lived in minute thatched hovels and worked on the local estate. For each piece of land a bullace tree and an apple had been planted. But on that first day I observed only the order and beauty of the place.

At the end of this magical road I came to a T-junction. In front of me rose a wooded ridge, beyond which I knew lay one of the 'boundary' roads of the village – and civilisation. This side of the ridge, however, there was a magic that was beginning to permeate my every sense. It was so quiet here; so beautiful; so full of sounds and sights that seemed to hold a range of meanings far beyond the tangible. Old Cruck Lane. I have walked down it many hundreds of times in many varied moods, sometimes in tune with my surroundings, sometimes dissonant with them, but always by the end of the road its peace and beauty have soothed my spirits, or raised, or heightened them. I hope that it never changes.

As I turned into the lane which led past the church and back up the hill to Knight's Manor, I leant into the wind, which was funnelling between the tall trees and ancient farm buildings that surrounded the church and the massive tithe barn opposite. Lifting my gaze to watch the leaves tumbling and spiralling down from the trees opposite the church, my attention was caught by a piece of paper that was flapping against the barn door.

HARVEST CELEBRATIONS

FRIDAY 13ᵀᴴ OCTOBER

7.30P.M.

ALL WELCOME

***

'Mark?'

'Mm?'

'Do you fancy going to a "Harvest Celebration" tomorrow night?'

I was washing up after supper. Mark was sitting with his back to the Aga, feet resting on another chair, playing a game with the dogs which involved hiding their favourite toys and then loudly encouraging them to 'find' them. The result was two frustrated dogs and much laughter from my husband at their confusion. He paused momentarily:

'Where did that suggestion spring from?'

'Oh, it was a notice pinned to the barn door opposite the church. It would be lovely to actually get to know people here Mark…'

'Tiring of my riveting company are we, Cheeks?'

'No. Don't be silly. Only, how many hours per day do I actually spend with you?'

'I've never calculated precisely – but quality is better than quantity.'

I turned my attention to the last of the cups and saucers.

'Oh, OK then – anything for a quiet life. Don't say I never take you out anywhere!'

***

I was ridiculously excited the next day. I tried hard to remember the last time I had actually been out somewhere and came to the conclusion that it had been to a little restaurant in Covent Garden several months earlier, when we had both worked hard and late and it would have been way past supper time when we arrived home. For a second I missed the excitement, the stimulus of my London life – but only for a second. I remembered the consistent expressionless turmoil of the London crowds; the unremitting pressure of commuting; the noise; the greyness of the ranks of suburban houses set row after numbing row, parallel to the train tracks.

I looked at my clothes, only recently unpacked. They seemed to fall into two very different groups: smart work clothes; and shapeless dog-walking and house-cleaning jeans and ancient jumpers. I didn't have a clue as to what was the appropriate dress code for a harvest celebration. An additional challenge was that I didn't know what the celebration consisted of. Was it a meal, a dance, music?

Eventually I chose a pair of black trousers, flat shoes (for dancing) and a longish grey shirt (with expansion room for a meal). Mark, arriving home for once relatively early, swiftly threw his business suit onto the bed and put on jeans, white casual shirt and a grey sweater. As usual he looked effortlessly elegant.

I was really nervous as we drove down the hill towards the tithe barn. This would be the first time we had met the neighbours that I knew existed, but had never seen. My imagination had attempted to populate the village with likely 'types' of people. Would there be a Lord of the Manor? A Priest? Young Farmers? Womens' Institute Domestic Goddesses? Such huge oversimplifications. In retrospect, how different were my musings from the vivid, unforgettable people we met that evening.

I was used to turning the corner before the church and tithe barn and seeing no light, no movement, and hearing no sound. But on that evening as we came into view of the ancient buildings there was, at last, huge life and energy and movement in this dark, remote and silent place.

The huge barn doors stood open wide to the black night and the cold stars piercing the frosty sky. The interior of the barn was beautiful, more beautiful than I would ever have thought possible. It soared to, perhaps, thirty feet. The heavy honey-coloured roof timbers, crafted with love and skill centuries earlier, were underlit by hundreds of candles, placed in jam jars to make them safe and protect the bales of straw placed as seats. Heavy golden hops swung from the giant timbers, like the most intricate and complex Christmas decorations but infinitely more beautiful, lending a bitter tang to the cold October air. Inside the barn, tables were set out in a pattern that at first seemed random but, on closer inspection, had been placed to accommodate the diverse social groups that thronged the extensive space. At the shadowy far end of the barn, the end almost overhanging the dense woodland, was a circular table, full already but for a single chair in the darkest segment of the circle, furthest from the candlelight. The people here faced inwards, talking quietly and, because of the lack of light in those far reaches of the ancient building, it was difficult to see their faces. At right angles to this curious table were long tables which swept down to the massive doors which stood open to the night.

I was overwhelmed. After weeks of being in my own company, in the limited light and warmth of the great house that we were restoring, the assault on my senses was acute. I was entranced by the light, the beauty, the scents and the sounds of this golden space.

'Stalls or Circle?'

'Sorry?'

'Hello!' grinned an extraordinary figure. He was small, very small, much shorter than my five foot four inches. He had an enormous head and a malformation of his spine which must have left him short of several vertebrae in his neck. Consequently, his head seemed to sit immediately on his shoulders. However, when you looked at his incredibly wide and warm smile and his bright blue eyes, the uniqueness of his appearance became unimportant.

'With the nobs, or the likes of us?' he repeated. Then looking my husband up and down slowly, he grinned again.

'Ah, I see, the nobs! To your left, ladies and gentlemen!' He made a mock bow. 'But don't forget the £8.00 entrance – nobs or not!' He held out a work-worn hand, fingers half-curled and calloused.

Mark took out a ten-pound note and, excruciatingly, said:

'Keep the change!'

Never had my husband's sense of humour been so ill-timed! This man, these people, were our neighbours!

'Oh, thank you!' I stammered, desperately trying to cover up my husband's rudeness. 'What's your name? I'm Kate Summers.'

'Jacob Wheatley! At your service, ma'am,' said the door keeper, bowing stiffly. 'You new to the area then?'

'Yes. Just moved into Knight's Manor.'

Jacob sharpened into attention:

'Knight's Manor?'

'Yes. That's right.'

'That's my house,' he said. Unsmiling now, he turned swiftly away from us to greet the next arrivals at the great barn door, leaving me confused and intrigued.

What on earth? Mark had already wandered off, gazing around him, apparently quite at ease – presumably looking for a table that suited him.

When I joined him, Mark had chosen to sit in the middle of the line of tables to the left of the entrance. There were many places to each side of Mark and I and no one as yet sat opposite.

'Why have you decided to sit here?' I whispered. 'Talk about no hiding place! Everyone can see us as soon as they walk into the barn!'

Mark gave his Cheshire cat smile.

'Well you wanted to get to know people, and we have a prime viewing position here. There is real entertainment ahead if all the inhabitants of Ashward are as odd-looking as that little man who met us at the door!'

'Mark, for Heaven's sake! Speak more quietly! These people are our neighbours.'

'So?'

On the other side of the barn, on the tables to the right of the entrance, almost all places were full. Hair newly washed and combed down hard, dressed in old-fashioned tweed suits, the men nodded and chatted together. Most held tall glasses of, presumably, cider or ale. The women all appeared to have nearly identical hair styles: neat, waved, short. Their dresses were all variations on the same theme: floral, fitted to their ample waists, with elbow-length sleeves. I tried to tidy my hair surreptitiously. It had grown to shoulder length in the months since I had last visited a hairdresser and was thick, dark and unruly. I was also conscious of my outfit, as I was the only woman wearing trousers. But I needn't have worried. These people were self-contained and self-reliant – only giving the scantest of flickering glances in the direction of Mark and myself as Jacob sidled over and presumably told them who we were and where we lived. Clearly these people knew the countryside, and each other, very well indeed. Their faces,

47

hands and body language all demonstrated that. There was an easy flow of conversation that only years of acquaintance made possible.

'How's your silage, Thomas?'

'And your uncle? Ah that was a sad day…'

'Poor Jenny Cooper. Have you seen how ill she looks tonight…'

And on it flowed. From farming, to health concerns, to reminiscence. I felt utterly outside these peoples' experiences and turned to Mark, expecting to see in his face some reflection of the interest and exclusion that I was experiencing.

He was smiling. Not a sympathetic or empathetic smile, but a superior, almost mocking, expression. I was certain that the residents of Ashward were receiving a less than glowing impression of their new neighbours.

Within the next half-hour the places next to us, and opposite us, steadily filled up. Without exception, the people who filled those places entered noisily, speaking loudly to their companions, quickly greeted others that they knew and laughed, once again loudly and intrusively, before taking their seats. They brought their own wine. They briefly acknowledged Mark and I but, quite simply, were not interested in people they did not know and whose status they were uncertain of.

When almost the entire barn was full, there was a slight flurry of activity at the entrance. The person who had welcomed us had actually sat down, almost ready to participate in the evening's celebrations. But suddenly he was on his feet and, in a couple of bounds, reached the door. He raised his right hand to his forehead in a time-honoured gesture of respect.

'Mrs Woodville. Good evening. How are you?'

'Oh, Jacob, I am well! Thank you. How are you? And May?'

I turned around and saw probably the most striking, poised and graceful woman I have ever met, inclining her head and smiling at the man who greeted her so warmly.

She swept in and smiled again – this time at Mark and I.

'Hello! My name is Helen, Helen Woodville. I don't think that we have had the pleasure of meeting?' Helen's voice was deep and melodious, with a definite mid-European accent.

Mark unashamedly and appreciatively scanned Helen's perfect figure before saying:

'Mark and Kate Summers. Delighted to meet you Helen.' My husband clicked his heels together and made a deep mock bow. I noticed that our new acquaintance had flushed slightly – whether in anger or embarrassment it was impossible to say. Certainly, her open smile tightened somewhat as she took Mark's proffered hand. As soon as she could, she turned to me.

'How lovely to have someone new in the village!' she exclaimed. 'Where do you live?'

'We moved into Knight's Manor – about a month ago,' I responded.

'Oh I love that house! It is like something out of a fairy tale. It has many faces too, Kate: a smiling face; a mysterious face; and a secret face.'

I laughed.

'Yes! But no one else has ever talked of the house like that! That's exactly what I think. I love it. It fascinates me.'

'How does one get a drink in this place?' interrupted my husband loudly, clearly irritated that, for once, he was not the centre of attention. Resuming her innate politeness immediately, Helen Woodville turned once again to Mark.

'Forgive me, Mark! Let me introduce my husband, James. He will show you where the bar is. It is quite tricky to find as the barn has hidden corners which the candlelight doesn't reach.'

She turned to present her companion: large, florid, dressed in a faultlessly-cut tweed suit and yellow waistcoat.

'Oh, pleased to meet you old chap! Let's find the whisky!'
And off they went.

'Kate. I would love to talk to you about your house, but I am formally "on duty" tonight.'

'Sorry?'

'Our vicar doesn't attend these celebrations and my father-in-law, James' father, who lives in the Manor House opposite, is away in Brussels until next week. So we have to host the celebrations this evening.'

She raised her perfectly arched eyebrows a little.

'It is so difficult bringing the two sides of the village together, and I cannot relax for a moment. But please do come and visit me at home. Come for coffee. I live at Meadow Farm, just around the corner from here.'

'Oh I have seen it, Helen. It's beautiful!'

And it was. Built in traditional Wealden style, as was Knight's Manor, it had handmade tiles the colour of terracotta and rosy bricks, but this time with a diamond-patterned overlay of the darker, locally-made Ashward bricks. Meadow Farm was lower and gentler than Knight's Manor, but probably built around the same time – at least that was how it appeared to me from the glimpses I had caught of the house from the lane. Helen continued to circulate gracefully, stopping to say a word to one group, giving a smile to another, shaking hands, gently touching the arm of an ancient villager in encouragement or sympathy. She fulfilled her role perfectly. The table at the end of the barn – set deep in shadows – she left until last. Squaring her shoulders and lifting her chin slightly, she stepped towards it. I was too far away to hear what she said or to see her expression, but her back was rigid and she did not linger long.

Whilst Helen circulated faultlessly, a bread and cheese supper had been served and a small group of musicians had started to play in one of the side aisles of the barn. The main doors had finally been closed against the frosty night and, at last, I started to feel a little warmer.

Some of the tunes I could recognise from my school days: *Oats Beans and Barley Grow, John Barleycorn, The Farmer's Boy*. But others were new to me. The feet of the villagers opposite started to tap in time with the age-old music that, no doubt, they had heard in this place, year after year, for perhaps more than half a century. As the candles flickered and the atmosphere in the soaring ancient building became increasingly smoky and dusky, it became more difficult to make out precisely shapes and colours. The faded floral dresses, the colourless tweed suits, could have belonged to villagers celebrating their harvest half a century ago, or almost at any time in the past.

Mark and James drank steadily. I could see no sense of the same social responsibility in Helen's husband as she herself demonstrated so clearly. He obviously felt that he had found a kindred spirit in Mark and they laughed together, gesturing and making comments about some of the people gathered together in the barn.

As the evening wore on and inhibitions were lost, villagers and some of the 'gentry', as Jacob would have called them, started to join in the country dances. I was itching to dance but, looking at my flushed, falsely jovial husband, I did not think that I would be likely to partner him that evening.

Suddenly the small, stiff figure of Jacob Wheatley presented itself.

'Come on lass, I know you want to dance. You have done nothing wrong and you need to feel welcome in the village.' He whisked me up out of my seat and proceeded to steer me very competently around the space cleared for dancing in the middle of the floor.

'Is your husband often like this?' he asked bluntly, looking up at me.

'Like what, Jacob?'

'Drunk and rude!'

I didn't really know how to respond to this, so said nothing, lowering my gaze slightly.

'He will be all right with them lot!' the old man commented, nodding towards the people that surrounded our table who were nodding, drinking and laughing loudly. 'But I am not so sure about you…'

'Oh, I'm fine!' I responded. 'I have my dogs and so much work to do on our house I don't think I will ever be able to complete it!'

'You seemed to get on well with Mrs Woodville.'

'She seems lovely.'

'She is. Kind and generous and a real lady. Worth a hundred of any of the other nobs in this room.' Jacob twinkled at me. 'But her father-in-law now… well, that's a different story.'

'That sounds intriguing,' I replied. 'I would love to know more.'

'Well, and you shall my dear. But not right now! One dance is all my rheumatism will stand these days.' He gave an awkward stiff bow and returned to his table.

I was touched by the old man's sensitivity. He seemed to be the only one prepared to interact with me that evening – and for that I was grateful. Mark was lost in alcohol and 'man talk'. Helen, never losing her poise for one instant, drank only water and circulated constantly. Whatever she did, I reflected, she would do perfectly.

And so, left to my own devices, I sat and watched, folding and refolding the paper napkin which had arrived with the supper before the dancing started. I noticed that there were two groups of people who did not fit into the sharply contrasting groups of 'nobs' and villagers. One was a table of three, sitting on the far side of the barn: a middle-aged couple and their son. He was attentive to a degree not often observed in someone in their twenties – especially to his mother. She sat pale, still and almost unmoving and, as she turned her head, I saw that there was a hollow at her left temple – clearly the sign of a recent operation.

The second group were the people who sat around the table at the unlit end of the barn. As I made concertinas, fans and waterlilies out of the long-suffering rectangle of tissue paper,

I became increasingly puzzled by their behaviour. Not one got up to dance, or to get a drink. There was a huge flagon in the middle of the table from which they helped themselves and which was refilled wordlessly by the person acting as barman that evening. There were, I counted, thirteen of them and, try as hard as I might, I just could not make out their features – although I could tell that some were women, some men. At the furthest distance from the light I noticed that the empty chair had a tall arched back and was much bigger than the others – but it remained empty throughout the dancing.

'Who are those people on that round table, Helen?' I asked, on one of the occasions she was able to return to 'her' table.

She frowned slightly: 'Just villagers… they meet together regularly. I'm not sure why Kate, but they make me feel so uncomfortable.' And she was off again as an ancient couple rose to leave the barn.

Mark and I were some of the last of the 'nobs', as Jacob would put it, to leave. Almost all the farmers had gone, including the family of three who had seemed so separate from everything that was going on around them. They left early and I noticed how gently the young man protected his mother as they walked to the door, shielding her from the flying elbows and feet of the dancers. I glanced one last time at the figures that remained. Almost everyone had gone now. James sat motionless, his chin resting on his cupped right hand, eyes closed. I wondered if he had fallen asleep. Helen and Jacob were talking quietly together, Helen nodding and smiling and Jacob grinning widely. I thought they were probably reviewing the success of the evening. I narrowed my eyes to see whether I could penetrate the darkness in the furthest end of the barn. As far as I could make out, the figures around the circular table had not stirred; but, surely, the great arched chair at the shadowy far end of that table was no longer empty? I lingered, trying to see more clearly.

'Can't tear yourself away from such intellectual company then, Kate?' mocked my husband, swaying slightly as he pushed back his chair and walked slowly to the barn doors, open once again to the bitter night air.

'Mark, you can't drive, you have had far too much to drink...' I started to say.

'Walk then, shall we?'

'Well I don't mind. It's safer. Look at the frost!'

'Oh for God's sake, Kate! If you don't want to come with me, you really can walk!'

Mark turned his back on me, opened the door of his car and, without even clearing the thick frost properly from the windscreen, accelerated up the hill to Knight's Manor.

Chapter 4

'You OK?'

It was Jacob. Clearly the evening was nearly ended. Helen and James had driven away in their car whilst Mark and I were arguing. The remaining people were leaving the barn in a thin trickle, turning up the collars of their coats and walking in the direction of their respective homes. Fortunately, only Jacob appeared to be heading in my direction. I was freezing cold – my coat had been in Mark's car – and was angry and upset to be so unceremoniously left at the side of the road.

He didn't wait for my response.

'Here, take this,' he grunted, removing his ancient and slightly smelly overcoat and throwing it around my shoulders. 'We'll walk back up the hill together.'

We started off, following the swerving tracks of Mark's car tyres in the frost. I wrapped the ancient coat more closely around me and bits of hay and dog hair floated off it as we walked. I just couldn't stop shivering – whether with cold or anger, or a combination of both, I wasn't sure.

'He's one of a kind, your husband, isn't he?' Jacob observed caustically.

'He has his moments, Jacob,' I replied eventually. 'Thank you so much for rescuing me. I probably would have been found frozen to the spot if you hadn't helped me out.'

Jacob didn't respond to my attempt at a joke. He seemed deep in thought.

'He needs to take a bit more care of what is his!' he muttered. 'Those back there,' he nodded to the barn, whose doors were closing again – but by whose hands it was impossible to see – 'are always waiting for the unprotected ones.' He shook his head, or rather his shoulders, thoughtfully.

'What do you mean?' I asked.

'I've said enough.' With a conscious effort to change the subject, Jacob continued:

'How are you getting on with Knight's Manor then?'

'Well, it's big and it needs sorting out,' I observed.

The old man nodded. 'Aye, so many changes since my day… That ugly great bit at the back of the house was built for the bathrooms,' he explained, grinning. 'Couldn't somehow see Mrs Reed in the old tin bath we used in front of the kitchen range!'

Despite myself, I laughed out loud.

'The old well was filled in too,' he muttered, 'and why that was done I don't know. The water came up fine and clear and cold and had done so since before my father's day. The only trouble we had was with newts – we did get the occasional newt in our water. But then, they are clean little animals. You wouldn't never catch anything from them!'

Secretly I was rather glad that the tap water came, presumably, from some mains water system. I like wildlife, but not in my drinking water!

'How long is it since you lived there, Jacob?' I asked.

'Me? 'Bout twenty years – but before that, Father was a tenant of old Lord Ashward. We had farmed our land since

Oliver Cromwell's day. But I decided that I would become my own landowner; so I worked all the hours that God sends and saved and I proved them all wrong! Aye, my schoolmasters, my father, the villagers, and Mr High and Mighty Woodville. They all said I could never succeed, because... because I am as I am.'

'Mr Woodville? Do you mean James, Helen's husband?' I frowned, trying to keep pace with his account of what clearly meant so much to him.

Jacob Wheatley's face changed subtly. His smile faded and the work-drawn lines, which had made him look like a benevolent gnome when he was smiling, now became grim and grey.

'No. Ralph. Her father-in-law, poor lady!'

Jacob paused, kicking at a stone frozen to the surface of the mud at the side of the road.

'Around 1953 – my old dad was still the farmer here then and me and my brother helped him like – old Lord Ashward died. He had become what you might call peculiar in his later years, although his kind have another word for it. "Eccentric" they call it! He never had children and we village folk never saw him. He shut himself up in the old priory and wandered around his garden and rode his horse all over his land – but we never saw him in the village. He had been Lord Ashward since the turn of the century and there was hardly anybody who had seen inside the great house. It is a rum building that! There is an old priory – well, what remains of it – and then some other old house joined on to it, not as old as the priory but grand enough!'

I was not getting a very clear picture of the architecture of Ashward Priory – certainly Jacob was no architect – but I imagined that, after the reformation, the titled family had repaired an ancient mediaeval priory and extended it in seventeenth-century style. But I really wasn't too sure.

We trudged on up the road, the wind whipping frost off the branches of the bare trees which arched overhead.

Jacob went on:

'Well, as I say, when the old lord died, there was no one obvious to pass the estate to and the priory and gardens were closed up for a time. About two years later though, we saw that the hedges and grass were being cut, the gates taken down and then replaced with ones that hung straight and fancy on their hinges. My dad came home one Saturday night from The Swan – Saturday night was always his drinking night – full of news.

'"Guess what?" Dad asked us. "We have a new lord of the manor! Them fancy London solicitors have found an heir. And guess what again? He is a vicar!"'

Jacob stopped to button up his tweed jacket and turn up the collar.

'And he is still our Vicar, now!' added Jacob.

'Is he called Reverend Lucas?' I asked. 'I saw his name outside the church on that little board.'

'Aye. That's his name,' my companion confirmed. 'But at that time, none of the villagers knew what was going on. The whole of the parkland, where we used to be able to go in the old lord's time, was closed off and 'Private' notices put up everywhere. Eventually this land agent came around knocking on doors and asked folk whether they wanted to be part of "a new venture". I ask you! When most of us were working all the hours that God sends just to make a living! Anyway, this "new venture" turned out to be turning the old priory into a "Spiritual Well-being Centre",' Jacob snorted. 'Whatever that might mean!'

It struck me as he was speaking that Jacob must have an almost photographic memory. Clearly he remembered exactly what was said, many years previously, even though it included words that were unfamiliar to him.

'It were a right funny do,' Jacob mused quietly. 'None of us knew what was going on. Strange arty folk and do-gooders came into the village from time to time, trying to talk to us and invite us over to their new-fangled place.

'And that's where Ralph Woodville comes into the story,' Jacob went on to explain, shaking his head sadly. 'Apparently Mr High and Mighty Woodville was a close friend of Reverend Lucas in London. He came down to Ashward and decided to buy it! Aye, and he thought he could buy the souls of the people in the village too!

'You should have seen him, looking down that long nose of his, as he looked around my house,' growled the old farmer. 'It was a bit mucky – but you can't farm nigh on 350 acres single-handed and worry about a few cobwebs! Woodville went here and there, tut-tutting at this, that and t'other. Finally he said, "Now, Wheatley, as *my* tenant the state of this property is unacceptable. It is filthy and dilapidated."' Once again Jacob was repeating, word for word, what he had heard years previously.

'You should have seen his face when I just stopped and faced him and told him, "Don't bother yourself. I want to buy Knight's Manor anyway! And if it is in such a terrible state, you won't be asking that much for it now, will you?" And I did buy it…'

By this time we had reached the woodland at the end of Knight's Manor land. I could see that Mark had got home safely because most of the lights were blazing out across the frozen fields.

Jacob Wheatley stopped and leant heavily on the field gate which was the lower entrance to our land. He looked levelly, almost fiercely, at the beautiful house.

'We called this flower field,' he murmured, almost to himself, 'and that next one was home field. The next meadow down into the valley is spring field. You wouldn't know that if you didn't plough and sow and harvest the land. This land is in my bones, and your Ralph Woodvilles and Mrs Reeds come along and buy it all – just like that!'

'I'm sorry, Jacob.'

He shook himself like an old dog. 'Why should you be sorry? You understand – and you will understand more before things are finished.'

'Jacob?' I prompted him gently 'Why did you have to sell again? You had worked so hard to buy all this.'

'Well…' he sighed sadly, looking intently at the lines of the beautiful old house that had once been his. 'Can't blame Mr Ralph Woodville for that. That was all my own fault.'

As we stood there, the lights in Knight's Manor started to go out one by one, and I realised that Mark must be finding his unsteady way to bed. Jacob was silent. Eventually we were left looking at the black silhouette of the house, a backdrop of stars providing the only light. He took so long to answer me that I wondered if he was ill. But eventually he muttered:

'I drink. Yes, all this… farmhouse… barns… 350 acres… cattle… animals. I drank them all away.'

There was nothing I could say, so I just laid my hand on his arm. Eventually, he shook himself again.

'Ah well! Must be getting to bed now! All respectable folk are indoors by this time.'

'Where do you live, Jacob?' I asked.

'Knight's Manor Farm: the bungalow back down the lane.'

I recalled the glimpses of our neighbours that I had seen when we arrived in Ashward those four short weeks ago. The dilapidated, grey net-curtained farmworker's bungalow, with the frail old woman collecting eggs from the overgrown garden, must be Jacob's home. He must have got planning permission to build his 'retirement home' before selling the noble, beautiful house for which he had slaved for so long. All that remained to him now was a sad dream and a great name.

Chapter 5

I closed my eyes and sighed. 'You know Helen, this is like coming back into civilisation for me. To be warm and fed and looked after... amazing! These biscuits are fantastic. Where do you get them from?'

Swinging back her pale golden hair, Helen Woodville smiled.

'Oh, James gets them from Fortnum & Mason. Would you like him to bring you some?' In the weeks since I had met James at the Harvest Celebration I had come to realise that he behaved more like a lapdog towards Helen than a husband, seeking to anticipate her every whim. She regarded him with good-natured tolerance.

'They are probably really bad for me,' I replied. Although I was slim, I would never, I feared, achieve the determined elegance of Helen's figure. She was absolutely perfect. Even in her 'country clothes' she looked stunning. Today she wore dark fawn cord trousers and a loose-fitting creamy mohair jumper with contrasting purple bands around throat and wrists. She had, astonishingly, knitted it herself. 'That's why the wrists and neck are darker,' she had laughed, as she had worn it for the first time several days previously. 'It saves washing it absolutely every time I wear it.'

What an extraordinary mixture my new friend was. During the previous three weeks I had walked down Old Cruck Lane many times to see Helen, inevitably with my larger than life dogs in tow. We would put them in the barn at the back of Meadow Farm and they would play quite happily for hours in the hay, hunting imaginary, or sometimes real, rats and mice and then crashing out in golden heaps, almost indistinguishable in colour from the hay on which they lay. Helen was immensely warm sometimes, but had a sharp, almost astringent aspect to her character – rather like eating a sweet sponge with a tangy lemon icing. She was beautiful, without a doubt, with the sort of features that spoke of centuries of refined and careful breeding. In one of our many conversations she had somewhat reluctantly shared with me that she was, indeed, a countess; that her homeland was Poland; and that she and her mother had sought refuge in Britain at the end of the War, when their lands had been taken and their properties destroyed.

Helen went into the kitchen to make more coffee and I had a few moments to look around her beautiful pink, green and gold drawing room. What a contrast to Mark's and mine!

Mark and I had both started from absolutely nothing financially, both from working-class parents. Mark's had run a corner shop; my father had worked as an office manager, desperately trying to maintain the respectability that had surrounded his own upbringing, always held back by my mother, who never worked because 'the home' took up so much of her time. I shook my head impatiently – why then was it never particularly clean, certainly never tidy? We had moved to our first flat in Mark's brother's car. I remember the most prominent item was a huge bunch of daffodils perched in a milk bottle on the rear parcel shelf.

In total contrast to the mish-mash of furniture that we had brought to Knight's Manor, Helen had brought her aristocratic taste to the decoration of her home. Everything that surrounded her was elegant, funded by the wealth of the family into which she had married. Each piece of furniture was chosen with great care. Matching green silk sofas invited one to sink into them. A beautiful inlaid Georgian workbox stood in the corner by the window. Vases of fresh, skilfully arranged, flowers were set in the deep windows. The curtains were graced with swags and tails of material. I thought ironically of how I had made my own and how they were held up with plain pine curtain rings on plain pine curtain poles, with not a swag nor tail in sight!

Meadow Farm was softer, quieter, more hidden than Knight's Manor, which fronted its land like a huge ship putting out into a stormy sea – defiant, a bit rougher than its near neighbour, more intractable and with much, much more character. I stood up and stretched, before walking over to the large windows perfectly framing the beautiful view of the Ashward woods.

'I love your view, Helen,' I murmured, as she returned with a laden tray. I always felt so secure, so sleepy, in this room.

'Mmm...' she mused. 'But Kate, it's so quiet! I still miss all the excitement, the challenge of my London office.'

'What made you leave London, Helen?' I asked, finally voicing the question that had been on my mind since we met.

'Ha! You cannot be a busy accountant and manage an estate the size of the Woodville kingdom,' she responded wryly. 'I've never fully explained to you the real reason why I am living in this quiet spot, have I? You are always flying off to decorate a room, or dig a flower bed, or put a casserole into the Aga. We never have very long to talk, do we?'

She was right. I felt guilty immediately, a feeling that came very easily to me, stemming from my childhood of apologising constantly to my mother.

'Oh Helen, I'm so sorry!' Involuntarily, I moved towards the door.

'No don't be – and come and sit down again! I know how much you love your new home and that brilliant husband of yours. Do please sit down again,' she repeated, as I still stood, undecided, in the middle of her beautiful room. 'I'll pour you another coffee.' I curled up once again on her immaculate sofa, my washed out jeans a contrast to the silk brocade.

'Are you sitting comfortably?' quipped my beautiful friend. 'Then I'll begin. Some two years ago, Ralph, James' father, found that he just could not keep up with the demands of his estate. He felt that with advancing age, the accounts, the trust that he had established and the consultancy work that he still occasionally does, were becoming too great a burden. It took him over a year to persuade me to administer his financial affairs. We arrived in Ashward only nine months before you did, Kate.'

'But I thought Meadow Farm was yours, Helen.'

'Nominally. On paper only,' she replied, her face as hard as it could ever become. 'Meadow Farm is a lovely bribe, offered to me by my devoted father-in-law in return for my agreeing to leave my career in London and my beautiful mews house in Chelsea to come and act rather like an estate manager. Ralph owns Ashward, Kate. Every tree that you see planted, every neatly cut verge in this village is at his instigation. It is his tractors, his money, that see to it all.

'Ralph moved here some twenty-five years ago, when Paul Lucas came down from London. Paul had recently inherited the Ashward estate and was on the verge of a nervous breakdown. He just did not know what to do. Ralph was his friend and mentor. He is considerably older than Paul and had attended the church where Paul was curate. My father-in-law is a chartered surveyor and Paul desperately needed his professional advice as well as his friendship. Well, things developed from there. Paul moved into Ashward Priory; Ralph moved into the Manor House. Ralph "bought" Ashward. Bought a whole village.'

My friend stood silent for some minutes, her back towards me, tracing and retracing with her finger the moulding on the wooden shutter folded back from the window.

'Helen?'

'Oh I am sorry, Kate. I was just lost in my thoughts, my memories. I had a brother once. It was wartime. We lost him because he had become weak through hunger... and couldn't... I will tell you the story one day.' She paused again and visibly made an effort to pull herself together.

'What I am trying to say is that the contrast between what my mother, my brother and I had then, and what Ralph has now... sometimes it is unbearable.'

She was looking steadily, with an expression that I found unfathomable, at the ridge which marked the boundaries of Ashward and the start of the outside world. I was completely nonplussed. I had never seen the woman I had started to admire so much, so moved. Her breeding ensured that she maintained an outward calm, but I could sense that she was deeply upset. I did what has always come easily to me. I went up to her, put my arms around her shoulders and gave her a hug. Where I would have turned, in tears probably, and returned the hug, Helen laughed lightly, patted my arm and turned away from me again.

'So there it is Kate, my loving friend. That is the reason I am here. Imported to do a specific job, with a golden carrot being held out to me.'

We sat, not speaking, in a motionless, companionable silence. I heard the little noises that made up Ashward: a tractor rumbling by; sheep bleating in the field opposite the house; the wind blowing, now loud, now soft, down the chimney. Cold rain spattered against the window and a few drifts of mist crept across the dark woodland on the other side of the valley.

'Helen, I must be going,' I said reluctantly. 'Mark will actually be coming home for a meal tonight. He does not have a client meeting, or a squash match, so I want to produce something really nice for his dinner.'

'Lucky, lucky girl! Do you know Kate, I am only seven years older than you, but I feel hundreds of years older than you in experience!' she exclaimed. Looking into the cool depths of her large hooded grey eyes, I too felt this experience. I suspected that she had passed through things that I could never have possibly survived. I also felt that there were things now, not quite as substantial as the loss of her brother, her home, title and position, but still terribly significant in her life, that were ongoing trials to her.

'You go home to your wonderful old house and light those candles and pour the wine and have a romantic evening with Mark. Whilst for me,' she turned away again with a sigh, 'my devoted James will return from London as usual on the seventen train. We will eat, as usual, what we eat on a Wednesday evening. He will sleep, as he always does, after his meal, in front of the television, and we will spend an unremarkable night together in bed, only for the whole mind-numbing routine to start again tomorrow. I envy you!'

I smiled, rather embarrassed that in one short afternoon I had discovered so much about my enigmatic friend.

I laid my hand gently on her arm. 'Goodbye, Helen. Thanks again for the warmth.'

We walked across the heart of her home, the beautiful central hallway. It was full of light and fragrance from the bowl of late roses she had placed on the circular yew wood dining table. It struck me then, as it had before, that the corresponding part of Knight's Manor was the only part of the house in which I did not feel comfortable. My central hall was dark. The oak linen-fold panelling absorbed any ray of light that had penetrated that far. There was a feeling of heaviness and staleness that no amount of window and door opening could dispel. I always walked quickly across this area.

We were nearly at her back door when, surprisingly, the doorbell rang. I could see the angular outline of a very tall, thin, slightly stooped figure standing outside. Glancing at the silhouette, Helen set her shoulders and raised her chin in her accustomed attitude of unconscious defiance.

'Why, Ralph!' exclaimed Helen, as she opened the door widely, 'what a lovely surprise! I thought you were in Brussels until Friday.'

'My dear, how good to see you looking so well. Clearly Ashward air agrees with you.' Ralph Woodville's voice was the first thing that struck me about him. It was low, well-modulated and incredibly cultured. Occasionally, the contrast between my roots in industrial Lancashire and my position as owner of one of the finest houses in the area struck me. It did now. Ralph's cold, pale blue eyes were looking straight at, or rather through, me. I knew what he must be thinking – my dress was, as usual, suitable for dog-walking and decorating, but not much else.

With icy politeness he turned to his daughter-in-law: 'Helen my dear, do please introduce us. I don't think we have yet had the… pleasure.' His bony hand was extended in my direction.

'Yes, of course. This is Kate Summers, who has just bought Knight's Manor with her husband, Mark.' Subtly, but quite distinctly, Ralph's manner changed towards me.

'Kate, I am delighted to meet you. What a magnificent property you have! Did you know that originally the house was mine, included in the village houses and farms when I bought Ashward? I saw Knight's Manor when that old reprobate Jacob Wheatley and his father before him had been tenant farmers. What the Wheatleys had done to that beautiful old house! It was filthy. There were even birds' nests in the bedrooms!' He laughed with derision. 'He actually asked me to sell it to him below market value because of the state into which his own family had rendered the property! Just imagine.

I didn't reduce it of course. He paid a full and fair price and I avoided the expense of renovating the house. So, as I said to him at the time, he was welcome to the place. Obviously though, his foray into property ownership was ill-considered, because he had to sell in the end, to Reed, who renovated it and made distinct improvements.'

As he talked on in his precise and haughty way, I thought of the defiant forthright figure of the farmer who had made such 'an ill-considered foray' into property ownership. Born with such disadvantages and yet working through these to such achievement, all scornfully dismissed by a man who had everything – birth, talent, fortune, position. I can't say that my initial impression of Ralph Woodville was particularly glowing.

Would this, I wondered to myself, be my Mark in forty years' time? Cold, hard, recounting his financial triumphs with scant regard for the personalities involved and with a complete lack of compassion and understanding. On and on Ralph talked, clearly determined that I would be in no doubt of his status within 'his' village.

Some five minutes after our introduction, there was actually opportunity for me to speak.

'Well it is so good to meet you at last, Mr Woodville. I have heard so much about you from Helen.' He directed a quick, hard stare in his daughter-in-law's direction, as if to gauge just what had been revealed.

'Oh yes. I am surprised that we have not yet encountered each other. I walk my lanes and check for damage to trees and hedges every week. No chance of travellers settling here, or of trees falling and blocking roads here in Ashward! My men would soon sort out problems of that sort.' Deliberately, he turned to Helen. 'My dear, Rebecca and I wanted to ask whether you and James would like to come to a little drinks party we are holding a week tomorrow night, to formally welcome you into the neighbourhood? I know it's short notice, but you couldn't possibly have any other important engagements on a Thursday evening. I assume that you will both be able to attend?'

Perhaps it was the assumption that she would come when he beckoned; or possibly that her father-in-law believed that he knew every detail of her social life; or maybe the deliberate omission of an invitation to me, that goaded Helen into saying what she did.

'Oh Ralph, I am so sorry. Kate and I had just arranged something for that very evening. Another time maybe.'

Two deep vertical creases appeared between the great man's eyebrows. His dulcet tones rose just fractionally. 'But Helena, I have already issued the invitations to the other guests. Now, let me think.' Then, turning to me, 'Kate, I have just had a most happy thought. Are you and your husband doing anything special a week tomorrow? It would be an ideal opportunity for you to meet your far-flung neighbours. Please, do say you will come.'

I looked at Helen under my lashes. She smiled.

'Thank you, Ralph, provided that Helen has no objections. I would love to come. I'm not sure about my husband Mark though. He is always so busy.'

Helen and I laughed together like schoolgirls as she ran me and the dogs home in her tiny Citroen, since my intended return walk had been delayed by Ralph's visit and the rain was now torrential.

'Do you know, Kate,' she chuckled, 'that is one of the few triumphs I have ever had over my father-in-law! And,' she grinned, 'it was *great!*'

Chapter 6

I looked out of the kitchen window at a wall of white. The mist of the previous afternoon had transformed itself today into a thick cold blanket of fog, obliterating everything. The only items of interest I could see from the window were the spiders' webs on the fencing posts, strung with tiny water droplets, which shimmered and shifted ever so slightly in the movement of the moisture-laden air.

I shivered involuntarily. The house was like an icebox. I didn't often resent my husband's rather individual take on life, but today, when I could see my breath inside the house, I was really irritated by his airy assumption that we could manage to keep warm with open fires and a range. Easy to say when he spent most of his time in a centrally-heated office or an air-conditioned squash court!

A strange cold torpor hung over the house, and there seemed to be an almost physical weight on my mind that I just could not shift. I decided to try to dispel the fog that had seemed to have penetrated my very brain by taking a brisk walk with my faithful dogs. I had, by now, several favourites and today I followed my usual path down Old Cruck Lane.

Jacob had fallen into the habit of calling in for a cup of tea two or three times a week and a couple of days previously had explained the origin of the name of the lane. Apparently, when he was a boy, the oldest house in Ashward was to be found some fifty metres down the lane. It was an early thirteenth-century thatched cruck-framed cottage, and could actually be seen from the upstairs windows of Knight's Manor. Jacob told me how one day, when he was getting ready for school, his father called out:

'Fire! Old Cruck's on fire!'

Jacob flew to the window of his bedroom at the front of the house and saw billowing smoke and tall red-gold flames rising from the roof of the ancient cottage. Jacob's father and several of his farmworkers ran down the land with pitchforks and pieces of wood, intending to dislodge the burning thatch and to beat out the fire from the reeds. But there was nothing anyone could do. The fire had taken firm hold of the old house and it was burnt to the ground. Only the idiosyncratic name remained.

On this gloomy foggy morning, instead of turning left to Meadow Farm, I decided to turn right and walked the shortish stretch of road which led to Ashward church and Ralph Woodville's magnificent manor house and the tithe barn which had been the setting for my rather uncomfortable introduction to Ashward society. Usually this collection of buildings was breathtakingly beautiful; and, as Ralph subsequently told me, has been described by Pevsner as 'the perfect manorial group'. On a sunny day, with every line of roof, wall and mullion lit with a clear golden light, you could see why. But today, it loomed from the thick fog – dark, amorphous, threatening, with as much aesthetic perfection as a gasometer. From the Manor Farm the little road rose steadily for about two miles back to Knight's Manor.

Not for the first time, the geographical relationship between the three main houses in the village struck me. The Manor House, Meadow Farm and Knight's Manor were set in an equilateral triangle, with my house at the top, Meadow Farm the bottom right and Ralph's manor house the bottom left.

It was a duty walk, taken only for the purpose of exercising the dogs. But even they did not show their usual enthusiasm and trotted quietly by my side, resignation evident in every line of their bodies. Re-entering our freezing house, they installed themselves on the old rug in front of the Aga, plastering their cold, damp bodies right up against its comforting warmth. I, however, felt much better: that mental oppression had lifted.

Clearly the dogs were fine until later. I gazed out of the window, considering how best to spend my time on such an unpleasant day. Finally, I decided to start a job that I had been meaning to tackle for weeks but was reluctant to face. I would try to improve the appearance of the cold, depressing, dark hall.

Armed with coffee in the largest mug I could find, some expensive wax polish and a pile of soft dusters, I left the cosy depths of my kitchen. Not content to rely upon the two overhead lights in the hall, I carried two reading lamps from the study and our bedroom.

This was going to take ages! I started at the foot of the stairs and decided to tackle a panel at a time. Much to my surprise, the linen-fold panelling started to improve markedly with my vigorous polishing. It would never become light and glowing, but amber depths were awoken in the wood as my dusters moved rhythmically over and over the fine carving. At least *some* light was now reflected from the polished panel and I was pleased. But after several hours of concentrated work, I realised that I had only covered about a metre of panelling. This renovation was the project of a lifetime! I stood up, stretching my stiff back and flexing my fingers.

I went back into the kitchen for more coffee and stood against the range, savouring the warmth. I would do two more hours' work, I decided, and then finish for the day. It was still only one o'clock. There was plenty of time, and what else would I do?

With renewed vigour I set about polishing the wood in the next section of panelling. When this was finished I would be about halfway across the hall. Time passed as I repetitively polished round and round, gently coaxing life into the filthy dark woodwork. Suddenly my duster snagged on a rougher part of one panel. This was in the darkest part of the hall – roughly midway between stairs and the long corridor leading to the shower room and garage.

'Oh blast!' I hoped that I hadn't done any damage. I was only too aware how the blundering efforts of an amateur could spoil and damage really valuable antiques. I gently pulled the duster back from where it had snagged and brought over one of the lamps to get a better look at the rough patches on the wood's surface. But when I looked – really looked – I could hardly believe what I saw: clearly ancient, sloping script ran neatly across one wooden panel. I gently continued cleaning and polishing in smaller circles until I believed that I had uncovered all the lettering. Incredulously I read:

Paul Ashward
1729

It was like meeting a character from history! My hands shook with excitement. Who was Paul Ashward? Why did he carve his name and this date here, right in the middle of the house, not in a prominent position on the outside, or over a fireplace? Thoughts were racing round and round in my mind. If I couldn't share them I felt as if I would burst. I went quickly over to the telephone, my first thought to speak to Helen. I rang her number, but her phone just rang and rang. Clearly she was out.

I simply must *do* something, I decided. I was far too excited to just stay polishing for the rest of the day. I looked at my watch. It was only one-thirty. I glanced out of the window – still dense fog! Suddenly I made my decision: I would go into Tentersley, our local town. Mark would not be home for at least six hours, probably longer. There would be people and lights and warmth in Tentersley, and I had suddenly started to realise how hungry I was. In my absorption with the panelling I had forgotten to eat. I quickly fed the dogs, then loaded them into the car before heading carefully down the twisting narrow lanes towards the town.

Tentersley is a beautiful place. Dominated by the massive Abbey Gateway, every house, every shop seems to be a miniature museum in its own right. I reflected upon this now, as I sat in the Cloisters Tearooms and looked up to the enormous timbers holding the vaulted roof. There was the kingpost, carved for all to admire, the pivotal point upon which all this huge heavy weight descended.

As I sipped my coffee and ate a sandwich, the question of what I should do with the rest of my day presented itself again to me. I still felt a bubbling excitement at my discovery and just had to find something to occupy my attention and energy. Idly my eyes flicked over the little posters and fliers displayed for customers of the tearooms to entice them to visit more attractions and nearby places of interest.

TALK ON THE HISTORY OF ASHWARD
and the
ASHWARD PRIORY ESTATE
by
William Deepdene

Tentersley Library,

Thursday 28 October 1981
4pm.

That's today! The very thing! Downing my coffee quickly and calling for the bill, I picked up my bag and walked swiftly through the swirling fog in the direction of the library.

***

The little reading room of the provincial library was hardly full: the residents of the town on this cold and foggy afternoon were staying firmly by their firesides. I would estimate that only some fifteen people were sitting, still in their outside coats, waiting with a sort of bored patience for Mr Deepdene to start speaking. I looked around. Some attempt at alleviating the deadly grey and white decor had been made by the posting of photographs and maps on the otherwise featureless walls.

I yawned. Whatever the other attendees thought about the lack of warmth in that reading room, to me, used to the sub-zero temperatures at Knight's Manor, it was positively tropical. I took off my quilted jacket, sat back and prepared to listen.

Mr Deepdene was small and neat, in a tweedy, checked suit and white shirt. He was fifty-ish, with short grey hair. He started very low key, giving some of his own background and explaining that he was a farmer. My knowledge of farmers extended only to Mr Wheatley and he was very different to this composed, articulate figure. William Deepdene still farmed with his brother the land called Barrow Farm, which lay on the parish boundary. He explained how he had become increasingly interested in the history of 'this beautiful and historical part of the county in which we live' in his early twenties. Since then he had written and published several monographs and short books on the history and prehistory of the area.

It really was warmer in here than I was accustomed to. I felt my eyelids drooping as my concentration wavered under the dry and monotonous delivery of the speaker.

'Here is a sketch map of what I consider to be the centres of historical interest in our parish,' pronounced Mr Deepdene, flashing up on the overhead projector screen a neat plan of, presumably, some part of Ashward parish. Suddenly my eyes opened wide. Never mind 'some part' – there was my home!

At the top left-hand corner of the slide, a neat irregular ground plan, shaded black, represented Knight's Manor. The relationship that I had thought of during my morning walk – of my home with Meadow Farm and the Manor House – was clearly evident on the sketch map. It looked almost as if Mr Deepdene had drawn the roads with a set square. Directly to the west of Knight's Manor lay Barrow Farm, and it struck me vividly how close this man's farm actually was to my home.

Unbelievably I heard the following: 'Knight's Manor represents the flower of the early Tudor period of building in this area. The magnificent proportions of the farmhouse are of a splendour unequalled in our parishes. Of special note are the chimneys, which dominate the southern aspect, and the superb eighteenth century linen-fold panelling which was added by Paul Ashward, a frequent visitor to the house and a patron of the family who lived there between 1701 and 1760.'

What? Paul Ashward? I couldn't believe this and listened intently, fully awake now.

'Apart from the superb architectural worth of this classic house, some of the stories which surround it are noteworthy. The tales of the notorious Paul Ashward would, if transcribed in detail, fill a substantial volume.' He smiled in what I suppose he imagined to be a winning way. 'And a selection of his exploits appears in my short work: *A brief life of Paul Ashward* which can be purchased for the modest sum of £5.00 from this library. Less dramatic, but equally fascinating to my mind, is the legend that an underground passageway leads from the cellars of Knight's Manor to the cellars of Ashward Priory. There is evidence that the aforementioned Paul

Ashward used these passages for his frequent and mysterious nocturnal forays.'

This man talked like a guidebook! But to me it did not matter at all. What was I hearing? The sort of information that sounded so fantastic that I would doubt its credibility in respect of a place and area I did not know – but in relation to my own home I was left amazed and listened with every atom of my concentration. Secret passages? A notorious figure from history? My mind was in turmoil at the host of images that these words conjured up. But one fact in this long tale of dramatic facts shook me most of all. This self-important little man was suggesting that a passage led from Knight's Manor cellars, of which I had never seen a trace, to Ashward Priory.

I brought my mind back firmly to the present and attended once again to the quiet, measured, erudite tones.

'In the cellars of Ashward Priory lies one of the least known aspects of its history. Away from the classical proportions and rich embellishments of the Priory and the subsequent seventeenth-century addition, lie the remains of much earlier building.' Here Mr Deepdene paused to clear his throat for what I felt was dramatic emphasis. Not that I needed further drama, my mind was utterly riveted.

'Remains not of a single previous dwelling, but of many! There is the fine mediaeval tiled flooring of the Priory itself, under which is a thick layer of ancient timbers – some of which are heavily charred – then Roman walling and, ultimately, traces of much earlier, pre-Roman habitation, like a slice of archaeological fruitcake.' Again, that pedantic smile! 'This proves that the site itself has been of lasting cultural, and almost certainly spiritual, significance for successive generations.'

Mr Deepdene moved on to Meadow Farm, explaining that Paul Ashward's daughter had overseen the building of this house during her lifetime, and ended with an encomium upon the Manor House.

'Within the stately pile that we now see, lie the remains of the original priest's house, which is, of course, contemporaneous with the building of Ashward church in the late eleventh century. Here, in the eighteenth century, Paul Ashward's wife, Lady Penelope, settled after the death of her husband, extending and altering the original humble dwelling until it was fitting for one of so exalted an origin.'

Well, I thought as I joined in the polite clapping, maybe this man's oratory would never set Rome on fire, but what a lot he's given me to think about. Of the many thoughts whirling around in my mind, the major thing that struck me immediately after this talk was the close historical relationship of Ashward Priory, Helen and Ralph's houses, and my own. The lives of the people who had lived in these great houses in the past were interwoven very closely, just as, I thought, my own life was every day becoming linked and twisted together with the lives of my neighbours.

I decided to remain anonymous and, having thanked Mr Deepdene for his talk, went to the librarian's desk in the next door room to buy a copy of his 'short work' on the life of Paul Ashward. Tucking the slim volume under my arm, I left the library.

The day had darkened into a virtually impenetrable blackness. It really was difficult to see for more than a few metres in any direction. Shop and street lights glowed a dull orange as I returned to my car and I wondered whether, after all, it had been sensible to venture out of my big safe stronghold on such an afternoon.

I switched on every available light that the Mini had and even then it was probably the most terrifying journey I have ever made by car. It wasn't too bad on the main road but, at the tiny turn to Ashward, I lost the cats' eyes and the white lines that had guided me along the busier route. Windscreen wipers going steadily, alternating between full and dipped headlights in a desperate attempt to see anything and going at no more than fifteen miles per hour, it took me thirty minutes to complete a journey that normally took ten. I negotiated the cattle grid which led into my courtyard with huge relief and considerable difficulty, since no lights were on in the house. I thankfully let the dogs out, locked my little car and, clutching bags of shopping and my book, went indoors, immediately flooding it with light.

Quickly I lit the logs set in the huge inglenook and looked at my watch. It was still so early, even though I felt as if I had travelled through at least a thousand years of history that day. Mark would be home in twenty minutes and I couldn't wait to see him! I crossed to the Aga and took out my heavy cast iron griddle, ready to cook the steaks I had bought for dinner. Apart from the dogs' steady breathing, everything was totally silent and still. I could almost feel the swirls of fog around the metre-thick stone walls of my house. Shattering the silence came the shrill ring of the telephone, which made me physically jump, so silent was the fog-bound world in which I was marooned.

'Hello!'

'Oh hi, Kate. Look, I won't be home this evening. I just have to complete the deal I was telling you about and need to stay on in the office to phone New York at five p.m. their time, which is ten p.m. ours. Sorry! Also, to be honest, I just did not feel up to negotiating those roads at midnight in this horrendous fog.'

'It's bad your end then?'

'Terrible.'

'Oh, Mark, I am so disappointed. I've got so much to tell you. Do you know what happened today?'

'What, the Aga blew up? Look, love, I am interested, but just now everything is happening here. Save it for tomorrow. It's Friday and we'll have a good chat then. Bye!' And he was gone. No wonder I had tried to telephone Helen earlier with my news of the carved name on the panelling, rather than Mark.

I slammed the receiver down and went back to my two faithful friends in the kitchen. Yawning, scratching, looking lovingly up at me, they were always the same. Always ready to give and receive love – unlike my husband. For a few seconds I longed for someone who did not operate on the same level as Mark: someone who listened to me as well as talking at me; someone who empathised with how I felt and what I did.

I carefully cut one steak into two equal parts and threw one each to the dogs. Wagging and gulping down the unexpected treat, Rupert and Emma licked their thanks to me. I cooked the remaining steak, opened the wine and sat down to my solitary meal.

Chapter 7

'A Brief Life of Paul Ashward,' I read, 'by William H.B. Deepdene.'

It was nine o'clock. Washing up done; fire blazing softly in the huge inglenook; dogs snoring loudly in front of the logs. Only the previous evening Emma had dislodged one of the blazing pieces of wood and it had rolled onto her back, singeing her quite badly. It is a testament to her incredible temperament that she just looked dazedly up, sniffed her smouldering fur, and only then gave out a half-hearted yelp. She was unhurt, but her coat now bore an unusual pattern of zebra striping on her right shoulder. I smiled again and almost involuntarily bent to stroke my loving friends. A few minutes previously, I had looked out of my window into absolutely nothing. With the absence of any surrounding lights, the fog had become almost tangible, an impenetrable barrier between me and the outside world. Everything that night seemed preternaturally calm.

I had decided to settle down and read Mr Deepdene's book before even attempting to go to bed. I knew what would lie before me if I did – hours of sleeplessness and longing for Mark, even though the fulfilment of that longing was, without exception, disappointing to us both these days. I stoked up the fire, took a sip of the red wine which I had poured for myself and started to read the book which promised to hold such fascination for me, almost hearing his clipped tones delivering the rather sententious content.

Chapter 1: The Earl's Early Life

Paul Beaupre de Ashward was born in the year 1700. He inherited the vast Ashward Estate which occupies a very substantial part of the county of Kent. To his parents' eternal disappointment he remained their only child, but he excelled in everything he did. His tutors spoke most highly of his attainments; and at the age of eighteen he attended Balliol College, Oxford. Here he read Classics and became one of the most prominent scholars of ancient languages of his day, being a key pioneer of the translation of the Anglo-Saxon archives held at the Bodleian Library. This he achieved, despite there being rumours that he had had a certain degree of involvement with the notorious Hell Fire Club, which was rife at that seat of learning in the early years of the eighteenth century. At twenty-one, Paul returned to help manage his father's estates.

All went smoothly for some five years, but when Paul was twenty-six his father, Frederick the twelfth Earl, died. A contemporary account, found in the diary of the incumbent of Ashward church, reads as follows:

November 1st 1726

'Was roused from my bed early this day by a messenger riding post-haste from her Grace at the Priory. Oh Tragedy! His Grace, the Earl, was found by the lower bridge this morning shortly after dawn, stiff and cold. My presence was required forthwith. When entering the chapel at the Priory, I saw what was obviously the corpse, decently covered with a black and gold

87

cloth, lying in front of the altar. Walking quietly to it, I knelt and prepared to uncover the body. What horror awaited me! The picture is imprinted still upon my numbed brain! The good Earl, instead of having embraced death with calm and the peaceful composure that one hopes to see seemed, in faith, to have been frightened to death. His great eyes stared at me, the white exposed to an unwonted degree around the pupil and iris. His lips were drawn back from his teeth in a horrid grimace, as if all the horror and pain and misery of the world had hit him at once in an unbearable wave which, quite simply, deprived him of the vital spirit. One of his hands was clasped around an object. I hastily re-covered the face, but gently prized open the fingers of his clenched hand. In there, held so tight that it had made an imprint upon the dead flesh, was a knuckle bone, crudely carved with a letter of some kind. It looked like a capital F, but with the horizontal strokes tilted slightly upwards.

'Her poor Grace! Let us pray to God that she forgets this terrible last sight of her beloved husband.'

I took another mouthful of wine. Ugh! The old parson had certainly known how to write! Emma shifted in front of the fire, moving closer to gain a little more warmth from the flickering logs.

Paul became the thirteenth Earl of Ashward and he managed the great estate with firmness, kindness and skill. He married Lady Penelope de Guise of Faversham Abbey and had, by her, four children: two sons and two daughters.

The thirteenth Earl became known nationally and internationally as a scholar and a paragon of nobility in these early years.

Chapter 2: The Middle Years

Sadly, such are the fluxes of this mortal life that when Paul, thirteenth Earl of Ashward, reached his fortieth year, matters were no longer in such a happy state.

It is reported in the journals and letters of his wife Penelope that her husband took increasingly to walking abroad late at night. Sometimes, she writes, he did not return until the following morning.

To her sister Agnes, Lady Penelope wrote as follows:

'My dear sister, I really do not know how to begin, or how to explain what I saw this morning. I was unable to sleep because of the heat and the absence – alas becoming habitual! – of my dear husband. Towards dawn, I went to the open casement to try to cool my bedchamber a little by opening it even further, when I saw Paul on the outskirts of the woodland. He appeared to be on his knees, but for what purpose I could not immediately distinguish. As the grey light grew a little, I gradually made out that he was not alone. He appeared to be bowing to a person or creature, standing still as stone, in the shadows of the thick summer foliage. It was impossible, at that distance and in such faint light, to make out any precise detail. All I could see was that the figure was still, huge and black. In the split second it took me to blink and direct my gaze again, the figure had disappeared and I saw my poor husband rise slowly and stiffly to his feet, to return, his eyes cast down, his gait unsteady, to the Priory.'

When asked for an explanation by his anxious wife, Paul replied, apparently in increasingly violent tones, that she should 'Mind her own business and allow him to mind that of the parish.' Along with these night time absences, Lady Penelope started to note a change in her husband's appearance. Paul's face began to show signs of ravage and ageing beyond his years. The rest of this section of my little book is taken almost verbatim from the journal of Lady Penelope. I have abbreviated some lengthy passages and have, somewhat, modernised the language.

I smiled somewhat ironically to myself – I could not detect any significant difference between the inflated language of the book and the way in which its author spoke!

One night Penelope determined to follow her errant husband. She dressed herself wholly in black – black dress, black hooded cloak, black gloves and boots – and waited in her room in the seventeenth-century part of the Priory for sounds that her husband was leaving his adjoining chamber. At around two o'clock in the morning. she heard those signs. Softly, she slipped out of her room, along the corridor and followed the Earl as, to her surprise, he descended the servants' staircase. This led directly into the mediaeval part of the building – the original priory itself – and down into the ancient cellars which lay under the twelfth-century foundations.

Most of these are now walled off for safety, but then they were extensive, with separate stone chambers and vaults to store cheeses and wines. The thirteenth Earl walked firmly to the far corner of the cellars, where the vestiges of far older buildings still remain today. He reached forward and opened a very ancient, small, arched oak door. The wood was black with age and possibly fire damage. Breathing quickly, Penelope followed him. She was aware of a movement in the cellar to her right – the part which held the majority of the fire-damaged timbers and their ashes. The movement was regular, rhythmic, like a pulse, or a heartbeat, or a breath.

Paul had a dark lantern which he held in front of him to light his way along the wet and slimy passage. They climbed steadily, Penelope following the tiny glimmer of light held in her husband's hand. On and on they went until Penelope felt that she was in a never-ending dream. She felt certain that by now they had left the purlieu of the park and must be under neighbouring fields or houses. At one point Penelope felt a distinctly cold draught to her left and assumed that another tunnel entered the main passageway at this point.

Abruptly the tiny glimmer of light ahead of her stopped. There was the noise of a key being turned in a lock and her husband opened a door. For a second, Penelope saw him silhouetted against a flickering red light, then a huge black shadow moved across the aperture, dwarfing the figure of her husband and obscuring the light almost entirely, before the door was shut and locked. Immediately, Penelope was plunged into total darkness and, it has to be said, a fair degree of panic. What was she to do? Wait for almost certain discovery; or try to return, slowly groping her way along the narrow pitch-black passage until she reached the sanctuary of her home?

As she stood, too stunned for a moment to move, she started to feel, rather than hear, a deep resonance that seemed to throb through the whole tunnel and the earth surrounding it, through the door and the air beyond it. It was not quite a hum, not quite a chant. It was as if the whole of Creation at this one spot had been changed and all elements were moving together for some definite purpose which was the antithesis of good.

Penelope waited no longer. Slipping and groping her way back down the passage – inky blackness before her and she knew not what behind her – she fled, falling and scratching her legs, arms and hands, back towards the safety of her own home.

My hands were shaking as I stretched forward to make up the fire. Emma was practically sitting in the inglenook in her quest for warmth! I had been so involved in reading, my imagination transported back nearly 300 years, that I had not noticed that the fire was almost out. I poured myself another glass of wine. Oh dear, half a bottle gone! But I actually felt as if I needed some Dutch courage this evening. Just exactly where had the second door led? If it was true that an underground passage linked Ashward Priory and Knight's Manor, did the door open into my house? What was the significance of the possible second passageway that entered the main tunnel? Involuntarily I looked around the shadowy sitting room. The wall lights sent flickering shapes across the walls. The chill in the great room seemed even more acute than usual. Could I read on? I was getting distinctly 'spooked up' as my pragmatic husband would say.

I looked at my watch: just after ten o'clock. Mm! Well, not much chance of sleep now I thought, at least not until I had finished learning all I could about the man whose name I had uncovered earlier that day.

Chapter 3: The End

For Paul Beaupre de Ashward, the end came as suddenly as for his father – but where his father's death had been shocking, Paul's death was extraordinary to a degree not encountered elsewhere by myself as an amateur researcher of local history.

For nearly twenty years, Paul Ashward's strange habits brought illness and misery upon himself and his wife and increasing unease to his estate. At the age of fifty-nine, no longer making meaningful communications with either his family or his tenants, Paul was a wild figure indeed. Lady Penelope writes that he seemed to exist on no sleep and little food. His hair, which he wore longer now, was totally white, as was his face, due to his only leaving his dwelling place at night. His eyes, red-rimmed and staring, frequently shifted sideways, as if they could catch sight of something that other mortal eyes could not see. Gamekeepers reported that when they glimpsed him walking in the grounds of Ashward Priory, he would stop suddenly and whirl around, taking a few sudden paces backwards as if appalled by what he saw. Occasionally, he would half-sink to his knees. Thus the fine man and scholar had become a wandering, silent ghost, unfathomable to his family and tenants alike.

One bitter February day, writes Penelope, Paul announced that he would be 'very busy' all day; and that no one – neither family nor staff – was to search for him. At around ten o'clock in the morning, two heavily-laden covered wagons were seen slowly descending the road to the lower bridge at Ashward. The wide woodland path, which leads through the thickest of the ancient ash and beech woods, was the route these wagons followed, with the drivers laboriously urging their teams of horses along the bumpy uneven tracks.

From time to time that day, sonorous sounds of hammers ringing on stone were heard in the woods. But of the Earl there was no sign.

At twilight the wagons were seen emerging from the deepest part of the woods, now bouncing along the track, relieved of their burdens. Of Paul there was still no sign.

That evening the Earl's family toyed with their food. Their husband and father had not returned home. There was no word, no sign, no indication whatsoever of what had happened to him. By now the long years of worry had taken their toll on Lady Penelope. The bold young woman who had followed her husband along that passageway two decades previously had been replaced by a chronically nervous individual who relied almost totally upon her children for support. During the long hours of that late-winter night, the whole family were sleepless. In the morning the Earl's two sons determined to search for their father.

The morning was bright and cold; frost rimed grass and leaf. The two viscounts walked almost reluctantly towards the lower bridge and the woodland track where the figure of the Earl had last been seen. These woods are ancient – part, it is said, of the huge tracts of native ash forest which dominated this part of the country in primeval times. On either side of the track, huge boulders were poised at impossible angles, tossed there by some retreating glacier.

It became darker and darker as the young men penetrated the woods. Despite the leafless state of the trees, their sheer number and size effectively blanketed out the weak light of that cold February day. On and on they trudged, passing a strange black carved shape – like a crouching animal or bird – to the right of the path. Suddenly the young men saw signs of disturbance. The bushes and plants of the woodland floor had been bruised and broken. The lingering bitter smell of crushed herbs filled the clearing – and then, rising before them, the size of a small cottage, they saw it: a stone pyramid.

Convinced now that the construction of this pyramid had been the mission of their father on that previous day, the two men haltingly walked towards the structure. On the west face only there was a break in the carefully constructed stone walls, where a small wooden door had been set into the stonework. On the wood had been carved the word:

Déaþscufa

Hardly daring to move, dreading and half-expecting what they would find, the viscounts slowly approached the door. They flung it open – needing almost to get over the necessary shock of what they would discover. But never in their wildest moments of fantasy could they have imagined the sight that was now before them.

Their father sat upright at a desk, head in dead hands. In front of him lay scattered a couple of dozen knuckle bones upon which characters were scratched deeply. Three words had been formed in front of what remained of Paul Ashward:

cwiclác ádéþ wyrgþu

The young men were utterly horrified by what they found. They had not inherited their father's scholarly interest in ancient languages and to them, the words, with their unfamiliar letters, were meaningless. However, the elder brother, now the fourteenth Earl of Ashward, transcribed them carefully into his pocket book.

To conclude this astonishing and tragic story: the pyramid remains; the Ashward family had it walled up without disturbing a single thing. As far as we know, today the Earl still sits in his chair, skull in bony hands, gazing sightlessly at the scattered characters before him.

One final note: for the uninitiated, the words can be translated as:

But I did not need the pompous farmer to tell me what they meant. I knew. The resounding, echoing, powerful Anglo-Saxon words spoke clearly to me over the centuries:

Only a willing sacrifice will destroy the curse.

Chapter 8

It was three a.m.

Four and a half hours earlier I had finally managed to get myself from fireside to kitchen, to let Rupert and Emma out. The fog was still so thick that it would have been impossible to make out their flying figures, even if my numbed brain had been in a fit state to register such things.

My mind was fighting to come to terms with what I had just read. It was as if fantasy, or fairy tale, and reality had been suddenly grafted together in my secure twentieth- century world and had formed an unsettling hybrid that I was fighting to understand.

My dogs had returned and, as usual, taken up their 'bookend' positions against the Aga. I had shot upstairs, washed quickly in the freezing bathroom and dived into bed. On this unusually quiet night, all the creaks and groans of the mighty old house which surrounded me were clearly audible. There was no wind or rain to distort or muffle the sounds. It was just too quiet. I had tossed and turned for over two hours, becoming more and more awake, reliving what I had learned of the man who had carved his name into the panelling in my hall, directly below my bedroom. At twelve-thirty I had given up and returned to the kitchen to make some cocoa – my mother's panacea for all ills! When I returned to bed I decided to take Rupert and Emma with me. I hauled their heavy basket upstairs and put it by the small inglenook fireplace in my bedroom, fluffed up their blankets, encouraged the dogs to lie down and, once again, dived into my ruffled bed. That was better. The physical presence of two solid living creatures, instead of the insubstantial shadows that had been inhabiting my brain, was immensely reassuring and I fell into a restless sleep.

But at three a.m. I awoke in a flash as I heard, with crystal clarity, light footsteps running along the long corridor outside my bedroom. They ran to the far end, returned and ran back again. The dogs were awake too. My fearless Rupert, who had to be walked in quiet areas so as not to terrify humans and animals alike, was standing facing the door, his lips drawn back over his sharp white teeth, his hackles up, his muscles tensed, a low growl rumbling in his deep chest. Emma, a pale echo of her mate, was smaller but formidable in her own way. They mercifully blocked the space between my bed and the door but, as the footsteps started to return, the dogs retreated, tails dipping steadily to come to rest between their legs. Their heads tilted, ears cocked, listening, puzzled. From the other side of the door there appeared to be a delighted giggle before the footsteps retreated once again to the other end of the corridor. Then silence.

***

'But, of course, my dear! You must come straight over.' Helen masked a yawn politely as she answered the phone. I had waited as long as I could, trying to maintain social conventions, but at seven a.m. exactly, I rang her.

The fog had cleared and given way to torrential rain. I charged down the road to Meadow Farm, soaking dogs racing along beside me. They would, I thought, soon dry off in the hay barn.

'Oh, Helen!' I gasped, 'I am *so* glad to see you!'

Heaven knows what I looked like. I had had a sleepless night, had neither bathed nor showered, wore no make-up and was soaking wet. She, on the other hand, had clearly taken the trouble to brush her hair and looked composed and ready for anything that the day would cast across her path. The coffee dripped comfortingly in the coffee machine as we sat in the kitchen and I told her every detail of my extraordinary day. Recounting it made it seem impossible that it had all happened within twenty-four hours. It should have filled a week.

Helen listened gravely, not interrupting once, as I sobbed and stuttered out my story. She placed a mug of coffee in front of me, but that was all. I was waiting any moment for her cool laugh and the expected 'But, my darling, we live in the twentieth century!' Instead she said: 'Right, Kate my dear, this is what you will do. You will come upstairs to my guest room. You will change into a towelling dressing gown. I will run you a bath. When you are ready, you will get into bed and I will bring you breakfast. Here! Take the radio and listen to some solid Radio 4 news whilst you are changing. That, if anything, is a bracing antidote to creatures of the night.'

I did exactly what I was told. My friend brought me a tray of croissants, fruit and coffee and sat quietly smiling as she watched me eat every last morsel. Then, surprisingly, Helen crossed the room and drew the curtains.

'And now,' she whispered softly, 'you will sleep.'

And I did – for eight whole hours. I awoke at four o'clock in the afternoon, when she drew back the curtains and placed a tray of tea and biscuits on the bedside table.

'I have telephoned Mark and he is coming home early tonight. You will both eat with James and me.

'I command you,' she smiled, leaning over my bed in a mock threatening manner, 'to stay here until dinner is ready and your husband has arrived!'

No one had looked after me like this for seventeen years, and even then my mother's care had been so different – more dutiful, more correct – not intuitive and loving as that of this woman who was fast becoming the dearest friend that I have ever had.

***

At first Mark was clearly sceptical. After dinner that evening, he leant back arrogantly on one of Helen's Chippendale chairs, glass in hand, looking with a disconcerting directness at me as I tried to explain all the fear and shock of the previous day. James had excused himself and retired to his study when it became apparent that the conversation was not going to centre around fishing or shooting.

I could see at once that Mark thought my account a terrible exaggeration. That is, until there was a natural pause in the conversation and Helen began to speak in her quiet, measured, slightly inflected tones.

'I don't think I have ever told you about Nicholas, my brother,' she said softly. 'He was a beautiful child, my mother tells me, so good, so loving, so brave. He was eight years older than me. The three of us – my mother, Nikki and myself – left Poland together around 1943, shortly after the death of my dear father. Mother carried me, but Nicholas tried to be the man of the family, striding ahead, despite weeks of undernourishment, which had clearly sapped his strength. We came to a roadblock where searchlights intermittently flooded the road with light. My mother realised, she has told me since, that they must have been on some sort of time switch, and she counted the seconds between each sweep of light: just sixty – one short minute. The road was wide and uneven, full of potholes and mud and there were high banks on either side. We crouched quietly in the darkness on the field side of one bank. We knew that we had to cross to give us any sort of hope for the future. Already all our lands, country and town houses and most of our goods had been confiscated by the Nazis. We must have crouched there for twenty minutes at least, whilst my mother assessed the situation. Suddenly, the silence was broken by my mother's hushed whisper:

'"Nicholas, it is for you to cross first. As soon as the searchlight has swept across the road, you must run, run for all your life is worth. Wait for Helena and me on the other side, behind the bank."

'Nicholas gave an exhausted smile: "Right Mother." He curled his legs under his thin body ready for the sprint that should have brought him to freedom.

'Once more, the searchlight swept the stretch of road with its merciless stare.

'"Go, Nikki," whispered my mother, "and God be with you," she added as he stiffly, awkwardly, scrambled the high bank, slowed by cold and lack of food.

'"Twenty seconds must have passed already!" my mother whispered clutching me tightly.

'"Ah!" I heard her gasp of indrawn breath as she watched her son, my brother, stumble and fall as his foot caught in a pothole. His frailty from lack of food was pitifully apparent, as his movements were slow and laboured. The blackness between the searchlight sweeps was inky.

'"Nicholas, Nikki my darling, please, please hurry," prayed my mother, as he dragged himself out of the hole and tried to stumble on. But even I, child as I was, knew that time was slipping by. Mother's hold on me tightened until it was almost unbearable. She stared into the blackness, desperately trying to make out what was happening. Suddenly she saw. It was all too clear. Nikki had just reached the far bank and was starting to clamber up it, when that deadly light struck again. Harsh shouts came from the roadblock as his pathetic little figure was seen clawing its way up the slippery, muddy slope. I saw no more. My mother crushed my head into her, putting her arms across my ears to try to block the obscene sound of guns firing, I knew, at the only brother I had'.

We were all totally silent. Only the soft ticking of the brass carriage clock on Helen's workbox marked the passing of seconds, as we all thought about the desperate attempt of that small boy, a lifetime earlier, to obey his mother and run to safety – and his tragic failure to do so.

'I tell you this, Mark.' Helen spoke softly to my husband, looking more serious than I had ever seen her, but still with no sign of a tear. 'Kate has been describing the unexpected experiences she had yesterday and I could see that you were sceptical, and so I must share this with you. When I was old enough to understand, my mother told me of a strange dream she had, years before Nikki died, when we lived in our fine house on the banks of the River Oder. She told me that she had seen my brother in a dark place, lying still. He was covered with layers of muslin, or some such thin material, so that she could not see his face. Suddenly, a bright light came into her dream. But this light was not comforting. It was cruel and held a deadly fear for my mother. Seven times the light swept over Nicholas and his thin body was illuminated; and each time a layer of muslin disappeared, almost dissolved, from his body. My mother remembers thinking with relief that soon she would see again the face of her beloved son. Layer after layer went until only the final layer remained to be dissolved. The light came for the seventh time, the cobwebby material was gone – but then my mother saw that my brother was dead, shot in many places; and that, instead of lying in a peaceful bed, he was lying in a stone coffin. Kate's experience was, I am convinced, supernatural; so was my mother's. Do not dismiss as nonsense everything which you yourself have not experienced.'

More deeply moved that I had ever seen her, Helen rose and swept from the room. Even my arrogant husband found it impossible to make any sort of retort or sarcastic comment to her controlled and deeply felt outburst.

We returned home in silence.

Chapter 9

Whatever else the previous owner of Knight's Manor had been, she had been no gardener! Mark stood with his left arm lightly around my shoulders, both of us drinking coffee, looking out of the front door of our beautiful home. All we could see was grass. No flowers, no shrubs, just acres of green, stretching away towards the belt of woodland which fronted Old Cruck Lane.

'Right, Cheeks!' said Mark briskly, in his larger than life tone, 'I think we'll tackle the pathways and the front flower beds today.'

I turned round to examine the front of the house, where grass stretched up to the rosy brick of the walls.

'But Mark, it will take all weekend!' I exclaimed. 'I thought we might go out somewhere together.'

'Well we've done all that, Kate. I mean, once you have visited somewhere, that's it, isn't it? You've seen it!'

I thought of Canterbury, of Faversham, with their fascinating buildings and history, all within an hour's car drive. But then I supposed that Mark had been away from his home all week in London. He deserved some downtime, even if this meant breaking yet more fingernails and further ingraining my hands with soil and other grimy substances.

Once I had settled into the work, I enjoyed it as usual. It was just that I was so physically tired. As I picked up my spade, I reflected that since we had moved in I had decorated, cleaned or worked in the garden every single day. When it was wet, I worked indoors; when the weather was fine, I was outside. All this, as well as walking the dogs every day. No wonder I had lost about a stone in weight since our arrival in Ashward. My muscles were aching slightly before I began, but this eased after about fifteen minutes heaving up turf and cutting the shape of two curving paths, which we intended to infill with old bricks, to be in keeping with the rest of the property. We had found the bricks in the corner of the walled vegetable garden, heaped carelessly by the fruit cage.

We started at ten-thirty in the morning; I crawled indoors at four in the afternoon filthy, damp and exhausted. Mark went straight to the kitchen cupboard which held 'the booze' as he called it.

'You'll feel better after this, love,' he pronounced cheerily, pouring me a glass of red wine as I lowered myself into a chair at the side of the Aga. Mark looked wonderful. During the week, the travelling and the pressures of work took their toll. By Friday he was pale and often looked very tired. But now he looked relaxed and full of life, his eyes bright with the fresh air and exercise – he was obviously in a wonderful mood.

'You know, Kate,' he said, quite seriously for him, 'I think it's great the way we work together on projects like this.' He gestured vaguely towards the front of the house. 'Other women wouldn't work in the same way. You are strong – for a woman.' So that is what he valued me for: work! Is that how he really sees me, I wondered – as a good investment, value for money, just as he regards property deals, or cars, or making innovative connections in the world of commercial law?

'Let's go to bed,' he announced suddenly. 'It's dark outside and freezing in! We need to warm each other up.'

'But how about the dogs?' I asked 'How about the state I'm in? I need a bath first, Mark. I really do.'

His face hardened. 'Ah well, any excuse I suppose. I think I'll ring up Robbie and see if he'd like a game of squash.'

Oh no, not another solitary evening. I simply could not bear it! So, pushing aside all my objections, I gave in to his blackmail.

Some hours later, awake, vividly awake, against my sleeping husband, I reviewed my life bleakly. Increasingly I never felt as if I shared in Mark's sexual experience. He seemed to be fulfilled – well, relieved might be a more appropriate word – but the heights of ecstasy which we had both reached in the early years of our marriage had long since disappeared. Renovating one of the great country houses of the district was all very well, but I needed more balance, more fulfilment in my life. I needed company, but above all I thought, full of self-pity, I needed a love that was deep and meaningful. Not merely the physical attention of someone who led entirely his own life and picked me up and put me down again when it suited him.

It had never struck me so forcibly before. No wonder I longed for a child – someone who would not look sceptically at me, or question my motives, or take violent issue with my opinions and grind my argument or point of view into the ground. It would be quite wonderful, I thought, to be with someone who would love me exactly for what I am, not what I could, or should, be.

Mentally I flicked through my diary for the coming week and realised with a shock how central Helen had become to my daily routine. Tuesday, coffee morning at Meadow Farm in aid of the local church; Thursday evening, the much laughed about evening at Manor Farm. Two social events; both centred around Helen. And in between times, walks with the dogs down to my friend's beautiful home.

This just will not do, I told myself. I absolutely must get to know a wider circle of people in this scattered settlement. I finally fell asleep with the question of how, practically, this could be achieved, going round and round in my head.

***

It was this last thought, I believe, that persuaded me to go to church the next day.

'Hmm!' grunted Mark. 'Hallowe'en – very appropriate!'

'Why don't you come with me?' I queried.

A rather bitter smile crossed his features.

'When I was young,' he answered obliquely, 'I used to go to Sunday school; and sometimes Mam – the Northern expression jarred somewhat with the sophisticated professional persona which he had carefully developed – used to take us to church. But Dad would never come. "You take the family, Gloria," he would say. "You get dressed up and parade yourself and the lads with the other best Sunday coats and boots that folk want to show off. I'll just stay out of the picture if you don't mind."' Mark looked immensely vulnerable and at that moment I wanted no more than to take him in my arms and love him; but, almost immediately, the spell was broken.

'So you go and represent the family, Cheeks,' he quipped, 'but make sure you clean up your hands and do something with your face and hair. You could learn a lot from Helen Woodville – she always looks good. Why don't you ask her to give you a makeover!' And, as was often the case, Mark laughed out loud at his own humour.

If I had needed encouragement to follow my resolve, then Mark unconsciously had just provided it.

Evensong was advertised outside Ashward church on the display board: to start at three-thirty I noted, as I flew past with Rupert and Emma later. There was just time to go home and change. I was really angry about Mark's ill-directed joke earlier. Helen had no need to walk dogs, or clean her house, or decorate, or garden – unless she wished to do so. The Woodville empire provided all this support.

I decided to put on a dark brown Jaeger suit and matching hat. I looked at myself critically in the mirror and thought to myself that, finally, I looked as if Knight's Manor could actually belong to me.

I had never before been inside the little, very ancient, church. I thought back to the talk at Tentersley library during which I had learned that the church was late eleventh century. I could well believe it. It was small, low ceilinged with huge oak doors and mullioned windows. It seemed to have grown organically from the stones and earth which surrounded it. Inside it was, quite simply, the most beautiful church building I have ever seen. Immaculate whitewashed walls, intricately carved rood screen and pews, magnificent oaken pulpit behind which was a grey slate plaque with the following words carved and outlined in gold:

> ***Love bears all things, believes all things, hopes all things, endures all things. Love never ends.***

The whole effect of unusual luxury and softness – almost like someone's earthly, rather than their spiritual, home – was heightened by dozens of fine wax candles which had been lit along the pews and in the deep window embrasures. Someone, I thought, has spent a fortune on this place.

An elderly woman was peering over her spectacles at the music which rested on the small organ, which she was playing competently, but without any real panache. Another elderly lady walked slowly over to her and rested her hand in a friendly and familiar way on the organist's shoulders:

'Now, Doris, Mr Paul is nearly ready,' she murmured in a soft Kentish voice.

'Right you are, Blanche,' replied the organist. 'I'll get my hymns organised.'

How lovely to belong, I thought. Clearly these two old girls had known each other for aeons. They probably went to school together, had worshipped in this church for decades, maybe were even related by marriage. My mind ran idly on, acutely aware of the distance which my status as owner of Knight's Manor and my birth and education, many hundreds of miles from this isolated community, placed between myself and the rest of the congregation. Well, not quite the rest. I looked with great fondness at Helen and her family, sitting in the front pew of the beautiful little church. This evening Helen wore a bright red woollen coat. From the back, with her immaculate blond bobbed hair and slim, almost boyish figure, she looked as young as her two teenage daughters who sat beside her. Jane and Ella both boarded at Roedean and I had only met them briefly the previous weekend. James sat, bulging over the pews, beside his elegant wife and daughters. Large, more than slightly overweight, a good-humoured smile was fixed, it would seem almost permanently, on his florid face. No – however hard Helen was trying, her family did not 'belong' either. And Ralph and Rebecca Woodville, sitting on the opposite side of the aisle to the younger members of their family, most certainly did not. Ralph, in every studied inch, appeared to be the aristocrat, in ancient but faultlessly-cut, grey suit. Rebecca, his wife, in dress and jacket, talked occasionally in deep cultured tones to her husband. I had yet to be formally introduced to Mrs Woodville senior. Both the elder Woodvilles had entered church only a few minutes previously by a private door leading from the south of the little building into an ancient porch, which faced the manor house. Something which, I thought, served to distance them yet further from the country people who made up the majority of the congregation.

Suddenly, the congregation was hushed as if by an invisible signal. Brisk firm footsteps came down the aisle from the rear of the church.

I don't know how I expected the minister of this gem of a church to look – perhaps rotund, placid, thinning hair, with a benign expression on his face. What I saw couldn't have been more different. Clerical robes billowing impressively out around him, grey hair thick and more than a little unruly, steely, thick glasses catching the soft light of the candles as he strode between the pews housing his flock, I first saw Paul Lucas.

He was tall – at least six feet and of medium build. Every action was purposeful: his firm stride, the way in which he arranged his notes on the carved pulpit, the impatient gesture with which he removed his glasses to address the congregation.

As the service progressed, I realised that Paul Lucas was a man of profound and searching intelligence. He quoted Latin and Greek in his sermon – not extensively, to be sure, but to an elegant degree. I was reminded of characters which I had encountered in the works of Jane Austen and George Eliot. He was like a 'classical' figure, cut out and preserved from a time I could only dream – or read – about, but not access directly, superimposed upon a simple rural society. What on earth did the likes of Doris and Blanche think about this powerful, authoritative figure who, at first sight, would appear to lack all humility and gentleness – qualities which I had come to think of as mandatory in the clergy.

Paul Lucas was leaning forward slightly from the pulpit. He had again removed his spectacles and was talking impromptu to his congregation, not referring to his extensive notes.

'Make no mistake,' he said, his beautiful well-modulated voice lowered to a deep intensity. 'Without doubt tonight the most appalling practices will take place – more dreadful than we could possible realise.'

Of course! Tonight is 31 October – Hallowe'en. I recalled Mark's sarcastic comment when I had told him that I intended to go to church.

In Paul Lucas' sermon were none of the watered-down phrases I had heard before in connection with Hallowe'en. This man went light years beyond the 'trick or treating' syndrome. He spoke with passion and directness of evil and spiritual death and he introduced me to ideas and concepts which, at that time, were only on the very borders of my consciousness.

The service was over. His sermon had taken me out of that perfect little church on to rough hillsides and into dark forests. In my imagination I had watched unmentionable practices and had felt loss and intense fear at the images his eloquence had conjured up.

Still fighting to come to terms with what this man's words had made me realise, I sat and watched the energetic, almost restless, figure striding once more down the aisle of this little country church.

I shuddered as I went outside into the dark, cold evening. Flurries of leaves swept down from the tall lime trees which bounded the church on its northern side, softening the angles of the mossy gravestones. In this ancient setting, shadows changed into menacing demonic figures, columns of swirling leaves into ghosts.

Thankfully I jumped into my faithful little Mini and locked the door. Even two miles of well-known road was potentially full of evil threats to my mind, still haunted with so many dark images. I drove quite slowly, because the road was muddy from the passage of tractors and cows. Suddenly, just on the junction of Old Cruck Lane and the road which led from the church back to Knight's Manor, I saw, away to the left where the land fell away to Barrow Farm, a line of dark red lights. They flickered – whether because they were naked flames, or intermittently obscured by trees and bushes, I wasn't sure. I saw them maybe for thirty seconds and then they were gone. Without thinking I had braked too suddenly and my little car had slewed sideways in the mud. Inevitably the engine had stalled. I tried to restart: nothing. I tried again: a mere flicker of life, then silence. I was going to have to walk home – fortunately only about two hundred yards or so. Well, actually run rather than walk! I swiftly locked the door of the little car and without looking behind me or down towards Barrow Farm, I pelted as fast as I could down the dark muddy road to the vast bulk of Knight's Manor, looming even blacker than the black sky.

Mark was whistling tunelessly in the kitchen, making himself a cup of coffee.

'Hi,' he greeted me non-committedly. 'Was it good? Do you feel spiritually cleansed and holy?' Then, because of my silence he turned to look at me for the first time. 'Are you OK, Kate? You look awful!'

And I must have done. I had lost my hat, my hair was tangled and I looked at my legs spattered with mud from the road. I told Mark about the lights and he just laughed. 'Rabbit catchers!' he exclaimed. 'It's just the night for hunting. Look, you sit down and I will go and rescue the Mini – and your hat, if I can find it.'

It was at times like this that I really thought that our relationship could return to the easy, happy times we had had at the start of our marriage. Smiling at the thought, I left the kitchen, intending to go to my bedroom and change my church clothes for something distinctly more 'doggy'. As I left the brightness of the kitchen to cross that gloomy hall of ours I heard, or thought I heard, an almost indistinguishable noise. Far far away, the soundwaves fluctuating because of what I assumed to be the distance, I heard a low chanting. Now I could just make it out; now it was gone. It seemed to have a life of its own, moving and shifting the reality of the hall and staircase.

Soon I heard the comforting crash of the cattle grid as my little car was driven at great speed by my husband, wearing my battered hat at a jaunty angle, into the courtyard and then the double garage.

'Mark,' I said quickly, 'will you come with me and be very, very quiet.'

'What?' retorted my husband loudly.

'Just come into the hall with me will you, and listen. Tell me if you can hear anything.'

We sat on the bottom stair and listened intently. We could hear the wind down the huge open chimneys; an occasional light tap as falling leaves struck the windows; and the whimpering sound of Emma having a dream. Of any other sound there was not a vestige.

'What am I supposed to be listening for?' enquired Mark eventually.

'Chanting of some sort. I heard it just here, as I was crossing the hall. I really did!'

'It must have been the dogs snoring melodiously,' joked my husband, pushing back my long-suffering hat on his head, and then paused.

'Look, love, I've been doing some thinking.' (Mm! I bet you have, I thought, after Helen's stern address on Friday night.) 'I'm going to get in a specialist firm of house restorers and have them remove all this dismal panelling. It *is* gloomy in here. Even I find it slightly depressing and so I can understand how you, being, shall we say, more attuned to these things, get spooked up in here. We will have it newly plastered and we will paint it a really light, bright colour. And guess what? To fund all this, I shall sell the panelling. It should fetch several thousand at least.'

I received this news with mixed emotions. A large part of me rejoiced that the centre of my house could soon be as bright and sparkling as that of Meadow Farm. Yet, a stubborn core in me was angry that I should not have been consulted about so important a change to the structure of a house whose very bones I was getting to know through my careful wallpapering and painting. However, I said nothing but: 'OK. And when is this going to happen?'

'In a month or so,' replied Mark. 'When McIntosh's are free.'

So he had already gone as far as speaking to a firm to fix a date for the work to commence.

I felt that I really should protest about not being included in these plans, but decided against it as at least this move suggested that he was thinking about me. Surely it was an indicator that he cared?

Chapter 10

The following week flew by. Almost as at the flick of a switch, the weather changed abruptly and November came with frosts and clear blue skies. My spirits lifted as I walked the dogs for miles across the bare, frozen Kent landscape.

Thursday was just such a day. I shopped, buying an expensive bouquet of flowers for our hosts-to-be that evening. I went to the Cloisters tearooms again, idly checking to see whether Mr William H.B. Deepdene was planning another address to his acolytes. Nothing – only a poster advertising some sort of spectacular bonfire party, on the following evening, to be led by the 'Tentersley Bonfire Society' with a 'Special Mystery Guest Appearance'. I idly noted that it started from the Abbey Green at eight o'clock.

Seven o'clock arrived and, amazingly, so did Mark. I had been so sure that business (or squash) would prove much more attractive than a parochial get-together, but no – just for once, Mr and Mrs Mark Summers would be seen to arrive together at a village function!

'I just hope that this will not be too boring,' muttered Mark as he drove his white Lancia down to Manor Farm.

So did I! I knew only too well how incredibly rude my husband could be if he judged that people were pretentious or pompous.

We parked in the church car park. There must have been a dozen or more cars there already. The Manor House was narrower than ours and taller, having three storeys. The windows were deep and had stone mullions, giving the whole place the appearance of a castle. On that evening, every light in the place was blazing. We walked past the pond in which the house lights were reflected, along the shingle drive and up to the large, white pillared entrance. We rang the bell and waited. No answer. There must be a lot of noise inside, I thought to myself. Mark was becoming slightly irritated at having to wait outside in the frosty starlight. He rang again and this time kept his finger on the bell-push long and hard. Doris, of organ fame, answered the door. She wore a black dress and white pinafore – for all the world like a Victorian maid! I reflected, as I often did, on the acutely visible social strata in this remote village where we had settled.

'Mr and Mrs Mark Summers,' announced my husband, whisking off his navy cashmere coat and paisley scarf and depositing them firmly across Doris' outstretched arms. When he was like this, he was magnificent – confident, demanding respect. No wonder he had come so far in his thirty-three short years.

We entered and followed Doris into a huge room, decorated with vases full of white lilies, crystal chandeliers and glasses catching the light from the log fire and the Chinese porcelain lamps placed strategically around the room. Dividing doors were folded back and the separate living and dining areas of the extensive floor space ran together. The room was comfortably full of people, certainly not crowded. I imagined that Ralph would have done some sort of complex calculation of the amount of desirable floor area per guest and issued his invitations upon this basis. I hoped that having to include Mark and myself had upset those calculations radically!

'Kate, how very good to see you!' Ralph stalked across the room, his profile keen and aloof. He eyed my husband from top to toe of his immaculate navy pin-striped suit, cream shirt and navy silk tie. Mark, to my embarrassment, did exactly the same to Ralph. Clearly Ralph approved of what he saw.

'And this must be your husband. Mark isn't it? How good of you to come.'

'How good of you to ask us. Ralph isn't it?' Mark riposted, echoing the rather crude welcome that he had received from our host. My husband was, I thought, going to play a civilised game this evening – even if elements of his acerbic humour remained. He seemed totally focussed, totally business-like.

We talked of niceties; and I could see Mark was stifling a yawn. So could Ralph.

'Let me introduce you to some of our guests.'

I had smiled and quietly waved across the room to James and Helen, who was looking towards me with a complicit smile. Apart from my dear friend, none of the people in this luxurious, sparkling room particularly attracted me, I have to admit. I recognised some of the faces that I had seen at the harvest celebration. They were similarly loud and self-important here, I reflected – talking of themselves, rather than listening to others. They gave the appearance of a self-confident eclectic club, evaluating newcomers with suspicion, almost with hostility. We circulated, and met the families that Ralph clearly regarded as the pillars of Ashward society.

There were Andy and Sue Reynolds, introduced by Ralph as having the largest family in the district – seven children in all.

'It was desperation really,' laughed Andy. 'I felt I just had to have a son and we kept trying until we did.'

Do these people live in the Dark Ages, I wondered to myself, looking at Andy's bonhomie and Sue's frazzled appearance. Michael and Daphne Woods ran a specialist plant nursery and designed gardens for those who could afford their huge fees. Michael's choleric good looks hid, I was sure, a violent and uncertain temper and his poor wife looked as if her delicate beauty had been frayed by her husband's volatility. Margaret Smith, as pallid as her name, hovered by the kitchen door. She looked scruffy and quite out of keeping with this exalted society. Alastair Loughland, an Anglican clergyman, was in animated conversation with Rebecca Woodville. He divided his time between the ecclesiastical college his father had founded in Auckland New Zealand and visits to churches in the UK to speak about his work. Gisela Lucas, Paul's wife, who was large and Austrian and jolly, provided a vivid contrast to her stern and ascetic husband. But it was with Estelle and Geoffrey Raymond, an elderly couple who had considerably more charisma than the others, that we finally settled to talk. Estelle was tall and thin, and wore stylish colourful clothes and heavy silver jewellery with great style. She smoked constantly, using a long elegant silver cigarette holder. Every time she lit a cigarette, she whisked a large spherical air freshener from her capacious handbag, which she referred to as her 'Smoke Ball'.

'Where do you live, Mrs Raymond?' I asked.

'Estelle, my dear. Down in Low Ashward, at Rose Cottage. As I told Geoff when we moved here, "I want the smallest possible cottage with the largest possible garden". And the dear man found me one. He even found me a cottage with a studio in the garden – invaluable for my art!'

'So you paint, Estelle. How fascinating.'

'Yes, my dear. I am an artist.' (Whoops! I have made a gaffe there, I thought.) 'Actually, Ralph has just bought one of my paintings. There it is.' She gestured to a small glowing oil painting of a wood in autumn. The composition was done in a riot of yellows, oranges, reds and golds. It was beautiful: impressionistic, but not abstract and, clearly, painted with great skill. Estelle was right: she was 'an artist'. She lowered her voice. 'He paid a pittance for it, of course. Quite ridiculous really! He obviously bought it as an investment.'

Estelle and I talked for ages. Mark wandered off and I noticed that he had made a direct line for Ralph Woodville. I was sure that Mark had a hidden agenda for the evening that, as usual, he had not shared with me.

My new acquaintance was fascinating. With an astringent, trenchant humour, she proceeded to intellectually dissect most of the people in the room, pricking their bubbles of pomposity with wicked fun. I learnt that Low Ashward was an area of the village which had once housed the brick kilns for the production of the locally-used black-glazed Ashward bricks. Her cottage had previously belonged to the Ashward Estate and she was systematically creating a garden which she intended to open to the public during the following summer.

'It is frightfully hard work of course, Kate, but I love composing borders. It is just like painting pictures in three dimensions – combining colours and shapes in the garden.' She was outrageous, often making a grand or shocking statement just to examine the effect that it would have.

'I'm thinking of having my hair cut really short.' She grinned mischievously, looking at her husband. 'The only problem of course is that people may mistake me for a lesbian!'

I heard the long-suffering Geoff mutter 'For God's sake!' under his breath, as he stood up and moved across the room to talk to Helen and James.

Although we had only met some twenty minutes earlier, she delighted in telling me about her 'dear old Geoff.' 'He is so boring now, of course, but I married him because he was quite startlingly handsome. We have been married for forty-four years and, believe me, the older he becomes, the more boring. If it hadn't been for the affairs, life would have been unbearable!'

Mainly, that evening, I listened to Estelle's sharp, sparkling conversation. Occasionally I added a comment or opinion of my own. I discovered that Mr William Deepdene was a near neighbour of hers – her cottage must lie about the same distance to the west of Barrow Farm as my own house did to the east. Estelle had a little King Charles spaniel puppy called Bonnie and 'that nice Mr Deepdene said I could walk her on his land whenever I wished,' she said, lighting at least her fifth cigarette since we had been talking. The 'Smoke Ball' must have been working overtime, I thought to myself.

'I do think that Bill is just a tad too easy-going though,' she drawled, exhaling deeply. 'There was definitely some sort of disturbance on Barrow Farm land last Sunday night. I thought it was some sort of bonfire party, but it was a bit early, wasn't it?'

'What sort of time did you see or hear anything, Estelle?' I asked, the hair prickling on the back of my neck.

'Mm... about five-ish I would say; and again, unbelievably, about midnight. My angina does tend to keep me awake and Sunday night was no exception. Still,' she smiled slowly, looking straight into my eyes, 'I *am* seventy-eight, and I have had a very full life...'

I'll bet she has, I thought. I was amazed at her age. Her brain was quick as lightning, her wit delightful, her artistic skills stunning. What an inspiration!

***

Later that evening my husband's 'hidden agenda' was revealed. With his Cheshire cat smile, he pulled me towards him in our freezing bedroom.

'You enjoyed this evening didn't you, Mark?'

'Oh yes, love. Ralph has asked me to produce a business plan for a new Christmas tree venture he is proposing. If he likes what he sees, there is real opportunity for my firm to review the commercial interests and opportunities within the village and become the legal advisors for his London partnership.'

So that is what it was! Not pleasure that we had done something together, but the usual drive to focus on business, to make more money. I gulped back a rejoinder and instead moved on to my conversation with Estelle.

'Do you know darling, Estelle told me something really interesting about Hallowe'en...' I started.

'For God's sake Kate, can't you ever leave your ghosties and ghoulies alone? Can't we discuss a topic that is in the real world for once, not the shadowlands of your imagination!'

Mark pushed me away from him, jumped into bed and pulled the duvet over his shoulders, deliberately turning away from me.

Chapter 11

'Helen, would you like to go to the Tentersley bonfire tonight?' I had telephoned my friend soon after Mark had left for work the next morning. He was still incredibly grumpy, seeming unable to shake off his irritation at me from the previous evening. He had announced brusquely that he would be 'late back.'

'Of course Kate, I would love to. Jane and Ella have a weekend home, so I am going to Brighton to pick them up at about four this afternoon. My mother is coming down from London a couple of hours later and so we can all go as a big party. James, bless him, will be too sleepy to attend!'

At seven-thirty prompt I turned my Mini into the drive of Meadow Farm and parked it in front of the hay barn. Helen had security lights installed at the rear of her property and the whole of the lawn and drive area was now illuminated. An elderly woman answered the back door. She had striking, haughty features which were an exaggerated form of my friend's and I knew at once that this was Helen's mother.

'Helena!' she called, 'here is Kate.'

'Kate, can I introduce Matilde, my mother?' Helen was dressed, as usual, perfectly for the occasion. The previous evening at the Manor House she had worn an elegant long black and cream dress with 'designer label' written all over it. This evening she wore checked woollen trousers, her red coat, a matching red jumper and black beret and gloves. She kissed my cheek warmly.

'It is so good to see you! You have been neglecting me this week, you naughty girl. I have missed you.' Why did this woman have an uncanny knack of saying just the right thing – exactly what I needed to hear at exactly the moment I needed to hear it! It was true. Apart from the coffee morning on Tuesday, when she had been working hard at her stall, I had not 'disturbed' her once. My new resolution had made me lonely and miserable; and it seemed had not benefitted Helen either.

'Have a drink of bonfire punch,' she offered and I drank gratefully from a small silver cup. It was freezing outside and this was just what I needed, both to warm my body and lift my spirits. Mark's quixotic change of mood the previous evening had haunted my day.

We all loaded into Helen's tiny Citroen, which sank dangerously as the doors were slammed shut. We laughed and talked inconsequentially as we drove into Tentersley and arrived a few minutes before eight o'clock, just in time to see the procession begin.

The bonfire had been lit already. It was massive and its leaping flames illuminated the centuries-old walls of the Abbey which rose austerely behind it. This peace offering to God of a long-dead monarch made a strange contrast to the pagan scene on Abbey Green. Figures became timeless as their profiles alone could be seen. Hats became Viking helmets; coats and scarves, hoods and robes; bending figures, distorted and foreshortened by the bonfire's light, became nameless monsters.

Suddenly a slow drum beat started from inside the Abbey gateway. The members of the Bonfire Society emerged, carrying heavy torches made of stout wooden sticks wrapped around with cloths soaked in bitumen and set alight. They marched, not in a haphazard tumbling throng, but in a stately and stylized procession. This was not at all what I had expected. This was not a twentieth-century catchpenny, but a tradition which went back, I was certain, to prehistory, to times beyond the Gunpowder Plot, to the primeval battle between dark and light, remembered at this time of the year in festivals of light across the world.

The procession cleared the confines of the Abbey and, as it emerged, I looked back, away from the members of the 'Society' to the end of the procession. Carried aloft on a sort of platform, was a huge black figure. It must have been seven feet tall, cloaked and masked. Was it alive, or some sort of guy? Or was it the 'Mystery Guest' advertised on the poster? Even the crowds had fallen silent as they watched the chanting men and the silent menace of the black figure crouching upon its bier. A collection tin was suddenly, loudly, shaken in front of my face, and I nearly screamed. Hastily putting a few coins in the tin, I stared again at the procession. They would, apparently, process through the town and return again to the Green.

There was excited suspense as the sight and sounds of the procession disappeared into the starry November night; and an almost unbearable sense of expectation as, some fifteen minutes later, the processing men and their strange 'Guest' returned. Three times they circled the bonfire, now blazing higher than it had done all evening. Then suddenly, they stopped. All eyes were fixed on the red bier which carried the enormous black figure. The crowd was totally quiet, waiting for what was going to happen next. In that uncanny silence, slowly the tall figure uncoiled itself and stood silent and overpowering – the focus of everyone's gaze. Children gripped their mothers' hands. Even teenagers with cans moved surreptitiously away.

In a hoarse deep voice, almost a whisper, but a whisper that commanded the attention of the audience, the figure began to speak.

'Tonight,' it intoned, 'I am returned to my lands! The most powerful! The one who conquers Fire and Water. The one who cannot die!'

Then, leaping high into the air, black cloak flying, the figure jumped straight for the blazing bonfire. Simultaneously, two things happened: mighty fireworks were set off, some on the ground, some shooting powerful streams of colour into the air; and almost without thinking most, if not all, of the crowd quite simply hid their eyes from what would appear to be the public burning of a living being.

When we looked again, the world had exploded into light and chaos. Of the dark figure, either burning on the bonfire, or standing with the procession, there was no sign. Immediately, the atmosphere had relaxed. People started chatting to one another, laughing in a frightened attempt at normality, all discussing the shocking climax of the evening.

I turned to Helen, about to ask her what she thought of the spectacle we had just witnessed. But one look at her face told me the answer. She was white to the lips and extremely angry.

'What a disgrace!' she exclaimed, 'frightening children and old people! We will go home immediately.'

We were very quiet during the drive back to Meadow Farm, each lost in her own interpretation of what we had just seen.

'Helen, what do you think happened back there?' I asked quietly. Jane and Ella, sandwiched in the back of the car on either side of Matilde, had finally started to talk again to their grandmother.

'Kate, I am undecided,' she replied softly. 'Maybe we saw a clever attention-grabbing trick; or maybe we saw real evil. At this time of the year, spiritual and tangible worlds are very close together. Sometimes evil breaks through the surface of what we call the natural world.'

'What is the Bonfire Society?' I asked again.

'Ah, now I can give you some information about that. James and I used to bring the children to Manor Farm sometimes when we lived in London. Several years ago we visited at this time of the year; and Ralph, who has made it his business to research the history of this part of the world, explained as far as he was able. Apparently the society is formed – allegedly – for charitable purposes. Its rules of operation are kept secret from outsiders and Ralph could discover only two further facts: firstly, members are elected, although upon what basis was a mystery; and secondly, it is a very ancient society, with its roots stretching back to prehistory – far beyond the time of Guy Fawkes.'

Back in the safe haven of Meadow Farm, we soon relaxed in front of Helen's blazing log fire. I realised that, here, the fire was only a focus, most of the heat being provided by a modern and efficient central heating boiler. In my home, one was warm only when sitting almost within the inglenook. We would really have to prioritise the updating of our central heating system, I thought ruefully. We drank hot chocolate and ate sausages, French bread, soup and gingerbread which Helen had, of course, provided, as always making an occasion out of what should have been the most ordinary event.

Matilde, it appeared, was always quiet, but had been even more silent than usual since our visit to Tentersley. Now, however, sitting quietly with her family by the fireside, she spoke – almost, it seemed, thinking aloud.

'Do you know what that "spectacle" back there reminded me of?' she murmured. We shook our heads. 'Years ago, when I was a child, we had a hunting lodge deep in the forests of the Carpathian Mountains. Around this time of the year, my father always took us to spend several weeks there. Snow had started to fall, but the roads were not yet impassable. The great rivers Biala and Tisza, which rise in those frozen heights, were still running deep and black and deadly cold – the ice which kept forming on their banks broken and carried away in the swirling torrent. At the little village of Orlat, a few kilometres from which lay our hunting lodge, they had developed their own brand of entertainment to lighten the darkness at this difficult time of the year. We did not have fireworks, but there were bonfires, and lanterns hung from trees. Candles were set in the house windows both upstairs and down, so that the whole place seemed ablaze with light against the extinction of life which was taking place outside.

'One year, I will never forget. We children were wrapped in fur blankets and hats and we piled into our horse-drawn sleigh to join in the village festival for banishing the dark of the year. The journey was incredible. Every detail is still as clear as crystal in my mind. The black shapes of the forest trees slipped soundlessly by, as the huge runners of the sleigh glided across the newly fallen snow. Overhead were myriads of silver stars and in front of us the dark profiles of the horses as they ran effortlessly along, taking us into the village. Orlat looked beautiful, as if trails of jewels had been laid everywhere. The village was bisected by a tributary of the Tisza, but even the swiftly flowing, freezing black torrent appeared softened by the reflection in it of hundreds, possibly thousands, of lights along its course. But make no mistake: the river was at its most deadly at this time of the year.

'As in Tentersley, there was a central area where a huge bonfire had been lit. Here, people stood talking and holding their lanterns, rubbing their hands together in the welcome heat from the fire. We jumped down from our sleigh and ran over to the fire, where we laughed and played snowballs with the children of the village.

'Suddenly, all the laughter and animation of the villagers was extinguished. Silently, a group of dark-clothed men emerged from an ancient stone building – it almost looked like a tomb – and at their centre strode a huge figure. He too was dressed in black, masked and immensely tall. Slowly, deliberately, the group moved over towards the bonfire and stopped midway between fire and water. The figure at the centre of the group stood even straighter and raised his arms, flinging back its huge head and crying out almost the identical words that we heard tonight:

"Worship me, the most powerful! The one who conquers Fire and Water. The one who cannot die!"

'He then turned and walked straight towards the river bank, never turning once. He disappeared into the black, deathly cold waters without a splash or a cry.

'This was the start of a change in that beautiful place. Men and women left their farms and were seldom seen in the village. Animals were neglected. Disease spread throughout the region. All the bad things in life became more frequent: theft, violence, even murder.'

Matilde turned her rather impassive features from the fire, in whose leaping flames I am certain she had been seeing again the figures and shadows of the events she had been describing.

'I agree with Helena,' she said. 'I too believe that dark forces are present in this world and that, from time to time, in certain places, they break through the restraints put upon them. Usually this is through the actions of human beings, but sometimes there is a flaw, a fissure, in Creation and evil is allowed to seep through into what we call the real world. At times like these, something is altered. Somehow the balance of Creation is upset, maybe a little, maybe cataclysmically. We see only part.'

Mathilde turned again to the dying flames of the fire. She looked timeless, as the flickering firelight filled her face with dark shadows, hollowing her cheeks until the bone structure beneath her features was accentuated.

Her sombre words had brought again to everyone's mind the horror – there was no other word to describe it – of the night's events. This time, warmth and good food could not dispel the unremitting and shocking image of that powerful menacing figure jumping, apparently, into the heart of the flames. Again and again it came unbidden into my mind. Little more was said and at ten o'clock I kissed Helen and bade her family goodnight.

Chapter 12

It was late November. I so desperately wanted to become involved in the life of the quiet parish in which we lived, that every Sunday I had continued to attend Ashward church. I was gradually getting to know my neighbours. Not the 'glitterati' of the village, but the people who farmed, kept houses, cleaned and worked in shops in Tentersley. I was still on the outside, looking in at their world, but at least I could now wave, or bid them 'Good morning' by name when walking Rupert and Emma. But above all, it was Paul Lucas who drew me to that lovely little church. Never before had I heard a man talk with such articulate passion about things not of this world. Always at the wise heart of Paul's sermons lay the complexities of humankind and I think that was the essence of their fascination for me. For the first time in my life, I became aware that Good and Evil are vividly and eternally in active opposition, like the ebb and flow of a powerful tide. At times the waves seem inexorably to engulf the beach; at others they seem, equally remorselessly, to be retreating.

I still attended the services without my husband, who never failed to joke about my 'increasing holiness'. 'Maybe you need to get religion to ward off your ghosties and ghoulies, Cheeks!' was a typical comment.

One Sunday, I was surprised to be approached by Rebecca Woodville.

'I have noticed that you do not stay to Holy Communion,' she stated in her direct way. 'It's a shame. You should participate in every aspect of church life.'

And this, I reflected, is why the Church has such bad press, but all I said was:

'I haven't been confirmed.'

'Speak to Paul. He will sort something out. Good evening.'

But actually I didn't speak to Paul, I spoke to Helen. She sighed deeply, shaking her head at the memory.

'When James and I were to be married, we had to go to "classes" with Paul,' she explained. 'Ralph insisted that the tradition of missionary zeal which had marked his predecessors should continue into future generations unsullied. James is not strong intellectually – and what does a Polish countess know of the Church of England? Paul went through all sorts of basic aspects of belief and we discussed with him any questions or doubts which we had. I expect that he would do something similar with you, Kate. Ring him up. Ask him,' she advised.

I did. And as a result I was now driving my little car down a bumpy track along which I had never been before. It led across Ashward Park to the back of the Ashward estate, where the stables for the horses and high-arched carriage houses were to be found.

My first impression of Ashward Priory was one of extreme activity. Everywhere I looked there were people, occupied in doing many and varied tasks. Some were completing the conversion of parts of the outbuildings into little houses; some were cultivating a massive walled garden; others were pruning shrubs and ornamental trees. Most of the people were in the age range eighteen to twenty-five. I learnt later that these were young people who came from all over the world to support the work at Ashward Priory during their vacations, in exchange for free food and lodging. I suppose it was a prototype 'gap year'.

I drove around to the front of the Priory. So this had been the home of Paul Ashward! And over there – I squinted towards the lakes and bridges set out by Capability Brown – over there must be the track into the woods leading to the pyramid which Mr Deepdene had described with such relish in his book, if indeed such a thing did exist!

The ancestral home of Paul Lucas looked so peculiar. The ancient heart of the house was the mediaeval priory. It had been built of the same rosy bricks as Knight's Manor, although their shapes were much more uneven and the surfaces worn and pitted, denoting their age. High-arched windows told their own ecclesiastical story, and there was even a cloistered area around a lawn, at the centre of which was a fountain whose water splashed into a stone basin. The haphazard original structure was at complete odds with the classical proportions and symmetry of the seventeenth-century addition, which was enormous and completely dwarfed the comparatively compact original Cistercian monastery. This was set at right angles to the Priory, to maximise the views of the river and meadows sweeping up to the wooded ridge which marked the boundary of Ashward. The setting was visually stunning – the Cistercians certainly had an eye for the beauty of creation – always combining the elements of water, hills, woodland and pasture into a perfect whole, as an appropriate setting for their ascetic regime of prayer and meditation.

Sometime after this first visit I sat on a slope opposite the house and compared what I could now see with a photograph of the original structure which Paul Lucas had inherited.

Years of neglect meant that much of the seventeenth-century structure had to be demolished, and much of the mediaeval Priory rebuilt. The first floor still housed the family's private apartments, whilst the ground floor consisted of huge, once magnificent rooms. These had been divided into smaller meeting rooms, so that here a section of finely-moulded cornice emerged at a strange angle, there a door was sealed shut against a bricked-up opening. After the Reformation, Ashward Priory's sole purpose was to be the magnificent dwelling of one of the kingdom's richest families. Even now, when its purpose was utilitarian, it still glinted, almost embarrassed, with signs of its earlier luxury.

But at the time of my first visit there I knew none of this. Extremely nervous, I locked my car and went inside. Surprisingly, I found myself in a bookshop. How on earth was I to find the man I was seeking in this labyrinth?

'Good morning,' I said hesitatingly to a tiny, neat woman busy writing new prices on a consignment of books. 'My name is Kate Summers. Could you please tell me how to get to Paul Lucas?'

'Well, yes I can,' she smiled directly into my eyes, 'but normally Paul is working at this time and doesn't like to be disturbed. My name is Jenny Fox. Can I help you in any way?'

We shook hands and I explained the reason for my visit.

'Oh, in that case,' Jenny laughed, 'let me take you up. You can meet my husband at the same time. My John helps with the accounts.'

We left the bookshop and followed a maze of corridors and passageways which eventually led upstairs to the Lucas' apartment. As soon as I had walked through the fire door which separated the working part of the Priory from this private area, I could see an astonishing transformation. Ralph Woodville's house was luxurious, but here I could see that some of the items on the walls were priceless. Carved Venetian mirrors glowed and reflected flattering images; silver candlesticks and picture frames were placed upon shining Georgian and Stuart furniture. Oil paintings, some of which I had seen catalogued in art books, glowed like deep-coloured jewels from the walls. In the corner, covered by a calico cloth, was a display case of some sort. Heavens, this place was like Aladdin's cave!

Jenny led me past these splendours to quite an austere office facing out over the bookshop.

'John, dear, this is Kate. She has an appointment with PL.' Jenny's husband stood up. He was quite elderly, but vigorous still. Originally he must have been at least six foot two, but years of, presumably, poring over accounts had caused him to stoop somewhat as he stood up. He pushed his spectacles back on his high-domed forehead and extended a well-kept hand.

'How good to meet you. I will get Paul for you.'

He proceeded to walk over to what appeared to be a bookcase and to knock on it. I reflected wryly that everything in my life had become so bizarre. People in this surreal world no longer knocked on doors – they banged on bookcases!

Soundlessly, the well-oiled mechanism of what was obviously a secret door slid back to reveal a tiny, snug inner office, almost like a priest's hole. Then, striding out of this private sanctum, came the man I had come to see.

'Hello, Kate,' he said, with a firm handshake. 'Jenny, would it be possible to rustle up some coffee? I am sure that Kate would like something to drink and I certainly would. Just knock when it is ready,' he commanded. 'We must get on.'

***

This was the first of many sessions. Paul's knowledge of religion was comprehensive. He had read Classics at Cambridge and had then chosen to go to a theological college. At twenty-five he had just been granted his first curacy when the shock of inheriting one of the most important estates in the country hit him.

'You know Ralph Woodville, don't you, Kate?' he asked one afternoon when we had left theology behind and had progressed to what I must admit I found infinitely more interesting – Paul himself and his background.

'I could not have managed without him, you know. He is very aware of his position in society,' Paul grinned widely, 'but he is a true friend. Coming here I was surrounded by a thousand questions of estate management for which I had never been trained. I was almost overwhelmed, but he was wonderful. Slowly, inexorably, he made me face my responsibilities one by one. If I did not understand what to do, he would explain and gradually I came to appreciate the great gift which had been given to me.'

I had learned that Paul was a great mimic and he caught perfectly Ralph's clipped tones, even his stance, right now.

'"Paul," Ralph said to me one day, "I would dearly love to buy Ashward. Do you think it could be arranged?"

'Of course I agreed, glad to have my friend and mentor so close at hand and, quite frankly, to hive off some of the responsibilities with which I had been landed. Since that day, twenty-one years ago, Ralph has lived in this hidden heart of Kent. Of course he has withdrawn now from the daily business of his firm in London, but for years his bowler-hatted figure was a regular sight, in all weathers, travelling to and from Tentersley station. I remember one day, he had to ask one of his farm workers to take him to the station in the snow. There sat Ralph, in immaculate suit, camel coat, bowler hat and briefcase, surrounded by straw and sacking.'

***

As weeks passed, from becoming tutor and pupil, the relationship between Paul and I soon developed into a real warm friendship, and the openness that we shared together was akin to that which Helen and I enjoyed. I had never made many friends and I could not believe that I had been drawn so quickly into two such precious relationships. Maybe things between Mark and I were not improving, but here, surely, were major compensations.

One dark December day I remember vividly. Although only three o'clock in the afternoon, it was very grey and overcast. The lights of the Priory were blazing and revealed little 'cameos' in different windows. In one were two large, fair female students giggling together; in another a dark young man was writing a letter; John Fox could be seen, as usual, poring over figures. Unusually Paul Lucas was in the outer office, the bookcase door of his 'inner sanctum' ajar. He was striding up and down, concentrating on a letter which he held in his hand.

'Ah, Kate my dear! Just the person to dispel an old parson's gloom. John, coffee please!'

We went into his tiny private office. A battered old desk and two chairs, one slightly higher than the other for work at the desk, and a small bookcase were all the items of furniture that could be fitted in.

'Sometimes,' he declared in a very non-parsonical way, handing me the letter that he had been reading, 'people make me sick!'

I didn't know what to say, so just sat quietly, scanning through the letter that he had given to me.

Dear Mr Lucas, (I read)

I am sure that I am speaking for many people when I say that your presence in our parish is really not wanted .

I know the practices that you get up to at Ashward Priory. Spiritual Well-being Centre indeed! You get people to pay you stupidly large amounts of money – to do what? To convert them from their own natural ways to your 'spiritual' ways.

You think that, because your friend owns my house and those of my neighbours, you both own our souls as well. Let me tell you that my soul is my own. I will live my own life. I follow my own way.

Why don't you retire and make way for some nice ordinary man to properly lead this parish?

It was signed *Mary Smith.*

'Why, I met her at the Woodvilles' house a few weeks ago!' I exclaimed. 'I wondered why on earth she was there, to be honest, Paul.'

'Ah, she is distantly related to Frederick Woodville, Ralph's great-great-something uncle who was a missionary,' Paul replied, 'and has wheedled her way into the Woodvilles' life. She is an unpleasant, gossip-mongering, negative troublemaker, to put a good Christian spin on it...' He smiled again and I realised that he had already put the unpleasant attack behind him.

'Paul, do you often receive letters like that?'

'Too often,' he replied, lapsing into seriousness again. 'Kate, you couldn't possibly understand. People want a comfortable existence – with a comfortable parson! Someone who likes a nap on Sundays and a glass or two of port. Someone who is not bitterly aware of all that goes on beneath the respectable surface of this perfect parish.' He whipped off his glasses and went to the tiny slit of a window which looked out over the dark lake and woods beyond.

'Paul, since I arrived in Ashward, my life has been turned upside down. My preconceptions have been shaken to the roots. You could tell me anything, without my turning a hair. Just try me and see!'

Paul smiled at me with infinite patience. 'Kate, I could tell you things that would turn your hair as grey as mine.'

At that moment our drinks arrived. Jenny brought them in and she had made a few sandwiches to accompany them.

'There now, Paul,' she fussed. 'You haven't eaten a thing today, and you know what Gisela will say if...'

'Thank you, Jenny, you are an angel!' he said, firmly ending her ramblings.

As we munched and drank together, he visibly relaxed.

'Look, I'll tell you what,' Paul said. 'Let's forget our confirmation session today. There are too many unworthy thoughts in my mind just at the moment! Please tell me about these experiences which have rocked your world.' The remarkable thing about Paul Lucas was that whatever you said to him, however extraordinary or unexpected, he would never ridicule or underestimate it. The contrast with my husband Mark was painful.

So I told him. As the final, dreary traces of light disappeared from the late November afternoon, I relived again the footsteps and laughter outside my bedroom and the dogs' behaviour. I told him about the lights and 'disturbance' at Barrow Farm on Hallowe'en and the deep chanting or resonance which I was certain I had heard. I mentioned Mr Deepdene's book about his ancestor and the hints of links between Ashward House and Knight's Manor. Finally I described the sinister figure at the bonfire.

He listened intently, without interrupting once. He nodded at certain parts of my tale and, at the mention of the strange climax of the Tentersley bonfire, I saw his knuckles whiten as he gripped more tightly the arms of his chair.

'And now,' he said quietly when I had finished, 'it is my turn.'

Chapter 13

'When I first came to Ashward Priory I wanted to give myself time: time to come to grips with the amazing inheritance which had so unexpectedly fallen into my hands; time to learn about the history of this great and historic house; and time to learn as much as I could about this forgotten and hidden part of Kent.

'I spent weeks – months – in the library here. You will know this now only as several meeting rooms, utilitarian with all beauty and luxury removed, but then it was quite extraordinary! Huge, double aspect, with elegant windows reaching from polished floor to gilded ceiling; each wall lined with oak bookcases filled with gold-embossed volumes. I ignored the Latin tracts and political satire and started fairly and squarely with the local shelves which contained my ancestors' diaries, books on local history and many of Paul Ashward's translations of Old English texts.

'It did not take long for me to be transported back to the roots of Ashward. There has been a settlement on this site for thousands of years. The early settlement here – of Viking raiders turned farmers – was built on ancient stone and tile, almost certainly Roman. And this, in turn, had been constructed on massive stone slabs dating back to the start of civilised settlement in this place. Did you know that the Anglo-Saxon mead hall was under the very spot upon which the great hall of the Priory was built in the twelfth century? And that the charred timbers remain, testament to how that ancient building met its end, by fire, more than one thousand years ago?

'Paul Ashward had translated parchment after parchment of the local Anglo-Saxon Chronicle, written by the monks of Faversham Priory in the mid-ninth century. Clearly the ancient history of this place had powerfully caught hold of his imagination. He hinted at an *ascúniendlíc árléast*, an "unspeakable deed" which had been perpetrated on this site and which had brought a curse on Ashward. Exactly what this was is uncertain, but my ancestor was absolutely convinced that witchcraft was involved. He was equally certain that the curse remained active and ongoing, preventing anything good or wholesome from flourishing in this place.

'In a margin of one of his diaries is traced faintly in pencil:

cwiclác ádéþ wyrgþu'

'Only a sacrifice will destroy the curse,' I murmured quietly.

Paul stopped abruptly, smiling at me with undisguised delight.

'You understand Old English?'

I nodded and returned his smile.

'William Deepdene's short account of your ancestor's life quoted these very words. And yes, I do understand Anglo-Saxon. It was part of my course at Uni.'

Paul rubbed his hands together and strode over to the window. He took up his story once again.

'Kate, I became almost enchanted with the works of Paul Ashward. I pored over the sketch plans of the parkland he wished to create. I read and re-read his hints and half-references to history. I was shaken by his writing about the immoral and disgusting practices of the Oxford-based Hellfire club to which he belonged and his intention to bring those practices to this beautiful and troubled place. As I read, it became clear to me that Ashward is like a great magnet of evil, drawing more darkness to itself.' Paul paused and looked again out of the narrow window. It was pitch black and he certainly could not see anything in the physical world. But, looking at his changing expressions, I knew that he was reliving the discovery of the secret and darker world of which his ancestor had written.

'Paul Ashward wrote in increasingly strange and eccentric terms as his diaries progressed. He explained how he wished to "extend the power in this place" to other houses and structures in the parishes and had removed useable timbers and other materials from the wrecked site of the Anglo-Saxon mead hall to be included in rebuilding or extending the other great houses in the neighbourhood. Some of those he mentioned have long since perished – but some…' he hesitated just long enough for me to anticipate what he was about to say.

'Knight's Manor has some of these timbers Paul, doesn't it?'

'Yes, Kate, it does.'

'Paul, what are the implications of this?'

'I am not sure. Ashward is one of those rare places where the barrier between the seen and the unseen worlds is gossamer thin. I know as fact that a coven of witches meets in the parish.

I believe it is near to Barrow Farm since I too have seen "disturbances" there. But they meet in other places too, sometimes on public occasions, like celebrations or midsummer fairs. That is why I am conspicuous by my absence – the only parson who doesn't support the traditions of his parish.' He hesitated.

'Paul, what? Please do not stop now!'

'Kate, Margaret Smith belongs to that coven and she knows that I have glimpsed her meetings, hence her venom towards me. That is the reason she wants some nice benevolent clergyman to jog along with his cosy flock, completely missing the raging battle between Good and Evil that continues to be waged here in Ashward.'

'So is it... dangerous... to live here?' I stammered.

'No. Not in itself. I do believe that certain acts can trigger tragedy, but living here, being aware but not becoming involved, this is as safe as life can ever be.' His voice cut firmly across my chaotic thinking, like an anchor to what we call the real world. 'Radiant good is evident here, just as strong as entrenched evil. Past and present flow close together here too. This house is built over centuries of memories and somehow there seems to be a universal consciousness, created by generations of people who have lived, loved, suffered and died here in Ashward. Things are felt and heard here from other times; and past actions continue to influence the present.'

He paused, removed his spectacles and rubbed his forehead restlessly.

'This must sound very strange to you, my dear'

'No. I understand exactly what you mean. Helen's mother feels it too.' And I repeated, as best I could, how Matilde had explained her feelings.

'Let me tell you of the other side of the coin Kate, the positive, shining side of what we call the spiritual world. In those early days I worked tirelessly with Ralph Woodville to restore Ashward church, which was in a total state of disrepair. Part of the roof had fallen in years previously and rain and weather had wrought havoc with the old building.

'It is an eternal monument to Ralph that he promised that he would restore the church before he renovated his own house. He spent a fortune, having the finest craftsmen produce their best and most imaginative work and giving specialist architectural salvage companies the challenging task of finding suitable pews and rood screen. The list is endless. And, true to his word, Ashward church was ready for worship again before Ralph and his family moved into the Manor House.'

I remembered my initial impression of the beautiful little jewel of a church – that it was more like someone's home than an ecclesiastical building.

'Ralph had finally been successful in obtaining a massive, weathered oak timber, almost a tree in its own right, to span the nave of the church just above the altar screen, as it was here that most of the roof damage had been done. The huge oak beam arrived on a lorry. The roof had been removed at this time, prior to replacement and repair, and a crane had been brought into the village to manoeuvre the mighty timber into place. We held our breath as the mechanism lifted the unimaginable weight high into the air and slowly, slowly began to lower it. Workmen stood on scaffolding ready to receive the supporting beam. They had it in their guiding hands and it was inched down towards the stone corbels which protrude on either side of the church building. Soon, however, we realised that something unthinkable had happened. The timber was too short! It failed to span the width of the nave by some fifteen centimetres.

'It had taken Ralph months of searching and enormous expense to find that timber, and we just gazed unbelievingly at the gap. The removal of the roof had been timed to fit in with the arrival of the timber beam. As I looked at my friend I knew that the same flocks of thoughts were in his mind as were in mine: could we somehow bridge that gap? No – because of the enormous weights and stresses involved. Could we obtain another beam? Well, yes, but not at short notice. What could we do with the open roof? And so on.

'The huge piece of oak was lifted out and rested on the ground. White but determined, Ralph said to me, "Paul, we must pray that it will fit. God knows that I am putting the church first in my life and He will honour this."

'That night we both kept vigil with Rebecca and we prayed continually that God would work a miracle.

'Kate, He did. The next day, the timber was lifted again into place by the sceptical crane crew and it fitted to the millimetre.

'I know that this sounds more than strange Kate, but the miracle shook me. I had been ordained for some eight years at this time and had found God a comfortable companion. Now I began to glimpse a power beyond the visible world which shook me to my roots.'

Deep silence reigned in the tiny room as our minds swept over the facts that Paul had just recounted. Paul strode the three paces' length of his study, turned and re-paced, as he relived the way in which the events that he was relating had impacted upon his life and belief. His brass carriage clock ticked away the slow minutes before once again, he took up his extraordinary story.

'For as long as I can remember, I have been fully aware of the strange rumours surrounding my ancestor, Paul Ashward. When I was a small boy I visited the Priory with my family. My uncle was a recluse as you know. He was a gentle reflective man, but there were two places that he would never go: the cellars of the house and the woodland track to the right of the bridge. Whenever he passed the latter he became cold, almost angry, and would quickly move on. As far as the cellars were concerned, he created a private chapel in part of the original Priory and positioned the altar and cross over what I estimate would be the oldest part of the hidden foundations of this great house. I had never been allowed to explore the cellars, nor the woodland track, when I was a child. I knew of both only from the writings of Paul Ashward and gradually I resolved to see whether I could discover something of the mystery which surrounded them.

'I had been here about a month. It was midsummer and there was a glowing beauty – a hush – across this golden countryside. I decided that the moment had come, took a powerful torch and went down into the cellars. There was an indescribable smell down there. Maybe dampness, probably dry rot, the faintest hint of charred wood, soil, decay. It was unpleasant and very, very cold. Compared with the balmy June day outside it was like walking into an open grave.

'My torchlight flickered along the walls. I am accustomed to ancient buildings – you can't be an Anglican clergyman and not see how each generation puts its distinctive mark upon its buildings – but this was different. There was dressed stone and brick and timber; and a layer of huge rougher stones. But one area, where the ancient mead hall had obviously been built, held something indefinable. I could sense raw power here: no doubt what had attracted the leader of the Vikings who settled here so long ago to build his hall, his own centre of power, precisely here in this spot, as had the Romans and the early prehistoric settlers before him.

'Instead of *giving* energy, however, this was an energy drain; a rare source of negative energy and I felt it sapping my spirit as I stood by the dank, charred timbers and the dripping stone walls.

'Kate, this part of the cellars is furthest away from any door or staircase and yet, as I looked, a tiny spiral of dust seemed to rise from the blackest part of the burnt wooden beams – just like autumn leaves blown by a breeze into a tight swirl. And, like leaves, the spiral subsided to the ground, only to rise again, momentarily, seconds later. It was almost like a breathing rhythm: inhale – spiral rises; exhale – it falls again to the ground. It was fascinating, horrible – and terrifying.'

As we looked, unspeaking, at each other, the quiet of the tiny office was shattered by the telephone. We both jumped violently, struggling to return to the present from the menace and darkness of the cellar, conjured up by Paul's vivid account.

He snatched up the receiver impatiently:

'Paul Lucas.' He nodded. 'I will be there in two minutes.'

He sighed, replacing the receiver, and stood for a moment, breathing deeply, his back turned to me. I had the impression that he was composing himself before speaking to me again and was consciously forcing himself into his pastoral role.

'My dear, a parishioner has had the temerity to decide to get married at Ashward Church and is here in person to insist that it is my priestly duty to marry him – even if it is the only time he crosses the threshold of my church, apart from the final occasion, which even I cannot refuse him! Can we continue next week?'

I tried to catch his humorous tone. 'If I can stand the suspense, Paul!'

He grinned and opened the door back into the world of responsibility.

Chapter 14

The next week was long indeed.

My dreams were filled with darkness, swirling dust and an indefinable horror which stalked my mind between the hours of two and four in the morning. I dreamt again of the terrible fire, the screaming, the unutterable sadness that had haunted my teenage dreams; and slowly the dream and the account that Paul had given me of his visit to the cellars of Ashward Priory started to merge and give life to each other.

Sadly, I shared nothing with Mark of my meeting with Paul. He was bright and breezily himself – quixotic, volatile, demanding, superficial. I, however, was acutely aware that I was undergoing a series of subtle, but irreversible, character changes.

A week after my unforgettable meeting with Paul, on an evening of deepest darkness which seemed to anticipate the next part of the account that Paul was sharing with me, my little car bounced valiantly along the pot-holed track that led to Ashward Priory.

'Come in, my dear!' Paul was smiling but, I sensed, tense, as he prepared to share with me the next stages of his growing awareness of the tragedy and evil that lay at the heart of the magnificent pile that he had inherited. With a deliberate effort to lighten the tone of what was to come, he welcomed me into his snug sanctuary with a gesture to a bottle of red wine that he had already opened on the scruffy desk.

'I have unplugged my phone, Kate. I absolutely must finish this story tonight.' He sat down, steepled his fingers and closed his eyes, preparing to take up again the story from the point where he had left off a week earlier.

'Almost against my conscious will, I left the cellars and walked back into God's daylight and sunshine. I was deeply disturbed that the foundations of this house, upon which I hoped to build so much hope for people in the future, were built upon a spot which sucked energy and life into itself. The swirling dust I could not, in any shape, manner or form, account for.

'Next, I turned my attention to the woodland track. The day I decided to uncover whatever lay hidden there was a perfect summer day: bright, sunny, full of birdsong. I looked at the magnificent house behind me and the wide sweep of lawn from house to lakes and once again started to recapture my initial euphoria. I must surely be one of the luckiest men on earth.

'It was about ten-thirty as I entered the woodland through which the track led. As the tall, heavily-leafed trees closed in around me, I experienced a strange sensation. It was almost as if I was leaving behind the world I knew and in which I was happy.

'Here there was no birdsong.

'My journey seemed to take me a very long time. It came to have a nightmarish quality and the unevenly strewn boulders, balanced at impossible angles, took on a menace and life of their own in my overheated imagination. After what seemed hours, I came upon a clearing. And then I saw it – at first looking like just another glacier-tossed boulder but, on closer inspection, revealing skilful joints and stone worked by human hands rather than nature's process: the pyramid of Paul Ashward. I sat down on what I thought was a sizeable tree stump. The land had obviously been cleared for many centuries, as the huge forest trees stopped in a dark line some twenty yards from the structure. I looked around and saw herbs: some culinary – I am no cook but I recognised parsley and thyme; some medicinal – feverfew, wormwood; and some, I guessed, for a much darker purpose. Hemlock grew there.

'Whilst taking in the scale of my discovery, my fingers moved idly over the object on which I was sitting. To my surprise I felt the lines and planes of rough carving! I knelt down for a closer look and saw… what do you think I saw, Kate?'

I found that I had unconsciously been holding my breath, so fine a storyteller was my companion.

'I haven't a clue, Paul,' I whispered, breathing in again deeply.

'It was a huge raven, roughly carved from a black piece of oak. Although split and distorted by centuries of weather, the shape was unmistakable.

'I suppose it was a sort of pride in me that made me approach the pyramid, to somehow make my presence known in this part, too, of my estate. I was amazed at how open the clearing was: there were no saplings. On the far side of the structure, I saw the place where the original entrance to the pyramid had been sealed.

'Although orderly and astonishingly well-kept, it was almost as if I was seeing the clearing in monochrome, in greys and blacks. The air here was stagnant, stifling, silent. But, as in the cellars, there was nothing more I could do here. The place made its own unpleasant statement. I found my way back to the world of life and sunlight, hungry and ready for my lunch – but when I looked at my watch it was four in the afternoon! I had been in the woodland for some six hours!'

Paul Lucas stopped, frowning and silent, reliving the unanswered questions that his explorations had raised. We each sat for a few moments in this small, safe space following in our imaginations the events that his vivid account had created.

'Let's pour the wine!' Paul declared, clearly wanting a break from the fascinating story he was telling me.

'Oh yes please, Paul.'

He poured the deep-red wine into what were clearly priceless crystal glasses which caught and refracted the light of the utilitarian angle-poise lamp on the shabby old desk: such a place of contrasts – such a man of contrasts.

We sat in companionable silence, swirling and warming the fragrant liquid before we sipped it slowly.

'It is getting late,' said Paul, glancing at his watch.

'Quite simply, Paul, I don't care if your story takes all night. My nerves won't stand the suspense for another week!' I laughed. So did he, and continued.

'From that day, my life changed. I became aware of an infrastructure of good and evil which underpins our life here. Sometimes good triumphs; but sometimes, and more often here in Ashward than in any other place I have ever known, evil surfaces. The people of this parish do suffer, Kate. Your experiences are a case in point. Do you really think that you would have seen and heard all that you have if you were in Wales, or Cornwall? Somehow the interface between the hidden world of the spirit and the seen world has been damaged here, or has not been properly sealed. It is thin, like the earth's crust in places where earthquakes occur.

'About three weeks later I suffered my first real setback. As I told you, I had entered into the renovation of Ashward Priory with tremendous enthusiasm. I was always at the centre of the action, whether it was planning with Ralph Woodville or helping with demolition. One Thursday a particularly delicate piece of work was taking place. There used to be one of the finest staircases in Europe here. It rose in a double sweep from the magnificent entrance hall of the seventeenth-century building, carved, glowing and stately. When I inherited, it was rotten with woodworm and I was told by McIntosh's, probably the best firm of wood specialists in the country, that it was in danger of collapse at any time. I particularly wished to retain the fine plaster mouldings on the walls on either side of the staircase and was keen to help supervise the removal of the fragile woodwork. As is often the case in these things, although rotten, the huge staircase was stubbornly resisting all efforts to dislodge it. Men with small metal tools worked away at the joints at the top of the stairs. I was standing in the main hall, near enough to see what was happening but, I believed, sufficiently far away for safety.

'Suddenly the staircase started to move. It was like an avalanche. The carved balustrades caved in; the stairs themselves, loosened from the central structure, started to fall together like dominoes. It was all too quick. I just did not have time to move away. Bannisters and balustrades hit me and I knew no more. When I awoke I could see nothing, but could hear voices.

'"Your Grace, are you awake?" a male voice asked.

'"Of course I am, but why can't I see anything?" I exclaimed impatiently. My hands went to my eyes and discovered thick pads and bandages. "In Heaven's name, what has happened to me?" I shouted.

'"Quietly now," spoke a female voice and I felt a prick in my arm and knew nothing more.

'When I awoke next – time had no meaning to me as I could see neither a clock nor the passage of daylight – I was calmer.

'"Would someone please explain to me what has happened?" I asked.

'"It would appear," said that same male voice, "that you were struck on the head by flying debris from the demolition of your staircase, sir. That was four days ago. You experienced a particularly sharp blow to the temple and," – he hesitated as he searched for the correct form of words – "you suffered damage to your eyes."

'"Just what exactly?" I desperately fought to curb my natural impatience.

'"Well, wood actually penetrated the right eye, and the retina of the left was detached. We have performed surgery on both your eyes your Grace, stitching the retina very satisfactorily and repairing the ocular tear as best we could."

'"Yes, yes," I snapped. "But in real terms, what implication does this have for me?"

'"I am virtually certain that you will regain some measure of vision in your left eye," said the voice.

'"And the right?"

'"I'm afraid I hold out little hope of vision remaining in your right eye, but this will only be confirmed when the bandages are removed."

'I was silent – and devastated. All the studying and close work I had to do; all the improvement of my estate and my ministry in the parish. Would I ever see anything again?

'The result was much as the doctor had explained. I have about 60% vision in my left eye. From my right I can see nothing.'

Paul sipped his wine. I would never have guessed that this was the case – but almost immediately my mind flicked to the occasions when Paul whipped off his spectacles impatiently, almost angrily.

He consciously lightened his tone.

'But it could have been worse, much worse. I could have been blinded altogether and would then have been even more ineffectual than I have been in this beleaguered parish!'

I so desperately wished to say something: to comfort, to support, to empathise. But anything that came into my mind was empty and meaningless; and I respected my companion too deeply to try to say anything that did not ring absolutely and completely true.

Paul and I sat in the little room, silent, lost in our own reflections. It was very late – long past midnight – and the wind had started to gust and howl around the gable end where his office lay. Suddenly the door was flung heartily open and Gisela appeared carrying a tray of cocoa.

157

'Do you two know what time it is?' she asked, with mock indignation. 'A quarter to two! This is no time for a respectable vicar and a kingpin of the community to be gossiping together. What on earth have you been talking about, anyway?'

'Oh, this and that...' smiled Paul.

'Well I am saying *this!*' smiled Gisela, '*that* Kate must stay the night. Her husband will be asleep by now – or away on business?' she asked, turning towards me questioningly.

'I think it was a late business meeting in town. He will be home and asleep by now.'

'There is no problem then. Come through and drink your cocoa in front of the fire. There is a little warmth left, still.'

Gisela's brisk and humorous approach to life was, I thought, exactly what Paul needed. He was academic, she was practical; he was serious on the whole, although I had started to detect a wicked sense of humour which flashed through his conversation from time to time; she was warm and funny.

It was two-thirty when Gisela firmly put the fireguard in front of the final glowing ashes. 'Bed!' she declared, hands on hips.

I really was exhausted – and very glad to be saved the necessity of driving home. My bedroom was a tiny octagonal one, reached by a spiral staircase in one of the old Priory towers. I just had time to appreciate the lavender-scented linen, the crystal bedside light, the paintings of flowers, the glowing mirror... before my eyelids drooped and I slept, deeply and completely, until the morning.

Chapter 15

I had absolutely no idea where I was when, in the first grey light of dawn, the sounds of the great house awakening roused me the next morning. But I quickly remembered and snuggled further down in the unbelievably comfortable bed. The wind still howled around the tower bedroom and I heard sleet spattering against the window.

The previous night I had encountered Gisela's motherly warmth, which I had thought to be the essence of her character. This morning, as I heard her brisk, business-like voice echoing up the winding staircase from the central hall of the Priory, it struck me how infinitely more complex people are than one initially imagines.

'Right, Jenny. We have a new consignment of books arriving at ten o'clock this morning. The rest of the stock needs to be tidied and checked against the inventory before we unpack the new ones. John, Paul has a deanery meeting at six this evening. This morning, he has parish visitors. Directly after lunch, Paul has told me that he wishes to finish the discussions that he had with our guest last night.'

Needless to say I reluctantly, but immediately, left the soft warmth of my bed, washed, dressed and was downstairs within ten minutes.

Gisela greeted me with a warm smile. 'Good morning, Kate! I have already telephoned your husband and asked him to deal with the dogs before going to the office. He was a little surprised, but agreed. So you can stay until early afternoon, I hope? You and Paul can finish your discussions then.'

There was no disagreeing with this! Gisela clearly organised each day like a miniature military campaign. I smiled at Gisela's use of the word 'surprised' and could imagine Mark's tone of voice and his amazement that I could be spontaneously away from home – as he was on more occasions than I could count. No doubt I would be the target of his sarcastic humour later that evening!

Paul was fresh and relaxed.

'I will have to keep you in suspense until later this afternoon,' he grinned. 'But I am sure you can while away a few hours... maybe in the library; or possibly watching the rehearsals of the Christmas play that we are putting on this year.'

'Is it something you do every year?' I asked.

'Yes. We try to. It is an opportunity for village and Priory to work together. This year it's *The Tempest*.'

Young people and older staff were everywhere. Some were decorating the huge rooms for Christmas with holly, mistletoe, baubles and paperchains. There was a tall tree in the great hall and a girl was tottering on a ladder, laughing to her companion who was standing on the bottom rung to keep it steady.

I wandered on. It was the first time that I had ever been in any part of the Priory beyond Paul's office and the bookshop, and I was enchanted by what I saw. Everywhere there was the contrast between the original beauty of design and the utilitarian purposes for which the once grand house was now used. I drifted past the library, the kitchens, the drawing room, following the direction of the voices I heard, raised measured and clear above the sounds of the wind and sleet outside.

The voices belonged to the young actors who were obviously running through a dress rehearsal of that strangest of Shakespeare's plays. The setting that they had chosen for their performance was the high-ceilinged stately, mirrored ballroom of the seventeenth-century house. A relatively small stage had been raised at one end of the room, and this was where most of the actors performed. However – and this struck me at the time as a brilliant idea – Ariel, 'the airy spirit', and Caliban, the dark and complex slave, spoke and appeared on either side of the central stage. Lights sparkled in the area inhabited by Ariel; but Caliban's space was shadowed and dark.

I sat, as quietly as I could, in an unobtrusive part of the room. Chairs were set out for the performance and side tables were laden with holly, Christmas roses and pine cones, presumably the makings of future table decorations. I hoped that the flowers and greenery might obscure me a little, so as not to disturb the actors.

They were very good. Miranda was played by a slight, blonde, attractive girl, whose quick movements and clear voice gave impact and poignancy to the well-known words.

'Oh brave new world, that hath such people in it!' Her wonder at the beauty of the newcomer to the island kingdom established by her father actually brought tears to my eyes – maybe of regret that my adoring love for Mark had lost its unquestioning innocence.

The interplay of light and dark between the two slaves of Prospero, Miranda's father, caught my imagination and seemed to gain a deeper meaning as I thought of Paul Lucas' sombre story, which was to be completed later that day.

But it was the central character of Prospero – authoritative, complex, commanding – that riveted my attention. The other amateur actors were good, but he was outstanding. He wore a golden mask that obscured his features, but his long dark hair framed and surrounded it, making the dividing line between fiction and reality difficult to discern clearly. He was tall and the flowing golden cape that he wore added to his presence and stature. He held a long golden rod and, even at this distance, I could see his finely-formed hands, the long strong fingers and expressive gestures.

The shutters rattled as huge gusts of wind blew across the grey winter fields and shook the windows – a fitting background indeed to a play which centres around a stormy island – and the actors had to raise their voices to be clearly heard. But, towards the end of the play, when the lights were dimmed and all figures except that of Prospero had left the stage, suddenly there was complete quiet. The actor playing Prospero stood centre stage, his robe glimmering and glinting in the few lights that remained:

'Our revels now are ended. These our actors,
As I foretold you, were all spirits and
Are melted into air, into thin air:
And, like the baseless fabric of this vision,
The cloud-capp'd towers, the gorgeous palaces,
The solemn temples, the great globe itself,
Yea, all which it inherit, shall dissolve
And, like this insubstantial pageant faded,

Leave not a rack behind. We are such stuff
As dreams are made on, and our little life
Is rounded with a sleep.'

His presence, the golden robe and mask, the beautiful cadences of his voice had certainly woven a spell in this room. No one moved – for much longer than the action of the play warrants.

'Kate, are you ready?' It was Paul. The morning had passed, lunchtime had passed, whilst I had been entranced with the words and action of the play.

'Of course, Paul.' I stood up unsteadily.

'Have you eaten?'

'Er, no! I was a bit involved with the play…'

'We will have tea in the library then. Gisela!'

A gloomy winter dusk had already started to creep across the countryside. Paul walked briskly along the corridor leading to the library, where a fire had been lit in the arching mediaeval fireplace. I sat down on one of the leather armchairs flanking the fire, trying to wrest my mind and attention from the beauty that I had just seen. Gisela soon brought in a tray with tea, cake and scones.

'Paul, you have just two hours!' she said admonishingly.

'Well then,' said Paul, 'I had better continue.'

Chapter 16

'On my return from hospital, I had to "take things easy" for a time. Dreaded words! There was so much to do. I solaced myself by retiring here, to the library, and reading – but even that was frustrating, because I could not let the one remaining eye with sight become too tired. The long months dragged by and summer slipped into autumn. In mid-October my surgeons pronounced me as fit as I would ever be and, once again, I launched on an active programme of visiting my parishioners and managing my estate.

'One glorious autumn afternoon I had decided to walk down to Low Ashward, along the track which leads from the stables back towards Knight's Manor. You probably drive along it, Kate. I had felt more optimistic that day than I had since my accident and I strode out with something that vaguely resembled my previous pace. I decided that I would walk down the long bridleway that leads to Barrow Farm. The scenery there is very striking. Have you ever been there?'

I shook my head, so as not to interrupt Paul's story.

'The track starts to rise gradually towards Knight's Manor, and Barrow farmhouse is set over to the right. Eventually, after about a mile, the origin of the farm's name becomes apparent, as the track skirts a huge barrow, on the top of which grows a copse of beech trees. The barrow is very striking, its shape smooth and oval. It sits under a rocky sandstone outcrop and seems to brood there like an animal waiting to spring. A huge, flat, sandstone block seals the barrow and faces the outcrop from which it was, presumably, taken. It seems always in shadow, always cold, always, somehow, threatening.

'The sun was starting to sink in the west and long low beams struck across the track I was following. Suddenly I saw a faint grey figure in the distance walking rapidly in the direction I intended to take. I cursed my diminished eyesight as I could make out only the shape, not the identity, nor the gender, of the person in front of me.

'I increased my speed and caught up a little with the figure I was following. I could make out longish, untidy grey hair and realised that it was Margaret Smith who was walking the same path as I was.

'She increased her speed to pull away from me somewhat, perhaps becoming aware that she was being followed. I just could not walk any faster. The months of inactivity had taken their toll on my physical fitness.

'I realised that I had misjudged the timing of my walk. The sun had very nearly set now, and Barrow Farm was still some distance away. Should I turn back? I admit that my curiosity was aroused. Where was Margaret going? And why so late in the afternoon?

'A cold wind started to blow open my coat, which I hastily buttoned. I stopped to catch my breath, thinking that I really must regain my physical stamina, if not my sight, when I became aware of other figures converging on the bridleway in front of me. They had come down through the wooded slopes on either side of this main pathway: some were male, some female.

'It is very difficult to describe, but it was as if some sixth sense warned me not to make my presence known to these silent   figures, becoming by the second more difficult to discern, as afternoon turned rapidly into evening.

'I stayed where I was for some fifteen minutes and then, as quietly as I could, followed the ancient pathway as it led to the barrow. There is a bend in the track just before the great mound is reached and I paused there. If I turned the corner, I would be completely exposed and all my senses told me that the people I had seen were somewhere close by. I stopped and, mixed with the rising wind and the sighing of the oak leaves, I became aware of a chanting, almost a resonance. Walking carefully to a dense clump of blackthorn, I managed to see around the last corner of the track. A fire had been lit opposite the entrance to the barrow, around which the figures circled in some sort of dance. But the most chilling thing of all was that a huge black figure sat motionless, apparently on top of the very flames themselves. It watched the bending, swaying ring of people as they bowed and circled the fire. It was completely dark by that time and I felt fairly confident that I was hidden from view. As I watched, the circling became faster and the figures half turned to the left, then to the right, in their hypnotic dance. Gradually they started to chant – slowly and quietly at first, but increasing steadily until the spectacle seemed to occupy my every sense. Then suddenly they stopped and formed a semicircle facing the entrance to the ancient burial mound.'

He paused and took a sip of tea.

'Paul, what happened next?' I asked breathlessly.

'I find it difficult to find the right words to describe what I saw next, Kate... You know how a photograph negative looks? You can make out shapes and some sort of substance, but the colour, the detail, is absent?'

I nodded.

'On the heavy sandstone slab a series of images started to appear. They drifted across the rough surface – hardly discernible in the darkness, but lit with their own dim light. The first was of a woman dressed in a light-coloured long dress. The dress was covered with livid stains which I took to be blood and she was tearing at her long dark hair, beside herself with grief. As the image shifted and changed, the half circle of figures shouted:

'"Worship!"

'At which cry the flames of the fire glowed more brightly and the monstrous figure in their midst appeared to grow even further in stature.

'Further pictures followed – like an ancient film being played. A huge, black bird flew across the rock surface; a haggard man with tangled, long white hair; a small child with silver-fair hair running and looking behind her. As each image faded, the blood-chilling shout and the growth of the great black figure was repeated.'

Paul was ashen. He lowered his head and supported it in his hands.

'It was the most terrible thing I have ever seen, Kate.'

We sat in silence for several minutes. Paul refilled our cups, and still we sat, and thought. He was clearly reliving that terrible spectacle; and I was desperately trying to understand the significance of what he had told me. Eventually I murmured:

'So, all the things I shared with you, Paul – the chanting, the black figure, the flames – they are all in your story too!'

'They are in my "story" as you call it, Kate, because they exist here. The coven, the worshipping of evil itself, the dark power which emanates from the roots of this very house are all real, my dear. All too terribly real.' He relapsed into silence, as we sat reflecting upon our own, and our shared experiences. We toyed with the scones, but it seemed that neither of us had any appetite.

'Should I continue?' he asked, smiling gravely.

I just nodded.

'I returned from that horrifying night as quietly as possible. Over the next months I read and researched as much as I could, trying to reach some sort of understanding of what I had witnessed. I came across considerable amounts of information concerning ancient religions, collected, no doubt, by my infamous ancestor.'

Paul stood up and gestured to the tall bookcases which stretched from floor to ceiling.

'Look, this section deals with "Ancient Religions". This one with "Society and Culture in the Bronze Age". So much knowledge. So much to learn and assimilate!

'I learned that in the Bronze Age, a form of worship grew up which was based upon the natural world. By Celtic times, the followers of this religion believed that there is a deep and mystical connection between our individual lives and the source of this planet's life. I spoke earlier about the dark energy drain here at Ashward: this place takes, other places give. In its simplest form, the spirits of earth, air, fire and water were worshipped in those ancient times. I believe that this happened here at Ashward. Some terribly significant event occurred here which combined the four elements – earth, air, fire and water – into some sort of spiritual reality that still has influence today. You have read Bill's book. You know of the curse that rests here. Such curses are made rarely and only when there is an unusual juxtaposition of elements, creating almost insuperable evil power. You have read also of the "sacrifice" that is necessary to escape the curse. But Kate, I feel as if I have put together a jigsaw puzzle without the centre. I know a curse has been placed; I know that a sacrifice is needed to lift it. But the detail of the story, the implications of the sacrifice, I have not yet discovered.'

'Have you read all of your ancestor's diaries and translations, Paul?'

'Almost. It has, literally, been a lifetime's work. I have read all his formal translations of the Anglo-Saxon Chronicles – the local newspapers of the time, if you like. But his journals and diaries run to dozens; and, as he got older, his writing deteriorated markedly – just like my diminishing eyesight!' he exclaimed sardonically.

'There are five notebooks containing his last attempts to record his ramblings, but these are almost illegible. I continue to try to find the missing pieces of the puzzle. But, realistically, two pages per night is the best I can manage.'

A slight sweat had broken out on Paul's forehead, which he impatiently wiped away. I was reminded again of his Hallowe'en sermon and the personal experience which I had thought, even then, informed his words. He glanced quickly at his watch.

'Kate, we really must draw our conversation to a close. Gisela will descend like an avenging angel in about five minutes.'

'I know, Paul! But one final question and then I will go. When we were at the Tentersley bonfire, Helen said that evil appears to be stronger at some times of the year. Why? Is this true?'

Paul grinned widely. 'Ah, I have taught her well! All worshippers of the Old Religion follow the "Calendar" based upon eight Sabbats, or days of power, occurring each year. Each Sabbat is the occasion for a feast and a huge celebration; and,' said Paul in a matter of fact way, 'that is why, at certain times of the year, the dark powers of this world can be seen to surface and actually impinge upon our conscious life. What we call in the Christian calendar "All Hallows Eve" – Hallowe'en – is Samhain, the Celtic New Year. On this night it is believed that the veil between this world and the world of the dead is drawn aside, and that "journeys" can be made between the worlds of the living and the dead. Our May Day celebrations are the Celtic Beltane, the celebration of fertility and new life.'

Paul stopped, lost in thought. What should have been an exploration of the polite world of Anglican convention had turned into the deepest and darkest story I had ever heard. What I had believed to be fantasy, elements of my over-heated imagination, had been shown to be stark and shocking fact – the framework of a world that danced just on the edge of my consciousness.

Chapter 17

That was the last of our sessions before Christmas. I saw Paul only at church for some weeks after this, but the extraordinary events that he had shared with me reverberated again and again in my brain. I found that since I had come to Ashward, I was seeing the world much more clearly – not just the surface, but the strong emotional and spiritual currents which ran beneath the surface of life.

Christmas that first year at Knight's Manor was unforgettable. The great house came into its own, as it was warmed by two fires and decorated with the heavy-berried holly that grew at the end of the orchard. Filled with food and drink, holly and presents and, above all, our new friends, the old house seemed to stop slumbering in the past and start to reflect the lives of those who gathered under its sheltering strength. Helen was, of course, a frequent visitor and we talked and laughed together over mince pies and coffee. We were drawing together in a way I had never before experienced with a friend. Although the weather was bitter, we often walked with the dogs through the snow, returning with glowing faces and freezing hands. No matter how long we spent together, our conversation never flagged. We talked of past experiences and future hopes; of Helen's daughters and their successes at school; of James' idiosyncrasies. Paul did not often come to see me: he was too occupied with preparations for Christmas, both at the Priory and in his church and parish. Jacob Wheatley continued to drop in two or three times each week, but only during his sober periods.

The old farmer was a mine of information. He would often reminisce about his earlier farming days and the grand parties which they had held in my kitchen, with the farm workers and their families dancing and celebrating the midwinter feast in ways established and rooted in age-old country tradition. His old face creased with smiles as he told of the impromptu musical evenings which he and his neighbours had organised.

'Old Ben Tolley now, he were amazing on the fiddle! We didn't need these fancy instruments, he could keep time and tune for hours on end,' he laughed.

Of his own personal life, he was strangely reluctant to speak. As time passed, I gathered that his wife, May, had originally come to the farm as his housekeeper. Jacob pulled out a creased black and white photograph one day of a young May, in a flowered cotton dress, hands folded, looking over the wrought-iron gate at the top of the stone steps which led between the two levels of the garden. She bore little resemblance, I thought, to the frail, stooped woman who flitted like a nervous ghost in and out of their squalid bungalow.

It was Christmas Eve and outside a few flakes of snow were falling from an icy blue sky. There was a knock on the door and Jacob walked in, muffled up to the ears with coat and scarf. He wore thick knitted gloves.

'My!' he exclaimed, 'I do believe that we are going to have another Christmas like 1947! It started to snow like this on Christmas Eve and continued up until the New Year. Then it froze for three months. What a year! It was impossible to feed the animals outside and we had them in the oast barn. They cost me a fortune in fodder! The land girls who had stayed on after the end of the War were freezing in the attic bedrooms. So much so that May had to give them extra blankets and hot water bottles. For food we used to take the tractor into Tentersley and buy enough for a month at a time. So many spuds that I wished that the old cellars could be opened up again!'

'So there are cellars here!' I exclaimed.

'Bless you my girl – of course there are. They are sealed in behind that fancy panelling yonder.' He gestured towards the central hall, now enlivened as much as it could ever be by an enormous decorated Christmas tree. McIntosh's, the firm that Mark had contacted, were coming in the New Year – probably mid-January – to remove the panelling. About the revelation of the cellars I had mixed feelings. At our ancient cottage, we had enjoyed a beautiful cellar, dry and sound and surprisingly sunny, thanks to a window at ground level which let in light and air. But here at Knight's Manor there was no window or air vent at ground level. If we had cellars, they must be dark indeed!

'So have you ever been in the cellars, Jacob?' I queried.

'Well, not directly like.' The old man scratched his head thoughtfully. 'My father and his father before him told of how him from the big house had the panelling built over the cellar door – years ago, before my grandfather's time.' Jacob leant forward and lowered his voice, almost as if he feared that we were being overheard.

'There were right strange goings on in those ancient times. Meetings in our cellars here. My dad didn't tell much and I didn't ask. Some things are best left unsaid. Anyway – must go.' And he stood up, buttoning his ancient overcoat around him and pulling on his old cap.

'Here y'are,' he grunted. 'This is why I dropped by.'

From the deep and slightly torn pocket of his ancient tweed coat he pulled a parcel, hastily wrapped in Christmas paper which had obviously been used before and was a bit too small. Part of the contents was visible and I could make out a large box of chocolates. I was deeply touched and quickly strode over to him, just as he was about to leave the kitchen, and impulsively gave him a kiss on his cheek. His gnome features beamed.

'Well, that's the nicest Christmas present I've had in years!' he laughed and turned, still smiling, into the now rapidly-swirling snow.

I knew how little Jacob and May had got and wondered what I could give to them. I hastily reviewed the contents of my 'Christmas cupboard'. Every year since Mark and I had been married, I had earmarked one of the kitchen cupboards for special Christmas food. Here I stored cake, puddings, mince pies, liqueur chocolates, and the other luxuries that I had bought, or had been given. Mm! The only things in there were either chocolates, which at best would appear to be copying the Wheatleys' really kind gesture and, at worst, would appear to be outdoing it; or alcohol, which was obviously inappropriate! Then I thought of the calendar which Mark had been given by a client. The company manufactured dog food and the calendar showed pictures of dogs in different poses. I loved it, but then so would Jacob who had a little springer spaniel which he adored.

I quickly wrapped the gift and put on my waxed jacket against the heavy snow which was now falling. It took only five or so minutes to walk down to Knight's Manor Farm and, turning my head away from the prevailing wind and the increasingly heavy snow flurries, I rang the doorbell on the grimy front door of the bungalow. Slowly I heard shuffling footsteps approaching – but it was not Jacob who opened the door, but his wife May, who shyly peered into the rapidly darkening afternoon.

'Hello,' she greeted me quietly.

'May, I have just brought this for you both,' I announced, holding out the calendar wrapped in holly-decorated Christmas paper. She looked very pleased.

'Do come in, Kate. I can make you a cup of tea,' she smiled gently.

'Thank you. I'd love to. But just for a few minutes,' I replied.

We walked into the sitting room. Quite frankly, it smelt terrible – of dirt, dog and alcohol. I swallowed quickly and chose a fairly clean chair to sit upon. Bess, the spaniel, was playing around on the floor with a bone, which she brought proudly to me. Looking at the state of the house, I hoped that I had not made a rash decision accepting a drink. I did not really relish the idea of having food poisoning for Christmas!

May soon brought in a tray with fairly clean-looking cups and a plate of biscuits. I would certainly avoid the biscuits if I could!

'Is Jacob out?' I asked, trying to open the conversation.

'Yes. He drove into Tentersley – straight from your house I think. He has gone to buy his Christmas drink,' May murmured.

I looked at May's work-worn arthritic hands supporting her tea cup, her downtrodden slippers and wrinkled stockings. I thought of what a difficult life she must have had with Jacob – never quite knowing whether he would be sober, or go into one of his drinking bouts.

Uncannily echoing my thoughts, May said, 'I just don't know what to expect over Christmas. He might be all right, or he might be in bed for days, incapable of caring for himself. You know,' she muttered, pouring herself another cup of tea, 'drink has changed him so much. When I first came to Knight's Manor he was such a fine man. So strong, so vigorous, such a sense of humour. You didn't notice his disability for one minute. His sheer force of character and determination took your breath away. I soon realised that I was falling in love with him, and was amazed when I knew that he loved me, too.' She gazed at the flickering coal fire, lost in her dreams of yesterday.

'We were married two years later. I loved that house, and I loved our life together there. There was only one thing between us: I longed for a baby and so did Jacob, but he was frightened to have one. He really believed that the baby might inherit his condition – such a cause of hurt and disappointment to him throughout his life.

'Well, despite everything…' May Wheatley was almost talking to herself now, speaking softly, still gazing at the flames in the small grate, '…I became pregnant and Jacob didn't know whether to be delighted or horrified. We went to specialists and they couldn't tell us for certain whether our baby would inherit his father's problem or not. Despite these worries, those nine months were some of the happiest of my entire life.' She smiled gently, looking straight into my eyes. 'To feel the flickers of new life inside my body, to feel the baby's strength growing day by day – it was wonderful.'

Despite myself, my eyes filled with tears. I had experienced three short months of 'motherhood', feeling none of the sensations that she described so lovingly. I bent over my teacup but need not have worried. May was clearly seeing the times of which she spoke pass like a pageant before her eyes. She had become unaware of me.

'May came, my birthday month, and the month my baby was expected. What a beautiful birthday gift! On 15 May I knew that baby was on her way. Jacob drove me to Ashford as fast as our old Austin 10 would go and there I had her.'

I was desperate to ask whether the baby had been all right, but felt that I couldn't interrupt her poignant story.

'When Jacob came into the labour ward it was all over. I could see the fear in his eyes as he bent over and looked into the little pink-blanketed cot. There lay our little girl, Emily – perfect! Nothing wrong with her whatsoever. And she was so beautiful with, even then, a fine down of silver-fair hair and little pink lips. People said that she looked like an angel. I saw tears in Jacob's eyes as he bent to kiss me and our little girl.'

'And does Emily live nearby, May?' I asked.

'Let me tell you. That child was a complete joy. From the day I brought her home, she smiled and gurgled with pleasure whenever she saw either myself or her dad. She would raise her little arms to touch or cuddle us and always, as she grew older, she would laugh, a delightful little giggle. You know the long corridor upstairs at the house?'

I nodded.

'Well, she had an old wooden trolley, full of coloured bricks, and she really taught herself to walk, pushing that trolley up and down the corridor, smiling and laughing to herself.'

Although May was smiling still, in a flash I knew what she was about to tell me.

'And then, it was Christmas Eve, thirty-six years ago today. Emily had been drawing Christmas pictures for her dad. We sat together in the kitchen. She rubbed her little hand across her cheek. "I hot, Mummy," she said and, for once, there was no smile on that beautiful little face. I felt her forehead and tummy and she was, indeed, very hot. I whisked her up in my arms and carried her to her nursery. We have never had very much, Jacob and I, but what we had we spent on that room. Jacob had carved some little farm animals and these were lined up along a big wall beam that ran alongside her cot. I had made a patchwork quilt cover and I tucked her up and kissed her. What I did not realise was that I was kissing her goodbye. The next morning – Christmas Day – I went in to wake her with the little gifts that we had managed to buy or make for her and,' May looked bleakly at me, 'she was dead. Meningitis they said.'

May continued to stare at me and I realised that all emotion, all feeling had, by the death of that one dearly loved little girl, been killed in her too. No wonder she was so frail, so lacking in contact with the real world. Her world had ended when her child had left it.

'I am gone seventy now... And, out of all those long years of what people call my life, I was only really alive for those three short years when my little Emily was with me. But if I was upset, Jacob was beside himself with grief. When her little body was taken away he stormed out of the house. It was four o'clock on Christmas afternoon; he didn't return 'til Boxing Day.'

I just couldn't speak. I continued to listen quietly to the heart-breaking story.

'He looked terrible. His face was white and his eyes red-rimmed from lack of sleep. He was unshaven and his clothes were muddy. He said not a word to me but took a bottle of whisky and disappeared into the front parlour with it. The next day, he did the same. It was the start of a pattern that has haunted him, and me, since then.'

'May, I don't know what to say.'

'You can't say anything to me,' she stated bluntly, 'that will give me one tiny bit of comfort. But the past is past. I just cope with each tedious year as it comes.' She continued to gaze at the dying flames in the fire, but said no more.

After a few minutes had elapsed, not really knowing what to do, I stood up. 'Well, thanks for the tea May, but I must be getting home to Mark.'

She didn't reply, or move. She just gazed into the fire embers, still lost in the past, rocking herself quietly to and fro and reliving her love for her child.

I left the mean little bungalow, treading steadily back along the deep untouched snow that had blanketed the Kent countryside. I thought again of my own loss – and how insignificant that had been compared with my neighbour's. I looked at the flakes of snow falling from the impenetrable darkness of the sky and thought how each one was unique, totally individual. I was cold and really upset. I thought about how, for each human being, there is a unique love which will transform them. For my father, it had been my mother. For my mother – I wasn't sure! Was there anyone? For poor May Wheatley, it had been Emily. For me, I had thought it was Mark, but so many doubts had started to enter my mind over the last six months. Had he changed so much? Or was it that I was perceiving life here in Ashward as I had never perceived it before? I had been overwhelmed by my husband; but increasingly was irritated, upset and belittled by his behaviour. Had his love transformed me? I didn't think so.

My thoughts raced. Treading quickly across the cattle grid I looked up at the north face of Knight's Manor and the windows which illuminated the corridor along which a long-dead child had walked and laughed and held up her arms to her loving parents. Had I somehow heard Emily Wheatley's footsteps and laughter that autumn night, when my dogs were so disturbed?

Transformational love? I ran quickly into the warm, bright kitchen of Knight's Manor and was met by licks and wags. Maybe all I could expect was the unconditional love of my dogs…

I sat at my kitchen table and wept.

Chapter 18

Mark finally arrived home at eight-thirty, over an hour and a half late. Looking at the mass of whirling, dense snowflakes, I was surprised and relieved to have him home again, despite the growing realisation that his attitude towards me had hardened and cooled over the previous eight years. He was piled with presents: gifts from friends at the office and from clients; and in a tiny russet velvet box, a gift for me.

'You would have laughed, Cheeks, if you had seen me,' he smirked, pouring himself a whisky. 'It was four-thirty and suddenly I realised that I hadn't bought you anything for Christmas. So I shot out of the office, hailed a taxi, went to Bond Street, asked the taxi to wait, bought your present and returned to the office all within thirty minutes. Good going, ha?'

I smiled without speaking. This was just box-ticking. I thought of Jacob's carved animals and the length of time it would have taken a busy farmer to make them; the patchwork quilt made by May's work-worn hands – so special, every stitch made with love. The contrast was bitter.

Christmas morning dawned bright and sunny. Looking out of our bedroom window, I saw a view that could have been taken from a Christmas card. A thick blanket of snow had fallen during the last twenty-four hours. Holly trees were lined and capped with snow. A robin perched, hungrily pecking at berries. Ice glazed wall and gate. Trees were etched with silver and the hills opposite were masked in snow. The lane had disappeared.

Suddenly the bells of Ashward church started to ring across the still and silent landscape.

'Happy Christmas, Mark!' I murmured, turning towards the tumbled warm bed.

'Happy Christmas,' came the grunted reply.

I made my customary trek downstairs through the freezing house to my warm kitchen, let out the dogs and laughed as I watched them shovelling up the snow with their noses, puzzled as to why they couldn't run at their usual speed across the courtyard. They bit into the cold whiteness, perhaps regarding it as some sort of enemy. After several minutes the coffee was made and I let them in again, to occupy their favourite winter place: the rug in front of the Aga.

Telling this story across the space of so many years, it is like stringing together sparkling gems: each scene so very clear in my memory. That Christmas day was no exception. It was as if at this height of the Christian calendar, evil could not surface. The snow almost became like a blanket that covered the dark world which bubbled up here in Ashward so often. After breakfast, we opened our presents. Mark had bought me a pearl on a fine gold chain. I put it on immediately. After a lot of thought, I had managed to get Mark a slim blue clock set in a silver rectangular surround on which a world map was etched. Time zones, shown on the map, would, I thought, help him in his international business deals. It didn't have quite the effect I had expected.

'Amazing what business toys they produce these days,' he commented humourlessly. 'Of course I can get this information from the Financial Times. Shame you didn't invest in another bottle of whisky!' And, with that, he filled his glass again.

Helen had bought us small, but perfectly chosen gifts. For Mark, a gold engraved matchbox cover; for myself, two tall gold candles.

At ten-fifteen we walked down to church. This was the only occasion that Mark would permit himself to enter the lovely little building. Perhaps this was the only time his father would ever attend church. I didn't understand his reason for accompanying me, and he didn't explain.

The exquisite ancient place of worship was aglow. Ashward church was so cared for by the Woodvilles that it almost seemed like a pampered cat, smiling quietly to itself, as it was cleaned, polished, adorned and filled with flowers and light. I was so happy here, sitting surrounded by more friends than I had ever had before. On occasions like this, Ralph and Rebecca Woodville opened their home to the congregation, with tea and coffee being served by Doris in their large, old-fashioned kitchen. The people who had attended the church service chatted happily and then we returned to our respective homes. It seemed that here, families spent Christmas Day by themselves.

Well, my family was just... Mark and I, so we did what we had always done on Christmas Day. We put the turkey in the oven and went out to take the dogs for their Christmas Day treat: an extra-long walk.

We decided to walk past the church again and turned right into the sparsely-wooded area of Low Ashward. A track led past scattered cottages and houses, and scenes of celebration were everywhere. Holly wreaths garlanded doors, chimneys were smoking cheerfully, and the dogs dived into snowdrifts and nosed small avalanches down from overhanging bushes.

At the end of the track, Estelle and Geoff Raymond's cottage lay to the left, whilst the path continued past Barrow Farm, off to the right. We intended to walk past without disturbing them, but were hailed by a loud 'Hello!' from Estelle, leaning precipitously from an upstairs window under the undulating line of the snow-covered roof.

'I say!' called Estelle loudly, with a wide smile, 'do come in and save me from terminal boredom with Geoff. He has been looking over his stamp collection for hours now and could easily bore for England!'

We walked around to the kitchen door, the dogs panting and steaming from their exertions in the snow. Estelle's kitchen was truly minute. It consisted of a deep butler's sink on raised brick pillars, a dresser and a small pine table with two chairs. Because of the kitchen's size, or lack of it, Estelle had had a conservatory built on to the back of the cottage. It was in here that we left Rupert and Emma, with an ecstatic Bonnie, who, overwhelmed by the unexpected company of two canine friends, rolled over onto her back and wagged, upside down, with sheer delight.

'A glass of wine, my darlings?' invited Estelle.

'Do you have any Scotch?' asked Mark.

'Geoff, do we have any whisky?' Estelle addressed her long-suffering husband in the habitual bored drawl which she invariably used when speaking to him.

'Yes, I think so – I'll just check.' Having discovered an unopened bottle, he poured Mark a generous measure and handed it to him. 'Here you are, Mark. A very happy Christmas to you both!'

Poor Geoff. I felt so sorry for him. He retreated to his study, where I could see his desk illuminated by a reading lamp, his collection of stamps set out for his perusal. What an ill-matched couple the Raymonds were! We chatted for ages, watching the sky deepen its colour to a peacock blue until, once again, a few flakes of snow began to drift down.

'I must show you my latest work before you leave,' smiled Estelle wickedly. 'It is in oils – only just finished – and I think you may be interested in the subject matter!'

'How exciting!' I replied curiously. Art fascinated me and Estelle's was outstanding: passionate and emotive. The lights of the cottage struck out across the patio towards her 'studio'. Actually this was just a glorified garden shed, with double doors. But for a woman born to a titled family, whose parents had built an aviary for her amusement in her childhood, she could never paint in a *shed*. It would have to be 'a studio'.

Her latest work was set apart because the paint was still drying. It was large, probably nearly two metres long and one and a half high. No wonder she had smiled! I looked with amazement – at my own house! The view of Knight's Manor was painted as if from within the wood at the end of our land and Estelle must have used photographs or sketches done in the Spring. In the foreground, bluebells and wood anemones

185

sprinkled the woodland floor and ferns were starting to unfurl. She had really captured the grace and symmetry of the southern face of the house. White clouds dotted a cool Spring sky and the daffodils under the hedge were just about to open their golden trumpets. The twisting shapes of the orchard trees just carried a hint of beginning blossom. It was beautiful and I was speechless.

'I must have it, Estelle!' asserted Mark, rather too forcibly. 'How much do you want for it?'

She smiled coolly at him and said: 'How do you know that it is not a commission for someone else?'

'Surely not!' he exclaimed impatiently.

'No. It is not a commission,' she said quietly, 'but please, Mark, do not assume that everything can be bought. There are some things that money just will not buy you know. My work is available, but we must negotiate an appropriate price.'

I couldn't stand this sort of conversation – it was like verbal fencing and I found it excruciating – so I said quietly: 'I will go back and chat to Geoff, Estelle, if that is all right with you.'

'Of course my dear, leave your husband to me! He will be quite safe you know.'

I doubted it! Walking briskly across the stone flags of the patio, I reflected sadly that it had given me a fair degree of satisfaction to see my husband gently but firmly put in his place. He really did believe sometimes that he could demand anything he wanted and get it through sheer force of character.

Poor Geoff looked anxious when he heard footsteps, but relaxed when he saw it was me, not Estelle, who had come through the kitchen door.

'Another wine, my dear?' he asked.

'No Geoff, thank you, Mark and I need to reach home safely! Tell me about your stamp collection.'

Pathetically, he was taken aback at my interest. Did Estelle never wish to share his interest with him? He proudly showed me his rarer stamps, explaining their provenance at length. I stifled a yawn. Where was Mark? The light was fading now and we had at least half an hour's walk back home.

Eventually Mark returned, with a rather fixed smile on his face – not his Cheshire cat grin, which always indicated total victory on his part, but looking slightly frazzled. I bet Estelle has given him a hard time, I thought to myself.

'I will bring my work over the day after Boxing Day, Mark,' Estelle said graciously, 'and you can let me have your cheque then. I am pleased that we have reached a satisfactory agreement.'

'Yes,' came the curt reply. 'I will see you then. Thank you for the drinks. Enjoy the rest of your evening. Goodbye.' And with that, my husband, rather unceremoniously, left the cottage, with me and our dogs trailing in his wake.

'Don't you think you were a bit rude, Mark?' I asked.

'To that old witch? No way! My God, she drives a hard bargain,' he said, a flush rising to his cheeks. 'Let's not talk about it anymore. After all, I got what I wanted in the end! That's all that matters.'

We walked quickly along the track that led back to Knight's Manor. I was quiet, thinking about Mark's conversation with Estelle and his comment just now that getting what he wanted was all that mattered. I thought also of Paul's story about the strange circling dance that he had witnessed by the barrow, which lay to our left, about 250 metres further on, blanketed in white.

Snowflakes whipped into my freezing face. By now the dogs were trotting tamely along by our sides, exhausted by the extra effort of ploughing through the deep snow. We would hear no more from them that evening. On the right lay Barrow Farmhouse, small and ordinary looking, with two dim lights shining in the kitchen. We glimpsed William Deepdene and his brother Albert eating their Christmas dinner, silently shovelling forkfuls of food into their mouths.

I pulled my collar up further against the swirling white flakes and thrust my hands in my pockets.

There it was. Nothing had prepared me for the intense cold that seemed to emanate from the barrow itself. I felt as if I were walking into a glacier. My steps slowed, so did my breathing and the air seemed tangibly heavy. Thank goodness I was not alone. Even Mark was quiet. 'Can't wait to get home for some food!' he exclaimed briefly.

We did not linger. I had dreaded that Mark would want to inspect the barrow, but no. His mind was clearly occupied with what he considered an unsatisfactory deal, and so he trudged past the crouching white mound, seeming almost as keen as I was to leave it behind and regain the comparative warmth of our home.

Fifteen minutes more and we had done just that. The dogs slumped in front of their favourite friend and so did we, glasses in hand.

'Happy Christmas, Mark!'
'Happy Christmas, Kate!'

Chapter 19

The deep snow continued throughout January. Estelle delivered her beautiful painting to us on the day after Boxing Day as promised, braving the treacherous road conditions. I saw another side to her character as she gazed directly at my husband, hoping that he would 'cherish the painting as it deserved'; and graciously accepting the staggeringly large fee that Mark had agreed to give her. I smiled, slightly anxiously, as her little car skidded away across the snowy frozen road. Estelle, imperturbable as always, waved from the driver's window, cigarette in hand, steering, if it could be called that, single-handedly back along the twisting narrow roads to her fairy-tale cottage.

Over the Christmas period I saw nothing of Jacob and May, and assumed that Jacob was reliving again the recurrent nightmare of that Christmas thirty-six years previously. Paul had a heavy cold and our weekly meetings were cancelled for the time being. Helen had gone to stay with Matilde in London.

'Kate, please come with us!' she had urged the day before her departure.

'Helen, I can't. Really. You know what a mood Mark would get into, and what would we do about the dogs?'

'Mark could stay in London for a couple of weeks, and there *are* kennels you know, Kate! It would do Mark good to realise that he could actually look after himself if he made the effort.'

But I didn't go with her.

McIntosh's couldn't make 15 January, the snow was just too thick, but the next week the snowploughs started to do their job regularly and on 24 January the gold and red van, with 'McIntosh' printed neatly upon the side, arrived.

Two very dissimilar men emerged. In fact, they were almost physical opposites. Joe, tall and thin, with a drooping moustache, was clearly the more senior of the two in years and position. His companion was called Tom. He was short, young and cheerful.

The men started work promptly at half-past nine, refusing my offer of tea. With painstaking care they removed the fixings and levered the magnificent panelling away from the walls. As each section of panelling was removed, they carried it carefully into the adjoining garage and stacked it on soft blankets, interleaving each piece with hessian, one section on top of the other. I looked curiously at the cobwebby back of the panelling: it had been in place for nearly 300 years and, as always with such things, I found it fascinating to be the first to see something which had been hidden for so long. I mused that archaeologists must feel like this when they opened a long-sealed tomb...

I grew cold just hanging about and asked Joe if I could do anything to help. By this time, it was eleven-thirty.

'A cup of tea would be a real help now,' said Joe. 'All this dust is making our throats dry.'

We sat on the stairs, drinking and chatting together.

'This is real quality stuff!' remarked Joe, rubbing his chin thoughtfully. 'I have only ever done a couple of jobs similar to this and in both cases the panelling had been joined roughly and patched. But this is beautiful. Reckon this Paul Ashward who wrote his name here had a pretty penny.'

'How else can I help you?' I asked.

'Well, you could brush off the back of each panel with this,' Joe replied, giving me something that looked like a large make-up brush.

This I did. Wanting as always the company of the dogs, I lifted the double garage doors and let them play in and out of the building, now galloping into the snow, now panting back to me for a stroke or a biscuit. Rupert sniffed the stack of panels suspiciously. I knew what was coming. Obviously not liking what he smelt, he lifted his leg casually and comprehensively pee'd against the panel I was brushing off.

'Oh Rupert!' I stifled a laugh. 'That must have been your most expensive wee ever!' Money meant nothing to the dogs – thank goodness.

'Mrs Summers! Can you spare a minute?'

'Of course.'

I returned indoors. Joe and Tom were standing looking at something that had been directly behind the carved panel which held Paul Ashward's name. They had uncovered a door. Small and narrow, it looked much older than the other doors in the house, which I suspected had been replaced in the relatively recent past – well, over the past 150 years or so! It was arched, made of oak, with a heavy iron handle.

'So that's the entrance to the cellars!' I exclaimed in spite of myself. 'I knew it must be here somewhere.'

'Well, let's have a look then!' suggested Tom cheerfully, turning the handle. It did not budge.

'It must be locked,' deduced Tom, peering into the large key hole. 'It *is* locked! I can see the key – it's still in place. But, hang on, how can that be?'

'Where is the other entrance to the cellars, Mrs Summers?' asked Joe politely.

'We don't have one…' I murmured.

'Ah… right… Well, we are not here to solve mysteries. We must get on,' commented the incurious Joe – and get on they did, finishing the removal of the panelling some six hours after they had started, just as the short, winter daylight was beginning to fade.

***

Joe and Tom had gone. The winter evening had closed in like a physical presence as their large, red and gold van pulled slowly away down the lane which joined the main road leading eventually towards London. I surveyed my hall. Without the sophisticated panelling it was almost as if I was stepping back into a less civilised time – the time when Knight's Manor had originally been built which, according to Mr Deepdene, had been in the late fourteenth or early fifteenth centuries. For what must have been the hundredth time I mused idly upon the name of my house: Knight's Manor. Which knight? A knight connected with Ashward Priory. A knight who had been given the land I now owned? It was easy to visualise these less civilised times when looking at the rough plaster which coated the uneven walls and, between the box framing that had become visible, the lath and plaster infill. When repaired and painted it would, I was certain, look much softer and less forbidding than the dark panelling had done.

I looked at the small, grey oak door and tried the handle myself – no, it was certainly shut fast. After all these months of knowing that this great house had cellars, to actually find their entrance was something of an anticlimax.

I was restless after being cooped up all day in the house. No Helen to walk to; no Paul to drive to; and the return of my husband from the office still hours away. The best way to dispel the restlessness was, as I knew from experience, to take the dogs out, even though it was now full dark and the deep chill of that January night had started to set in. Stars blazed in the sky already, made brighter by the frost that was starting to form on grass and twig.

I decided to walk down to the church. In that peaceful spot, locking the building wasn't necessary and I knew how to turn on the lights. If Ralph Woodville did leave his warm hearth to investigate, he would, I knew, be pleased that someone appreciated the church sufficiently to visit it on such a bitterly cold night.

The dogs and I crunched our way down the road. The snow had started to freeze and ice crystals chimed and shattered under paws and feet. I reached the beautiful building within twenty minutes and soon flooded it with light. This place never seemed cold! I really believed that it was warmer than Knight's Manor. Idly I sat in the pew which I normally used – the fourth from the front on the left-hand side – and let the timeless peace of the place wash over me. Usually I was occupied with people-watching during the services but, for the first time, I looked properly at the carved oak and monumental brasses which lay within the nave and chancel. Some were really beautiful; all spoke of love between the person commemorated and the person who had chosen the words whereby that love should be remembered.

The Light went from my world when you passed on…
Beloved mother and wife…
The flower of his age and the adornment of his family…

Bitterly, I asked myself how I would commemorate Mark, and wondered how he would remember me. He never seemed to take life seriously enough to express meaningful emotion. What would I remember of him, were he to die? His sarcasm, his criticism, his ridicule?

I shivered, turned up the collar of my coat, put on my hat and gloves, switched off the lights, and returned home.

Chapter 20

At seven o'clock I heard the crash of the cattle grid heralding Mark's return. He came in, his face pinched with cold.

'It's brass monkey weather out there, Cheeks!' he exclaimed, striding over to the Aga and opening the two hob covers to let out maximum warmth to his chilled body. In several layers of jumpers, I was, finally, warming up after my evening walk.

'How does it look then?' he asked impatiently.

'Good. Or it will. But you will never guess what? They uncovered the door to the cellars!'

'Ooh, real *Boys' Own* stuff, eh?' he sneered. 'And what did you see? White shapes through the worm holes; steaming pitchforks through the keyhole?'

'No!' I replied, as patiently as I could. 'Because the keyhole is blocked. It is locked – from the inside.'

Even Mark's sarcastic banter was cut short by this blunt observation. Then, he cursorily dismissed what I had said.

'Nah, can't be! Who did McIntosh's send?'

'Joe and Tom. They were very nice and experienced and they both said…'

'Hm! Brains of Britain no doubt, both of them! Well I'll bet you that the "locked" door is really a "blocked" door. Some piece of ancient debris will have become lodged in that keyhole, you mark my words. I'll get my crowbar after dinner tonight and I'll soon open it. You wait and see.'

'But, don't you think we ought to wait to…'

'Er, sorry to be difficult, but do we have anything to eat this evening?' Mark interrupted.

Oh no! In my involvement with the removal of the panelling and the discovery – at last – of the entrance to the cellars and then my bitter walk to the church, I had completely forgotten about cooking an evening meal!

'Oh for God's sake, Kate! What am I supposed to do – eat dog food?'

'We could have a meal at the pub, I suppose,' I suggested.

'Do you know,' he exclaimed, striding to the door, 'sometimes I think you regard me as just a meal ticket. What do you do with your time all day? Chat to your precious friends? Daydream? Walk your stupid dogs?'

I felt that this could easily develop into the sort of argument that we always seemed to have these days and so decided on the easy course.

'Sorry,' I said. 'Please forgive me.'

Once I started to plead, you could see the bullying, arrogant aspects of my husband's character come to the surface.

'Of course I forgive you.' He used a silly, whining tone, presumably aping mine. 'But you just need to bloody well pull yourself together. A day in my chambers would sort you out, I can tell you!'

In the end we went to the Swan Inn – our 'local'. We sat in the huge window at the back of the ancient building, looking out over the white landscape and the frosty stars, eating a bar meal. Gradually, as Mark ate and drank, he regained some measure of good temper. The cold immensity of the Kent countryside was really apparent from this viewpoint. We had been to the pub several times during the daylight and I knew the extent of the view. Quietly I identified the source of some of the lights glimmering on that intensely cold night. Closest of all was Fortune Farm, where the lights glowed from milking parlour and hay barn. Further away, to the left, were the greenhouses of Michael and Daphne Woods' nursery. Furthest away, blinking its warning to the ships out on the unimaginable black vastness of the sea, was the sporadic beam of the lighthouse at Dungeness.

All too soon it was half-past ten and the landlord was looking pointedly at us as we lingered, the last of his customers, basking in the warmth of his central heating and his log fire. We had to leave. The Lancia windscreen was coated with ice and, laughing, in good spirits again, we scraped it off with Mark's credit card.

Mark looked resolutely ahead as he expertly negotiated the bends and twists of the narrow lane.

'You know, I still intend to open that door tonight.'

Not wanting to spoil the feeling of something like warmth which had flickered between us again that evening, I said nothing.

Completely misinterpreting my silence, I felt Mark relax.

'I knew you would come round with a bit of good food inside you!'

It was nearly one o'clock. For two hours in that frozen hall, my husband had been working away with a crowbar and screwdrivers of various types. It was so cold that ice patterns had begun to form on the inside of the staircase window.

Finally it seemed as if all his efforts were taking effect as the ancient wood groaned under the pressure which he was applying. I had sat with him for most of the time on the bottom step of the staircase and it was almost as if I was caught up in a play or film. I felt powerless to say anything to Mark, because I knew that, in the stubborn and determined mood that he was in, the slightest remark would provoke a savage verbal attack. My energy to resist these attacks was growing less, I reflected sadly. So I just sat, wrapped in my outdoor coat, and watched.

Suddenly there was a loud *crack* and the old door timbers splintered. The noise reverberated through the house, seeming to echo and re-echo, magnifying and swirling through the freezing air. A gust of foetid air came from the cellar. Its stench was indescribable and I was reminded of Paul Lucas's phrase, used to describe how he felt when entering the cellars at Ashward: it was like entering an open grave. It even made Mark draw back.

'Phew!' he exclaimed. 'It's just as well we did get this cellar opened up. We could have had a serious dry rot problem on our hands. There is obviously a total lack of ventilation in here.'

He attacked the weakened door with a vengeance until the splintered wood lay over the quarry tiles of the hall floor. The space where the door had stood gaped wide.

Laughing, Mark picked up the piece of wood which held the latch and keyhole.

'Here you are!' he began with his usual confidence. 'There is absolutely no sign whatsoever of the door having been locked from the inside… oh!' He stopped abruptly and actually had the grace to look embarrassed.

'Well actually, this is odd. The door *was* locked from the inside.' He removed a very large, rusty, clearly ancient, key. 'I wonder, how on earth…' his tirade petered out. Swiftly he changed the subject.

'Come on! Aren't you excited? Let's explore the only part of our house that is new to us.'

'No, Mark. Not tonight. You don't know what you might find in there.'

I was tired. The hall, stairs and half-landing were filthy – as was my husband. All I wanted to do was to crawl into bed and get warm. Opening the cellar door had somehow made the house seem vulnerable. I remembered the chanting I had heard on my return from church on Hallowe'en.

'Ah! Vampires, demons, witches…'

I was too tired to argue.

'I meant priceless historical information, Mark. I think we ought to call in an expert.' I was angry at the glib way in which my husband dismissed the delicate spiritual journey I had been drawn into since entering this parish.

'Bill Deepdene would be fascinated to see what you have just uncovered. Call him. Call him tomorrow. I am going to bed.' And, with most uncharacteristic firmness, I did exactly that.

Surprisingly, Mark followed me.

Chapter 21

Even though I had felt exhausted when I stalked up to our freezing cold bedroom, I found that sleep was a million miles away. I replayed in my mind the events of the day... again and again.

Without the sophisticated and edgy conversation of Helen and the intellectual stimulus of discussions with Paul what, I asked myself, did I actually have here in this beautiful, isolated place? The relentless sarcasm and disinterest of my husband? The loving companionship of my dogs? I thought through the long day that had just passed and felt only disenchantment.

I just had to get away, and thought again of Helen's invitation to stay with her in her mother's home in London. As soon as it was light the following morning, I spoke to Mark. I told him somewhat tersely that I was going to stay with Helen and her mother; that there was ample food in the freezer for at least a fortnight; and that he had to look after himself. This I suspected would be for the first time ever, as he had lived with his mother before marrying me. I phoned Estelle and asked whether she could possibly look after Rupert and Emma for a couple of weeks. She replied laconically that, at this time of the year, nothing much was happening in the garden and so the dogs could chase each other until they were tired. I didn't know quite what sort of state they, or her garden, would be in when I returned, but it was a genuinely warm and kind offer. I walked them over to her cottage, returned home, then caught a taxi to the station.

On the train my brain was still working overtime. I had so enjoyed packing my beautiful London clothes. I realised with a pang that it had been months since I had had the occasion to wear them. Just feeling the soft, expensive material and the lingering scent of my favourite perfume took me back to the heady days of non-stop partying Mark and I had lost ourselves in after my miscarriage. Such a lifestyle was unsustainable and empty – we had both realised that – but here, buried in the depths of the country, I felt that I was in danger of losing my own identity. Our dream of establishing a home that we could make beautiful and love and fill with our future family had not quite turned out as I had expected. The truth of the last six months was that I had worked physically very hard indeed to transform a large, cold, unloved house; and that my husband had worked equally hard to earn the money to enable the transformation. But, I realised sadly, our paths were diverging. He was becoming more firmly fixed in his London life, whilst I was becoming increasingly enchanted by, and deeply involved with, the beauty and history of Ashward.

I knew that I was different now to how I had been when we arrived. I had experienced Helen's wisdom and friendship, Paul's erudition, and a frankly bizarre array of events that intrigued me deeply. Walking the lanes of Ashward was to encounter history at every turn: past and present ran together here.

***

Matilde's cottage in Wimbledon was about five minutes' walk from the Common. It was tucked down a side street, Georgian, tiny and exquisite. When I walked with Helen down the paved front garden in early February, clumps of snowdrops fought bravely against the overcast day. Helen opened the deep-green painted front door into the spacious sitting room, and I saw immediately that her good taste had been inherited from her mother. The room held a large gold sofa and two green armchairs. The elegant marble fireplace was surmounted by a gilt, arched mirror and fresh flowers were everywhere. It was like Meadow Farm in miniature! This front room led through to a small dining room, with French doors leading on to an enclosed patio. Here the external walls of the cottage and the adjoining property had been whitewashed to reflect every glimmer of light back into the dining room. Jasmine rambled up a small trellis on the south-facing wall of the patio and I knew that in summer the house would be flooded with its scent. A minute, immaculate kitchen completed the ground floor.

Matilde took me to my bedroom at the back of the house, overlooking the jasmine. It was so small that it could only contain a bed and bedside table apart from the fitted wardrobe. It was warm and soft and comfortable – and I realised how much I had missed these basics since my arrival in Kent some five months earlier. Sinking down into the delicious softness of the bed, I remembered with a shiver the chill lift of the valance on my bed back at Knight's Manor, moved by draughts and never heated.

Being with Helen in Wimbledon was like enjoying the company of the sister I had never had. We got up early and walked together to the bakery on the corner to buy fresh croissants, or rolls, still warm from the oven. We used to wrap them in a cloth to retain their heat. We talked late into the night, sharing a bottle of wine together, or sometimes hot chocolate. I heard more about her childhood; and when she told me how she had met James and about her disappointment in their marriage, I wondered to myself whether any marriage is truly happy. We went on a river cruise in the snow, watching the well-known landmarks pass us by through a falling veil of white. We shopped, went to art galleries, the Tower of London and the Houses of Parliament. In short, not one minute of those two weeks passed without a conversation or new experience lifting my mind and spirits. It was exactly what I needed. Although London was stimulating and exciting, I realised how much I missed the quiet, the peace and the beauty of the countryside which surrounded me back in Ashward. I missed my dogs, my house, my garden and the church. Did I miss Mark? Bleakly, I had to admit that I did not.

***

In Helen's tiny white Citroen we clanged across the cattle grid into the courtyard at the back of Knight's Manor. The idyllic, but unrealistic, fortnight in London had ended. It was a Friday evening in mid-February and, at five o'clock there was now enough daylight to light up the rosy bricks and soft cushions of moss on the ancient walls of my home. The Aga chimney puffed faintly aromatic steam into the early Spring air. The snowdrop and daffodil bulbs which I had planted in containers around the courtyard were showing, some just thin spears of green, others fully developed flowers. Everything looked perfect, homely, dearly loved and unremarkable.

To say that I was surprised to see the back door open and Mark step out with a cheery grin on his face and a wooden spoon in his hand, would be an understatement. Never before had I been met by my husband on a weekday evening, and certainly I had never seen him look so domesticated!

'Good to have you back, love!' he exclaimed, giving me a kiss on the cheek. 'You should see the washing! I have used all my shirts I think. You are back just in time!'

So nothing changes really…

'Dinner's ready – just,' he said, disappearing indoors rapidly. He had picked up the dogs and they gave us their usual rapturous welcome. Well, I was certainly home!

Mark had lit the gold candles that Helen had given me at Christmas and had opened a bottle of wine. He had cooked the only meal he could actually produce – steak and salad – and it was very good. The three of us ate quietly and hungrily at first. Mark insisted on clearing away the plates and then brought in cheese and biscuits. He had bought grapes to eat with the cheese, which he knew I loved – and I was really touched.

We relaxed and laughed together as the daylight faded and the first stars appeared. It was good to be home. The carefree break with Helen had been amazing. Yet coming back to Knight's Manor, I realised that my heart, soul and spirit were at peace here. This is where I needed to be. Cutting across my reverie, Mark suddenly announced:

'I have been busy. Come with me!'

We walked from the dining room, through the kitchen and into the hall, where a new oak door had been fitted to the wrecked doorframe. The rendered panels between the timber box framing had been skilfully repaired and painted. Mark walked towards the replica of the original arched door and flung it open, in typical Mark manner. He stepped down into the cellar and immediately the whole area was flooded with light. I don't know how much wattage had been installed down there, but it was dazzling!

'Old Deepdene came over and we found something really fascinating, actually,' he said. 'Come and see.'

We needed no second bidding. We followed Mark through the first cellar, then came to another door, almost identical to the one destroyed by my husband's fervour that cold January night: small, arched, made of grey weathered wood. Mark unlocked this and we walked through. We followed a passage that I estimated was directly underneath the drawing room, and on into an enormous circular space. The ceiling above this circular room was supported by huge black timbers, arranged like the spokes of a wheel and meeting an upright post set in the centre of the floor. Around the curved walls were thirteen alcoves, all with pointed tops, like the ancient door into the cellar. Above the apex of each alcove was a carved symbol.

Neither Helen nor I could speak. This was incredible! I had never seen a space like it. It was cold and, quite frankly, immensely threatening. Helen and I both felt it. Mark, however, seemed completely impervious to the feeling of the place, the *genius loci* as Paul would have described it.

Here too lights had been installed. But their shrill insistence did nothing to lessen the overpowering heaviness of the place.

'Just look here!' Mark exclaimed proprietorially. In the stone-flagged floor were circling patterns, overlapping and intersecting each other. They appeared to be worked in brass and were immensely complex and skilful. In places the metal was bright and worn.

'Deepdene explained that these almost certainly relate to gatherings here and show the importance of positioning in ritualistic dance. In earth magic, movement makes the chanted words more powerful. He believes that this is, or was, a meeting place for some sort of sect. He wasn't exactly sure which sect...'

I thought of Paul's encounter with the suspected witches' coven near Bill Deepdene's own farm and was astonished that the historian could be so pedantic and, at the same time, so utterly lacking in spiritual perception.

'Anyway, he told me that he has never personally seen a space such as this. Apparently, he has read that there was a similar area in Delphi. I didn't understand all he was saying... but this is the gist of it,' he stated, rather defensively.

I really could not speak. I think the central thought in my mind was that this cold and threatening space lay close to my drawing room. No wonder the eastern part of this room never really got warm. I felt that there was a spiritual and physical drain to any warmth or positive energy generated above.

Helen, typically, broke our silence.

'Have you spoken to Paul about this, Mark? Bill Deepdene is all very well, but I feel that there is a coldness and oppression here that goes beyond what you see. Paul may well be able to give you some deeper, more relevant information about what has been discovered.'

Mark would have torn apart this suggestion if I had made it. But, since it was Helen who had calmly pointed out the limitations of the only opinion he had yet received on the origins and possible uses of this strange circular room, he accepted the suggestion without quibble.

'OK. I will ring him right now.'

'But, Mark, it is nearly ten o'clock!'

'Oh, I am sure the old man will still be up. He will probably be slaving over his Sunday sermon.'

We gladly left the strange, deeply disturbing space, watching with relief as Mark locked the inner and outer doors.

Both Helen and I naturally gravitated to the warmth of the kitchen and looked at each other with complete understanding. We both felt the coldness and oppression of the circular room. We both felt the latent threat, and also confusion and concern about how the hidden space fitted in with the lives of people who lived in Ashward. It seemed to us both that the space was a tangible symbol of the unseen spiritual world that lay just under the surface of what we call reality. We had talked, interacted socially, laughed, read, drunk tea and wine just metres above this timeless space, whilst activities were taking place here that may have directly or indirectly influenced the outcomes of our everyday lives. How often was this situation replicated? How often did acts of goodness on the one hand, and evil practices on the other, impact upon the routine of existence?

We heard the mainly one-sided conversation between Paul and my husband. It ended with the words, 'That's great Paul. Many thanks. See you tomorrow.'

He came into the kitchen, grinning widely:

'See, no problem! He is coming over tomorrow.'

'I must go home, Kate,' smiled Helen, stifling a gentle yawn. 'James will have been asleep in the armchair for hours by now. He needs to be woken and sent to bed.' And with that, she kissed us both lightly on the cheek and left.

***

Paul looked concerned. He had whipped out a powerful magnifying glass almost as soon as we had entered the underground room and was busy examining the symbols which were carved into the stone above the pointed arches surmounting each of the thirteen alcoves. He examined them closely and in silence for some time. To the alcove directly opposite the door through which we had entered, he paid particular attention. He ran his fingers expertly around the stone moulding and scrutinised the vertical joints minutely.

'Right!' he exclaimed eventually, with typical briskness. 'Let's get out of here!'

The three of us went back into the daylight. Once again I felt real relief as we shut and locked the doors behind us.

'You are literally sitting on a time bomb!' Paul announced forcefully.

'What do you mean?' asked Mark, frowning.

'The room is a meeting place for the witches here in Ashward. A coven consists of thirteen members and there is a place for each member in the room we have just been in. Over each niche is a cabbalistic sign, and together they will make a spell. I cannot decipher the signs and I certainly am not able to "read" the spell. However, I can take a pretty accurate guess as to what the spell relates to.'

We listened without speaking.

'I believe it relates to an ancient curse which was made in this parish, and which is still working its way through Ashward society today. Perhaps it is intended to strengthen the curse – perhaps perpetuate it. Witches look for evil and rejoice in it. We wish to bring about joy and fulfilment in life; they wish to bring about destruction and misery. Once again, making a fairly confident guess, I believe that those blackened timbers are from the burnt, ruined building in the cellars of Ashward Priory. Do you remember, Kate, I told you that my ancestor, Paul Ashward, brought some of these timbers to Knight's Manor, to transport some of the "power" he had discovered in the foundations of the Priory to other places within the parish?'

I nodded.

'Well, this power was obviously evil, connected with the ancient building that had been destroyed centuries ago by fire. I further believe that the circular room, which forms such a singular part of your historic property, was the room to which Paul Ashward exited, from the passageway that leads from the Priory to Knight's Manor, when followed by his wife. The thirteenth alcove, directly opposite the entrance to the room, contains a secret door, skilfully hidden in the stonework. Finally, I believe that the distinctive chanting noise that Kate heard on Hallowe'en evening came from this meeting room. The stone ceiling, the massive timbers and the substantial space between the floor of your house and the ceiling of the circular room all mean that much of the sound generated underground is deadened.'

Even Mark was silent as Paul delivered his information with clarity and emphasis. It would have been impossible to interrupt him. And certainly totally unthinkable to question or contradict what he was saying.

'If you are physically ill you go to see a doctor,' continued Paul. 'Since you asked me to come here and give you my opinion on this newly discovered aspect of your house, in effect to advise you on your spiritual well-being, these are my recommendations.' He looked Mark straight in the eye, no shadow of a smile on his face.

'I have lived here long enough and encountered enough evil to be categoric in my advice. You must try to remove, as best you can, all traces of your presence in the hidden room. You must remove the lighting, seal the room and try to forget that it is there. Any notion that you may be harbouring of maximising the value of this property by drawing public attention to its unique cellars would be foolhardy in the extreme.'

I noticed Mark's sheepish smile – Paul had correctly read his intention.

'You can only hope to co-exist peacefully with the people who follow the evil way in this parish,' continued Paul. 'There may be a totally unexpected way to escape the impact of the curse that threads through the lives of all the people here, but I do not have a crystal ball to foretell the future.' He smiled grimly, without humour.

'What I am absolutely certain of, however, is this. God has absolute power and a plan to protect his people. However difficult, if you stay true to His rules, He will, somehow, find a way to protect and cherish you – to safeguard your spiritual integrity and well-being. But now, I must go. I have other work to do. But, Mark, heed what I have said. Kate has encountered much of the spiritual turbulence in Ashward, and you have ridiculed her for it. Do not...' he paused for emphasis, '...ridicule what I have said. Goodbye.' And with a very warm smile directed at me and me alone, Paul strode out of our kitchen and into the car, where Gisela had sat waiting for the duration of his visit.

'My God, I need a bloody drink!' said my husband, running his hand through his hair and heading for the drinks cupboard.

I didn't know what to feel. Paul had confirmed all my worst fears. But equally he had given a reasoned way to cope with the unwanted secret we had recently uncovered. I just hoped that Mark would pay attention to his vigorous and unequivocal advice.

He did.

'I can understand the effect that old parson has on you, Kate,' he said, finishing the second whisky which he had poured for himself. 'I am going to seal up the cellar door – making sure, of course, that there are sufficient air bricks to avoid dry rot, and so on.'

I was astonished, and so relieved.

***

I shared everything that Paul had said with Helen first thing on Monday morning. She listened quietly, looking deeply concerned.

'And Mark actually took on board what Paul said?' she asked.

'Absolutely!' I exclaimed. 'I was surprised too, Helen.'

She thought for some time, her lovely face shadowed, thoughtfully sipping her coffee. Finally she said, 'I think you have to come to terms with the presence of that room under your house, Kate. I don't see what else you can do. Put it out of your mind. Trust what Paul said – that God will protect you if you live the life He expects you to live.'

We sat in silence for some minutes, both lost in the implications of what she had just said and the reality of doing what Paul recommended. Eventually, desperate to change the rather oppressive thoughts that were crowding around us, Helen said:

'You will never guess what Ralph did the other day?'

I smiled. I loved this woman so much. I tried to respond in kind to her conscious lightening of tone. 'Bought a new car?' It was a cause of constant amusement to us that Ralph, millionaire though he was, drove around in an ancient Ford Fiesta, which reeked of his small dogs.

'No. He bought an etching from that new antique shop in Tentersley. It was very fine, very expensive and it shows a grand Palladian mansion called Woodville Court.'

'His ancestral home?'

'Well no. That's the amusing thing!' exclaimed Helen. 'Ralph does not have an ancestral home. He is the first of his family to have amassed a fortune. But nevertheless, he has hung the etching in the entrance hall at Manor Farm, to create that exact impression.'

As we laughed together at the pretentiousness of Helen's father-in-law, once again I felt relief that the hints of evil which lurked beneath the surface of society here had been brought to light by Paul Lucas. In the brightness and clarity of

Paul's exposition, Mark had no option but to face the complex reality of the spiritual flaw at the heart of Ashward. I wondered whether our relationship would now enter a new and more positive phase. One where he would acknowledge and respect my opinion, and where I would experience again some of the warmth and excitement of our early marriage.

Somehow, I rather doubted it.

TIME IS

TIME WAS

ASH

Chapter 22

2014

Ash Cooper ran his fingers through his dark spiky hair, took off his glasses and closed his eyes against the permaglare of the computer screen. His birthday! That's a laugh. Woke up alone, had breakfast alone, working alone in his chaotic office. From his family, one birthday card. The girls couldn't even manage to buy him one each. Slowly, reluctantly, he opened his eyes again. What a mess! Files, contracts, empty coffee cups littered the small, stuffy room. After fifty-three years of hopes and dreams and idealism – this! Photos were stuck in haphazard places, an executive summary of his life. His parents in front of the white, weather-boarded farmhouse where he was born; the girls when very young; a Thai restaurant he loved when he lived in Bangkok, with the owner beaming above a plate of steamed vegetables; the band he had managed...

And where was he now? In a dingy rented flat over a garage, seeing his daughters every fortnight for four hours, paying over to his rapacious ex-wife nearly all he earned. What a mess!

The gentle chime of an incoming email momentarily took his attention. Oh God! More work, more things to do when really all he wanted was to sit and do nothing at all. He had cancelled his flight to Atlanta. He couldn't face the trade fair, the incessant talking, the meaningless promotion of, what? Everything was meaningless…

Wearily he put on his glasses and looked at the email.

'I think we knew each other a long, long time ago…'

He frowned. Refocused. And really looked…

She was unmistakable. Lighter hair, thinner face, but the same intense light blue eyes, the same direct gaze, straight into his exhausted mind. The gaze took him back, thirty years back, to that golden summer held deep in his memory like a jewel from a forgotten world. He closed his eyes to remember more clearly that bright spring day, a lifetime ago, which had changed his world.

On that far-off morning he had recognised her as soon as he had seen her lying, relaxed and vulnerable, in that field full of early Spring flowers. He had seen her previously through the eyes of the mask he had worn during the Christmas play at Ashward, when he had watched her slip silently into the huge gilded ballroom. Moving with unconscious grace, she was obviously anxious not to disturb the performance and he had been taken immediately by the way she looked at him and the other actors, honestly and openly and without guile. Her eyes were beautiful, a clear blue, like sky or sunlit water. Her face and gestures were mobile, her mouth ready to smile, hands swift to brush back her shoulder-length brown hair, swift to reach out, to touch, to help, to give…

Chapter 23

1982

Spring had definitely arrived. Having been brought up in the north of the country, I could never get used to the way in which, in Kent, primroses appeared in February; and by April, catkins flourished, birds were nest building and even tulips were in full flower.

It was a Saturday, exactly a week after Paul Lucas's visit. In the woodland which marked the boundary of Knight's Manor land to the south, the wild cherry trees spattered the browns and patches of acid green with their creamy whiteness. With the gathering light and life of the year, it seemed to me as if nature herself held new hope and expectation.

Our latest purchase was a ride-on lawn-mower. I had seen these used in suburbia for what amounts to just a large lawn and had laughed at what seemed to be an expensive affectation. But here, in our developing three acres of garden, it was a necessity. Mark loved the machine. He roared up and down the expanse of lawn, wind ruffling his thick dark hair and flattening his stained T-shirt against his slim body. As I watched him systematically covering the vast area of green, starred with the whites and yellows of daisies and buttercups, I reflected upon my volatile, charismatic husband. His life continued to move away from mine with a speed which frightened me. His job was becoming much more demanding and his clients now included major international companies, involving frequent meetings abroad. He had to stay away from home more and more and, on these occasions, I always took Rupert and Emma up to my bedroom. Never again, however, had my sleep been broken by the running footsteps and that heart-breaking laughter which echoed from moments of joy experienced long ago. Had the 'haunting' stopped? Somehow I didn't think so: it was too enmeshed in the very fabric of the house to have simply disappeared.

As our life together progressed, I had become aware of something else in Mark which disturbed me greatly. At times his spirits were irrepressible, almost manic. But in stark contrast, he would suddenly become silent and morose, his mind elsewhere entirely. His behaviour seemed to veer between these two extremes and he could never seem able to reach a happy balance of either quieter enjoyment, or happier reflection. As charismatic as ever, still staggeringly attractive, I had to admit to myself that, however hard I tried – at improving my personal appearance, at producing a meal, at planning room decoration – as far as Mark was concerned, it was never quite good enough.

We were shouting to each other, striving to be heard above the noisy engine of the lawn-mower.

'Where do you think I should put this rhododendron?' I yelled, balancing the small, deep red-flowered plant in my hands and surveying the rockery that I was in the process of creating to cover the steep fall in the land between the roadside rose garden and the higher levels which stretched in front of the house to the south.

'You can stick it where the sun don't shine for all I care!' bellowed Mark; and laughing loudly at his own humour, he executed a sharp turn to head back once more, away from the house towards the woodland.

This was exactly the sort of response that was beginning to annoy me intensely. I wanted to share decisions with my husband, even small unimportant ones. But it seemed to me that, with the increasing profile of his professional work, everything that was dear to me – my home, my garden, dogs and friends – were regarded by Mark as being too insignificant to concern himself with.

I turned my back on the carefree flying figure. Some of the slabs of sandstone which formed the rockery had been in place already, presumably found on Knight's Manor land at some time by Jacob or a previous owner. I was trying to create pockets of colour around these stones, scooping out the earth and planting in sheltered spots. It was hard, dirty work, because sometimes the stones did not sit just right on the soil and I had to heave them slightly to one side or the other. Sometimes an area just begged for an additional outcrop and I had to wander off around the perimeter of the land, seeing if I could find any more sandstone lying on the surface. My hands were filthy, as were my jeans and T-shirt and, watching Mark's sheer enjoyment as he drove effortlessly along with a cool breeze ruffling his hair, I felt more than a stab of annoyance.

I pushed my hair back from my face and got slowly to my feet, bending backwards to ease the stiffness in my neck and shoulders. I shut my eyes against the sun and turned so that I was facing directly into the gentle southerly breeze. I simply had to have a break so, choosing sloping land with a gentle curve into which I could comfortably fit my body, I lay on my back, closed my eyes and basked in the warm, early Spring sunshine. The dogs, never very far away, hurtled up to me and started to lick me busily, probably imagining I was ill or, I thought crossly, collapsed through overwork. Panting heavily, they slumped on the grass next to me. The sunshine was having its effect on them too: they were tired and hot. Soon they had shifted onto their sides and were breathing slowly and rhythmically, quickly asleep.

An early bee started to buzz lazily around the rhododendron I had just planted and my thoughts drifted towards the edge of consciousness. This, I thought sleepily, used to be called 'flower field' by Jacob and his farming ancestors. I was half dozing, half dreaming on the borderline of sleep.

Suddenly a dark shadow blocked out the sunshine. I was alert in an instant and sat up, embarrassed to be found in such a vulnerable position. I jumped quickly to my feet and, shielding my eyes against the light, tried to see the features of my visitor. The bright Spring sun sat directly behind him, creating a dazzling nimbus within which it was impossible to discern anything clearly. The smell of cut grass, the warm breeze, the Spring sunshine, the height and breadth and shape of my unexpected visitor – surely I had been in this situation before? Surely I had seen all these things, heard all these sounds… the bee buzzing, the wind in the trees… my head started to swim. Perhaps I had stood up too quickly?

'I'm really sorry to disturb you,' said my visitor quietly, 'but I just called by to introduce myself. Dad said you are new to the area and he hasn't had time to call. I'm Ash Cooper. I live down the lane at Fortune Farm, the last building before the Tentersley road. Well, my parents do. I do sometimes, I'm at Uni and come home when I can.'

He was tall – a couple of inches over six feet – slim, with broad shoulders and the most beautiful hands I have ever seen on a man, not too slim, not too broad, with long, straight strong fingers. He had long dark hair and as soon as my eyes adjusted to the light, I saw that his eyes were dark brown and, well, the only words to describe their particular quality are brilliant, or shining, or lustrous. Certainly it was his eyes that I noticed most of all. I judged that he must be in his early twenties.

I desperately tried to gather my composure. I felt foolish on two counts: firstly, that I had been caught almost totally off guard, and secondly, because I looked more of a mess than usual. As I shifted my position so that the sun was not directly behind my visitor I suddenly recognised him.

'We have met, Ash, actually – although we didn't speak. I believe you were at the Harvest celebration in the Church Barn last October? Were you there with your parents?'

He smiled quickly: 'Yes. Mother had just come out of hospital and I was guarding her rather fiercely if I remember! And you are right – we have met, more than once. You, I believe, were the audience for our dress rehearsal of *The Tempest*.'

'I was! But who were you?' As soon as I had asked the question I knew the answer. 'You were Prospero, weren't you?'

Ash nodded, smiling.

'Well, I'm really pleased to meet you properly,' I replied, extending a grubby hand whilst trying to tidy my hair with the other. 'My name is Kate Summers. That distant figure, passing and repassing on the horizon, is Mark, my husband.'

Ash smiled again without comment and seemed at once to relax. Perhaps he was expecting a more formal, less honest greeting? I desperately tried to think of a suitable topic for conversation, as I still felt distinctly disoriented.

'Ash. Is that short for Ashley? It's not a name I have come across before…' I babbled.

My companion nodded. 'Yes it is.' He hesitated. 'Actually there is a story behind my name. Do you happen to know Bill Deepdene? He is a historian as well as a farmer and he and Dad meet occasionally for a pint at "The Swan."'

'Yes I do.'

'Well, apparently, when Mum was expecting me, Dad got into a conversation about local names with Bill, who was doing some research on the Anglo-Saxon origins of Ashward. Bill said that he had discovered that originally Ashward was called *Æscwyrd* – meaning fortunate, or fateful, settlement in the ash forest. Since we effectively live in a clearing in the ash forest, he suggested that Ashley would be a suitable name for father's first and, as it has transpired, his only son. Apparently the "ley" bit of my name means clearing… sorry, how boring I sound.'

I gave Ash a warm smile, realising that he, too, was feeling self-conscious and was doing his best to make conversation. Compared with my husband's hard arrogance, his uncertainty was immensely touching. I pulled myself together.

'Would you like something to drink?' I asked.

Flicking back his dark hair in a mannerism that I later came to know so well, he smiled.

'That would be good. Thank you.'

We both looked south towards the end of our land and saw the little red tractor heading back towards us.

Mark jumped off and cut the engine. He walked towards our visitor, grinning.

'Hi, I'm Mark Summers; this is my wife, Kate.' Did he, I wondered, imagine that I had just stood, dumbly, as our neighbour arrived? Ash, bless him, picked up the covert insult.

'Yes, Kate has done the introductions already. I'm Ash Cooper. Pleased to meet you.'

Mark and Ash sat under a lime-green conifer that provided welcome shade on that warm Spring morning. I trailed indoors, my dogs at my heels, to make coffee, which took, as always, an interminably long time to filter. Whilst waiting, I snatched the opportunity to wash my face hastily at the kitchen sink. Eyes half-shut, I felt my way to the Aga, for a warm towel to dry my face, but was unexpectedly met halfway by the towel itself, being held out by someone's hands. Dashing the water from my eyes as quickly as possible and drying my face hastily, I smiled into the face of the person who had been so thoughtful – Mark, I thought, wasn't so bad when he relaxed and stopped being 'the dynamic businessman'. But it wasn't Mark. I smiled straight into Ash's eyes.

'Mark asked me to see whether there are any chocolate biscuits,' he said apologetically, clearly embarrassed. As I placed coffee and biscuits on a tray, we chatted inconsequentially. He told me about his Uni course: Music and Drama. He loved the ability to combine speech, gesture and movement to express his feelings. He was in his final year at Manchester, and had relished every minute of the past two and a half years.

'The only problem was when Mum was so ill,' he said quietly.

'I can imagine,' I responded mechanically, juggling coffee, milk and biscuits.

'Yes. She had a brain tumour. Dad was finding it difficult to cope and I had to come home really frequently,' he murmured.

I thought of my nominal visits home when at Uni. Twice per year, if that.

'How often did you manage to come home then, Ash?'

'Oh, as often as I could. About every three or four weeks.'

'From Manchester?'

'Well, yes. They both needed the support, but she is much better now, thank goodness. Anyway, enough of me! Tell me about yourselves.'

I tried, I really did. But all I could seem to talk about was Mark. Mark's life, his successes, his status, the firm he worked for. Ash listened patiently, but when I said, 'Coffee's ready now. Let's take it outside shall we?' he rested his hand on the door handle for a few seconds before opening it for me, and replied:

'With one proviso. That one day you actually tell me about *you*. What you are interested in; what you think of Ashward; *your* friends; what you do here, buried in this beautiful isolated village.'

I hadn't blushed for years but, unexpectedly, I did so now. I was so used to being brainwashed by Mark into thinking that prestige, position and wealth were the only things that really counted. It suddenly struck me what a shorthand for life this attitude actually was. There were many commercial lawyers, many successful businessmen – but only one Kate Summers. When I felt able to turn and face my visitor again, I did so with a smile.

'I will do that. Thank you. But we had better go out now to Mark with the coffee. So another day, perhaps.'

Mark was lying in the sunshine, basking with his T-shirt off, eyes closed, oblivious to everything, it seemed to me, but the thoughts in his own mind.

'Ah, what excellent service!' he declared predictably, as he heard us approaching.

I watched the two men as we all sat talking – mainly, I was embarrassed to observe, about Mark's work and Mark's squash. Of the two men, Ash seemed the more mature, without question. He listened carefully, responding spontaneously to what either Mark, or infrequently I myself, had to say. He seemed self-contained and yet ready to relate to others freely and without constraint. Compared to Ash, Mark appeared loud, self-centred and opinionated.

We had been talking – well, Mark had been doing most of the talking and Ash and I had listened – for a long time. It was still only March and I became aware that the afternoon had turned chilly. The wind had crept around from the south to the east and was blowing directly from the direction of Barrow Farm, from the chill hollow where the dark burial mound lay. I shivered – not only at the cold – and stood up.

'Well, sorry to be a killjoy, but I must be getting on with our evening meal,' I said, looking at my watch.

Ash leapt up.

'Sorry,' he echoed, 'I have wasted your afternoon.'

Anything but, I thought to myself! I had been touched and intrigued by the combination of perception and empathy in Ash's character. But what I actually said was, to say the least, somewhat banal.

'Not at all! It has been lovely to meet you. You must call in any time you are passing.'

I was somewhat preoccupied as I started to prepare our supper. Mark resumed his grass cutting. As my hands followed routine tasks, my brain was in overdrive. Meeting Ash Cooper had really shaken me. It was years since I had met a man to whom I had been attracted; and yet here, in this remote place, I had very suddenly encountered one. Not only did Ash Cooper look like a figure from a mediaeval ballad, but he was nice, really nice – the sort of man my parents would have approved of. My mother had never come to terms with my marriage to Mark. He was too eccentric, too loud and moved in a world light years away from her own experience.

I was quiet as we ate, my mind replaying parts of our earlier conversation which hinted at the character of the man I had just met. Eventually my silence penetrated even Mark's egotism.

'Planning complex dog walks are we? Or how to hang wallpaper straight? Or some other equally intellectual exercise…'

His constant needling really got to me. I suppose it was a bitter contrast to the gentle understanding of Ash. So I retaliated, rather pathetically.

'I hope you haven't got anything planned for us both this evening,' I said. 'I thought I would start something I have wanted to do for years: a verse translation of *The Wanderer.*'

'What?' exclaimed Mark. 'What are you talking about?'

'Well, the subject should make about as much sense to you as your endless talk of arcane points of law makes to me,' I retorted sharply. 'You may have forgotten, but Old English was part of my English degree. *The Wanderer* is one of very few non-religious poems that have survived from the period. Many translations have been done, but not a decent one in verse. It is a challenge I have been promising myself for ages and tonight I am going to make a start.'

My immature outburst brought a not unexpected response.

'Well, do as you like. I have a squash game booked anyway.'

***

The chill easterly wind had brought rain, bitter slanting rain, which drove against the windows of the drawing room. Most of the time I was able to push away the knowledge of that sinister space which lay under my house but, sitting there by myself with a wind that howled down the wide chimneys, it was very difficult to do so. I had turned my chair resolutely towards the inglenook and curled myself up, with a writing pad on my knee and a musty volume from my university days propped against the arm of the chair. Emma was lying by my feet, oblivious to the danger of falling logs. I smiled as I stroked her fur, still faintly singed from her previous encounter.

The ancient resonance of the Anglo-Saxon words sounded in my head.

What fate has befallen the fine leader?
Seats stand empty at the solemn feast;
Fine festivities have flown far away.
How those times of rejoicing have retreated
Becoming dark under night's curtain
As if they had never been!

The logs in the fireplace shifted and settled, sending up a shower of sparks. My mind wandered. I saw pictures in the flames: blackened wood, shooting fire, the howling wind – or was it cries of utter despair? I pressed my hands against my eyes and, unbidden, the image of our visitor earlier that day came strong and bright into my thoughts. It was as if my mind was split and one part looked scathingly at the other: the way in which my emotions were reacting was being ruthlessly analysed by my rational mind. I got up and went restlessly to the curtains, to draw them a little more snugly across the draughty windows. Grasping hold of the material before drawing it tightly across the black rectangles, I gazed out sightlessly, despising my inept reaction to our earlier visitor, and the stupid, empty gesture I had tried to make in retaliation to my husband's belittling comments. My attempt to translate one of the most difficult of Old English texts had not been an outstanding success: *'How those times of rejoicing have retreated… As if they had never been!'*

What, I thought blackly, was the purpose of life? Would I gradually turn into a Daphne Woods – beaten into quiet submission by her husband's powerful dominating personality? Or a Rebecca Woodville, haughty and conscious of her position, bought by the wealth of her husband? I returned to the fireside, all fascination with the past gone because of the wild turmoil of the present.

Laying aside my faltering translation of the ancient Anglo-Saxon poem, I started to write on a clean white sheet of paper. I wrote clearly and carefully, not in my usual untidy scrawl, pressing strongly into the white paper. I somehow wanted to capture the beauty of character which I had glimpsed in Ash earlier that day. I wanted to write of the poignancy I felt, because I could only watch from a distance all his direct, unspoilt approach to life, all his sensitivity and, I had to admit it, all his dark beauty. All the images of Spring that had been bursting into my mind during the morning, as I had fought to create the rockery and wandered over my land to search out appropriate stones, now flowed from my pen as I wrote the first poem I had written for years.

La Domaine Perdue

You live in my lost domaine.
You quietly turn the key
In the morning, to let me in
To the heart-stopping beauty of birdsong;
And in the dark of night, you create again
The silver patterns of stars.

You quietly lead me

Down morning-wet pathways
Of crushed grass
Where flowers smell sweetest.

You just being there
Opens the mind-cells
Of memory and desire...
Your hands enclose a pre-fall Eden
Where dreams still live
And golden promise flowers with the rose.
Your eyes are wells
Where my soul reaches
For rest and comfort.

I took the title from a book I had studied for my French 'A' level. When I had read it all those years earlier, my imagination had felt deeply the poignancy of innocent, deep love and the tragedy of not being able to sustain it in the face of the demands and disappointments of everyday life. I stared at the words I had written, forming together new patterns of meaning and felt now, in my own life, my own experience, the deep disappointment of hoped-for love which comes to nothing. My tears fell and the blue ink smudged and ran, words merging together.

Chapter 24

Mark smirked over his morning coffee.

'How's the poet laureate this morning then?'

He had returned the previous night long after I had gone to bed, restless and dissatisfied with just about everything: my lack of skill in translating Anglo-Saxon poetry; my own verse; but above all my reaction to meeting Ash the previous day. Much to my surprise, I had slept soundly for a good seven hours.

'Bored with your stupid sense of humour!' I responded with, for me, unusual asperity.

My husband just smiled and ate his toast. As was his habit though, he just could not let a point go and, half turning on his way to the car, announced that he was intending to translate the *Financial Times* into blank verse on his journey to London.

I was certainly in no mood for Mark's sarcasm this morning and slammed the kitchen door shut with such force that the dogs retreated, afraid that they had done something wrong. As usual their naivety touched me deeply.

'Oh, come here you sillies – you're lovely!' I exclaimed, dropping to my knees to cuddle them. 'Come on! Let's go for an extra-long walk this morning.'

I threw on an ancient dog-walking coat and headed off down our land – for once, directly away from Ashward Priory and Barrow Farm, into the dense woodland which hid the bottom of the valley.

The dogs, as usual, engaged in their uniquely doggy play. They picked up sticks and galloped along together, each holding an end and trying to tug it out of the grip of the other. They jumped into the stream that meandered along the valley and followed scents that they picked up in the undergrowth.

Usually they returned pretty quickly to my call, but a particularly strong and interesting scent seemed to be fascinating them on that chilly grey morning. They took several minutes to return, rather than just seconds. I walked on, head down, deep in thought and, in retrospect, certainly wasn't as careful of my dogs' whereabouts as I usually was. I suddenly realised that their loud, crashing games had ceased and that I could neither see, nor hear them. Rain had started to spatter on the leaves.

'Rupert! Emma!' my call echoed loudly in the steep-sided, wooded valley, but neither appeared. I repeated my call – it must have been for at least ten minutes – and finally saw Rupert bounding through the undergrowth towards me. Of Emma there was no sign. I slipped on Rupert's lead and retraced our steps towards Knight's Manor land, calling continually. I must have walked to and fro in the woodland for at least an hour, calling Emma's name at regular intervals, but there was no response.

The rain had started to lash down by now and the wind had got up so that the trees were swishing and bending around us, scattering even more raindrops over us. We were both soaked and Rupert trailed along, tail and head down, a picture of total dejection.

By this time, I was beside myself. What if Emma was lost – really lost – or hurt? It didn't bear consideration, and I could hardly crawl through the undergrowth looking for her. Finally, I reluctantly gave up and ran back as fast as I could to the house.

Even before drying myself off, I telephoned the local police to explain that my dog had been lost in the woods. The ponderous and pedantic police constable took minute details and predictably reassured me that 'everything possible would be done' to find my missing pet. That was it. I hung up the receiver and finally, shivering, went upstairs to towel myself off and change.

Rupert lay quietly against the Aga, raising his head occasionally and looking around in a confused way for his companion. I sat by him, stroking him absent-mindedly and wondering just what else I could do. I knew the woods were extensive and stretched for miles towards Tentersley and the main London road. If Emma followed a strong trail, her mind, I knew, would be on this and not on potential danger. I ran my fingers through my hair again and again, thinking about her utter faithfulness and her idiosyncrasies, her singed fur and her smiling face.

By three-thirty in the afternoon I felt that I would go mad if I couldn't speak to someone and so I telephoned Mark. I thought of the quiet Sunday morning three years previously when we had responded to an advert for yellow Labrador puppies in the local paper. We arrived at a sprawling Kent farm a couple of hours later and were entranced by the fat, wagging puppies and their calm quiet mother. With Emma, it was love at first sight: she was the smallest and least bold, but won my heart immediately. Mark would, I was certain, be as deeply concerned as I was.

I got through to his secretary, Claire, without any difficulty and asked to speak to my husband.

'Is it urgent, Mrs Summers?' asked Claire.

'Well, yes, it is.'

I held on for a couple of minutes and eventually heard Mark's voice, impatient and abrupt.

'Yes?'

'Mark, Emma is lost!' I was poised to embark on an account of the unfortunate walk that morning, when he cut across me without preamble.

'And you rang me to tell me *this!* I am in the middle of a most complex discussion concerning a US tax case and you bother me with a lost dog!'

'But it's not just any dog Mark, it's Emma.'

'Stop wasting my time, Kate.' And he hung up.

***

When he arrived home several hours later, his black mood had not lifted.

'Your thoughtlessness probably lost my firm a huge amount of money,' he said coldly, regarding me without a flicker of warmth or humour. 'What is the stupid dog worth anyway? £300? Small change! And you have lost me tens of thousands of pounds. I am going out – because I can't stand to see your pathetic face tonight.'

A year ago this verbal attack would have devastated me, but now I was almost relieved when the routine of door banging and car revving had been gone through, and peace reigned again.

Although it was only around eight o'clock, it was pitch black and I knew that there was little, if any, hope of finding my lost pet. Nevertheless, I grabbed a torch, slipped on Rupert's lead, threw on my waxed jacket, and ran quickly down the fields towards the woodland, calling Emma's name repeatedly. Thankfully, the rain had stopped and the gusty wind had died down. It was silent, and I was grateful that there was a full moon, which almost made the torchlight redundant.

I did not know the tracks well enough to venture into the woodland at night and so I stopped at the gate to the woods and just shouted my dog's name as loudly as I could, completely focussed on listening for any sound at all from the direction in which I had headed that morning.

This is hopeless, I told myself, near to tears by now. Emma must be miles away, or injured. I pushed back my hair, which the wind was whipping across my face, when I heard a quiet voice.

'Kate?'

What on earth? Was I hearing things? I whipped round.

'Ash! What are you doing here?'

He smiled. 'I was just about to ask you the same thing. I just needed to get out of the house. It's really difficult sometimes seeing Mum struggling to be as she used to be… struggling to be herself. I just needed to clear my head. But enough about me. What's wrong?'

I told him; and he listened with quiet attention.

'I see. Kate, I know these woods well: they were my playground, my Sherwood Forest, when I was a boy. Fortune

Farm land runs right up against their eastern edge. Poachers still set snares in here, unfortunately. Ridiculously, it is still not illegal! Let's go and look for Emma together – right now.'

In the bright moonlight we opened the wooden gate that led into the woods. Ash's talk of snares had really frightened me and I was quiet, as I bit my lip hard to control my emotions. Ash talked quietly, with the intention, I am certain, of stopping my imagination from working overtime. We went much further into the dense woodland than I had gone earlier, moving from larger, to smaller, to hardly discernible tracks. Gradually, as he tried to distract me with his quiet conversation, I started to glimpse further aspects of his character and his past.

'My sister and I built a shelter here, of fallen tree branches. She was Maid Marion to my Robin Hood,' he laughed quietly. 'We lit a fire and boiled water from the stream, putting grass and other plants in it to cook. I remember we were both really ill the next day! Mother was not pleased. She was cross with herself I think, because when we were younger – before she became ill – she came with us to the woods. She was so funny in those days, wearing cut-off jeans and an old T-shirt.'

'We carved our initials in this beech tree. Look!' He stretched up and flicked on the torch about two metres above his head. The distorted initials 'AC', carved twice, in slightly different childish script, were still clearly visible. He looked pensively at the reminder of his childhood.

'Yes, the same initials for both of us: Ash and Anne.'

The woods were utterly silent; the breeze now non-existent. Everything was in monochrome: darker trees and branches, lighter grey leaves, colourless sky. Suddenly we both heard a slight noise. Unmistakably, it was a whimper.

'Oh no, Ash! Is it Emma?'

He swept the torch around in a slow arc. Sure enough, lying quiet and still, her head on one paw, the other caught in a wire that had cut deeply into her leg, lay Emma. Blood stained her soft golden fur and her mouth and whiskers, as she had clearly been worrying at the wire and licking her wound, from which blood still dripped. At our appearance, she looked up and even managed a slow wag before her head sank again to the woodland floor.

'Oh God! Is she all right?'

'I hope so, Kate. I will know more when I have cut off this foul wire.' Ash whipped out a penknife and soon freed Emma's right paw from the snare. He felt it carefully.

'She is in shock and has lost a fair amount of blood.' Ash stirred the beech leaves, which had been stained red. 'But the good points are that the paw is warm and her foreleg is not broken. If she had not been so calm, she could have done herself such damage. Her temperament has probably saved her.'

'We must get her to the vet immediately.'

Ash smiled grimly. 'Easier said than done. She isn't light! And she may well struggle if we try to carry her in our arms.' He thought for a few moments.

'Take off your jacket, Kate. We will zip it up, put two branches through it and use it as a stretcher.'

In an absolute daze, I did exactly as Ash had said. Soon we were carrying Emma back to the woodland gate and then up the fields to Knight's Manor. Rupert's tail was firmly between his legs as he trailed along, occasionally sniffing his motionless companion.

Knight's Manor was in total darkness. It was ten-thirty and I would have thought Mark would have finished whatever he was doing by now. With difficulty we loaded my injured pet, who was now, worryingly, unconscious, into the back seat of my Mini. Ash had got in first and carefully received Emma's inert body, which he held carefully as I drove as fast as I could into Tentersley.

***

It was past one o'clock in the morning when we got home. My thunderous knocking on the door of the flat above the vet's surgery had brought Mark's squash partner and our vet, Robbie, to the window – and then, quickly, to the door. He had confirmed exactly what Ash had said, but was concerned that Emma had been traumatised for so long.

'I will keep her overnight for observations. But she is young and strong and I am pretty certain that all will be well. You two look as if you could do with some medical treatment, though!' Robbie exclaimed, 'Or at least a good shower and some food. Get off home now. She is fine with me.'

'Ash, I can't thank you enough,' I murmured as we drove into the courtyard at the back of Knight's Manor. He had resolutely refused my offer to drive him home.

'It's just a short walk and a car arriving at this time of night would disturb my parents. Mum really isn't too good yet.' He rubbed his hand across his eyes in a weary gesture.

'Oh, Ash! That was the reason you found us this evening. And yet it has been all about me and my dogs! I am so sorry.'

He smiled. 'Well, it's just as well I *did* find you! Emma had been in that snare for over eight hours. I don't know how she would have been if we had postponed our search until the morning. Her blood loss was slow – but steady. But I must go. Goodnight, Kate.'

'Goodnight, Ash.' And his dark figure melted into the night as he stepped silently over the cattle grid.

To my surprise, there was still no light on in the house. Clearly Mark had not returned. I let Rupert out. He was thoroughly downcast and trotted slowly over the courtyard for his final pee of the day, clearly exhausted. Him and me both! The bath could wait until morning.

***

Mark rolled up breezily at six o'clock the following morning.

'Hi, Cheeks,' he said loudly, as he crashed into the bedroom. 'Having a lie-in?'

I half opened my eyes as he strode about the room, slinging off dirty clothes and dumping them unceremoniously on the floor, then whistling as he went into the bathroom to shower. I didn't speak. I couldn't. Through his selfish ill-temper I had nearly lost my dog. He hadn't even noticed Emma's absence!

Chapter 25

As that Spring progressed I realised that I was happy – really happy – happier than I could ever remember. I watched with joy as Emma regained strength and confidence, even though she hated the comical plastic collar that she had to wear until her damaged leg had healed. The day after she had returned from the vet, Ash dropped by, waving a bunch of bone-shaped biscuits that he had tied, bouquet-like, with a red ribbon. He knelt by her basket, stroking her softly and repeatedly, and smiling with satisfaction as she wagged her thanks. He was returning to Manchester the following day and wanted to assure himself that 'the patient was improving.'

I compared my present happiness to my state of mind in the fraught early days of my marriage when I was trying to understand and interact with a man who struck me dumb with adoration. Then it had been like trying to understand a chameleon, a restless, ever-changing creature with a fluid identity. My thoughts moved on to the deep happiness of my fleeting pregnancy, all too swiftly followed by the miscarriage which, in retrospect, had been the beginning of the disaffection and disassociation between Mark and myself. So sad, so incredibly sad…

At first I attributed my happiness to the circumstances of my life in Ashward. For goodness sake, I told myself, I was the joint owner of one of the most beautiful houses I had ever seen. I had friends, real friends, not just acquaintances, who loved spending time with me. I had a remarkably good social life, bearing in mind the intensely rural nature of the environment in which we lived. I had my lovely dogs, and so on.

But gradually I came to realise that the source of this surprising happiness was Ash. It was as if a missing part of the puzzle that was my life had been found, swiftly and completely. He was involved in his final exams during the early part of the summer, but still found the time to come home and check that his parents were all right, especially his mother. And within those precious weekends he always called in to Knight's Manor to see us. The three of us sometimes sat in the kitchen talking. I remember one day, Mark had a new camera, inevitably the latest model, and was playing about with it, photographing me, the dogs and Ash. The picture of Ash is the only one I still have from those days. He is sitting, cross-legged on the kitchen work surface, explaining something. He is frowning slightly, flicking back his hair, emphasising a point with an expressive hand gesture. As I look again at the fading image I feel my heartbeat quicken, my breath deepen: he was so beautiful, so young, so unspoilt.

I remember my sense of irritation and irrational loss when Mark and I had been out shopping in Canterbury and came back to find a neat square of paper posted through the kitchen door: *'Sorry I missed you. A.'*

One April Saturday I woke late – for me. The sky was heavy with thick grey clouds and rain was falling steadily. From the sheer lack of daylight I thought it much earlier than

241

the eight o'clock it actually was. Mark groaned and turned over.

'Fancy getting the breadwinner some coffee then?' he mumbled. I thought it was a measure of our relationship that I just let the sarcasm wash over me without comment.

I wrapped my fleecy dressing gown around me, slipped on a pair of warm socks, and went sleepily down to the ever-warm kitchen. Yawning, I let the dogs out. Even they hesitated in the steady downpour before trotting sedately, Rupert keeping pace with Emma, around the corner of the house and into the field.

I put the kettle on the Aga and leant against it, revelling in its warmth. My half-awake thoughts flickered over the kitchen with its shadowy corners and its heavy old beams. I thought of the generations of people who had been born here and lived and died here. How many had realised the influence of the hidden subterranean room? I walked across to the window and watched the drip of rain into the pond opposite – each drop causing widening circles on the surface of the water that intersected with others until the whole surface was dynamic, almost hypnotic in its movement. So many facets of life here were almost archetypal, elemental. How many women had watched the rain breaking the surface of this pond, from this window? I thought of May Wheatley, almost certainly holding her beloved child in her arms as she watched – for three short years only – the awakening buds in Spring, the summer sunshine, the glorious golds and reds of autumn and the bitter swirling snow as winter took the world in its grip.

I was brought sharply back to the present as the cattle grid at the back of the courtyard clanged its early warning. Who on earth could it be at that time of day – and on a day like this?

Fully awake now, I stepped quickly across the room to the window which looked out over the courtyard. When I saw Ash's car I almost panicked. It seemed always to be the case that he saw me looking my worst – filthy from gardening or bedraggled from searching for my dog. I hadn't even washed my face, for goodness sake! Could I pretend I wasn't in? But no, there was no escape, the dogs had arrived back and were mobbing him as he got quickly out of the car and strode towards the back door. He bent and caressed Emma's silky head with both his hands.

One of the most intensely unusual things about Ash is that he consistently seems to see the essence of you. And so, as he smiled into my eyes, I knew he wasn't registering the messy hair, the dressing gown or the lack of make-up, but he was seeing my surprise and embarrassment – and my evident pleasure at seeing him.

'Coffee?' I asked, desperately trying to regain some sort of composure.

'That would be lovely. Thank you. I need something to warm me up! I am sorry to descend upon you so early, but this revision is driving me mad! I have just got to get some fresh air, and you were the only person I thought crazy enough to want to go on a walk with me on this foul day!'

Despite myself I laughed. 'Thanks for the vote of confidence! I'd love to! Just let me deliver Mark's coffee and put some suitable stuff on and I will be right with you.'

My husband did not flicker an eyelid as I went back to our bedroom, dragged out some old jeans and jumpers and shrugged them on quickly.

Despite the waterproofs that Ash and I had put on, we were soon feeling distinctly damp. It was typical late Spring weather and the wind had started to gust strongly as we walked down the road after a very swift coffee. Soon we reached the track that led across the fields, past the old iron-smelting furnace, intending to call in to see Estelle and then eventually to loop back to the pond opposite Knight's Manor. I soon gave up trying to hold my hood in place. Instead I let the rain blow my hair back and the wind stream into my face.

'What a sight I must look!' I exclaimed and then, inevitably, tried to apologise. 'Sorry!'

'What are you saying sorry for?' Ash asked incredulously. He stopped, put his hands lightly on my shoulders, and turned me to face him. He smiled gently as he stroked the long, wet tendrils of hair from my eyes. 'You look… beautiful.' And he stooped and gave me the lightest of kisses on the lips – like the touch of a butterfly's wing, soft and fleeting. I thought he was joking and looked in his eyes for the flicker of sarcasm that I knew would have been in Mark's. Instead I saw a deep gentle stillness.

'Race you to Estelle's!' I challenged. As I ran away along the slippery wet track as fast as I could, I realised that I had never felt the excitement – the 'butterflies' as my mother would have expressed it – and above all the rightness, the completeness, that I felt with this man. The years of containment, professional determination, proving myself in a difficult financial work environment, fell away. I could have been any woman, with any man, at any time, in the relatively recent history of the world, feeling more alive and real through the presence of her companion than she had ever felt in her life before.

Estelle was mildly surprised to see us. 'Hello darling!' she cried. 'Dump Rupert in the garage. Come in and have a drink!'

We crammed into her minute kitchen. 'And who,' she twinkled as she looked at Ash, 'is this?'

'Someone trying to avoid concussion on the beams of your delightfully warm kitchen!' he smiled.

I remembered a conversation that I had had with Estelle some months previously when she had recently returned from staying with a widower friend in London, her junior by many years. 'If only I was twenty years younger, Kate, I would still be there…'

I had laughed at her frivolity then, but looking now at her sparkling, utterly charming, interactions with Ash, I could well believe what she had said.

'Let's open a bottle of wine!' she declared. 'Just the day for it…'

I saw Ash glance at his watch. It was, after all, only ten-thirty – coffee, rather than wine, time. But he soon moved into the easy way he has with people, of making them feel comfortable and at ease rather than awkward. The contrast with the last visit I had paid to Estelle and Geoff's fairy-tale cottage was vivid. Then the edgy banter between Mark and Estelle had been excruciating; now the conversation was gentle and warm, the interactions stress free.

'Great idea. We will float back to Knight's Manor after that!' he exclaimed.

The day grew darker if anything. The timber frame of the small cottage shook in the powerful gusts of wind that blew up from the coast.

Ash relaxed and was clearly enjoying the intelligent, flirtatious behaviour of Estelle. For a woman of her age, she was formidable!

'Tell me about yourself,' she invited.

'Just someone living off the state and waiting to be a wage slave,' he teased.

'Well *that* I don't believe!' Estelle retorted. 'Kate has *far* too much taste to waste her time with someone who fulfils that description.'

Estelle turned to me. So did Ash. And I saw the direct challenge in the eyes of one; and the intense tenderness in the gaze of the other. Swiftly Estelle glanced towards Ash, catching his expression.

'Kate, do you remember that painting I wanted your opinion on?' Estelle asked.

'No I don't, Estelle.'

'Oh you silly girl, of course you do. Its upstairs. Please spare me a minute of your time my dear.'

Puzzled, and yet suspecting an Estelle plot, I went upstairs with her.

'My darling – he is gorgeous! Where did you find him?'

'I knew you were up to something, Estelle,' I sighed. 'We sort of found each other.' And I described the initial encounters between us, Emma's rescue, the walks and the conversations that had followed.

She listened carefully and seriously – one of the few times I ever saw her in this mood. When I had finished she laid her hand gently on my arm.

'You know, my dear, you need someone who will love you to distraction. Who will cherish you and place you at the centre of his world. You need an intelligent, adoring companion and lover who will give you children, not expect you to take dogs out in all weathers and work like a slave to run a big prestigious house! You deserve so much better than this, Kate.'

I was surprised to find that, once again, tears came to my eyes. I did so miss being cherished. Estelle was right.

I nodded without a word and gave her a hug.

Time slipped by as Ash and I laughed and talked with Estelle about her life in this flowery paradise she had created.

'I would go quite mad if I didn't have my art to stimulate me!' she sighed. 'Oh, and by the way, how does Mark like his latest acquisition, Kate?'

I mumbled something along the lines of, 'Oh, he loves it…'

Estelle shook her head slightly, almost imperceptibly, and turned to Ash.

'You wouldn't believe it, but Geoff is out at a stamp auction in London today. I could suggest a million better things to do in London than to buy stamps!'

Eventually, Ash looked at his watch and sighed. 'We must go, Estelle. It has been really lovely. I just hope I can write an essay that makes sense after that wonderful wine!'

'Oh, nonsense my dear. It is the stuff of inspiration! Equal only to love of course. That is the ultimate inspiration.'

He laughed, put his hands on her shoulders and said, 'You are a wicked woman!'

We put on our waterproofs, which had dried somewhat, and reluctantly went out again into the incessant downpour. Predictably, the wine had made us warmer, and so we walked at a reasonably slow pace. I did not want my morning with Ash to end, to return only too soon to some sort of scheme that Mark wanted to drive forward in his limited leisure time, which would invariably involve me in becoming exhausted and filthy.

'You have never fulfilled your promise you know,' said Ash teasingly. 'I know your name, where you live, a little about your friends and a lot about your dogs! But nothing really about *you,* your childhood, your life influences, your likes…'

I threw him an embarrassed smile.

'It's not very interesting. My life is not very interesting.'

'I find you fascinating, Kate. Please help me to understand you better.'

And so I told him, as well as I could, about the frustrations and limitations of my childhood. My difficult relationship with my mother, the feelings of always falling short of expectations that had been laid down in my character in those early years and which still haunted me. I relived my joy at going to Oxford, the years I spent reading, translating and researching Anglo-Saxon texts, and my love of poetry in particular. I revisited my time in London and the fairly lucrative, but intellectually barren, career in financial administration. I captured again the excitement of meeting Mark and the way in which this seemed to fulfil my childhood dreams of position and prestige. I mentioned as briefly and unemotionally as I could the miscarriage I had had, and tried to paint a picture of the empty years that followed in London.

'The rest you know, more or less. We came here to Ashward last September. I met Helen soon after I had arrived...'

'And me just five weeks ago. Well properly I mean,' he mused, looking at me intently. 'Kate, you say you are not interesting, but strange though it may seem, I do not know anyone else under sixty who can read or translate Anglo-Saxon poetry! I don't, come to think of it, know anyone else who has been to Oxford, especially not from a family without connections or significant wealth. Neither do I know anyone who apologises quite so much, or quite so frequently.' And with that, he put his arm lightly across my shoulders and gave me the gentlest of hugs, dropping his arm almost immediately.

'I am really sorry about the baby too,' he said quietly. 'My sister Anne had a miscarriage a couple of years ago and it is a terrible, empty, exhausting experience. My brother-in-law has had to be consistently patient, loving and understanding. And it affects her still, even after this length of time.'

I didn't reply. I thought through Mark's response to the miscarriage... flippant, embarrassed, blaming me...

After this, Ash and I walked back almost without speaking to Knight's Manor. As always he was sensitive to my mood.

'Thank you for your company today,' he said quietly as we jumped across the cattle grid. He glanced at Mark's white Lancia parked next to his own car. 'I won't come in. But I *will*...' he emphasised, holding me lightly by the shoulders, '...be thinking of you.'

And with the lightest of pressures from his long, strong fingers, he was gone.

Chapter 26

Mark was restless and was determined to involve everyone in his mood. Since his sphere of influence was limited to the dogs and myself, the result was that they were bringing him every toy imaginable. They also kept pawing at each other and the kitchen door, and I was becoming increasingly irritated at his evident boredom.

The rain poured down. Since that early burst of warm Spring weather it had been unremittingly wet and, as a result, my daily routine seemed to centre around cleaning the kitchen floor! I thought again of Estelle's words to me…

'I love this house, but the country is a godforsaken place when it is as wet as this,' Mark grumbled, kicking at the red rubber bone Rupert had just brought to him.

'We need to *do* something.' He looked bleakly out of the window at the rain-heavy trees, the muddy patches in front of the flowerbeds where I had been working, the low cloud, the lack of view.

The minutes ticked by as his gaze took in the waterlogged grass, the black sodden stone wall, the pond… 'I know. We'll have a party!' he declared.

'Why?' I asked, taken aback. Our birthdays were in the autumn and I could not think of an occasion that justified a party.

'Because everyone else in this bloody dump is probably as bored out of their brains as I am – apart from you and your airy-fairy ideas and precious friends! You all drive me mad. Get out into the real world where you have to fight for money and position. You wouldn't last five minutes.'

I knew Mark in this mood. Until he had experienced some intense activity, he would be impossible. I knew what was coming: it would be either a very fast run in his car or a violent game of squash.

I walked quietly away.

'I'm going out!' he yelled, striding to the cloakroom for his coat and car keys. A few minutes later I heard him start the car. He hurtled out of the courtyard and I could hear the whine of the engine as he accelerated, far too fast, down the lane towards the main road to Tentersley.

Once again, I was relieved that he had gone. Almost automatically I walked out of the kitchen and looked around the shadowy spaces of my house. All was quiet, almost as if the very fabric of the house was listening, waiting. The cold swirled around me as I stepped out of the comforting warmth of my kitchen and I smiled wryly as I looked at the walled-up cellar door. I used to be so terrified of what lay behind it – of the dark history that I felt pressing upon me. Probably for the first time, I consciously realised that I had moved on and that, now, there was more balance in my life. Had the pragmatic approach of Helen been right? Was it that loneliness and lack of things to occupy my mind had made me obsess about the cellar and the intense feelings of evil and darkness that used to wash over me? Or was I actually becoming spiritually stronger, able to repel these forces of evil? In my mind's eye I saw Paul Lucas's wise smile, and realised that increased spiritual strength was certainly not the reason for the shift in attitude and atmosphere here in this enigmatic and compelling house. I leant my forehead against the cold glass of the window at the turn of the stairs, trying to puzzle out this very distinct change in me. Quite unbidden I thought of Ash and I realised that it was his steady presence at the centre of my life that had started to keep the darkness at bay for me.

It was at that moment that I think I fully understood that what we call life is merely the surface of things. Under the visible, sense-perceived world, lies a nexus of unseen forces – not limited by time or place but, existing out of both, infinitely more potent. Sometimes, in birdsong, or starlight, or in the face of someone we love, we glimpse this eternal beauty. Equally, we can be caught unawares by darkness or by despair, and even a glimpse of evil, real evil, makes our senses reel. Both light and darkness existed vividly in this rambling old house that we had bought. Maybe it was because of fairly recent tragedy – I thought of the Wheatleys. Or maybe it stemmed from unimaginable events across aeons of time that had somehow defined the place. Never had I been more aware of the subtle battle being constantly waged under the surface of our life here. I thought of Paul Lucas and his tight-lipped silence on certain subjects. I thought of Helen, tolerating the life she secretly despised.

***

Mark returned about an hour later, his jovial mood fully restored.

'We'll have a May Day party! This weather has got to improve some time and the house is big enough to stay indoors if it's pissing it down outside. May Day Eve is a Saturday, so everyone can come.'

***

But the weather was perfect. Almost like moving through the door of summer, the morning of the 30 April – May Day Eve – dawned clear and fragrant and beautiful. The dawn chorus seemed to lift me physically through the sheer beauty of the blackbird's melody, the thrush's persistence, the robin's ubiquitous call. I lay for a few precious moments drinking in the brightness and the joy of the day and drew my knees to my chest, hugging to myself my wonderful secret – that a short distance away, barely two miles, lay someone who had suddenly and unimaginably become the centre of my world. I was gently drifting back into sleep when my husband leapt out of bed.

'Come on, Cheeks!' he exclaimed loudly. 'Loads to do!'

I took a deep breath. He had not used his pet name for me for months. Maybe Mark's ambitious party was going to be a success after all!

We had invited Helen and James, Lizzie and Steve Jenner, two couples from church with their exquisite teenage girls – and Ash. I had come across Steve and Lizzie occasionally but, to be honest, stood a little in awe of them. They lived in one of the converted outbuildings at the Priory and worked within the community, helping vulnerable families. Steve was staggeringly good-looking but, I thought, rather arrogant. He and Mark, not surprisingly, got on really well together. Lizzie was quiet, mousy and heavily pregnant with their second child.

Paul and Gisela had declined. Paul had shaken his head slightly when I had walked over to deliver an invitation in person.

'Kate, you do know the origins of May Day celebrations?'

'Only vaguely, Paul. It's something about being outside and welcoming the dawn isn't it?'

He smiled wryly. 'That, my dear child, is the tip of a very potent iceberg.' He took down a battered green volume from a high shelf in his study, thumbed through the discoloured pages and gestured for me to sit down. 'Let me read you something.'

"Many of our modern day celebrations have their root in the pagan past and May Day is no exception. Beltane was the pagan festival that marked the beginning of summer, when earth energies are at their strongest. The name comes from the Celtic god 'Bel' (the Bright One) and the Gaelic word for fire – (teine). May Day, or Beltane, celebrates fertility – of the earth and of men and women. The symbolic union of the Goddess of Spring, Flora, and the epitome of male fertility, the Green Man, lies at the heart of the celebration. The union of these two symbolic figures is always consummated and Flora will become pregnant. Couples leap together over the Beltane fire, which is lit when all other fires are extinguished in the village and this marks their spiritual union – their 'handfasting.' Couples then spend the night in the woods and fields..."

'And I will leave the rest to your imagination,' he grinned, closing the book.

'So you see, my dear innocent girl, as is so often the case, what appears to be simple "good fun" has its roots deep in the past and carries a significance that we can never fully appreciate. If I came to your party, I think my parishioners would revel in having yet more ammunition against their parish priest!'

'Paul, why do you know so much about the pagan past?' I asked him directly a question that had been growing in my mind over the past months. He seemed at once both knowledgeable and respectful of traditions and practices that should not, I thought, naturally form part of the knowledge of a parish priest.

He looked at me without smiling.

'Because, quite simply, I have had to learn. I have shared my dark discovering with you, my dear. I could not just encounter and pass on. I had to research, because of my academic training. You know some of what I have encountered... but, Kate, you are young and the world is all before you, and you want to hold a party! The most natural thing in the world! Now off you go to that quixotic husband of yours.'

'Could I borrow your book please? If you could research the past here, then so can I. It might help me understand more deeply the complexities of this place. I have learnt already that so much from the past influences the present; there is so much darkness and sadness as well as beauty and joy.'

He handed the book to me, enclosing my hands with his.

'Be careful. Stories play themselves out over the millennia...'

As I walked home across the park to Knight's Manor, carefully carrying the battered volume, ideas were jostling together in my mind. There was so much to learn; so much to talk to Paul about; so much to do, if the party was to be a success.

* * *

Yawning, on the edge of sleep, I reviewed my conversation with Paul as Mark whistled tunelessly down the stairs into the kitchen. I heard him clanging about as he filled the kettle with water, put it on the Aga and yelled: 'Rabbits, Emma!' a phrase she always responded to by circling wildly, then digging wherever she happened to be. Since that was the kitchen, I really could not imagine the scene that was taking place downstairs! I was just grateful that she was fully recovered from her accident.

I had scribbled the various stages through which I hoped the day would run on the back of a shopping receipt. It looked like this:

10.30	Helen to come over to help with the party cooking
1.30	Lunch
3.00	Start to collect greenery and decorate the house
6.30	Costumes – get them ready and get them on!
9.30	Guests start to arrive/ party
3.00	Light the May fire – the Beltane fire
4.00	Dawn – dancing outside
6.00	Breakfast

As I showered, I realised that I was excited. Something seemed to be bubbling just beneath the surface of this beautiful day. There seemed to be a layered significance: the seen, the obvious, overlaying the unseen and significant.

Helen was in a teasing mood. I loved her like this. Seldom did she lay aside her seriousness, which she wore like a mask – but when she did, she sparkled! We laughed together, drank coffee, cranked up the ancient range until it was persuaded to produce the cakes, quiches, sausages, chicken and baked potatoes that we needed to feed eleven people.

We eventually sat down shortly after one o'clock, warm and flushed from the heat. Quite suddenly, she put her arm around my shoulders and pulled me to her.

'I love you, you know. Whatever happens, I love you.' And she gave me a warm, maternal kiss in my hair.

As usual, I was taken off guard by this display of direct emotion. I think I hugged her back and said something about being very fond of her too – something quite unsuitable to the intensity and significance of what she had said to me. What I would give for that lost time to be retrieved – for an opportunity to say what I really felt! That she was the most precious friend anyone could wish for. That I loved her like a sister. That I could not imagine life without her at my side, sharing the good and bad times together. The words of a 1970s folk song are vivid in my mind now as I write:

'We can't return, we can only look behind from where we came
And go round and round and round in the Circle Game...'

The complex business of feeding James called Helen home and Mark was singing loudly outside, chopping wood. I wasn't particularly hungry, as cooking always took the edge off my appetite, and so I went outside into the orchard and sat under an apple tree with the dogs. Absent-mindedly I fed them bits of bread and cheese as I felt the sun beating with real warmth on my flushed cheeks.

To be honest, I expected Ash to turn up that afternoon. I knew he was at home and I would so love to have gone with him in search of dark bitter holly, the unfurling glory of beech, wild cherry and precious Spring flowers. His presence seemed to lend such a beauty to the simplest of actions. But the afternoon passed and he did not come. Mark crashed about in the woodland at the end of our land, brandishing secateurs and filling the wheelbarrow with armfuls of greenery.

It was so natural to decorate the house with the leaves and flowers that its land had produced. The huge beams were like living trees themselves and lent their own beauty to the offerings that we brought in to prepare the old house for the festival where fertility and new life were celebrated in all their transient, intense, temporary glory.

At half-past seven I was still twisting tendrils of ivy and early wild clematis into the crevices between the beams and the lath and plaster ceiling. Mark had long ago left me to the final decoration as he had gone upstairs to put on his costume.

That must do, I thought to myself, as I slipped cyclamen into a tiny vase on the windowsill and turned towards the door which led into the hall. And there stood a very striking figure indeed...

Mark had evidently discovered the book that Paul Lucas had lent me. There were various line-drawings scattered through the text and clearly Mark had based his costume on one of them: the Green Man. He wore a long green wig and beard, which curled wildly around his head making him completely unrecognisable. His outfit, which must have been hired or bought from a costume specialist in London, was amazing. The tunic and leggings consisted of rows of leaf-shaped pieces of material in all shades of green, and he wore long, soft, green suede boots.

I didn't know whether to laugh out loud or to admire him for his attention to detail.

'You look extraordinary!' I exclaimed.

'Good, eh?' He struck a pose with one hand on his hip. I noticed that he had used some sort of make-up or dye and his face and hands were walnut brown.

Extraordinary indeed!

'It's time for you to go and get ready too, Cheeks. You don't want to be mistaken for the gardener!' Mark declaimed loudly, going into the kitchen, laughing at his own wit, to pour himself a chilled beer.

I had plenty of time. The day was still holding its golden light, although the sky was now becoming turquoise instead of the heart-lifting clear blue of the morning and afternoon. I went slowly upstairs, past our bedroom and, quietly opening the door to the attic rooms, I went into the high remote corners of the great house. I stopped for a few minutes at the attic window and looked out across Barrow Farm to the coast over the acres of lush Kent countryside. I was in a dreamy mood; and I knew that Mark would be ready to ridicule me if I could not somehow snap out of myself and become a decent host for the evening and morning that followed. But I would give myself just a few more minutes to follow my own thoughts. The landscape was like a tapestry, I mused, with rose-red cottages, dark green trees and hedges, and lighter green fields. The pale pink blossoms of the flowering cherries in the garden below where I sat were almost luminescent against the glowing sky and the darker blue of the pond opposite. I loved embroidery and it seemed to me that the timeless view I was looking at was built up of layers of thread – the present, vivid and glowing and vibrantly alive; the near past of the Wheatleys, visible under the present layer, just dimming slightly; and the far past in layer after layer of embroidery thread until colour was lost and stitches became formless. The game of life was played out again and again – by different actors, in slightly different ways – but the main themes remained: love and death and tragedy, and birth and new life. The person who had created the sun-dial on the front of Knight's Manor knew what he was about when he expressed his philosophy of the complex nature of Time in the honey-coloured stone.

TIME IS

TIME WAS

TIME IS NOT

Shivering, despite the sunshine filtering through the dusty window, I thought resolutely that I *must* pull myself together.

Slowly I walked through to the second attic room where I had left my costume. I had found the dress in a vintage dress shop in Tentersley: it was a plain cream soft material, full length, with a fairly low neckline and long fitted sleeves. And, because May celebrations were all about fertility and abundance, I had embroidered in the long afternoons waiting for Mark to return like a whirlwind from the cut and thrust of his time in London, a fine deep shawl. I had woven all my observations of the exquisite countryside which surrounded me into that shawl: the bluebells, the roses, swallows, celandines, a robin, early blossom, forget-me-nots and other flowers that I cannot now recall to mind. The scarf was gossamer thin and it had taken every ounce of my care and patience to weave the coloured silks into a representation of the flowers that I loved so much. But I was pleased with it. I had gathered bay and beech and woven them into a circlet for my head – I just had to collect the early roses that I knew were in the hedge at the bottom of our land and thread them through the greenery and my headdress would be complete. Not quite so striking as Mark's, but perhaps easier to wear, I thought with a smile.

The light was fading a little as I put on my costume and turned to look at myself in an old, foxed mirror in the corner of the attic. It was probably the light – or lack of it – but I felt that I looked different. It seemed to me that my eyes held a more direct gaze, that my skin was whiter, my hair darker and that, in keeping with the extraordinary quality of this day, I too had somehow changed.

I collected a pair of scissors from the bathroom and walked quietly downstairs, slipping out into the orchard before Mark could intercept me. I cut just five roses and wove them securely into the greenery of my circlet. Taking a deep breath, I walked back into the kitchen with just ten minutes to go before the first of our guests was due to arrive.

'Bloody hell love, you look gorgeous!' exclaimed my husband from the depths of his greenery. 'Shame it is only a few minutes to kick off, otherwise me might have a spot of dalliance beforehand!'

I turned away, very relieved that we did not have time for something that these days was so infrequently given and so unwillingly received.

Chapter 27

At nine o'clock precisely, Helen and James arrived. It seemed that they too had picked up on the traditional dress theme. James wore a tunic which only partially hid his expanding waistline, and Helen looked amazing in a long dress in shades of blue, which seemed to change and shift as she moved. Seeing me, she stopped quite still:

'My dear, you look utterly beautiful!'

'I'll say!' agreed James, giving me a rather too hearty hug.

I was genuinely embarrassed. I had always felt that Mark's startling good looks had deserved a much more striking prize than me and so I turned away, asking them what they would like to drink, as we drifted from the hall into the drawing room. We had lit a log fire in the huge grate and placed candles on hearth, wall niches and windowsills. The room was warm and welcoming and quite, quite timeless. We could have been sitting in a scented forest, I thought, looking at the effect of the flowers and greenery tumbling down and around the huge wall and ceiling timbers.

By ten o'clock all the guests had arrived – except Ash. I was in turmoil at every step into the hall, every sound made by cars coming into the courtyard. Surely, surely he would come? He had never let me down and I did not believe that he would do so now. But, as the minutes ticked on, it seemed that this was likely to be the case.

Mark was in his element. He stomped around in his green knee-high boots, laughing loudly and making direct, and sometimes highly inappropriate, comments. To the father of one of the beautiful teenage girls he winked and said:

'I would lock her up if I was you – tonight all sorts of things might happen.' Since the father in question was a churchwarden, this comment did not go down terribly well.

'In that case Mark, perhaps we ought to leave now,' he declared and, gathering his protesting family about him, he did exactly that. Soon after, the other couple who had come with their daughters also made their excuse to leave.

It was by now eleven o'clock and I had completely given up any hope of Ash joining the party. Our much diminished group had chatted and played the usual vacuous party games and I was wondering quite how we were going to keep the momentum going for another seven hours when, in a lull in the conversation, we all heard a sound. Not loud, but strangely pervasive. It was the sound of the sweetest harp music I had ever heard. The entire group moved to the front door of the house and we stopped, as one, looking at the circular lawn which I had created. In the centre of this grassy area sat a tall, dark figure. Dressed in green, with a green cloak, long dark hair lifting gently in the sweet Spring air was… was it Ash? His hair was encircled by a silver band and his long, strong sensitive fingers moved lightly across the strings of a small harp. The huge silver constellations hung in the sky behind him like embellished wall hangings in the largest Great Hall imaginable. The figure was like, but unlike, the man I had longed all day to see.

From beyond the stars I come
To sing to you this night
To tell you of a timeless love
That made the darkness bright.

Like twisted ropes of ivy
Two lovers became one
When one was cut, the other died
The Evil had begun.

We were entranced. Even Mark was quiet. The beautiful music, the chanted words, conspired together to draw us into one unforgettable and complex part of the immense fabric of the human story. It sounds totally far-fetched to try to describe the scene now after a lapse of so many years, but perhaps it is simplest to say that it was a part of the deep magic of that most enchanted night.

Unbidden, we sat in a circle on the soft cool grass and were drawn remorselessly into a tale of radiant love and tragic loss – told against a pagan background of sacrifice and death – and a curse that echoed down the centuries.

The song ended. I had no idea of the time. The great constellations had visibly swung across the sky and slightly, very slightly, dawn was lightening the expanse of sea in the east. We were all held in the spell of the desperate story of love and death that the figure had told. At one moment, looking at him, I was absolutely certain it was Ash. Every aspect of his appearance was branded on my brain and I knew that I couldn't be mistaken. But then the look, the stance, the voice, at times held aspects of unfamiliarity. I was utterly confused.

He put his harp down quietly and lowered his face. His long dark hair swung over his features, blurring and obscuring them.

'It's time for fire-lighting!' announced my husband, leaping to his green feet.

We all, without exception, physically jumped, feeling the sudden violence of being pulled back into the twentieth century. As one, we looked at Mark as he picked up a bucket of twigs and a box of matches which he had placed in the front porch earlier that day. And then, as we looked back to where the singer-poet had sat – a little distant from the group – we saw that he had gone.

I was even more confused as, in a whirl, Mark grabbed my hand and started running towards the wood at the end of our land. The spell was finally broken. I was back in the pulsing, thrusting world of action that Mark was determined to create around him.

There is a clearing in the middle of Knight's Manor wood. One day, prior to that extraordinary evening, Mark had spent an enjoyable afternoon with a chainsaw, chopping branches from trees and clearing a significant space. It was, I had thought at the time, a miracle that he had returned to the kitchen at tea time, starving and with arms and legs still intact. It was to this clearing that he led us now. I remember reading once about the trees creating a 'cathedral of the woods' with their delicate beauty and tracery. At that moment, looking around me on that most memorable of Spring dawns, it struck me how human beings take the best of the natural world and strive to replicate it in their homes. I thought once again of the poem-song we had just heard and the beginning world it had painted, where the floor of the great hall was covered with rushes, its walls were made of timber, its wall-hangings covered with flowers and stars.

But now, Mark was definitely in centre stage.

'Right! Stand at least two metres back – everyone please. I will light the fire and then we will start the traditional dance.'

I was brought back again abruptly to the present – embarrassed, wishing I was elsewhere. What did my pragmatic, tone-deaf husband know of dance, or tradition for that matter? He lived aggressively in the here and now, most definitely in the material world. What did he really understand of the elemental feelings that twisted through the fabric of this unforgettable night? I turned to him.

'Do be careful Mark, please! We could start a serious fire if you are not careful.'

'Oh be quiet woman!' he hissed under his breath. 'We have had your arty-farty friend entertaining us with his rubbish. Let's have some solid entertainment now, shall we?'

So clearly Mark thought that our singer had been Ash. Why was I still unsure?

The fire started to crackle and spit. I noticed that, for once, Mark had planned every practical detail. He had excavated a fire pit and cleared the ground around this. He was right: there was no real danger of the fire spreading. He had contained it well. But I was at a loss to know what to do next. I loved dancing, but did not know exactly what was expected of me.

Then suddenly my right hand was taken. I knew at once that it was Ash. I could tell his cool, strong grip anywhere.

I whirled towards him and the relief of looking directly into the darkness of his eyes was almost too much for my poise.

'Where have you been?' I whispered, agonised, my hands tightening their hold on his.

'With Paul earlier… too long. I had to take his advice. And we talked… but then I came.' He frowned slightly, looking puzzled.

'So it *was* you then, you *were* the singer?' I looked past his face to his clothes: the green tunic and cloak, the silver circlet. 'I just wasn't sure…'

He frowned slightly and led me towards the fire. We started to move around the low, crackling blaze, slowly and deliberately at first. But then, through his guidance, I started to undertake complex patterns of steps that at first seemed haphazard, but then began to form an immense, mesmerising pattern. I looked swiftly up at the fading stars and I knew suddenly of what the dance reminded me – the unfathomable orbits of planets, appearing random, but tracing a regular dance through the heavens over a huge span of time. Gradually the others joined us: Helen, guiding the hefty form of her husband through the delicate mathematics of the steps; then the Jenners. Lizzie's delicate features were beautiful in the flickering, darting flames, as she lost herself in the rhythm of the dance, and I could see for the first time how her husband had been attracted to her.

Faster and faster we moved. I wondered how we would look to a passing stranger. Grey shapes threading and re-threading in a dance that I knew to be aeons old, that I dimly suspected told some elemental story. Would the unsuspecting onlooker believe we were ghosts? Or spirits from an earlier age, caught forever in a dance that repeated itself on this most powerful of nights?

And then in a fluid movement Ash held me around the waist with his right arm and we seemed to fly over the low fire as my partner leapt high. We were followed by Lizzie and Steve, who, for once, was clearly enjoying himself, his patronising attitude forgotten in the rhythm and complexity of the dance. I looked at Helen and James, really concerned that James's bulk could actually clear the low flames. But as he was hanging back, looking confused, I saw Mark hurtle into action, grabbing the unsuspecting Helen and literally giving her a fireman's lift over the fire. Her beautiful dress was dragged far too high, showing her long white legs. She was too poised to lose her temper but, when he set her down on the far side of the flames, I saw her cheeks flaming and her eyes blazing. James's broad smile soon disappeared as he saw the expression on his wife's face.

'James and I have promised to complete this dance together, Mark. I would be grateful if you could remember this.' Regal as always, she smoothed down her ruffled hair and her creased dress and took up again the hand of her husband, nudging and coercing him to follow the complex moves.

We had completed one entire cycle which had culminated in the heart-stopping leap across the fire, and had nearly reached the same point again. Mark had stood sulkily by himself, poking the fire with a long stick and glaring at those of us who were totally immersed in this age-old ritual. Suddenly I was conscious that he had flung the stick aside. Then without warning he came dashing towards Ash and I, seconds before Ash prepared to leap the flames again. Mark pushed Ash hard, then grabbed me and, as he had done with Helen, flung me over his shoulder. My scarf, embroidered with such anticipation and enjoyment, slipped from my shoulders, catching on the rough twigs of an ash tree. This time, however, Mark ran, not towards the fire but away from it, into the deepest part of the wood. I heard Helen calling my name, clearly shocked – but on and on Mark plunged until the faint glow of the flames and the voices of my friends became lost in the wakening sounds of the early morning.

He flung me down on the damp ground and looked at me with what I can only describe as disgust.

'You think you are so special Kate, don't you, with your perfect friends and your weird mystical ways. But you know what you are? My property. Mine. No-one else's. Like the rest of the house and the land. Mine. You know what the lord of the manor did years ago, don't you? Took what was his, again and again. And especially on this night.'

For the second time that strange evening, there seemed to be a transformation. Instead of the glib, attractive, fashionable businessman that I knew, suddenly I saw only the green inhuman figure before me, his face contorted with lust, hauling my skirt high above my waist, and ripping off my underwear.

'If I cover your face it's easier to do this,' he panted. 'But at least you looked vaguely attractive tonight – at least some seemed to think so!'

And there, in the melting beauty of that perfect May Day, the Green Man took Flora in an archetypal act of procreation, a fertility rite that had nothing to do with love, or selflessness or sacrifice. But was passionless, driven by lust and part of the age-old cycle of progeneration and renewal.

Chapter 28

The Spring blossomed into summer, a summer that glows in my memory like a picture from a mediaeval manuscript: vivid, exquisite, sometimes more real than the life I am now living.

The strange, half-real events of May Day were dealt with by all of those who had experienced them in very different ways. Mark had returned to the group left nonplussed, standing around the embers of the fire, to explain that I had a sudden migraine and had gone to bed. Which was where I did go, when I had managed to drag myself back from the wood, entering the house by the side door, creeping like a thief into the cosy room that had been the Wheatleys' nursery. I ripped my clothes off and bundled them into a cupboard, pulling on my warm dressing gown. I showered and showered for longer than I could ever remember and then returned to the safe little room above the kitchen and locked the door.

Mark never referred again to his behaviour on that night, but returned to his superficial, jovial self. It was as if, for him, it had never happened. Helen called round first thing on Monday morning and I shared everything with her. I remember her face still, absolutely quiet and expressionless, nodding without a word and holding me close. Steve smiled knowingly when he next saw me in church; whilst Lizzie simply came over to me and squeezed my arm in sympathetic

271

understanding. Ash went back to university. And I… well, my love for my husband died in the midst of the springing new life of that surreal May Day morning.

The perfect sun-filled weeks slid by. Ash stayed in Manchester, completely involved in his final exams. May moved into June and still I had not seen him again.

Lying one day spread-eagled in the sunshine, by the spring in one of our lower fields, I glanced towards the thickest part of our wood and reflected sardonically on the book that Paul Lucas had lent me about the act of fertility at the heart of the Beltane ritual:

The symbolic union of the Goddess of Spring, Flora, and the epitome of male fertility, the Green Man, lies at the heart of the celebration. The union of these two symbolic figures is always consummated and Flora will become pregnant.

'And Flora will become pregnant.' Really? Even when earth magic was involved, I thought bitterly, this did not apply to me…'

***

It was Midsummer Day and, for once, the day lived up to its name. I was having difficulty sleeping and, as usual, woke shortly after four o'clock to the dawn chorus rising like the most perfect oratorio from the depths of the heavy leaves and blossom of the trees which surrounded our garden. I crept quietly to the window, which was wide open because of the intense heat. Acre after acre of Kent countryside stretched, luxuriant and seductive across Barrow farmland, up to the ridge which protected Ashward from the intrusion of the real world, dipping away to the Kent marshes and rising once again to the distant coast. It was breathtaking!

A sudden grunt brought me back to the room:

'For God's sake, Kate, shut those bloody curtains! I've got to get up in two hours. Talk about thoughtless! *And*, I have a client meeting this evening. Have you packed my overnight case?'

I had. I shut the curtains without a word – but there was no way I was going back to bed when everything about the world outside was beckoning me.

My faithful dogs were, as ever, ready and waiting for exercise. I didn't even bother to put on their collars and leads. Traffic was never a problem in Ashward, and certainly wouldn't be at a quarter to five in the morning. Mark could get his own breakfast for once!

We walked down Old Cruck Lane. There was something about the day – that day – that felt like the first day that had ever been created. It was incredibly bright, luminescent; each flower, each tree, etched in a loving bold line that made its unique beauty totally precious.

As I turned the gentle corner just before Meadow Farm, I realised that I was not the only person who could not sleep on this most perfect of mornings. Helen was sitting on a flowery bank, her eyes closed, her face raised to the rising sun, totally quiet, totally absorbed in her own thoughts. I felt such love for her as I looked at her beautiful face; but this quickly turned to concern as I saw that she was crying – properly crying, not just the glisten of a tear in her eye which she forbade to fall. Without a word I put my arms around her. She didn't resist. It was almost as if she had known that I would come.

'What's the matter?' I whispered.

'Oh it's the perfect beauty of this morning! It seems like the start of Creation when everything had the potential to be perfect. I just could not sleep. The whole of the world was calling to me: birds, morning light, the very day itself. Compared with all this, my existence just seems so futile and my marriage to James so very empty. It is like living with a puppet, Kate. I have tried to push away the hurt over the years by organising my life like a military campaign, by running my household like a feature article from *Vogue*, with overwhelming love for my girls. But if there is one thing I could wish for, it would be to know the sort of love that poets write about, that legends are made of... that we heard sung about on May Day.'

The sunlight was growing stronger now and we watched swallows swooping low to catch insects. The whole world was, once again, taking up its reassuring daily rhythm.

She stood up suddenly. 'Oh, I am so sorry,' she sighed, with a sad half-smile. 'I am being middle-aged and maudlin. Forgive me!' In an instant she had slipped on the mask that she almost always wore: eminently capable, eminently practical, always in control.

'Come back for breakfast with me,' said Helen. 'James will have left for the station by now.'

For hours we hardly spoke. We just sat together in perfect understanding, each of us reflecting upon our less than perfect existence. But eventually we were able to start to talk, to articulate our feelings and our intense disappointments. It was one of those rarest of moments when it was right to share everything.

Around midday I stood up and stretched. 'Mrs Woodville, I *must* go home!'

'How are things between you and Mark since… since the party?'

'It was the end of a chapter, Helen,' I said, without further explanation. But I knew that she understood precisely what I meant.

Walking back up the hill with my panting dogs, I thought about the morning. I believed that I had been completely and utterly in love with Mark when we married. But I now knew that I had fallen in love with a figure of my imagination, rather than reality. His throwaway comments used to seem so witty and amusing. So too did his complete disregard of other peoples' feelings, which often bordered upon rudeness. I had changed – I had changed so much. How far he had changed had been demonstrated less than six weeks ago. Had our move to this isolated place affected us to such an extent? Was I being influenced by the people I had met here: Helen, Paul Lucas, Ash…?

Suddenly, with absolute conviction, I realised that I had found my soulmate. During the two or so months that we had been friends I had discovered how intuitive Ash was, with a lightning intellect and a quirky sense of humour. We shared absurdities with a look; empathised with people and situations without words; fulfilled each other so completely it was, quite simply, breathtaking. The moment when we leapt across the fire that unforgettable morning, I had known that, as the tattered book given to me by Paul Lucas had said, we were 'handfasted'. Whatever paths our lives took in the future, a part of us would always belong together. Beltane fertility magic may not have worked on me, but I knew that I had found the man whom I would always love.

I ate a cheese sandwich, most of which I crumbled and gave to Rupert and Emma, and started upon the first job on my list for the day – weeding the vegetable garden. Riveting! I dug with more fervour than precision, thinking through the reality of my marriage with Mark. My dawn conversation with Helen replayed in my mind: 'But if there is one thing I could wish for, it would be to know the sort of love that poets write about, that legends are made of… that we heard sung about on May Day…'

Chapter 29

'You do realise you have just dug up some horseradish?' Ash smiled gently down at me. I had not seen him since that May Day morning and I just did not know what to say, so I found my refuge in the banal.

'I thought it was dock.'

'Are you free?'

'What, now?'

'Yes…'

'I am, Ash.'

We went on our favourite walk to Barrow Farm.

'Do you want to talk about what happened that night?' he asked quietly, looking down at the flowers and grasses along the green track we were following.

'No,' I replied shortly. 'I want to forget it.'

He was deeply troubled I could tell and so, to ease him from what could develop into the most silent of walks, I asked, 'Ash, please tell me what you and Paul talked about that night. Please explain what happened. I still don't fully understand.'

He looked up swiftly from under the long sweep of his lashes, and I saw the pain in his eyes. He pulled himself together.

'Well, I don't fully understand either, Kate,' he frowned.

'I went to see Paul to ask his advice about something and clearly Paul had been expecting me to come and see him. You know he has this extraordinary ability to anticipate. As soon as I entered his study I realised that he was very serious, very concerned. He was also clearly deeply moved and almost "excited" about something. He was pacing to and fro in the cramped space, reading and re-reading a creased and obviously very ancient document.

'"Have a look at this, Ashley!" There was not a vestige of a smile on his face as he handed me the worn and discoloured scrap of parchment on which were written the most incomprehensible words. I copied them down to see if I could research their meaning later. Ash took a small blue notebook from his pocket and handed it to me.

I read:

Darkness. Darkness everywhere. The light had only just come. But in some places, in this place, darkness would always remain.

Swirling blackness; a miasma of evil concentrated until it condensed upon the bare earth, until it dripped off the stark branches of the just-beginning trees. A tangible breathing, feeling evil.

Nothing good that came here could survive. Nothing grow. Nothing flourish. The unnamed darkness would always prevail.

Tenebres nocti. Tenebres unnamae…

I frowned and handed the book back to Ash. He continued:

'Just reading those words seemed to drain me of energy, Kate. I felt desolate, confused and totally out of my depth. I asked him, "Why are you showing this to me, Paul? What does it mean?"

'He ran his hands through his thick white hair and said: "Ash, I think that I have found the missing pieces of the spiritual jigsaw puzzle that has been taunting me for years. I have at last reached the final notebooks of my ancestor, Paul Ashward. This enigmatic distillation of evil was folded into the very last page of his last book. It confirms everything I have come to believe about the nature of the place we live in. I don't pretend to understand it; I certainly do not know where Paul Ashward obtained it; but I am absolutely certain of its significance. I believe that this unpleasant scrap of history makes a statement about the intrinsically evil nature of this place. Ashley, it is critical that you listen carefully to what I am about to say. You are going to the party at Knight's Manor tonight, aren't you?" He really didn't need my affirmation. He knew I was.

"'Ash, you are... close, to Kate, aren't you?" I nodded. "Ash, I don't know the precise details, but she is in danger – not the gross physical danger that we immediately think of in life, but the insidious spiritual danger that is so much more corrosive – so much more devastating. She needs to know that here, in this place, a story is played out again and again and again – across the centuries, across the millennia. This story itself reflects the central destructive problem of Ashward – this 'great and wonderful estate' as the guide books call it. Whatever I do, whatever anyone does, this story seems intent upon replication and repetition. There is no escape." Paul had become pale, almost grey, as he said all this to me. I said nothing, just continued to listen with every atom of my concentration

'"Once, long, long ago," continued Paul, "there was a beautiful woman and a fine young man. Their story is archetypal. They fell in love and loved with a pure passion that lit the life of all who knew them. Then a terrible drought came to the settlement where they lived. The father of the woman, who had brought civilisation and security to the settlement here in Ashward, became desperate and turned back to his pagan gods. In order to petition these gods to provide water again for his people, he agreed to human sacrifice."

'Paul stood up and strode to the window, whipping off his glasses and wiping his hand across his brow as if trying to banish the truth of the terrible story he was telling.

'"Through the twisted and evil intervention of the local 'wise woman' – but witch is a more appropriate word – the betrothed of his daughter was sacrificed. It was terrible. The whole settlement was shaken, even though the rain came – but what a victory!

'"His daughter, once so beautiful, became like a wraith. She walked only at night. She never spoke. Until the night when her father was dying. And then all the agony of the past years flooded from her lips. It was then that she cursed this place.

'"She cursed her father, her people and the people that were to come. She set fire to the great hall whose embers lie beneath this house. I have seen them, Ash! The black layer that seems still to tell of the misery and death of that night over a thousand years ago. And do you know, the curse worked! It destroyed my ancestor, Paul Ashward; it has nearly destroyed me; and it has affected others. I do *not* want it to claim another victim. As I say, Kate is, I believe, in danger. And I think you understand how this can be. Surely I do not need to spell it out to you?" And Paul looked directly at me, not with anger but with frustration, with deep concern and with love.'

"'Tell this story at the party, Ash," he exhorted. "Here is the translation. I finished transcribing it last night from my namesake's very last diary. There is no more for me to read now. My journey of discovery is done."'

I whirled around, stopping and taking both Ash's hands in mine and forcing him to shake back his hair in that gesture I loved so well and to look at me. 'What? What are you trying to tell me?'

'I don't know. I don't fully understand. I had learnt the technique of speaking poetry to music as part of my course, Kate, but never had the words and poetry of something moved me so much. I started to sing the poem in front of Knight's Manor but, as the night moved towards dawn, it was as if someone else was speaking through me. You asked me if it was I that came that night. It was. But I was...' he clearly sought for the appropriate word, '...augmented by someone or something else. I had to share that tragic story with you that night. I had to take it to my own heart too. We need to try to work through the significance of all this for us, Kate.'

Chapter 30

He was so young. I looked at his creased forehead, the concern clouding his eyes. I had never loved him so much, but, equally, had never so acutely realised that, actually, despite his spiritual maturity and depth, he was a very young man whose life was just beginning. So much beauty, so much integrity, so much love and care and spiritual discernment and intelligence and talent... I pulled myself together. For the first time too I saw clearly the gap between us. I was nearly a generation older than Ash. I had been married for eight years. I was a householder... and on and on the inexorable bleak truths came. I had to say something or otherwise I would just run away from him, physically and mentally run away from the facts that were tumbling through my mind.

'Well, we have the entire day!' I said, as light-heartedly as I could. 'Let's walk and see where the day takes us.'

We passed the barrow, and the way in which our present lives encountered past belief was no longer a surprise. As I relaxed in his presence, I poured out my heart. I told him of the happenings of Beltane – but he knew already. I pushed my fists into my eyes as I recalled the horror of the physical reality of that morning, which contrasted bitterly with the mythical beauty and timelessness of the rest of the evening. Ash was totally quiet, totally absorbed in what I was telling him. And as I spoke, his face told the story of his emotions. But then, gradually, he overcame his own feelings in order to nudge me gently away from the drama and pain of that May Day morning. Although clearly shocked and angry, and hurt at my hurt, he tickled me with long strands of reed. He ran away from me, feigning disappearance as he raced into the trees. He doubled back behind me and flung his arms around my waist in an embrace that I longed to return, but felt unable to.

We walked for hours. We talked about the myths and pagan beliefs surrounding Midsummer. We reviewed again the astonishing story that he had sung. We shared poetry we had read and had written. Eventually, as the first stars were dimly lighting the sky, we sat down, tired at last, in a field where the grass lay in fragrant heaps ready to be bound into bales. We seemed to have covered a lifetime in a day.

Swathes of flowers lay cut and mingled with the grass; and flowers too still stood around the edge of the field.

After the tumult of our earlier conversation I was at peace, and so happy that I can still recapture the joy and beauty and vividness of that early evening.

Ash said nothing and, shielding my eyes against the golden and scarlet sunset, I looked up to see what he was doing. He was quite simply looking at me.

'I love you, Kate,' he said quietly – not smiling, not making a movement towards me – just looking at me with a gaze which held mine and drew me. I can't remember how long we stayed like that. Our gaze was like something tangible; it was as if it could never be broken.

Everything I could think of saying seemed trite and unnecessary. And so I said nothing, knowing that I could stay here forever, in this place, on this earth, with him, out of time.

I remembered once again the inscription on the old sundial on the fair southerly face of Knight's Manor:

TIME IS

TIME WAS

TIME IS NOT

But even as his eyes held mine I was aware of a subtle shift in the atmosphere of the meadow and the surrounding hills and woods. Almost impossible to describe, it was as if a tremor had passed through tree, flower and earth. Of course Ash sensed it too.

'Stay just like that.'

Swiftly he stepped away and bent several times to gather what I imagined were flowers.

'Don't move!'

Gently he placed in my hair a circlet of St John's wort, bird's foot trefoil, vervain, rue and wild roses.

'The legend is that if you place these flowers under your pillow on Midsummer's night you will dream of your true love,' he laughed quietly.

It sounds strange, but we talked no more. I carried the flowers back to my house where, without touching me, he said simply:

'Goodnight.' I also heard the words '… My own dear love…' but whether I had imagined them or whether he had whispered them or whether they were in the very air of that enchanted night, I still am not sure.

As the weeks went on, we held the knowledge of our love for each other quiet and still in our hearts. I felt as if everyone could see the way in which we had absolutely completed each other. We met at friends' houses, at church, at Ashward Priory and the wonder was we did not have to be near to each other for reassurance – we did not even have to speak. Our love seemed as if it had always been there, from the beginning of time, and would last until time was no more.

Chapter 31

With characteristic vigour, Paul Lucas suddenly stood up from his desk. My Mini was being serviced, so Mark had dropped me off at the Priory on his way to an early evening squash match. With half an hour to spare, my husband had, atypically, accepted Paul's invitation to have a cold drink.

'Be interesting to see where you have your indoctrination – I mean, confirmation – classes, Cheeks,' Mark smirked.

Paul appeared restless. We had been talking for some time about minor events in the village, when he had jumped to his feet having finally, it would appear, made a decision about something that had been on his mind.

'It's time we formed another Ashward study group!' Paul declared.

I smiled. 'Tell me more!'

'Years ago when I inherited this... vastness,' he gestured vaguely and expansively around him, 'I had an idea. What if, from time to time, we formed a study group, composed of people who live in the village or from guests here, to research a philosophical or theological question?'

'Whoa!' I protested. 'There is no way I am a philosopher or a theologian.'

'That's true!' exclaimed my husband. 'About the only claim to fame Kate has is to translate Old English poetry, something about someone who was lost or something...'

'Ah, you mean *The Wanderer*?' mused Paul gently.

> *'How those times of rejoicing have retreated*
> *Becoming dark under night's curtain*
> *As if they had never been.'*

For a moment a shadow crossed his face.

'Yes, Paul?' I prompted gently.

'Sorry. The rationale behind such a group is not as obscure as you would imagine,' he smiled. 'We discuss such questions as "Why do you think that Good does not always overcome Evil?" or "Does Evil have an identity of its own?" It's really interesting. Choosing the members of the group is key: it's the interaction of people that creates an innate enquiring energy as the months pass. Someone's ideas spark off a reaction in another person. Sometimes friction between opposing personalities brings about really intuitive discussion.'

Opposing personalities, I thought wryly to myself... Mark and Ash... Ash and Mark. The one so gentle, funny and supportive; the other harsh, aggressive, sarcastic.

'Kate?'

'Oh, Paul, I am sorry. I was lost in my own thoughts.'

'Oh, here we go,' interjected Mark. 'Away in fairyland as usual!'

Paul leant quickly across to me and patted my arm.

'Gisela always says I don't see what is right under my nose!' he said. 'But,' and here he fixed me with a direct and very discerning look, 'I am always here if you want to talk to me. Anyway, just to finish what I was saying, sometimes groups really cohere and start to share worries, tragedies, hopes, dreams.' The distant, abstracted look that occasionally crossed his features flickered there now for an instant, but he quickly pulled himself back to practicalities. 'I suggest that members of the study group should keep a diary to record thoughts, or discoveries – about themselves or other people. You will find it helpful to refer to them during the six or so months that we meet, and again in years to come.'

Mark looked pointedly at his watch – a new Rolex. 'Sorry, count me out of this conversation, although it might be an interesting exercise to see how much Kate has actually learnt over the past months!' he commented mockingly. 'I must be making tracks. My squash game is booked for eight this evening. That's the philosophy I understand! Thanks for the drink, Paul. See you. See you later, love.' And with that he was gone. Minutes later we heard the powerful engine note of his new Lancia and the scattering of gravel as he sped off.

I shut my eyes, trying to compose my thoughts. I was really upset by my husband's easy dismissal of something that promised to fascinate me.

'Paul, I'm sorry! Mark is…'

'Not a word. I think this calls for some sherry! You are walking back aren't you, Kate? Can't have you drunk in charge of a bike or a dog or something.'

'Yes I am,' I grinned. My friend always had the power to make me see what mattered in a very clear light.

'Do you have any thoughts on our group then, Kate?'

'Well, Helen would be great,' I suggested.

'Why does that choice not surprise me?' he teased.

'I will come, of course, and possibly Mark? From what he just said, it sounds as though he might possibly be interested.

288

You. How about Ash Cooper?' Even speaking Ash's name sent a flicker of excitement through me, as I recalled that someone had once said that when you are in love with someone, you want to talk of them constantly.

'Good choice. Also Lizzie and Steve Jenner.' He hesitated. 'Kate, did Ash speak to you about our conversation?'

'Yes, Paul, bless you! He did. Thank you for your love and concern. But we – I – am all right.'

'Oh, my dear!' exclaimed Paul. 'If only I were sure of that!' And, uncharacteristically, he stepped swiftly across the room and gave me a hard hug. Shaking himself visibly out of the direction our conversation had taken, he returned to the planning of the study group.

'That makes seven: a perfect number!'

***

Our first meeting was a month later – towards the end of September, the month that stands half in summer and half in autumn. I had walked the dogs long and hard that afternoon, through the woods on the road to Tentersley. We had seen a young stag, surrounded by the flame-coloured leaves of early autumn, looking with disconcerting attention at Rupert. Even diversions such as this were not sufficient to stop the thoughts relentlessly circling in my mind. Fortunately the stag turned away, but there was no escape from my recalling the conversation I had had with Helen on Midsummer Day: 'My existence just seems so futile and my marriage to James so empty'.

Increasingly my marriage to Mark seemed, quite simply, a waste of time. We never held a meaningful conversation. We did nothing together. He constantly poked fun at me; and he seemed to be involved in work and squash to the exclusion of absolutely everything else, apart from an occasional, somewhat apathetic, involvement with church. Increasingly my time was spent with Ash. We walked, we talked, endlessly exploring ideas and concepts together. I was at peace and had finally left behind the constraints of my childhood, filled with my mother's suffocating love and my father's ineffectual gentleness. The years working in London building a career, and buying ever more expensive houses, were as nothing compared with one minute of time with the man I loved.

I replayed these thoughts as I followed the track from Knight's Manor to Ashward Priory for the first of our meetings. It was, I reflected sadly, probably the last time I would be able to walk to the group until the Spring. The evenings were drawing in and, as I turned to follow the ancient rising footpath to the Priory, already dusk was leeching the colour from the landscape.

Everyone was there when I arrived. We met in the library and Steve gazed disconcertingly right at me as I walked in, but said nothing. Lizzie got up with difficulty – I had never seen anyone quite so pregnant!

'Oh hi, Kate!' She greeted me breathlessly. 'I am so glad you could come to this group.'

'Me too,' I responded, embarrassed because I just did not know where I stood with this couple. Trying to make conversation, I said tentatively, 'Did you manage to arrange a baby-sitter then?'

She smiled and I realised again how her delicate features could have appealed to her more obviously attractive husband.

'Yes, thank you for thinking of us. Jennet Hayes has offered to babysit for us.' I had come across Jennet during church services and trips to the bookshop at Ashward Priory. She was a young woman who presented that most unusual combination of extreme beauty and an apparently endlessly helpful and pleasant personality.

'I am really pleased,' I replied – and felt that, potentially, here was another friendship waiting to grow and develop.

Helen got up regally and gave me a gentle embrace. Ash remained seated, his glance holding mine.

No Mark! He was intending to arrive straight from his commuter train and, inevitably, he was late. I would have been surprised if he had *not* been late, but in any event I apologised, 'I am so sorry, there has probably been a delay on the line.'

'Not to worry,' said Paul briskly. 'Let's have a cold drink and start to consider the initial question for this first session.'

He handed a piece of A5 paper to each of us which read:

'Gustav Flaubert said that there is no Truth, only Perception. How far do you agree with this?'

After a few moments of complete blankness, we soon became totally involved in trying to put our thoughts into words. Inevitably Ash and I were drawn together and, as we became more immersed in our discussion, I felt the usual electric spark of ideas and counter-ideas flash between us. His eyes became darker – whether because of his feelings for me or his deep and utterly unshakeable faith, I did not know. I relaxed totally and laughed and gestured without constraint as I usually did in his presence.

Suddenly I was shaken out of my spontaneous self by a cool hand on my shoulder. It was Helen.

'And what are you two so passionate about?' she teased.

I blushed, completely taken off guard by the ambiguity of her comment, 'Just… erm…'

Helen smiled gently. 'I understand,' she said.

Mark arrived at nine-thirty, just half an hour before we were due to end our meeting. Our discussions had become less animated. We had moved into a quieter and more reflective stage. Lizzie looked exhausted. Helen was checking her watch and I knew that she would be thinking of her husband arriving home to the cold supper which she had prepared for him. Steve looked slightly bored, giving the impression that all this was just a little beneath him. Ash and I were still involved in our discussions.

'What are you holding here?' Mark enquired raucously. 'A séance?'

It was one of those moments when everything freezes. Helen and Lizzie looked concerned for me; Ash took a deep breath and looked down; Steve gave a sarcastic smile – which could mean either he thought Mark an idiot, or applied that judgment to all of us. Paul, as always, picked up the entire array of responses in the room.

'I believe you know what we have been doing, Mark,' he said quietly. 'You had agreed to be part of this group.'

Mark had the grace to look a little shamefaced at this gentle rebuke. Not fazed for long, however, he turned to Steve with a quick grin:

'Just bring me up to date mate, will you?' he quipped. 'I'm a quick learner.'

And so we progressed through the autumn, meeting fortnightly in Paul's exquisite flat. More often than not, Mark didn't attend, making work or squash a frequent excuse. When he did join us, he was often intent on debating an insignificant point of interpretation, just to try to catch out Paul. Of course, he never did. Paul Lucas was a wise and thoughtful man who regarded Mark's attempts to 'get one over him' as no more irritation than swatting away a troublesome fly. On the scale of Paul's experiences, Mark's arrogance hardly registered.

Apart from Mark playing his mind games, the rest of us talked, laughed and reflected together, all the time drawing closer as a group. I don't quite know what I had expected, but the reality, as the evenings became darker, colder and wetter, was quite different. Paul had talked about a group sharing its 'worries, tragedies, hopes and dreams' and for each of us these emerged quite clearly, like a series of short dramas which were taken up by the other members of the group. It was as if a collective consciousness was, as Paul had intimated, beginning to develop: each felt the others' joys, triumphs and tragedies. We sought to support one another, to listen and to understand.

The diary that Paul had suggested we keep was invaluable to me. In recording the events, I was able to reflect and order them. In that process of reflection, I was struck once again by the parallel unseen influences that ran strongly beneath the social meetings and intellectual discussions, beneath the conventions of coffee and conversation. The past was still a reality in this place: Good was made quintessentially greater and Evil still held its dark pervasive sway.

My 'Ashward Diary' was very precious to me. I bought a notebook which held blank pages interspersed with reproductions of paintings by Victorian artists who sought to represent the idyllic country life through an over-simplistic shorthand. But at that time it seemed beautiful to me, and entirely appropriate for the context in which I lived. Ash and I shared the book. It seemed important that he should read my reflections on our discussions. Occasionally, he inserted a comment; but more often a little drawing, a sketch of a bird or flower.

Chapter 32

2014

Ashley Cooper felt his grip on reality slipping away as he looked closely at his computer screen. He enlarged the photograph as much as he could until he could see the fine lines that had not been there when he had walked with her, talked with her and loved her. Her eyes held sadness and, enlarging the image again, he realised they still had the power to draw him in deep, deeper, until he lost his sense of self and they became again one consciousness. He closed his eyes and smelled again the heady scent of cut grass, of roses; and saw her astonished gentle smile as he handed her the flowers – bird's foot trefoil, St John's wort, and wild roses. That enchanted Midsummer, so long ago...

Slowly, he turned from his computer and crossed the shabby room. He knew exactly where to find it. Lifting dusty files and ring binders from the furthest corner of his office, he found what he was looking for: a cardboard folder, tied shut with green string and marked, diagonally, with a single word – 'Dead'.

Gently he untied the string which had become brittle with time. He lifted aside a faded programme for *The Tempest*; a golden mask, battered and dulled so that the once bright gold was rubbed and tarnished; a poem written in red ink; an exquisite embroidered scarf, rescued and cherished by him where it had caught on an ash tree on that unforgettable May morning. It was folded above dried flowers – yellow St John's wort, faded pink wild rose – which he lifted to see whether some lingering perfume remained. It didn't. He carefully moved aside a small blue leather box, and then he came to what he had been looking for: a square book. Gently opening it, he traced again with his finger her bold individual writing: 'Ashward Diary 1983'. He turned the page, smoothing down the thick cream paper carefully.

> *All other things to their destruction draw*
> *Only our love hath no decay*
> *This no tomorrow hath, nor yesterday…*

'Much better than I could ever write! These words of Donne for you, my love. K x'

And there, in the middle of the dust and paper and memories, he cleared a space on the dingy brown carpet and began to read…

31 October 1982

What an extraordinary evening! We met tonight acutely aware of the date! For once Mark was on time – he had actually made the effort to catch an earlier train. Lizzie arrived alone. She looked awful – pale, deep shadows under her eyes, pitifully thin apart from her pregnancy, her hair dull and unwashed.

At first Paul tried to ignore how ill she looked. Typically, he jollied everyone along, asking for feedback from the previous session and any thoughts or reflections which had occurred to us since our last meeting. Lizzie said nothing. She just sat, with eyes almost glazed. She was somewhere else in her mind and wherever that somewhere was it was an empty, bitter and challenging place.

In the end Paul could stand it no longer. He moved quickly and energetically, kneeling in front of her, in order to establish eye-contact and said quite simply:

'My dear – what is wrong?'

I have never seen anyone cry silently before. Lizzie covered her face with her hands and her slight body shook with misery. She turned her head from side to side in denial of something and clung to Paul's outstretched hands as if they were a lifeline.

She was so gentle, so vulnerable and deeply, deeply shaken. Paul sat next to her, putting his arm gently around her shoulder.

'You must share with us. You are safe here.'

'Steve is having an affair,' she whispered and, gulping through her sobs, she told us what had happened. She spoke simply and directly, almost like a child telling a story she couldn't quite believe.

'I came home earlier than expected from an antenatal appointment today and couldn't immediately unlock the front door. I took out my key and tried again – the door still would not open. I knocked and Steve came to the door and let me in. He seemed preoccupied. I tried to talk to him but just got monosyllabic answers. I asked if he would like some tea and

some of the cake I had made the day before. He said "yes" rather vaguely and stood with his back to me looking out of the front window at the rain sweeping across the fields. I moved to the back door, meaning to go out to our utility room to get the cake I had made and put in the fridge out there. As I opened the back door, Steve spun round and grabbed my arm.' She held out her right arm and showed the bruising where his fingers had gripped her wrist.

'"Don't go out there!" he said forcibly.

'I was hurt and angry and shook him off.'

'"I will go there if I wish! It is my home, too," I told him and twisted away from his grasp. Well... I opened the utility room door and Jennet Hayes was there. She smiled without a shadow of embarrassment.

'"Well, I will be off now, Steve. See you!"

'I can't recall the words, but at least Steve was honest with me. We have not been as close as he would wish since the start of this pregnancy and he is fed up, really fed up.'

She subsided again into that dreadful silent, shaking sobbing. She had told her story, bleak and starkly simple.

I had never seen Paul Lucas angry before – but he was now. He stood up suddenly, running his fingers through his thick grey hair.

'You poor child!' he exclaimed. 'I think that your husband needs to be reminded that he is here to do the work of this establishment, not follow his own desires. Helen, Gisela has made some chocolate cake – please could you make some tea? I will be back in a few minutes...' and he strode from the room.

Everyone was shocked. Helen, with her unfailing poise, swept into the kitchen of Paul's flat – the whole world felt safe in her presence, I thought to myself. Ash was white and quiet, eyes downcast. I longed to feel his arms around me, blocking out the world; but then he looked up and his gaze locked with mine – he was troubled. Was the tragedy being played out this evening just too similar to our own situation; or was he just empathising with Lizzie and Steve? He was closer to both than I had ever been. Even Mark was quiet – totally out of his comfort zone. He started to flick through a 'Country Life' magazine. I just could not stay in the room with Mark and Ash in this charged atmosphere and followed Paul into the small drawing room next to the library. I don't know what I expected to see, but his intense agitation was surprising. So too were his words:

'You think I am so bloody holy, Kate. I really am not! I could knock Steve Jenner into the middle of next week for what he is doing to his gentle, patient wife!' He paced to and fro, breathing deeply and clearly trying to regain his composure. Eventually, after several minutes, he turned and smiled his almost boyish grin. 'That's better! I can be the priest again!'

The rest of the evening dealt superficially with the topic of study for the session. All our minds were preoccupied with the story that Lizzie had shared with us. We were subdued as we bade each other goodnight. Ash avoided my eyes. 'Let me give you a lift home, Lizzie,' he offered gently.

Mark and I drove back to Knight's Manor in silence. He had recovered his thoughtless good humour.

'Cautionary tale, eh love?'

I just couldn't respond.

Ash put the book down, closed his eyes and was immediately back in the middle of the desperately sad situation that had played itself out all those years ago. Yes, he had been shaken. Probably for the first time, the enormity of what he felt for Kate and what he knew she felt for him had struck him like a blow in the face. The perfect purity of their feelings for each other, the sort of love that he well knew comes only once in a lifetime had, for a moment, been distorted as he had regarded it through the eyes of others. It was from that evening, he remembered wryly, that he had been determined that his relationship with Kate would not work itself out as a sordid, tawdry affair.

Did he have the energy to continue to read? He knew the outcomes of this complex story, knew in his head the twists and turns in the lives of the small group of people who lived and loved and suffered together over three decades ago. Could he bear to see the open, bold script of the woman who was life and light to him, to read her expressions of love for him that still shone from the pages after all these years? Almost as if in a dream, he turned the page and saw the gift tag he had fixed to Kate's Christmas present that year. It said simply: *'To Kate from Ash x'*. It had been a book of Donne's poetry.

15 January 1983

Well, Christmas is past again and Mark is very buoyant! He has been offered the promise of a partnership with his present firm. I expected him to be absolutely full of this and himself tonight, but to my surprise he is quieter than usual.

Our first meeting of 1983! Steve has been much chastened since Paul's 'conversation' with him. Lizzie just cannot get much more heavily pregnant: it's impossible! Helen delivered her perfectly wrapped and presented Christmas presents and is calmly entering the New Year with its challenges of university for Jane and a new school for Ella.

The session tonight was most unusual in that Mark had prepared for it! He had read, thought and talked to me about the theme for discussion. I was deeply surprised about his approach to this. Perhaps Paul's belief, that the energy created by the group would inspire its less committed members, was actually true!

Mark was slightly late for the session and we had all found seats in the warmth of the beautiful library, arranging ourselves in a semicircle around the fire. We had already started preliminary discussions, but Mark soon joined in with comments and the outcomes of his research. I became aware that Paul Lucas was gently drawing him into the centre of the discussion, encouraging him and affirming his opinions. For the first time in this group, Mark was genuinely holding centre stage. The amount of preparation he had invested in researching this question was clearly evident and, watching and listening to him, I could almost see again that energetic attractive man I had married. The other members of the group were similarly enrapt and listened with genuine respect.

Paul smiled gently. This meant a lot to him. As the evening drew to a close he warmly congratulated Mark on his efforts:

'Mark, I think we are all agreed that you have led our thoughts and the direction of our discussions tonight. It is really affirming that the acute business brain that you employ

so effectively in legal argument has revealed to you some deep philosophical truths which are immensely valuable to us all. Thank you!'

I expected to see the usual grin of self-satisfaction appear on Mark's face. But no. Instead of this he started to sob – quite unashamedly.

'I'm just not good enough for this,' he muttered. 'Not good enough for anything...'

Paul looked at me, clearly expecting me to go and comfort my husband; but to my horror I just couldn't move. I was embarrassed and ashamed of this display of emotion from someone who criticised and mocked emotion in others. Paul frowned slightly and was about to say something, when my lovely, empathetic Helen stepped forward to Mark and, laying her hand lightly on his shoulder said, 'Come my friend. We all have our limits!'

We drove home in silence. What was happening to me?

Reading once again Kate's account of Marks's emotional breakdown, a wave of absolute misery washed over Ash. How he had wanted to snatch her by the hand and lead her away from what was obviously absolute torture! He closed his tired eyes tightly and recaptured the way in which she had withdrawn into herself at the emotion that Mark had displayed. It was like watching a delicate flower curl into itself, when it couldn't physically face cold rain and wind. He could recall with absolute clarity the smooth curve of her cheek, as she lowered her eyes and shut them tight against all that was happening around her. Her long thick lashes drew him in – to touch, to stroke, to comfort. How had he ever let her go?

He picked up the gossamer-thin scarf that Kate had embroidered before the Beltane party, which had made him hate Mark with a violence that frightened him. He lightly touch the embroidered flowers of Ashward and delicately traced the aspects of the natural world that was so dear to her. He knew at the time that she felt the difference between their ages, but she was so naïve, so unspoiled, that her timelessness had entirely filled his mind and soul. He had wanted her then with a pure, life-consuming passion; never a tawdry one. She was so precious that he had been terrified of putting a foot wrong.

21 February 1983

If I had known what revelations this group was going to uncover, perhaps I would not have been brave enough to join it!

Tonight it was Paul's turn. Mark was working late and I had walked over to Ashward Priory by myself as the evenings were, finally, starting to lengthen. I had shared a thought with the group that I had about how all that is best and beautiful in life can be mimicked by what we call Evil; how things which seem sound can actually be fallacious and rotten. This reflection – deep for me – had been brought about by pruning an oak tree. I had noticed the tree had a mixture of acorns and oak apples and the startling difference between the fertility and promise of the acorn and the disease and threat held within the oak apple struck me forcibly. Paul had been unusually quiet during the evening and, equally unusually, he suggested that we should end the evening with sherry, rather than the tea or hot chocolate with which we usually ended our meetings.

There was a lull in the conversation and Paul said quietly, 'I have to share something with you.' We all looked up politely, some smiling. Paul took a deep breath. 'Your words, Kate, about what appears to be sound being, in fact, rotten, stirred me deeply. When I inherited this vast pile I almost had a breakdown. There were twelve separate floors on different levels, fifty-two principal rooms and 365 windows. Yes,' he laughed bitterly, 'a physical representation of the months, weeks and days of the year had been created by my ancestors. It was as if the earls of Ashward had tried to capture Time and recreate it here within their own control. Lords and masters of all they surveyed, including Time!' Paul stood up suddenly and walked to the window. He looked out, but I knew he wasn't seeing the black, dark night nor hearing the buffeting wind around the tall windows.

'When I came here I was overwhelmed. Not only did I have 30,000 acres of land to manage but, somehow, I had to meet the death duties that had to be paid; and had to manage the house as well as overseeing the spiritual well-being of my parishioners. I took up my duties as priest of the parish immediately but, as 'Lord of the Manor', I did nothing for three years. I struggled over what to do with the vast legacy which had been left to me. My uncle had amassed a huge library, with manuscripts and books dating back over a thousand years. The monks at Faversham Priory had been charged with the task of writing the local newsletter of its time – the Anglo-Saxon Chronicle – and, as Ash knows, some immensely powerful stories are told in this.

'It appeared that there had been an Anglo-Saxon settlement on this very site. There was a legend that priceless treasure was hidden either in or under this house, or within the park surrounding it. I read about the legend as it grew and became more detailed through the centuries. One of my most interesting ancestors, Paul Ashward, had become almost obsessed with it and used to wander around the estate, especially at night, muttering and chanting to himself. It is said that his favourite walk was down by the lake, across the bridge that leads into the wood, where I believe he now has his last resting place.' He involuntarily shivered.

'I am ashamed to say that I became too interested in this fable. I walked and sought for this treasure when I should have been concentrating on what to do with the property that had been left to me. I ignored the pressing needs around me – for too long – and became lost in dreams of what could be, instead of what actually surrounded me. The idea of setting up the spiritual well-being centre here had just started to grow in my mind. But I couldn't see how I could afford to finance all this, plus the restoration of this huge pile, as well as settle the devastating death duties that were being demanded of me. If I could but find the legendary "treasure", I believed that I could put it to the best, most positive use.

'And then, one night, I learnt what that "treasure" was. It was a dark November evening and I was working in the library, addressing once again the nigh-on impossible task of classifying the priceless collection of books and documents that I had inherited. It had been cold and windy all day, and the wind had increased almost to gale force as the light faded.

The huge shutters on the library windows rattled, even moved slightly, as the house met the full force of the blast.

'But even the loud rattling of the shutters was drowned by a thunderous knocking on the front door. Gisela was upstairs, cooking our evening meal, and the children at that time were away at school. Since we do not have a butler – he smiled wryly – it was left to me to answer the incessant banging on the door.

'I opened the front door with difficulty, holding it firmly against the tugging of the howling gale that enveloped the house. To my surprise, Margaret Smith stood on the steps with another figure – a figure that I had seen before but in a very different context.' Paul stopped and passed his hands characteristically through his thick white hair. *'You will find this hard to believe, but it is absolutely true. The figure was abnormally tall – all of seven feet – cloaked in a black, deeply hooded, garment. In fact the hood was so deep that it fell forward, obscuring the face of this striking person.*

'As soon as the door was opened they walked through and, without invitation, made straight for the library. I followed, feeling angry and, I must admit, rather foolish, that they led and I followed in my own home. Once we were all in the library, Margaret closed the door. The tall black figure stood in front of the fireplace, his back to the flames, which seemed to reach out and dance around his very person. His height and bulk blocked the firelight and the whole room seemed suddenly darker, diminished by the power of his presence. Yet it was not he who spoke, but Margaret.

'"Our leader says that he knows what is in your mind for the future of this place. He warns you that if you do not leave

our people alone, he will utterly ruin your plans. Your centre for the spiritual well-being of humankind will never exist if you interfere with what takes precedence here. The power that lies in this place – that, over the generations, the common herd has trivialised by calling it "treasure" – is the black energy over which your house is built. Blackness feeds from blackness. The light can never prevail in this place unless a sacrifice is willingly made, even though it is the antithesis of what the person who sacrifices desires. Listen and remember these words."

'*Margaret then opened the Library door, inclining her head slightly as the dark figure swept through; and they both disappeared into the night.*

'*I had not uttered a word. I felt violated and exposed – and in my own home...*'

For the first time ever, I heard Paul's voice falter. He had turned away from us, lost in his thoughts, his fists clenched tightly.

'*And so, "the treasure" is something abhorrent – a terrible destructive power that wipes out goodness and joy. I had spent fruitless months searching for something that is the antithesis of everything I believe in. What a fool I was! What a fool I am!*

'*About a week later Ralph Woodville drove over for tea. It was 1960 and it seemed that the country was at last awakening from post-war difficulties and was becoming a land of milk and honey, the promised land...*

'*Ralph and I have always been exceptionally frank with each other. That afternoon we had talked trivia for some time when Ralph looked up and said, in those tight, clipped tones of his:*

'"Paul, if you do not attend to this mouldering pile soon, it will fall down. I strongly suspect that you have dry rot."

'"What!" I gasped. "Why haven't you told me about this before?"

'"Paul, I have. You are just so wrapped up in histories and mysteries that you are deaf and blind to what those who care for you are saying. Come with me. I need to show you something."

'We went up the beautiful sweeping staircase that, in those days, faced one on entering the   seventeenth-century part of the Priory. On the second floor, Ralph opened one of the small guest bedrooms. Walking slowly over to the window shutter, he opened it and, taking from his pocket a small pointed knife, started to scrape away at the wood surround of the window. It fell to dust. We repeated this exercise in several rooms and, in each case, the dusty disintegration and the tell-tale spreading web of dry rot were only too painfully apparent.

'"You have closed your eyes to this, Paul," said Ralph, not reprovingly, but sadly. "And now I fear it is too late to save this beautiful piece of history. Your foolish dreams of treasure have destroyed this."

'To cut a painfully long story short, Ralph's firm did a complete survey of the house and identified the parts that were beyond repair. These were taken down and a mutilated, maimed vestige of the once-magnificent Ashward Priory now remains. Have you read the commentaries about the "thoughtless destruction of one of the most historically important buildings in England"? They are all true. It was through my neglect, through becoming obsessed by what appears to be, rather than what actually is, that this happened.

'So, when people praise my priestly sermons, my selfless Christian work, my writing, what they do not know is that I *was seduced by a fable. I am a fraud. Sacrifice was needed, not self-indulgence. If I had worked ceaselessly, put duty before daydreaming, who knows – the house may have been saved. And not only that, I have never, as some here know well, really addressed the question of witchcraft being rife in my parish. I could not forget that direct threat to my ministry and work here. Both are fatally flawed. Who would know what I could have achieved if I had not been such a coward?'*

What a story! Paul's bitter comments about the opinions of his parishioners, his less than perfect life, the sadness that lurked just below the surface – all these things now came into clearer perspective.

'Please don't try to comfort me,' he concluded. 'That is impossible. I just needed to be honest with you – at last, after all these years, to be honest. And now, forgive me if I bid you goodnight.' And, with that, he rose abruptly and left the room.

The words rang hollowly across the decades: *'unimaginable sacrifice... a sacrifice that is willingly made, even though it is the antithesis of what the person who sacrifices desires.'* But really, thought Ash, did it matter? Did sacrifice ever really work?

Inexorably the diary went on. He knew what the next entry would be.

6 March 1983

Helen!

The single word entry under the date echoed like a cry of despair down the years.

Chapter 33

1983

I had walked back to Knight's Manor after Paul's revelations, feeling confused and disappointed. I suppose that I felt that the man I had come to admire deeply as a spiritual mentor actually had feet of clay; and I was trying to assimilate the latest, rather more human, aspects of the friend that I had idealised. It was bitterly cold and the wind started to whip sleet into my face as I followed the track across Ashward park. I was wet through and absolutely chilled to the bone when I reached, at last, my wonderful, warm kitchen. Mark was sitting morosely by the Aga, whisky in hand.

'How was the holy of holies tonight then?' he said sarcastically. His brief evening of honesty and doubt was long forgotten. He had not been to our meetings since he had so uncharacteristically shown his vulnerability.

My teeth were chattering uncontrollably as I tried to answer.

'So cold!' I shivered and ran as quickly as my frozen limbs would carry me up into the bathroom, meaning to run the deepest, hottest bath imaginable. I turned on the tap and only lukewarm water fizzled out.

'Sorry dear!' sneered my husband. 'I just got a bit damp walking in from the car. Thought I deserved a bath after my day in the big smoke.'

I just couldn't get warm. I rubbed myself vigorously with a rough towel and changed into a lambswool jumper and fleece, thick socks and tracksuit bottoms. I was still shivering as I walked downstairs.

'You look attractive!' grunted Mark. 'Trying to seduce me are you?'

'I'm trying to get warm,' I replied quietly.

It seemed that the quieter I was, the more provoking and shocking Mark tried to be.

'What were the revelations of St Paul tonight then?' he asked.

'Actually, Paul did reveal quite a lot about himself,' I answered quietly. 'About mistakes he had made and how he wishes he had not.'

'My God!' exclaimed Mark irreverently. 'I wish I had been there. So the old fox is human after all?'

Fighting back my tears, I said, 'I'm going to bed – in the nursery.'

'In the nursery… In the nursery…' Mark mimicked. 'Some bloody hope that we will every fill *the nursery* with your holier than thou attitude. You would freeze the balls off a bronze statue, you are so frigid.' And he poured himself another whisky.

Not surprisingly I caught a really bad chill and, to my surprise, this turned into full-blown flu. I ached in every bone. I wanted to sleep all the time. I lost my appetite. Ash and Helen were amazing but, unsurprisingly, Mark had just shrugged his shoulders when I told him how ill I felt.

'Oh pull yourself together, for God's sake,' he had said with distaste, as he paid a cursory visit to my small, warm bolthole.

My friends walked the dogs, they did my shopping, Helen even did my cleaning, even though she herself had a cleaner.

'Mm, I don't quite know what to do with all the dirt that the dogs bring in, Kate,' she told me anxiously. Her kitchen floor was never less than immaculate and she regarded the large muddy paw prints with absolute horror.

Gradually I improved, but it seemed to take for ever. Then one night – Mark was away again, this time in the States – Helen called round. This was, in itself, really unusual because it was 'James' food-preparation time'. Many times, the faithfulness and duty of my friend struck me. I knew that she did not love James, that she merely tolerated him. But day after day she did what was expected, what her position in this tight-knit society demanded.

We sat companionably together as the grey afternoon darkened to evening.

'Kate, I need to talk to you – really seriously.'

Immediately my old habit of feeling guilty kicked in. What had I done to offend or upset my dear friend? I looked quickly at her and replied:

'Of course.'

'You know Ash and I have spent a lot of time together over the past couple of weeks?'

I nodded. 'And I can't thank you enough, Helen. I simply do not know what I would have done without you both.'

'Do you know there is not an occasion when I have met him that Ash has not talked of you. He brings you into every conversation – even the weather!' she smiled gently. 'It is pretty obvious he adores you, Kate.'

This was absolutely not what I had been expecting. I stood up quickly and walked to the kitchen window, from which I watched the clouds scudding across the sky in the bitter easterly wind. I said nothing. Soon Helen stood up and came quietly over to me, placing her hands gently on my shoulders.

'Please sit down again. I am not going to express disgust, or condemn you, but I do need to talk to you.'

We sat down together, and she moved the chair from the other side of the Aga next to mine.

'Nearly twenty years ago, I had made up my mind to leave James. We had been married for several years and the tedium of no conversation, mechanical sex and no creative discussion had driven me to the brink of making this decision. I researched the sort of divorce settlement I would get, but it was woefully small, as we then had no children and had been married only a relatively short time in terms of apportioning an estate. I couldn't speak to my mother. She had been so pathetically happy that I had at last found financial security, that she set aside the intellectual and personal limitations of my husband and tried always to praise him whenever she could. But she knew – oh yes, she understood.

'I found a small cottage that I could afford on the outskirts of Maidstone and put down a deposit on it. But I was distraught and deeply unsettled about the huge step I was about to take. I had always trusted Paul Lucas and felt that he was the only person I could talk to honestly. And so, next time we came down to Ashward, I drove over to see him and opened my heart.

'You know Paul, Kate – at least as well as I do. He sat and listened and looked quietly at me as I went through my reasons for making the decision I had. He let me talk and talk. Then he sat without saying a word for minutes! I thought he would never break the silence. But eventually he did.

'"There are more ways to love than one, Helen," he said gently. "I love Gisela dearly, but I love my children more. Every relationship has its limitations. Gisela is impatient with my academic thinking, with my short-sightedness – both metaphorically and actually – and we have had stormy times. But if you put aside personal gratification and if," he looked candidly at me "you do your duty to your family and remain true to your marriage vows – the public promises that you made in the presence of witnesses – you will, I promise you, you will be blessed."

'I knew that what he said was right. I had known it in my heart – even during the search for the cottage that would have been mine, a place of peace and beauty. But I now knew what I had to do.

'Kate, it was hard, so hard, but I rang the agents and withdrew from the rental of the little cottage and I threw myself wholeheartedly into my bleak marriage. I reminded myself of the blessings of status, and security for myself and my mother, and the stimulus of eventually inheriting the Ashward estate and managing it. Just five months later I became pregnant with Jane, and Ella followed. My love for my girls is overwhelming. I would, literally, do anything for them. Without question they are the "blessing" that Paul promised would be mine.

'Now I have to come to the most difficult part of what I have to say to you. You must not leave Mark for Ash. You too must do your duty. And then, as the years go on, you and I will look at each other in the knowledge that we have overcome temptation and that we have woven and made beautiful our part of the huge tapestry of life that is being created here in Ashward. Mark knows that you have stopped loving him. He is calling out for love from you. He has pushed himself too far in terms of his work because he feels that he no longer has a role in your life. When he broke down at our group meeting, it was painfully obvious that he is still emotionally immature. He needs his 'toys' – his Rolex watch, his car, his house – as substitutes for your love. I beg you,' and, shockingly, because Helen never implored, hardly ever showed deep emotion, my dear friend knelt in front of me, taking my hands in hers, 'think carefully about what I have said. Ash is very young, only five years older than my own daughter. When he is thirty, in his absolute prime, you will be forty-two – probably past childbearing. When he is fifty, you will be sixty-two – a pensioner, when he is probably at the height of his career. Kate, it won't work. You will step aside from your duty and your fate into a relationship that will last only a short time. Please my dear, dear friend, listen to me.' For the second time in our friendship I saw that she was crying. And I was too.

We stayed quietly together for what seemed like hours. Certainly the last light had left the sky when my friend stood up and smoothed her elegant skirt.

'I love you, Kate. I always will,' she said gently, kissing my forehead.

And then she was gone.

Usually I would have put on a coat and taken my dogs for a long walk to clear my mind. But I didn't want to get pneumonia, so I paced the kitchen, going through everything that Helen had said. Thoughts kept repeating themselves like a train on a circular track – round and round and round they circled, getting nowhere.

I just didn't think I could do what she asked. I had held the thought of Ash like an oasis in my heart for nearly a year. This thought had inspired and comforted me, as I finally believed that all the characteristics I had always longed for in a partner had come together in this beautiful, quiet, gentle man. To set this aside, I thought, would break my heart.

I spent a sleepless night. There was a bitter frost and the stars shone like jewels over the dark countryside. I thought of the Wheatleys' little girl; I thought of my miscarriage; of Helen's devotion to duty; Estelle and Geoff's loveless marriage. So much sadness, so much tragedy...

As dawn came, I knew that I just had to get out of the house. I flung myself out of bed and put on as many jumpers as I could, jeans with leggings underneath for extra warmth, boots, gloves and hat and slipped out into the bitter dawn with my faithful dogs.

The road was like glass – the dogs' paws skidded as they tried to run on the black, icy surface. I laughed to see their puzzlement as they literally ran on the spot in their haste to explore the hedges and fields.

We walked down the lane towards Fortune Farm. I didn't want to see Ash, but just to be near him. As we came close to his parents' house, I heard the lowing of the cattle as his father moved them into the milking shed. I smiled as I thought that

316

sometimes, even though he had showered, Ash smelled of cattle feed, but was not aware of it! Over the intervening thirty years no-one has ever realised that that smell takes me back to the low, white weather-boarded farmhouse and Ash's cool contained beauty. It seemed impossible that this routine farming task should be running along smoothly when there was such turmoil in my mind. Enough! I had to return to Knight's Manor. I was freezing.

Even my dogs seemed glad to be back indoors again. I actually felt hungry for once and I turned up the Aga and beat together eggs to scramble. Automatically, my mind still fully occupied with the conversation I had had with my dear friend the previous night, I put the kettle on the hob and bread in the toaster. Suddenly there was the usual volley of barks that heralded someone's approach and I saw that Jacob Wheatley had appeared at the back door. His figure was silhouetted against the morning light and I could not see his expression clearly.

'Come in, Jacob!' I called. 'Tea?'

He did not respond with his usual easy jocularity, but plodded ponderously across to one of the chairs that flanked the Aga. I saw his face then. It was ashen. He sat down, expressionless.

'Can you take a blow?' he asked.

'What do you mean? What on earth has happened?'

'I was just listening to the local news. They said a woman has been killed just outside Tentersley. They gave her name as Helen Woodville and said that she was forty-three. She was taking her husband to the station. He survived without injury.'

317

He repeated verbatim what he had heard. He seemed incapable of relating the facts to reality.

I shook my head in disbelief. How could this be? Less than twelve hours earlier she had sat exactly where Jacob was sitting. I closed my eyes and her vibrant loveliness seemed still to be with me.

'No, Jacob, no! This just cannot be. There must be a mistake.'

'There isn't,' he said tonelessly. 'There are police at the Manor House.'

I sat down suddenly on the other chair and I remember thinking that this was impossible; this could just not have happened. My mouth was so dry that I found it hard to speak, but I managed to whisper eventually: 'Sorry Jacob, could you let me have some space please?'

The old man stood up and came slowly across to me, placing a hand on my shoulder.

'I am so sorry. Why do these things happen?' And, walking slowly to the door, shaking his head sadly, he left me to try to come to terms with the absolute blank wall in my mind. I just could not take it in. I remember sitting for hours mechanically stroking the dogs, not able to move or speak, or do anything. In those hours I experienced in my imagination the friendship that Helen and I would have continued to share together. The little things we did habitually – had done habitually – walking, drinking coffee, shopping, laughing. But I thought too of the things that now would never be: the children she would not be godmother to; the fortieth birthday weekend that I had already started to think about – just her and me, somewhere sparkling and lovely – Paris maybe. I thought of how we would not grow old together, supporting each other as we found grey hair and wrinkles and… all the silly minutiae that make human life special and precious. All the tiny little things that make up the sort of friendship that you encounter maybe once in a lifetime – if you are lucky.

Chapter 34

2014

Closing the thirty year old diary abruptly, Ash knew he had to have a drink. He put on the kettle and looked sightlessly out of the grubby window which looked over the car workshop and yard. Dropping in the teabag and mindlessly stirring as he poured in the boiling water, he remembered every heart-wrenching detail.

After the milking had been finished on that terrible morning he had, inevitably, been drawn to the woman who had become the centre of his world. He had driven slowly down the treacherously icy lane towards Knight's Manor, anticipating as always the warmth of her welcome, the generosity of her smile and the brilliance of her eyes as she would greet him. No need to hurry. They had their lives in front of them to learn about each other, to cherish, to discover each other. He knew that she did not love Mark. He felt desperately sorry for the man, but was constantly puzzled by his total lack of support or respect for Kate. Ash had passed through the stages of excitement, disbelief, deep concern, denial and, ultimately, absolute acceptance of his relationship with Kate over the past eleven months. He knew now that he would love her, quite simply, for ever.

After thirty years he could still recapture the joy of that slow drive. And the abject misery that followed.

Chapter 35

1983

Haven driven over the cattle grid, Ash walked, smiling with happiness, to the back door. He often looked through the window into the kitchen, hoping to catch the woman he loved unawares, because he loved her every aspect. But concern gripped him as he saw her sitting, completely motionless, by the Aga, with her dogs' heads resting on her lap. She could have been a statue. And then he saw her face: white, colourless, expressionless.

He hammered on the door. Was she ill?

As if in a dream, Kate walked to the back door like one from whom all life had been drained. She looked at him, without speaking, her eyes introverted, blank.

'For God's sake, what's the matter?' For once he acted without restraint and pulled her strongly to him. She leant her head, without seeming to be able to prevent it, on his chest and closed her eyes.

'Are you ill? Speak to me. Please my love. What is the matter?'

'Helen,' murmured Kate. 'She is gone.'

'What do you mean? Has she had to go to London? Do we need to do something for her – for James, for the girls? What is happening?'

'She is dead. And my life is dead too. I have lost everything I hold dear. Everything that makes me, defines me… I don't know what to do, Ash.'

For hours they sat there – Kate in the chair by the Aga, he kneeling in front of her, his arms wrapped around her, holding her, loving her, until his legs became numb and his back ached.

Kate just couldn't speak. Words were totally inadequate to express what she was feeling. It was as if she had encountered an elemental blackness that had extinguished all life and hope. At the moment Ash was her anchor, her only support. She herself seemed dead. He was all life to her.

The day passed. Ash shook his head as he remembered. They were like a statue together. He had seen *The Pietà* by Michelangelo at St Peter's on a holiday with friends in Rome, years ago. Like that, he thought – frozen together in pain and love forever.

Eventually he thought she had fallen asleep. Stiffly, slowly, he got to his feet and, when life had returned to his limbs, he lifted her up and carried her upstairs to the nursery. Softly, gently, he moved back the bedclothes and laid her – his most precious burden – on the bed, covering her carefully, almost as if he was a parent, she the child. He lay quietly beside her, on top of the duvet, desperately wanting to impart his warmth and his energy to her exhausted body. Eventually, he remembered, he too had slept, breathing in the sweet scents of her hair, her clothes, her body.

He remembered the vague feeling of irony that he should be where he had longed to be for almost a year. Holding the woman he loved in his arms whilst she slept. But instead of passion and joy there was exhaustion and misery.

Dawn broke. It was like Spring, such a bitter contrast to the previous day. He could hear the birds singing, feel the gentle breeze blowing through the window, which Kate always opened to sleep. He looked down at her pale face. She could be dead, he had thought, so still was she.

Slowly the birdsong penetrated her deep sleep. Kate felt as if she had indeed died – or a part of her, at least, had died. Ash thought she would be confused, disoriented, but instead, she looked him directly in the eyes and said:

'We must part, my love. I love you with every atom of my being. I love your mind, I love your spirit, I love how you are, how you look...' and she lifted her hand to his face and gently, so gently, stroked the outline of his strong, high cheekbones, the curve of his jaw, his curtain of dark hair. 'Everything you are, I love. But Helen made the ultimate sacrifice. She died doing her duty. Please don't try to dissuade me. I am being torn apart. I feel as if I am dying too, Ash. I will love you always – as long as I live. But this must be the end – you must go.'

And he had gone. Dazed, desperate, not hearing the birdsong so bright in the air, nor seeing the golden Spring sunshine, nor the burgeoning buds on the trees. He had not consciously registered the familiar landmarks as he had driven back to his parents' farm and gone out, like an automaton, to help his father, in the comforting routine of milking and feeding the beasts.

He had managed at lunch, he remembered, to eat a very little and then went to his room and crossed to his desk under the window. Here he unlocked the top drawer where he kept the poems Kate had written to him, the Ashward Diary they shared, some dried flowers – so little – so few reminders of the life-changing encounter that he had had with her. In the back corner of the drawer was a little blue leather box. It was her birthday present. He had had it specially made in Canterbury: a plain silver band, because she never wore gold, with words engraved around it:

My Beginning and My End

TIME IS

RACHEL & ROSIE

Chapter 36

2014

2 February 2014 – her thirtieth birthday! For a few minutes, after her alarm had gone off, Rachel lay with her eyes shut, hugging the thought to her. She couldn't believe it. She had dreaded the day for months, almost for years. It seemed such a milestone, the gateway to true maturity, and she felt so unready!

When she finally opened her eyes to bright winter sunshine, the first thing she did was to look closely in her magnifying mirror, turning her lovely face this way and that as she looked at the fine lines that had developed around her eyes. Her mother had laughed when she had expressed her concern about these: 'But darling, they are laughter lines! You show your character on your face – it tells the story of your life.'

Rachel had smiled back into her mother's eyes and it was almost like looking in a mirror. They were an unusual piercing light blue, the iris surrounded by a darker band of colour. She loved her mum and in just two short hours she would be meeting her off the train from Brighton to see an exhibition, do some shopping and then have dinner in their favourite restaurant in Covent Garden.

She thought about her mother's words – that your face tells the story of your life – and thought about her mother's face.

What story did it tell? Her eyes were almost as bright as ever; hair carefully highlighted; lines yes, but kept at bay by the most expensive face products she could afford. She did yoga, swam most days, and gardened frenetically in the perfect little plot behind her gem of a cottage, and was still an effortless size ten. She seemed so composed, so 'together'. But sometimes, when sitting quietly, Rachel could see shadows cross her mother's face as unbidden memories interfered with the focussed drive and professionalism that she had had to develop since she and Rachel's sister, Rosie, were children. And always, her mother was, 'Fine darling! Just thinking about work.'

It had been the three of them for so long now. Rachel had been seven when her mother had left her father, on Rosie's fifth birthday. They had had a desperate couple of years, living in rented accommodation. Rachel still remembered her mother's determination to forge a new life for them all, since her father resolutely refused to give them more than the very basic minimum demanded by the divorce solicitors. She remembered one evening when her mother was really angry. Rachel had been very young and was aware only that her mother had received an official-looking letter. 'I'll show him!' her mother had vowed. And, thought Rachel, she had.

Ironically, her mother had chosen to take a law degree and had become a solicitor, just as their father had been for some years before the divorce. But whereas Mark, their father, was a commercial lawyer and highly respected barrister, Kate, their mother, had become a human rights lawyer. Rachel knew that often their mother worked for no, or little fee, because she felt so passionately the position of 'the underdog'.

I watched the patchwork of grey-green fields flicker past the train windows. February is such a bleak month and I smiled because, when nature it at its quietest, its most dormant, both my beautiful girls were born.

I reflected on how a story never really ends. As one part draws to its conclusion, another starts, with an expanding cast of characters, linking with the past and foreshadowing the future. The same, or similar, themes echo and re-echo across the ages: the great themes of birth and death, good and evil, sacrifice, everlasting friendship and transformational love.

I thought of the conversation that I would have to have with Rachel this evening. It was going to be difficult, but I had run my family of three so closely – ever since I had left Mark over twenty years ago now. I had probably shared too much with both the girls as they grew up, but the result was a bond that went beyond that of the usual mother/daughter relationship.

As always on the girls' birthdays, I thought of their birth. Rachel's had been so protracted, so painful, seeming to reflect the loss and pain of what had happened to me just months before. I conceived Rachel in May, just two months after I had thought that my world had actually ended. Sex with Mark was mechanical and had no vestige of love in it, but at that time I had felt like a zombie, just a body with no emotion. Quite simply I didn't care what happened to me and if that included Mark using me as he wished, then so be it.

As the dreary winter landscape flickered past the train windows, I recalled the day after Helen's death, as I had on countless occasions, with disconcerting clarity.

Chapter 37

1983

When Mark came home from his business trip he was visibly shocked at what had happened. By this stage in our relationship he had become almost totally unemotional but, at the news of Helen's death, he squared his shoulders and turned swiftly away as he poured himself a whisky.

I knew that we were both fully awake that night as we lay listening to a pair of owls calling to each other in the trees outside. The moon was bright and the night full of stars, clear and very cold. I had replayed again and again in my mind the events of the past couple of days. I had quite simply lost the two people who meant the most to me in the world: the man I loved and my dearest friend. Looking back, I suppose that I was in deep shock, but at the time my brain just seemed paralyzed. I felt numb and unable to do even the simplest thing. I turned for the hundredth time towards the radio alarm clock with the illuminated figures. It was half-past two: the time when that dreadful dream used to visit me when I was a child; the moment when Ash and I were transformed in the Beltane fire dance. This night was endless.

Suddenly the phone shrilled loud in the stillness of the night. As I suspected, Mark had been as awake as I had. He leapt immediately out of bed and ran quickly down to the hall. I heard him announce our number and then listen for what must have been about thirty seconds.

'Right, Paul. I will be along immediately. See you outside the church.'

What was happening now?

'James Woodville has disappeared with a shotgun. Paul Lucas is organising a search party. You stay here.'

Quite honestly, I was incapable of doing anything else. How much more misery was going to play out? I lay thinking that only twenty-four hours previously I had slept in Ash's arms; and I relived again the absolute desolate conviction that I had had, and its consequences. Round and round chased my thoughts. I recalled with heart-breaking clarity the friendship that bound Helen and I together, and the love that Ash and I had shared – still shared. I was absolutely convinced that this would remain always. I must have dozed off eventually, because my next conscious thought was hearing Mark's loud shouting and clapping to call the dogs back to the house. It was full daylight.

I slipped on my dressing gown and went down to the kitchen.

'It's OK. We found him. He was in the woods opposite Meadow Farm. He is all right. He was sitting on a fallen log, howling like an animal. He had put down his shotgun.'

'Poor James! Where is he now?'

'With his parents. The doctor saw him about an hour ago and sedated him. He is in shock.'

I sat down by the Aga, thinking once again of how Ash had knelt in this spot, just in front of where I sat, holding me, for hours and hours. Unconsciously I gently reached my hands forward.

'Would you like some tea?'

'Please.'

I seemed incapable of doing anything and for once, Mark, if not sympathetic, at least did not ridicule me. But it was as if he just did not know how to behave in the face of deep emotion. He made me tea, then announced that he was off to play an early squash game. He showed no sign of being concerned about leaving me alone.

I just sat motionless for hours, still in my dressing gown, my body immobile, but my mind frenetic.

A knock on the door cut across my mental turmoil. It was Paul and he looked terrible: white, unshaven, looking every one of his sixty-odd years. He didn't say a word, just gave me a big, fatherly hug.

It was the catalyst I needed. I just started to cry and cry – not speaking, just sobbing out my inarticulate misery.

'Kate, I can't begin to understand how you feel. I know how you loved Helen. We all did. She was an amazing woman who inspired and will continue to inspire us as long as we live. She would not wish you to be like this. You know she would not. Just think what she would do and say if she were here with us now. She would smile that beautiful smile of hers, lay her hand on your arm and say something along the lines of, 'Come, my friend, this will not do. There is life to be lived, people to be cared for…' Paul's voice faltered and I saw that he too was blinking back tears.

'You are right, Paul. That is exactly the sort of thing she would have said. But there is something else too, Paul.' And I told him that I had lost not one, but two people, who literally meant the world to me.

He nodded and listened carefully.

'I knew that you and Ash were close, Kate. I spoke to him last year about you. Mentioning your name was like lighting a flame in his eyes. I saw him this morning and suspected that something was wrong…'

'What? Is he all right? Why did you see him?'

'He joined the search party.' Paul stopped and considered carefully what he was about to say. 'He told me that he is leaving Ashward. He is going to work in London for a music company. They offered him a job, months ago, but he wouldn't commit himself, even though the offer was very attractive. He told me that he felt that he couldn't leave Ashward just at the present time. I know why now. The job promises everything that he could possibly be looking for: real prospects of promotion, foreign travel, even living abroad for lengthy periods. He intended to leave at ten this morning.'

'I see.'

'I must go my dear. Be careful.'

It was now ten-thirty.

Outside it seemed to me that the whole world had changed. It seemed quite empty. The abundant life that I had experienced over the past year seemed to me quite extinguished. Never again would I discover Helen picking wild flowers for me; nor Ash striding towards me with all the promise of gentle words, loving laughter and deep understanding. I didn't know how I could bear it.

***

The framework of our lives in Ashward remained, but the tapestry of our relationships had been roughly torn apart and those remaining had to fight hard to patch and mend the destruction.

The main change for me, as the days, weeks and months rolled relentlessly by, was the study group. Of course this ended. It had been changed and spoiled beyond repair. Lizzie had left Steve. Helen was dead. Ash was gone. And I was empty. But my visits to Paul still continued, although our friendship had changed radically. I no longer hero-worshipped him as I had before that evening when he had admitted his fundamental weakness in failing to challenge the grip of Evil within his parish. A nagging thought at the back of my mind was whether Helen would still be here if he had been stronger. My fondness for him remained, however, and I still valued the intellectual conversation that we inevitably had together.

It was as if Ash had never existed. No one heard from him. I was not sufficiently close to his parents to ask them about his whereabouts or his well-being. There were no social media in those days: no Internet, no Facebook to research and check how someone was.

Ralph and Rebecca withdrew significantly from society. Rebecca had always been reserved; but Ralph was now only seen at church on Sundays.

The opportunity for Mark to invest more energy and thought into our relationship was missed. He continued exactly as he always had. I saw him seldom and we shared so little together. It seemed to me that he had sex with me only when he absolutely needed to: there was no tenderness.

And so time went on. The bitter Spring moved seamlessly into early Summer and I had to face anniversaries that mocked me with the joy and beauty that had been – only a short year previously. May Day came and passed with memories of the timeless, ethereal beauty of the ballad that had been sung and the elemental dance, when it seemed that Ash and I had moved as one. The fire pit that Mark had dug in the woodland remained as a scar, but was rapidly being hidden by the emotionless and inexorable rhythms of nature: ferns and flowers filled and hid the unsightly black rectangle.

I was dreading Midsummer Day. I knew that it would be impossible to forget my time with Ash in the ancient hay field full of cut grass and flowers, and his unforgettable words to me. Almost mechanically, as I left Knight's Manor that morning to walk the dogs, I made my way to Barrow Farm, to the secluded oval field where we had laughed and talked and he had told me that he loved me. I had felt a bit unwell when I had got up that morning, really queasy, but hoped that the fresh air would settle the feeling of sickness. It didn't. It got worse and became so bad that I actually had to stop walking and sit down. I tried to continue – I think I had some idea that I needed to see whether the flowers that Ash had picked for me were still growing in that fragrant field. I did just make it to the field when I knew for certain that I had to be sick – and I was.

Ugh, horrible! Just the finishing touch to spoil my perfect memory of that perfect day, exactly a year ago. I sat down on the warm, scented grass and gradually felt a bit better. What I would have done without my dear dogs, I do not know. They fussed and sat close to me, licking my hands and resting their heads on my lap. When I felt able to stand without risking another bout of sickness, almost without thinking I picked again for myself bird's foot trefoil, St John's wort and roses. As I looked at the fresh beauty of the flowers in my hand, I knew with utter conviction that, even if I slept with these flowers under my pillow for a thousand years, I would dream only of Ash, the man I loved and longed to be with.

I sat there, shredding grass, for a long time, until the sun was obscured by clouds and the day had become cooler. I still felt pretty grim and returned sadly, slowly and thoughtfully home. How different to the joy and promise of that day, just a year ago! I thought about the differences that a year could bring, that ten years could bring, a hundred years, a thousand years. I knew that even if I lived a million years I would never forget Ash.

My sickness continued. After a couple of weeks, during which I vomited daily, I thought I had better go to the doctor. There must be something wrong. I was never ill. Was this curse now going to affect my health? It had already decimated my happiness. Honestly, at that time, I don't think that I would have minded whatever happened.

'Well, Mrs Summers I have good news for you: you are pregnant.'

'What!' I sat up, totally shocked. 'Pregnant?'

'Yes. It's good news I hope?'

'Unexpected...'

The doctor went on professionally. 'I think you are about twelve weeks...'

It must have happened in that catatonic period just after Helen's death and Ash's departure.

'For morning sickness, just simply tea and a plain biscuit before you get up in the morning may well help. Ask your husband to bring you tea in bed. All husbands are only too pleased to do anything they can at a time like this.'

All husbands? Including mine? I could imagine his sarcastic comments...

'We will arrange antenatal appointments for you, of course. It is really important to attend them, especially as you are... How old are you?'

'Thirty-five.'

'Especially as you are older than the average mother. Make sure you have enough rest. And now, congratulations, and goodbye.'

I went to the Library. I just needed some time to myself. I was, once again, in shock. Pregnant? How could I be? I thought making a baby involved loving the father... Had I made a terrible mistake, believing that Ash and I could never be together? How would he react if we were together and I told him I was expecting his baby? I could imagine. How would Mark react?

That evening, after dinner I said to my husband:

'Mark, I have some really important news for you.'

'Yeah?'

'I'm pregnant.'

'What? How long?'

'Twelve weeks.'

'Well, I hope you can keep it this time.'

What? Was this all?

'I'm tired Mark. I need to sleep.'

'Ah well'. Mark made a stale joke: 'Expectorant mothers need to be cherished!'

I went to bed in the nursery.

My pregnancy was difficult. The sickness continued. Mark, despite his jokey 'declaration' that pregnant women need to be looked after, simply continued his life just as it was before. Friends from church took it in turns to come and sit with me in the evenings when Mark was late at work, or playing squash, or whatever else he did.

Chapter 38

2014 and 1984

We were getting closer to London now and the checkerboard of fields and hedges had given way to suburbia. My thoughts drifted on…

Against all the odds, less than a year after I had sacrificed my love, I had held Rachel in my arms. She was utterly beautiful. I smiled as I remembered the way that people used to stop me in the street when I was wheeling her in her red pram, ready to admire, ready to praise. And how that automatic human response changed to genuine delight when they actually saw just how beautiful she really was. The beauty has continued: people of both sexes smile as they look at her – slim, vibrant, with her father's dark thick hair and with my eyes and energy.

I really believe that Rachel brought me back to life. Who could brood on the past, when a small demanding person depended upon you for their every need? Gradually, I was able to move forward, focussing my thoughts entirely upon my love for my daughter. We used to walk daily down to the manor house and the church. I planted hundreds of snowdrops on Helen's grave and thought how she would have smiled and loved them.

Estelle and Geoff Raymond left Ashward when Estelle's heart condition suddenly worsened. Rachel was about a month old when I saw the old lady's car veer sharply into the courtyard at the back of Knight's Manor.

'Hello, Kate my dear! I have come to say goodbye. My little gingerbread cottage is all packed up and my garden is already driving me to distraction as it faces the annual invasion of weeds.'

'Oh, Estelle, I shall miss you so much!' I murmured, as I put my arms carefully around her increasingly frail body, to give her the hardest hug I dared.

Estelle smiled thoughtfully as she bent down to kiss Rachel, laying her hand gently on top of the soft, pink blanket which covered my sleeping daughter. She traced the peachy curve of Rachel's cheek with her forefinger.

'Do you remember that conversation we had when you and your delicious young friend Ash came to visit me?'

I felt the usual, almost physical, constriction in my chest at the mention of Ash's name, and nodded. Estelle looked at me shrewdly, straight in the eye.

'So you have your beautiful baby, Kate. But are you cherished? Are you loved by Mark beyond all other things? My useful life is over! Geoff and I are off to a townhouse in Chichester with a garden roughly the size of one of the flowerbeds in my cottage garden. But your life, my dear, whatever you believe, is just beginning. In the years to come, as you pass my cottage, remember that rainy Spring day, remember my words.'

Estelle's cottage was soon sold. The centuries' old apple tree, exquisite rose beds brimming with fragrant pink and cream roses, the tiny red cyclamen that flowered under the hedge in the early Spring, all were soon destroyed by a kitchen extension at least half the size of the original building and a double garage which obliterated the cottage from view.

***

Rachel had just passed her first birthday when the last key figure from those enchanted years in Kent disappeared from my life.

It was Sunday. Mark was in the States again on business and I sat in church with Rachel on my knee, entertaining her with some coloured plastic keys, which she loved to shake or chew as the mood took her. It was Whitsuntide and Paul had been speaking about the birthday of the church, about it being the time for change and opportunity. The building was pretty full as usual and I noticed that Alastair Loughland and his wife Jane were in the congregation, right at the back. I did not know them very well, only having met them a couple of times at the Manor House, so I simply smiled and nodded to them as Rachel and I came into the beautiful small building. Inevitably my eyes rested for a painful moment on the empty front pew: no poised and elegant figure with perfect hair and bright red coat, speaking easily to everyone, but smiling at me with especial warmth.

The sun filtered through the glowing stained glass windows, illuminating dust motes in the air and the wood of the rood screen and pews. I had, to be honest, not listened to Paul's sermon with all my attention: my baby was constantly the centre of my life. Right at the end of his sermon, Paul paused for an unusually long time. I raised my eyes from Rachel's face and looked at him. He looked incredibly sad, but quite resigned: his energy, his immense vitality seemed dimmed somehow.

'Some of you will know this already,' he said slowly, smiling, but without any real humour. 'I have to have an operation which will take me out of circulation for some time, maybe four to six months.'

What? What operation? Rachel immediately felt my tension and her face started to crumple – changing from smiles to tears with the speed of windblown clouds flying across the sun.

'In view of my advancing age,' – he had regained his usual composure and sense of humour – 'I have made the decision to retire from the ministry and to move with Gisela to Devon, nearer to our eldest son. As, ironically, this benefice is mine to grant, I have asked my good friend, Alastair Loughland, to step into my place. The operation is timed for the end of the month and Alastair will become priest-in-charge two weeks before that.'

There was absolute silence in the church. This was a totally unexpected announcement and, whatever the opinion of his parishioners as to his ministry, people – especially country people – find change very difficult indeed. I glanced around and saw a shadowy figure at the back of the church. Margaret Smith, at least, made her feelings very clear indeed – she was smiling.

'I would like to say,' continued Paul, 'that every day serving the people of this parish has been a complete privilege. Getting to know you, some better than others, has given me some of the most precious friendships of my life.' He paused and swallowed hard. 'This is the last time I will be preaching in this exquisite little church. And so, goodbye, and may God bless you all.' Slowly and deliberately, as if putting into the gesture every ounce of feeling that he could, he made the sign of the cross, looking more tired and grey than I had seen him since the day after Helen's death.

One final time, his black vestments billowing around his tall frame, Paul strode down the aisle of the church, looking straight ahead.

The end of an era indeed...

***

If Rachel's birth was surprising, Rosie's was nothing short of a miracle. Thinking back to that day twenty-six years earlier, when I suspected I was pregnant again, I remember thinking to myself – how? But then I recalled that on one occasion, and one only, Mark had returned late from London, clearly having had a few drinks on the train or in a club somewhere, and had come into the nursery. It had almost been a re-run of the nightmare ending to that enchanted May Day morning.

But the difference was that, when he left, without a word, to return to the main bedroom that had become his and his alone, I felt a complete and overwhelming emptiness because, this time, there would be no comfort for me. No Helen to look at me with love and to understand. No Ash to focus all his energies on changing my mood, on lifting me out of the desert of introspection into which I was drifting.

***

I got out an envelope from my handbag. I smiled at my approach to the evening ahead with Rachel. It is always good to have visual aids!

I pulled out a photograph of my two girls. Rachel's dark beauty shone from the page, in total contrast to the pale, Pre-Raphaelite loveliness of her sister. Rosie has vivid red hair, her father's eyes and gestures, but my character – almost entirely. I reflected on how the voids of my twin loss had abundantly and entirely been filled over the years: with Rosie's quick understanding and emotional empathy; and Rachel's gentle love. I remembered the last conversation that I had had with Helen, and how she had shared with me that she firmly believed that the blessing she had received from sacrificing her chance of freedom from James lay in her two daughters. I shut my eyes: if only she were still alive, how much we would have to share!

***

When I told Mark I was pregnant again, he was clearly shocked. Perhaps he too found it difficult to reconcile with the non-existent physical side of our marriage. Perhaps, I had wondered later, he believed that Rosie was not his child… I don't know, but in characteristic fashion he looked at me, almost in disgust, and spat out the words:

'No bloody sex for a year again then!' before turning from me abruptly and slamming out of the house. Unusually, when he returned he was in no better mood, and drank more than ever that evening. As the months went by, however, he convinced himself that Rosie was going to be a boy, someone whom he could influence as a tiny carbon copy of himself, and so gradually he came to terms with my second pregnancy.

His words when Rosie was born shocked me:

'It's a girl, and it's got red hair...'

No pleasure, no wonder, no love.

***

It was at that moment that I most seriously doubted my decision to stay with Mark. I had followed my duty and sacrificed a love that was still as vivid in my mind now, recalling the twists and turns in the story of my life, as it had been thirty years earlier. During the intervening years I had, many times, wondered what the outcome of my sacrifice had actually been. And, building gradually, over the years, the answer had come sweet and clear: out of that sacrifice had come my girls, and new love had been born. As always Helen had been right.

I just had to snap out of this. Today was supposed to be a major celebration, not a wake. And, at the edge of my mind, a lovely positive glimmer of excitement flickered silently.

'In two minutes we will be arriving at London Victoria...'

Chapter 39

There she was, a small slim figure just getting off the train, walking with quick, light footsteps towards the ticket barrier. Rachel noticed that, as soon as Kate spotted her in the crowd, she noticeably quickened her pace.

'Hello darling! Happy birthday!' and with that she gave a solemn mock bow and presented Rachel with what was clearly a laptop case.

'Oh Mum, you got it for me!'

'Darling, don't be daft, of course I did! Let's go for a swift Prosecco and then back to your flat to dump this' – she gestured to the laptop – 'then off to the exhibition!'

Rachel knew that her mother felt years younger when she was with her or Rosie. Always the burden of work and responsibility for their well-being was visibly lifted when she was in their company. People commented on how expressions, voices, gestures and laughter were mirrored when she talked or walked with either of them.

'Oh come on darling, please let me buy this for you! You look gorgeous.'

'Mum, you have already spent hundreds of pounds on my laptop. Stop it!'

'Well, I could buy one for me too, if it would make you feel any better!'

'Mum!'

Seven-thirty soon came. They walked to Covent Garden from Oxford Street. Kate had teased Rachel about the amount of walking they always did in London.

'Do you know,' she laughed, 'Rosie reckoned she walked 18,000 steps with you the last time she came to see you! She has that app on her iPhone that counts steps.'

'Keeps me fit, Mother!'

Laughing, they sat at a table near to the window.

'I thought it might be interesting for you if we had a look at these,' said Kate, pulling out an envelope from her handbag.

'Ooh, Mum – photos! Yes please!'

'I have tried to arrange them in some sort of order,' said Kate, taking a deep breath.

'Mother, you are such a methodical lawyer, always assembling your evidence!' laughed Rachel.

'Here is Knight's Manor, where you were born.' Her eyes softened as she looked at the photograph of the beautiful, elegant house. 'I thought this was our home forever Rachel, but your father extended himself financially – just too far. It became unsustainable.'

***

Tears blurred my eyes as I looked once again at the beautiful house, every square centimetre of which I had cherished with my own hands, as I had repaired and repainted the gracious, neglected rooms. And I remembered that Friday evening in May when Mark had come home in a mood even worse than his usual black moments.

He had crashed over the cattle grid, parked his Lancia and, for once, had come quietly into the house.

'Hi, Mark, Rachel's had a difficult day today, I have just not been able to stop her from crying. I know the doctor said that she had three-month colic, but she is now nearly four months old...'

'Oh for God's sake, shut up!' said my husband without even an attempt at interest or concern.

I walked quietly away from him, holding Rachel close to me. Thank the Lord I had her, her little warm body, her wide blue eyes, her funny baby ways.

Mark drank even more than usual that night. He shut himself in his study with a bottle of whisky that was almost full. When I tidied around last thing at night, after he had stormed off to bed, it was empty.

I had been married to Mark for long enough to realise that he would, in his own time, tell me what was on his mind and, sure enough, the next day he sat looking into his breakfast coffee morosely.

'We will have to move,' he announced without preamble.

'What? Why? What do you mean?'

'I'm sure you wouldn't understand the ins and outs of the matter but, to cut a very long story short, I was offered a "too good to miss" business opportunity, a new venture which sounded so attractive. A little risky to be sure, but you will never make money if you don't take a calculated risk. So I arranged a second mortgage on the house and invested the money. The venture failed.'

I couldn't believe it. I was hurt, betrayed, deceived – all those things.

'But you didn't tell me!' I said, unbelievingly. 'How could you just carry on, gambling our home?'

'I'm going out.'

And, as usual, that was that.

***

The house did not take long to sell – just four months from the day it was put on the market until completion. The removal vans had driven away, following Mark, and leaving me in the house I loved so much, now just a beautiful, empty shell. I took one final tour of the gracious rooms, so full of memories, carrying Rachel in my arms. I had so wanted her to grow up here, eventually to have her children here and bring joy into the old house's shadowy corners. Finally, I walked into my kitchen and looked at the golden beams, the window overlooking the pond, and the ancient Aga around which so much of my recent life had been led. I reflected that my time here had now become history, linking with the histories of the countless generations of people who had lived in Knight's Manor.

Taking a deep breath, I closed the heavy front door with a sound that echoed heavily through the empty house. I carefully strapped Rachel into her baby seat and drove the Mini up to a folly called The Lookout, which is built on land belonging to Ashward Priory. I held Rachel in my arms as I looked over the countryside to which I no longer belonged. A light autumn mist made the view even more unearthly than it was usually. Lifting out of the mist, some two miles distant, proud and beautiful, like a ship braving the turbulent ocean, was Knight's Manor: one moment clear and glowing; the next partially obscured like a house in a dream. Much nearer, to my right, was Helen's home. I would always think of it in these terms. It was quiet, closed, silent and the laughter of easy friendship was no longer heard there. The fragrant roses that we had planted together were almost hidden by weeds. To the left was the Manor House: tall, austere, cold. Three houses, so closely linked in a story that moved between them, linking past and present and, I had thought, future. This story was ended. I turned my back on the exquisite, heart-breaking scene, held my baby close to me for a few minutes, and then drove away.

***

Rachel had seen the photograph of Knight's Manor years earlier, but had looked at it then with a child's eyes.

'Mum, it's enormous! And so beautiful. What is that thing on the front of the house?'

'A sundial.'

'Is that a design around it?' asked Rachel, looking closer.

'No – words. It says: Time is, Time was, Time is not.'

'I see. Which means…?'

Rachel saw the accustomed shadow pass over her mother's face. Clearly she was re-living or re-thinking something that Rachel could not reach.

Hesitatingly, Kate murmured: 'The words mean that there are certain things that are eternal; that go on from generation to generation; that do not change, although time and circumstance change…'

'Oh Mum, you are such a romantic! Love you though! Come on, let's move on from the sundial. Tell me about when you and Dad came to Knight's Manor.'

***

As well as she could, Kate told her faltering story, trying to recapture the excitement of the challenge of restoring the great country house and the delight of getting to know the people who became her friends. She recalled the promise that her life had held when she had driven on that September day down the twisting lane to Knight's Manor; and the way in which, gradually, over the years, Mark had changed – subtly at first and then more and more dramatically.

She had done the same a few days earlier with Rosie and had stopped in frustration.

'Oh, this is impossible! I sound as if I am reading a book. I just cannot seem to capture the essence of anybody!' she had exclaimed with impatience.

'Well, it's difficult, Mum,' Rosie had said. 'It's ages ago, a lifetime! It must be really hard to remember all the detail. I think you are doing really well.'

And in typical fashion, her daughter, sensing her difficulty, had put her arms around her mother. 'I do love you, Mum. It doesn't matter what happened so long ago.'

'But it does matter! The past does influence the present Rosie; and you both need to know the background. So… that things can move forward,' Kate had replied, frowning slightly.

'Mum, something has happened,' Rosie had observed, with quick intuition.

'It has darling, but give me time. I have to talk about the things that happened all those years ago for you to be able to understand what I need to share with you tonight.'

And now, in London with Rachel, Kate took out carefully a picture of Helen. Her lovely, wise smile shone from the photograph although, Kate noticed with pain, the colour was fading a little. Her hair was a much softer gold than this, her grey eyes held greater depth...

'Mum, she's beautiful!'

Throughout their childhood, Kate had spoken often to her daughters about her friend and both girls were familiar with Helen's features. Sometimes they both felt that they could even glimpse something of her character, as their mother's face lit up whilst speaking of her friend. This time, however, when Kate spoke to her daughters, she held nothing back. She told of Helen's disappointment in her marriage, her determination to do her duty, her faithfulness as a friend, and her death on that freezing March morning.

Rachel stopped eating. She had always thought of her mother as just that – Mum: always there, always reliable, always ready to listen to troubles or worries. But, during that conversation high above the noise and bustle of Covent Garden, she started to see her mother as an individual, someone who had had a life full of incident, joy and sorrow, before she had been born.

'That must have been terrible!' she whispered, her eyes full of unshed tears, as she reached over the table and placed her hand reassuringly on Kate's.

'It was.'

The waiter silently removed Rachel's plate and served the main course.

***

I thought to myself, I just can't do this. I desperately wanted to maintain my credibility with both my daughters. Rosie had understood, eventually, exactly what I wanted to say. But she had never been remotely close to her father. Rachel, on the other hand, had some memories of shared games and bicycle rides with Mark. There was much more work to be done with my elder daughter. I couldn't risk the possibility of alienating her.

As we chatted about Rachel's work, her latest boyfriend, and a film that she had seen the previous week, my brain was working overtime. I thought back to Tuesday night when my world had been shaken to the core.

I was in the middle of a long and detailed report. It was vital to get every word correct, as the report would become a public document in due course. It was nearly midnight and I had been working since eight that morning. I was tired and needed a glass of wine. I just had to give my brain a break!

I went over to the fridge. I had just bought it – a pale blue Smeg – and I had smiled as I thought of what I had achieved for my girls and myself. It was still a triumph when I bought something that we had longed for. I poured my wine and recalled how excited we had been when I had managed to buy our first table and chairs for the little house we had rented. Prior to that, we had just sat cross-legged on the floor for meals. The girls thought we were picnicking; I felt that I was failing.

I returned to my study. Glowing like a jewel on the wall of my cottage was one of the very few items that I had managed to salvage from the happiest period of my life: the wonderful picture of Knight's Manor, painted by Estelle. I lightly touched the trees and flowers in the woodland where we had lit the Beltane fire; the lime-coloured conifer under which Mark had reclined when Ash first called to formally introduce himself; the sundial which relentlessly marked out the hours, decades, centuries, proclaiming its philosophy that Time is a fragile human construct... I would spend just fifteen minutes on the Internet, looking at holiday cottages, I thought. I could do with a break! I saved my work document and clicked onto Google.

I played around with a few holiday sites, but nothing really caught my attention – and then I did something that I had thought of many times before, but had never actually done, I typed into the search engine 'Ashley Cooper'. In the seconds that followed I wondered what I would find. Was he still in the UK? Was he married? Was he still alive? All these thoughts flashed like lightning across my tired brain.

Images of a hundred or more 'Ashley Coopers' flashed onto my screen: tiny images of, mostly smiling, men. He must have changed so much, I thought. Would I recognise him, even if his picture were to appear? There were so many varieties and types of feature, I thought idly; so many different shapes and heights. Here was a young Ashley Cooper with blond hair and blue eyes, good-looking in a vacuous way. Here was a paunchy middle-aged man: right age, but surely the man I had loved so completely could never have become something that looked like that! Here was another middle-aged Ash Cooper, almost completely bald this time ... and on it went. There was no one who stirred even the remotest memory.

I tried Facebook instead and found fewer faces, only a couple of dozen this time. About half way down the list, suddenly here was someone who held my attention. Dark hair, short and spiky, his unsmiling face looking straight at the camera, resting on his hand, fingers strong and slender, heavy dark-rimmed glasses almost, but not quite, obscuring his eyes. But it was his eyes that convinced me: dark, deep brown, mesmeric.

It is frighteningly easy to research someone on the Internet. The outline information was that he lived in Tentersley and had worked for several music companies.

I closed my eyes. I thought back to the man I had loved so much, then opened my eyes again and tried to match memory with present reality. There were differences – hair and expression being the main two. But the intensity of gaze, the sense of peace and self-containment that surrounded even an insignificant electronic image, the long strong fingers whose touch I could still remember, I was certain that it was the Ash that I had loved.

Instead of allowing myself just fifteen minutes' break, I had spent nearly an hour flicking through images that held in themselves no reality. What was I doing, I asked myself angrily? I had a job to do, a document to finish before the morning. Tomorrow I faced more meetings, more decisions, more responsibilities.

I poured myself a second glass of wine and swirled the golden liquid around. Into my mind came a picture of myself as I had been: romantic, full of hope, passionate, embracing each day as a great joy. It compared pretty bleakly to how I am now, I thought, preoccupied with meetings, decisions and responsibilities…

Maybe it was the wine or perhaps the relentless pressures that I fought with daily but, spontaneously, I decided that I would send a message to this man who reminded me so vividly of the greatest joy and loss in my life, a lifetime ago.

I found a recent picture of myself, taken at a wedding, and wrote: 'I think we knew each other a long, long time ago…' and sent it. If it wasn't the man I had loved, or if it was and he no longer wished to know me, he would just ignore the message. But if it was Ash, my Ash, and he did want to know me again – the implications were immense.

***

It was this that I had had to explain to Rosie. I had told her, as best I could, of the love Ash and I had for each other, but the magic and mystery, the elemental rightness, I could not capture. She understood the facts, but not the essence of that strange story that had unfolded before she had been born. As to contacting the Ash Cooper I had found on the Internet, to my surprise she had laughed.

'But we do that sort of thing all the time, Mum!' she exclaimed. 'Don't get so heavy about things. He will probably fancy you to bits – whether or not you knew each other back in the day. You still have the ability to turn heads, Mum. Don't you realise that?'

How would Rachel take this? That I had contacted a man I had so very nearly left her father for?

We had ordered dessert wine at the end of the meal. As the waiter tactfully withdrew, I opened my envelope again and took out my final picture – the one of Ash, sitting cross-legged on the kitchen work surface at Knight's Manor, talking with great animation. Dark jeans, thick navy sweater, dark hair… hands clearly being used to emphasise a point. I handed it over the table to Rachel.

'Wow! Who is *this?*' she asked appreciatively.

I came right out with it.

'Someone I was in love with, Rachel, when I was married to your father. Before you were born.'

She studied the creased photograph for some moments.

'He looks lovely, Mum. Why are you showing me this?'

And I told her.

'I thought you would be shocked at what I have just done – contacting him I mean. It's not like me, Rachel.'

'No. You are hardly the scarlet woman, Mum. We do this sort of thing all the time.'

'Yes, Rosie said that too.'

'I have never understood why you didn't leave Dad, you know Mum. He was very strange. I never knew what sort of mood he would be in when he came home from work. How he left you almost every night to look after us by yourself, I just can't understand. At school my friends' fathers always played with them after work, or read to them. Dad – never. You deserve some happiness for *you*. I hope he contacts you.'

So, as simple as that! Totally accepted by both daughters. Perhaps I had not done such a bad job of bringing them up after all.

'Look Mum, I promised I would meet some friends in a rooftop bar about now. Do you mind if I go?'

'Course not, darling. My train leaves in about half an hour anyway. It's perfect timing.'

My mind was in turmoil on the way back to Brighton. It seemed an interminable journey and I was exhausted. Over the past few days I had re-lived the intensity of life that I had lived half my lifetime ago; and had been surprised to find that the feelings I believed long dead were not. If Ash contacted me… my heart soared at the thought.

Chapter 40

2014

Carefully, his strong slender fingers almost caressing each object, Ash Cooper replaced most of the items he had removed earlier from their resting place. The small blue box he kept in his left hand. He felt as if his emotions had been ironed out, taken up and examined, and shredded in the last twenty-four hours.

He returned to his computer, the centre of his life these days, and clicked on the email message Kate had sent to him. He looked intensely at the image, enlarged it and examined it minutely.

He re-read the terse words – saying nothing, saying everything. Did he have the emotional strength to contact her? Was she still with Mark? Would she still think the same about him, damaged and vulnerable as he was? Could he risk his emotional stability? He thought back to the barren years of his marriage to Tricia. He knew only too well that he had been attracted to her initially because of her superficial likeness to Kate: slim and small, with dark hair and blue eyes. They had married quickly – after only six months. There was a sort of desperate loneliness in Ash that craved companionship, someone to fill the aching void he had felt, constantly, after he had left Kate. The marriage had lasted only a few years. Ash grimaced as he remembered how, at every turn, aspects of

Tricia's character were polar opposites to Kate's. Tricia needed the latest clothes; she insisted upon manicures weekly; she was self-centred and hated animals... and so on. Increasingly he had thrown himself into his work, which involved staying abroad for lengthy periods of time; and, eventually, on his return he had started to notice a tangible coolness on Tricia's part.

But his two daughters were the delight of his life after his loss of Kate. He smiled, even then, at their beauty and innocence. But he had been deprived too of his children. On returning from a particularly long and exhausting trip to Hong Kong, he arrived at his house to find it empty and a terse note which said:

'I have left you. I don't love you anymore. I have taken the girls. My solicitors will be in touch.'

Ironically, it was propped against a mug which the girls had given him as a Father's Day present. Its lettering read: *The Best Dad in the World.*

After this, his life had truly dissolved. For months he was incapable of work, fighting for his sanity and his daughters, through a bitter divorce.

As he had said to himself, again and again since receiving the brief message from Kate, if he met her again, would she want to know the damaged, hurt, vulnerable human being he had become?

Night came. Every fifteen minutes or so he refreshed the image as his brain played and replayed the priceless memories of his time with Kate. It became almost a healing process. Looking at her direct gaze, her open face, he remembered the unfailing love, the energy, the laughter that they had shared.

Back then, at the start of his adult life, the whole world had seemed so very precious because it had held Kate.

From his flat, he could just about see the stars that made the night beautiful. He recalled that night when he had sung the ballad to Kate and, at the very end, the utter joy of holding her in his arms. He remembered her direct look – straight into his eyes – just as she looked now. How could anyone be so unchanged?

As dawn broke, he opened the small blue box and traced with his forefinger the words he had asked to be engraved on the ring, words that still showed clear through the tarnish of the last thirty years:

My Beginning and My End

He slipped the silver band on to the little finger of his left hand which closed protectively around the ring. Gradually his head sank onto his folded arms, to dream of flowers, of an injured, long-dead, much-loved pet, and of stars swinging across the sky on the stillness of a short summer night...

Chapter 41

The flicker of hope that had danced in my mind around the time of Rachel's birthday – that there was a possibility that I could see Ash again – quietly receded as the weeks passed. I had loved Ash from the moment I first saw him silhouetted against the Spring sunshine – that moment when time seemed to shift. For a few weeks I had snatched at a beautiful dream in which he loved me still. But as time passed, this dream faded.

For so many years I had closed my mind to the ecstasy and anguish of my years in Ashward and had focussed solely on the practical necessities of bringing up my children. But, by my foolish behaviour on the Internet, I had opened the floodgates to that extraordinary time. I replayed each aspect of my brief, life-changing relationship with Ash until my brain was exhausted.

It was one wet Sunday. Rachel had gone to Paris with her current boyfriend – quite honestly I couldn't keep pace with them – and Rosie had gone to the Brecon Beacons with friends from Uni. I sat and tried to work, but couldn't concentrate. So I paced the floor for a while, then went to the corner shop and bought the *Sunday Times*. What had been intended as a distraction merely added, however, to my unrest. I had brought home such a monumental pile of newsprint to wade through and I had so much work to do. It was relentless! My gym opening times were ridiculously short on a Sunday, so swimming was out of the question.

I was so restless, more restless than I had been for years. I leant my forehead on the cold glass of my study window and watched the rain driving across my vegetable garden, my roses, the little archway with battered jasmine that I had put up across the pathway from the garage. I felt completely desolate and so utterly alone

I thought back to the intense life that I had led at Ashward. I remembered my wonderful dogs, always there, always ready to lick or lie on my feet until they went numb. No possibility of having pets now, because the demands of my professional life made this impossible. I thought of the ancient mystery and wonder that had threaded through my life at that time. It was almost unbelievable – no, it was actually unbelievable – that I had come across witches and a curse: an unforgettable bonfire procession; a magical Beltane dance; and a midsummer of such intense tenderness that its mere memory raised my heartbeat and deepened my breathing. Was that really me? Was that really my life? And what did I have now? A job that helped others – good; that made it possible for me to live fairly comfortably – good; that ensured my daughters had decent Christmas and birthday presents – certainly. But what of me? What of the bubble of excitement that, despite my best efforts, rose and sparkled whenever I thought of Ash?

It was then that I made my decision. I would go back to Ashward. I would lay the ghosts of the past; see Knight's Manor again; visit Ashward church and Helen's grave; perhaps even follow one of our favourite walks. It could surely not be more excruciating than revisiting the place in my imagination.

I had closed my eyes against the black night as I listened to the spatter of raindrops on the glass. But in an instant my reverie was broken by the shrill of the telephone.

'Hi, Mum.'

'Hello, Rosie. How lovely to hear your voice! How's things?'

'Well, I was just about to ask you the same thing!'

'Oh, OK darling,' I said, fighting to keep the exhaustion from my voice.

'Mum. Stop working! It's half eleven. Bed time!'

I smiled.

'So who is the mother?'

'Mum. Did that old flame of yours ever contact you?'

'No – no, darling. He didn't.'

'I see! What a shame. What are you doing at the moment then?'

'To be honest, looking out of the window on to the wet garden.'

'Mm! Not particularly riveting. Are you working?'

'…ish!'

'Mum. Go to bed. Have a drink and get out a good book. I have actually taken precious time out of a convo with friends to talk to you!'

'Oh darling! What would I do without you? Actually, don't fret. I have a plan.'

'Which is?'

'Well, it is probably silly and you will think I shouldn't do it.'

'What is it, Mum?'

'I am going to pay a short visit to Ashward. It is the anniversary of Helen's death next week. I have not been back for thirty years, and it is about time!' I joked lamely.

'I think that is probably a good idea. Book yourself somewhere lovely though, not just a pub or something.'

'Don't fuss darling. I will!'

'Promise?'

'Promise.'

And so it was decided.

TIME IS NOT

KATE & ASH

Chapter 42

It was lunchtime on 5 March when I arrived at the 'luxury bed and breakfast' that Rosie had insisted I stay in. The weather was foul. Although only one-thirty, the afternoon was dark and cold, with heavy clouds which sent sleet over the acres of deep Kent countryside that I knew so well. My accommodation was an old rectory situated on a high ridge with sweeping views back over the dipping valleys to Ashward. I had booked the most expensive room they had – the Ashward suite. Much to my surprise, I was not disappointed in the slightest at the quality and spaciousness of the accommodation, nor the warmth of the welcome. Rosie, and Rachel, would certainly have approved.

'We have the best views in the house from this room,' said Mrs Floyd proudly. 'Just look!'

I looked. The undulating landscape swept across the river valley and, shocking because it was there in reality and not in my imagination or in my dreams, I could just make out Ashward church and the Manor House and, finally, the unforgettable shape of Knight's Manor. A hard lump rose in my throat as I tried to respond. Coughing, I murmured something about it being 'stunning'.

'Well, I will leave you now to get settled, but will bring you up some tea in about half an hour. Heaven knows it is so cold you need something to warm you! If there is anything else you need, just let us know.'

My eyes strained over the miles between my rented room and the magnificent rose-coloured face of the house I had once owned and loved so much. Was this visit a good idea? I just didn't know. Already I felt a sense of pensive melancholy start to descend upon my mind and could almost hear Mark's trenchant: 'Come on. Get back into the real world!' Good that I could now dismiss without emotion his all too predictable words.

***

I just could not believe it the next morning, the anniversary of Helen's death, when the weather was an exact replay of the freezing March day which took her life.

I forced myself to eat breakfast, to drink coffee, thinking all the time of the many occasions when my dear friend and I had laughed and chatted and planned our lives together so many years ago, just a few miles away across those frozen grey fields.

I had decided that I would visit the church and place flowers on Helen's grave and wondered how the church and graveyard would look, how they would be changed with the passage of the years.

Once again, echoing bitterly the bleak morning when I had slipped and slithered with my beautiful long-dead pets down the road to Fortune Farm just to be near to the man I loved, the roads were like glass. I drove slowly, taking in every aspect of the countryside which, I was shocked to realise, I still knew like my own hand, even after three decades. Properties had been subtly smartened and renamed; 'Keeper's Cottage' had become just 'Keeper's', and so on. I consciously took a deep breath as I turned the corner to pass Meadow Farm.

It was inhabited. Indeed it was full of life. Two small girls, wrapped in warm coats and scarves, red wellingtons and gloves, were holding on with all their strength to two yellow Labrador puppies, which were pulling and jumping to lick their faces. They were running in circles and giggling, clearly waiting for an adult to emerge from the kitchen door to take the pups for a walk. Would they be going up Old Cruck Lane? Would there be early primroses to pick, as Helen had picked them for me? There were so many memories crowding my head that I could hardly breathe.

Before going on I had to stop my car. Sleet was falling steadily and my windscreen wipers slowly shifted the grey slush. I shouldn't have come. What a mistake! All that new life at Meadow Farm. What did they know of a wise, quiet woman whose grey eyes had seen so much, and whose life was taken on this very day, thirty years earlier?

I took a deep breath and rounded the next corner. There was Ashward church, where I had first met the man who had opened the horror and the mystery of this place to me. I opened the boot of my car and picked up the bouquet of palest pink tulips I had bought for Helen. Then I clicked shut the doors of my car and looked at the exquisite little building. It had always seemed so vibrant to me, so alive. But now it slept again, slipping back into the centuries of disuse and dormancy from which Ralph Woodville had awoken it. I looked at the noticeboard: services once every two months. What! Not every week?

I foolishly still expected the priest-in-charge to be Alastair Loughland, but how old would he be now? No priest was mentioned.

Almost in a dream, I lifted the latch on the old oak gate and walked along the uneven stone path to the church door. I felt as if my movements were unnaturally slow: it was like walking in a dream. Inside the church it was dark, musty, almost disused. I thought of the freshness and light that used to fill the ancient building, the glow of candlelight on polished wood, and almost wept with loss. Hesitatingly I sat in my old pew, fourth from the front on the left-hand side of the church, and sank my head in my hands.

If I opened my eyes, would I see Helen and her young family again? Would I hear the steady footsteps of Paul Lucas as he strode down the aisle, his black clerical robes flowing behind him?

Nothing. Nothing except the sighing of the wind around the church and the battering of sleet on the windows.

This was terrible. One by one the precious golden moments of the only time in my life when I had felt truly alive were being obliterated. But I had to continue. I picked up the bouquet that I had brought to lay on Helen's grave and left by the south door, the private entrance that the senior Woodvilles had used to enter 'their' church. I registered that there was a large, ornate tomb dedicated to them, just to the right of the pathway to the Manor House. They were in sight then, of the house and church they had loved and now lay midway between the two ancient buildings.

The last time I had seen Helen's grave, Rachel had been a very small girl. Today, the snowdrops that we had planted there together were just fading: could anything be so forlorn? But I quickened my step as I saw that, finally, a headstone had been erected for my dear friend. Wiping the rain from my face, I bent to read the words that her daughters had finally chosen for their beautiful, amazing mother.

Helena Woodville
1941 – 1984
Love Never Ends

I knelt in the freezing wet grass and laid the tulips against the headstone. These were the right words. Whatever monumental changes I had experienced in my life, love remained: the love that I had felt for this woman and she for me; and my love for Ash as we had laughed with Estelle, cut Emma free from the snare in the woods, danced the mystical Beltane dance, looked into each other's eyes for an eternity by Barrow Farm on Midsummer's Day and held each other in the final, desperate minutes of our relationship together.

A sort of infinitely sad peace came over me. I kissed my right hand and placed it on Helen's bitterly cold headstone. I got to my feet and walked slowly to the gate. Just to the left I idly noticed a dark, overgrown plot. All the other graves were well kept, with flowers or bulbs planted on them. But this was covered with brambles and tall rough grass. Whose could this be? I knelt and read, scratched roughly in the saturated grey stone:

Margaret Smith

That was all. No dates. No inscription. But surely, a scratched carving of some sort? I shuddered, remembering her bitterness and the darkness of her life here in Ashward. I looked more closely, refusing absolutely to touch her last resting place and finally made out the shape of the pentagram. Shivering, I turned quickly towards the safety of my car. Things had not changed then, not fundamentally, here in Ashward. I swiftly went through the gate and looked back one more time at the desolate grey churchyard. I was unsurprised to see a drifting grey figure by the headstone of Margaret Smith, that disappeared almost as swiftly as I perceived it.

As dusk firmly fell, I left Ashward church for the last time and decided that I would return to Brighton in the morning.

I was physically shaking when I got back to the warm comfort of the old rectory and could have embraced Mrs Floyd as she met me, virtually on the doorstep, with a glass of brandy and a cafetiere of very hot coffee.

'Come in my dear, you are as white as a sheet! Are you all right?'

I muttered something about having got too cold and accepted the drinks gratefully.

'I have a beef casserole for your dinner, dear. Go and have a hot bath and it will be on the table when you come down.'

I did – and it was. And, washed down by half a bottle of red wine, it was one of the most wonderful meals I had ever had.

***

Extraordinary! The next morning was bright and clear and cold. Just as the day following Helen's death had been. Was life playing a series of bitter tricks on me?

I thanked my hosts sincerely for their concern and hospitality and, after breakfast, got in my car to return to my safe, anodyne cottage – but two things remained. I just had to look once again on the house that had brought me and my then husband to Kent, and make one last visit to the place that held the dearest memories for me of anywhere on earth.

When I saw once again the serene southern face of Knight's Manor my heart, despite itself, lifted. How beautiful it was! And to think that once, this had been mine. I slowed my car right down and drove past as slowly as I possibly could. Just as I came to the cattle grid, I glanced into the courtyard behind the great house and saw how much had changed. An oak-framed barn faced the entrance and the gardens, now professionally landscaped, swept away into the distance. I thought with affection of my younger self, desperately trying to create flowerbeds and rockery, with little knowledge and no expertise. But now, the exterior of this most beautiful of houses had been transformed by money and time and expert understanding.

How had the current owners dealt with the underground room? Had they decided to ignore its disturbing presence under the very foundations of their home, or had they usurped its purpose for something mundane – a home cinema perhaps? Did the centuries-old practice of coven meetings still continue? My mind teemed with questions that I knew it would be impossible to answer during my short visit.

I parked my car and jumped over the stile that led to Barrow Farm. The day was warming and the sky was a crystal clear blue. This was the last place in my pilgrimage. This had been held in my heart, as a beautiful secret, for so long.

There was still a dusting of frost on the grass under the hedges, riming the primroses and blackthorn blossom. I walked swiftly downhill, leaving far behind the little lane and the great proud house, once so intimately known to me, but now subtly unfamiliar, changed and altered by the hands and minds of others.

Soon I reached the ancient oval meadow, used each summer for haymaking because of the quality of its grass. As yet there were no roses here, no St John's wort or bird's foot trefoil: these would come later as Spring moved steadily into summer.

I walked to the spot where, as far as I could remember, I had sat, at Ash's bidding, whilst he had collected those precious flowers for me. I closed my eyes and let the Spring sun fallaciously persuade me that it was, once again, midsummer. Once again, I daydreamed, I would open my eyes and see the intense dark loving gaze of the man I loved – I still loved – his tall figure silhouetted against the golden hay, his strong hands holding out the flowers to me.

Almost inaudible on that silent, early Spring morning I heard my name:

'Kate!'

This, surely, must be part of my imaginings… and so, wishing to maintain the fiction for as long as possible, with the slowest movement, I inched my hands away from my eyes and turned, once again, as in a dream, towards the low early morning sun.

He was unmistakable: tall, slim, broad-shouldered, his hands once again holding flowers.

'Ash? Ash!'

The tremor that I had felt pass through that same field, those same sheltering trees, grass and flowers, when we had last stood there together, came once more. The world shifted – infinitesimally moving out of and back into focus, to settle with brighter colours and perfect clarity.

We each took two swift steps towards each other and soon I was in his arms, the handfuls of primroses that he had picked falling around my shoulders, crushed between our bodies, until their spicy scent filled that whole timeless place.

The years rolled back and we were once again as we had been: and, as has always been the case with us, we said nothing. There was no need. Time ceased to exist. Time did not exist. Past and present and future came together in a moment as certain and unshakeable as anything on earth or beyond.

Eventually, I said, 'How did you know I was here?'

He smiled and murmured, pressing his face into my hair, 'Rosie!'

Minutes, hours, passed as we stood together, just conscious of the cool Spring sun warming us slightly and a breeze, full of the heady promise of the summer days to come, playing around our hands and faces.

'Do you know what primroses signify?' asked Ash.

I shook my head, still in the safety of his arms.

'That I can't live without you… and to prove it, with something that can't get crushed and battered so easily, I have this for you.'

Ash reached into his pocket and pulled out a small blue leather box. He opened it and lifted out a silver ring.

'Read it my love, please.'

I read:

My Beginning and My End and

The words circled eternally, as sure as the seasons, or as the passage of time on the face of the sundial on the fair southern face of Knight's Manor.

TIME IS

TIME WAS

TIME IS NOT

'I had this made for you – years ago – but there was just room for the second "and" to be added by the silversmith, because we passed from life to a sort of death to life again. In you I begin again; and you in me.'

***

Across the frosty fields, through the great Ashward Priory, deep in its cavernous hidden cellars, a spiral of ash rose in a corner, rose and fell, encircling and enfolding a blackened, twisted and tarnished object – almost unrecognisable as a ring – and was eternally still. The willing sacrifice had been made; the agony was over; the spirit silent.